HIS ENTERPRISING DUCHESS

ENTERPRISING WOMEN, BOOK 1

Peri Maxwell

ARE YOU SIGNED UP FOR DRAGONBLADE'S BLOG?

You'll get the latest news and information on exclusive giveaways, exclusive excerpts, coming releases, sales, free books, cover reveals and more.

Check out our complete list of authors, too!

No spam, no junk. That's a promise!

Sign Up Here

www.dragonbladepublishing.com

Dearest Reader;

Thank you for your support of a small press. At Dragonblade Publishing, we strive to bring you the highest quality Historical Romance from some of the best authors in the business. Without your support, there is no 'us', so we sincerely hope you adore these stories and find some new favorite authors along the way.

Happy Reading!

CEO, Dragonblade Publishing

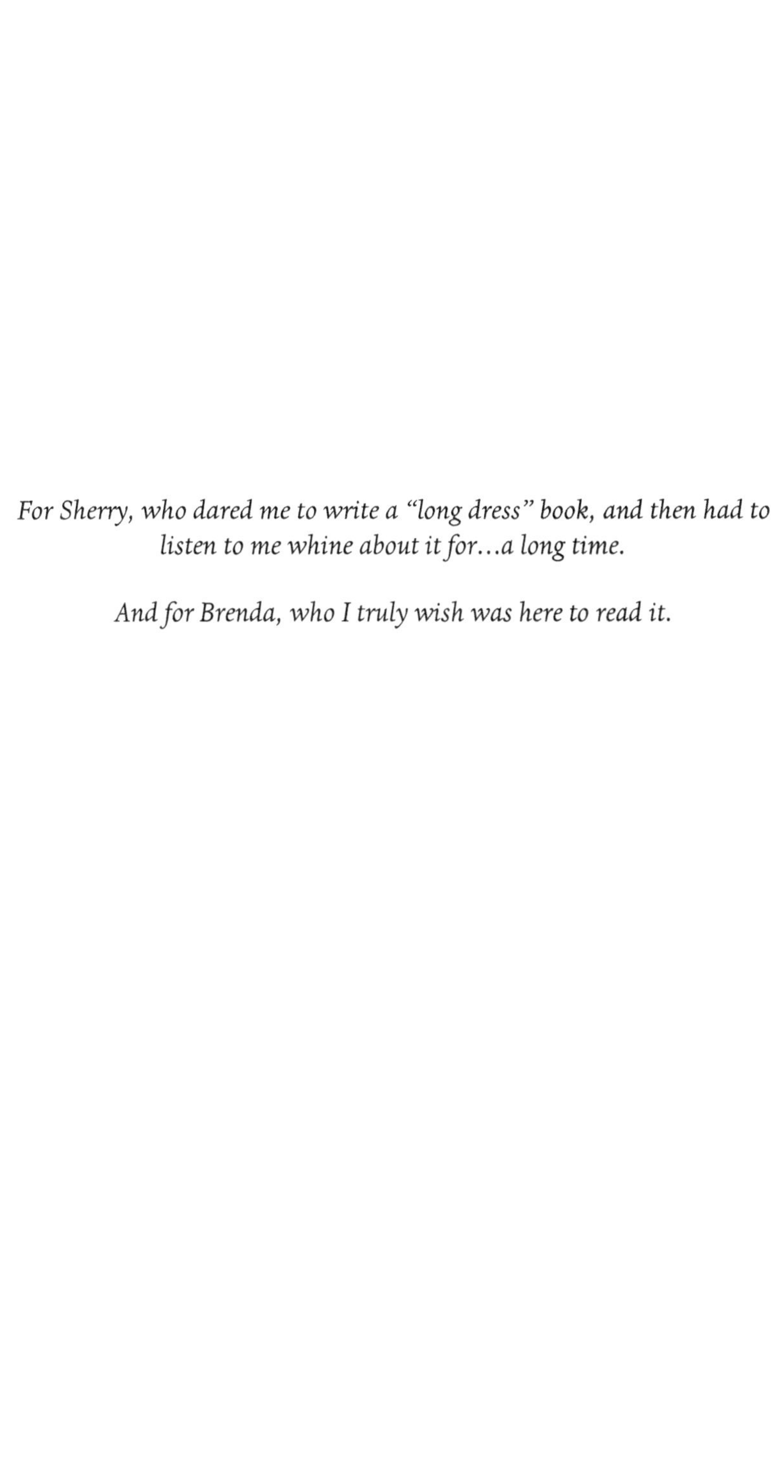

For Sherry, who dared me to write a "long dress" book, and then had to listen to me whine about it for…a long time.

And for Brenda, who I truly wish was here to read it.

CHAPTER ONE

Norfolk, England: July, 1845

OLIVER HAWKINS WAS home.

Or back in England, anyway.

The landscape outside the carriage window was no longer the mammoth trees of the Canadian wilderness he'd loved from the moment he'd landed there. Instead, he saw stooped and crooked saplings starving for the water that had turned the road to a thick, gooey mud that sucked at the coach wheels like a living thing.

Those trees could be healthy and strong if they had a chance for sunshine. The older trees looming overhead gobbled up everything in their fight to stay alive.

With the right kind of care, this forest could last for generations. The challenge danced through Oliver's brain. It was something Garrett never would have considered, but now…

Oliver flexed his fingers, and the too-tight black gloves scraped his knuckles. They'd been delivered by Emmett, who'd been waiting on the dock in Ipswich. *"Lord Garrett died while you were at sea, m'lord."* With that, Oliver had inherited his brother's gloves, cravat, and title without question or explanation. Their trip now had an urgency borne by duty.

"Look, Papa! An elk!"

The excitement jerked his head right to the four-year-old with his nose pressed against the glass, wobbling on his feet as they hit a bump in the road. "Get away from the door, Simon."

Instead of obeying, the little boy twisted farther, craning to see behind them and using the door latch for balance. "But, Papa—"

Oliver snatched him up and plopped him onto the seat. The leather was worn shiny by generations who came and went regardless of their personal desires. "Sit still."

The last thing he needed was to get Simon across an ocean only to have the carriage squish him into the mud so near to the end of their journey.

Dread pooled in his gut, cold and murky like the puddled ruts they splashed through. And, when he heard the sniffle behind him, guilt thickened the mess.

Oliver pinched the bridge of his nose and closed his eyes, but the rocking made him seasick—worse than the month aboard ship. He should have hired a nurse, someone to distract the boy and give *him* the pleasure of moping.

The traitorous thought made Oliver's already weary shoulders droop lower. He didn't need a nurse. Simon was his child, and the boy had dealt with enough on this adventure he'd regretted the moment they'd lost sight of the shore.

Oliver knew the feeling. Twice over.

He sat and put his arm around his son's thin shoulders. "I know you're tired, *hijo*. I am, too. But when we get there, you can run all you want."

Oliver's brain twitched at the lie, but the father in him dug in his heels. Simon would not be condemned to *his* childhood. Oliver had made that vow four years earlier, and he was going to stick to it. "Shall we find your elk?"

Tears forgotten, Simon crawled into his lap and the two of them stared at the trees behind the coach. A large stag, by Suffolk standards, crashed through the underbrush. Oliver lowered the glass, but the sound was swallowed up by rain, hoof beats, and the jangle of harness.

"Did you climb these trees, Papa?"

The boy had been full of questions since they'd entered the carriage. *Did you stay there? Did you build that? Does your old house look like that?* The amusement had worn thin several miles back.

"These were too far from home."

The carriage emerged from the forest and slowed to a halt under the worn and battered sign announcing The Pewter Owl. The inn, like the surrounding landscape, hadn't changed for the better in the last six years. Its low wall, more mortar than stone, surrounded a cramped, scraggly garden.

"Do you stay here when you were little?"

Not when he was little, but he had stayed here. Memories tightened Oliver's lungs, helped along by earthy smells on the damp, cold air.

Thea. Smelling of roses and rain.

Oliver stuck his head out as much as he dared, as if his past would grip him by the collar and hang him from the upstairs window. "Emmett? Can we drive on, please?"

The old servant peered down, water cascading from the brim of his hat. "I thought you'd be wantin' to stop at the first possible place, but the food is better up the road at The Galloping Goat. So's the crowd. Shall I stop there, m'lord?"

The formality chafed. As a child, the Felton House servants had been more like aunts and uncles. That had ended this morning when he'd become an earl.

God help him.

"Yes, thank you." He raised the window and locked it tight to keep the ghosts at bay.

"Are we almost there?" Simon asked.

"Almost." They were a good twenty miles yet, but the truth would only make the little boy whine. Oliver couldn't blame him. They'd been cooped up far too long. "We're going to stop for food first." He shrugged out of his restricting tailcoat and coaxed his son to his side. "How about a story?" He smiled when the pouting boy nodded grudgingly. "There's a good man. Now…how do I start?"

It was a game they'd played for weeks at bedtime, piled together in a hammock because Simon considered a sailor's bunk better than a berth in a cabin. Oliver's back hadn't agreed.

"Once upon a time," Simon said.

"Right. Once upon a time…" Oliver forced his exhausted, hungry brain to spin a story. "There were two young princes who thought of nothing but adventure, and they played in a forest full of ancient trees that stretched as far as the eye could see. Until…the oldest prince was captured by an evil queen who carried him away to do her bidding."

"Was the other boy lonely?"

Not as much as he should have been. "Yes. He was quite lonely, but then one day he met a princess—"

"Was she a fairy?"

She was a red-headed harridan, all wild curls and gangly legs, who'd bested him at math and science and made him look past his selfish, aristocratic nose. "She was a mermaid. She lived in the lake and waited for him every day, and they became the best of friends."

Better than friends. More than friends.

Until she'd forgotten him.

"What happened?" Simon asked, his words garbled by a yawn.

"The young prince left for a faraway country, and the mermaid was captured by a pirate who carried her away to the other side of the world."

"Was the prince sad?"

"He was. But then he met a beautiful fairy with eyes like a summer sky that healed his broken heart, and they lived happily ever after."

If only life were as simple as a fairy story.

"What happened to the mermaid?"

That was a question Oliver had tried for years to ignore. "She lives in the West Indies, where she goes barefoot every day, wears a ring on every finger, and eats mangoes for breakfast, like a monkey."

Rather than eliciting a giggle, the ending garnered a muffled snore.

Oliver laid his little boy across the empty seat and covered him with a coat. At first, he'd been irritated his parents had sent Emmett to greet them rather than coming themselves. Now he was glad for one last gasp of normal. He stretched his legs straight and leaned back. The rocking coach and the drumming rain hypnotized him until his breaths slowed and mingled with his son's.

God, he missed his wife. Julia, a wood sprite with clear blue eyes and a laugh like sunshine. His hope for happily-ever-after.

They'd gotten the happily, just not the ever after.

She'd been gone four years now, more than twice as long as he'd had her. But she'd left him Simon. The little boy had her dark hair and quick mind, though Oliver hoped the boy got *his* size. Julia would have been so proud of her son, and she would have been a doting mother.

She would have reminded Oliver of what was important. She wouldn't have let him dread what was coming closer with every creak of the axles.

Even though the countryside hadn't changed, everything was different. Garrett was gone. Thea was gone. Richard, the business partner who'd become a brother-in-law and then a live-in uncle, was in Quebec. His servants were going to treat him like an earl, and his mother…well, Father would be there to intervene.

If not, for the first time in his life, Oliver would be alone.

Maybe that was why he'd been dreaming of Thea since their first night at sea. He'd never felt alone if she was near.

He should be focused on his family, on his brother's death, on the lumber mill he'd promised his father, not on a woman who had forgotten him as soon as he'd sailed for Canada. Besides that, it was wrong to be haunted by memories of another woman when Julia had been the one to help him overcome his anger.

The coach stopped next to a low, whitewashed wall, and Oliver knelt next to his sleeping boy. Simon's hair was matted to his temples in sweaty whorls, and his pudgy cheeks were rosy. Oliver warred between letting him rest and keeping him from starving.

"Si?" He stroked the blue-black springy curls Julia had bequeathed their child and stared into his groggy eyes. "Are you hungry?"

The boy nodded and kicked free of the coat with an enviable burst of energy.

After straightening their clothes, they descended onto the squishy turf. A brightly painted sign swung quietly overhead. The neat wall and lush gardens reminded Oliver of his grandmother's cottage.

Emmett led the way through a red front door and into a large dining room. The sideboard was loaded with bread and butter, cheese, and bowls of crisp pears, juicy peaches, and berries and cream. The patrons were a mix of travelers, working men, and farmers. A few looked like servants from nearby houses. Everyone stared at him—the only gentleman in the room, the only person with a child, the only one in mourning clothes.

Oliver took a seat next to Emmett at a smooth, clean table and put Simon between them on the bench. A girl came 'round with a pitcher and filled three pewter tankards that looked suited for ale instead of bracing spring water.

A low fire crackled in counterpoint to the rain pelting the windows and the low murmur of conversation. White walls and crisp lace curtains were bright barriers against the cloudy sky, and the floor was dirtied only by their wet footprints.

The meal arrived, and the smells made Oliver's stomach rumble. For six weeks, their provisions had been dried, salted, or pickled. The tender food made him whimper with pleasure.

He was savoring a bite of potatoes, cutting Simon's beef, when every other man at the table wiped their faces and straightened their posture. The little boy stared like he'd seen an angel.

A woman stopped on the edge of the room to instruct the maids in quiet, measured tones. She was taller and thinner than fashionable, but her long limbs and fingers gave her an air of elegance as she moved through the room to check on her guests. Her dress was simple but clean.

She was more lady than innkeeper, and the sight of her heated Oliver's blood until his ears burned.

Her hair was coppery gold, but it would go lighter if she spent too much time in the sun without a bonnet. The fine hairs close to her face would curl if she went out in the rain. She hated bonnets and the rain.

Thea.

Oliver's pulse thundered as he leaned back, using Emmett as a hiding place. Was he going to have to face her with only a four-year-old as protection? Was her husband here, too? She was getting closer. He was going to have to talk to her.

"Hello, Missus," came the general rumble around mouthfuls of food.

Hello, Thea. Imagine finding you in an inn. Again. I have the life I always told you I wanted. I bought you a house another woman called home. That she died in.

Oliver gulped his water and coughed as it went down his windpipe. And coughed again, and then more. Everyone was staring. *She* was staring.

"Papa?"

He closed his eyes and focused on drawing in one deep breath after another until the tightness in his lungs subsided. "I'm fine, Si," he wheezed.

"You should chew slower." Simon patted his back. Laughter rippled across the table.

"I should, thank you."

Oliver raised his eyes to Thea's. Just like all those years ago in her father's schoolroom, he felt the pull of her.

Her wide, glittering, gaze flitted between Simon and him, as though she'd exiled him across the ocean and never expected to see him again. He would have gladly stayed there rather than be stuck on this damned island with her.

Oliver stood, stepped around the table, and faced the woman who had haunted him for years. He weaved his napkin through his fingers and tightened his grip. He wouldn't reach for her again. "Hullo."

Her bobbed curtsey matched the flex of her throat as she swallowed. "Oli—er, Lord Ol—Lord Elveden. My condolences on your brother's death."

It was all jarring. Elveden. The villagers knowing of Garrett's death before him. That, if possible, Thea's voice was prettier than he'd remembered. Deeper, perhaps, but just as affecting.

He dipped his head, glad of the formality that put a barrier between them. "Thank you, Miss Fow—umm Mrs...." He'd never cared to ask her husband's name.

"Smith," she finished. Her gaze darted again to Simon, who was pressed against Oliver's leg. His outgoing little boy had chosen now to be shy.

Oliver bent to lift the child to eye level. Simon hated to be talked down to. However, Thea was already on her knees, breaking every rule of polite conversation. She'd always been good at that.

He knelt as well, showing off the most precious thing in his life while using him as a shield against the smell of roses. "Simon, this is Thea, er, Mrs. Smith."

"How do you do?" Simon stuck out his hand, making Oliver proud of his manners. "Did you climb trees, too?"

"I was better at racing," Thea said as she shook the boy's hand. "It's a pleasure to meet you, Lo—"

"Just Simon," Oliver whispered. He looked at his son and spoke louder. "Th—Mrs. Smith—ran so fast her braids streamed behind her like a horse's tail."

"And your father pulled them to make me lose my footing."

"It never worked," he chuckled. It was easy to laugh with her.

It reminded him of the last time he'd seen her. They'd picnicked in an upstairs room at The Owl while rain had battered the windows and their clothes had dried in front of the fire. They'd whispered confessions and plans in the middle of the night.

The dining room had fallen quiet. Everyone was staring. Thea's laughter faded, leaving a brittle smile in its wake. She refocused on his son.

"Did you enjoy your travels from Canada, Simon?"

He nodded enthusiastically. Oliver, sensing a litany of tales, tightened his hold in a request for quiet.

"Another time." That couldn't happen. Oliver was pressing his luck as it was. "Perhaps."

Simon looked up at him, a frown knotting his tiny dark brows. "But she asked, Papa."

Oliver stood. His hand was out before he could stop it, and her touch singed his skin past his elbow. He jerked away as soon as she was upright.

"We need to finish eating, Si. We have a distance to travel yet, and Mrs. Smith has work to do."

He made himself walk away from her. Again. He ate his food, he answered Simon's questions, and he made small talk with those around him. All the while, his fingers tingled from where he'd touched her.

Thea came and went, her jaw set as she refused to look his way.

She'd done the same when he'd bested her at lessons. Then he'd chased her down and teased her until she'd smiled. He ached to do it again. He wanted to regale her of stories from his adventures and watch her eyes light up. He wanted to hear her stories. Just like all those summers when he'd come back from Eton.

Though now her stories would include another man.

The gravy soured on Oliver's tongue. He wasn't a school lad

any longer. He'd lived six years without Thea, and he could continue to do so. She could be just another villager—someone else's wife. He wouldn't darken this door again while he was here, no matter how good the fare tasted.

After finishing supper, aware that his little boy was waving goodbye over his shoulder as they left, Oliver nodded his thanks as Emmett opened the carriage door.

A basket sat on the floor, and Oliver lifted the lid, half expecting a snake to slither out. Instead, he found a light snack and a flask. Condensation soaked the cloth insulating it.

For Simon. The note was written in Thea's clear, fine hand. Despite himself, Oliver lifted the paper to his nose. He smelled only ink. Years of searching the post for a letter from her, and all he had were two words addressed to his son.

As soon as the broad-shouldered almost-stranger with the charming little boy had gone, while she could still hear the carriage creaking and the harness rattling, Thea strode back to her kitchen. Warm, clean, and orderly, it soothed her jangling nerves better than any herbal tea.

She sat beside the exhausted girl, Petra, who carefully placed her utensils on the table but protected her plate like a hungry kitten.

"I've chopped everything I could find." Petra wiped her mouth with a napkin. "Mrs. Snow said I could eat."

Not that many years ago, Thea had been hollow with hunger and terrified of being alone. "Of course you can."

The girl retrieved her fork and dug into a mountain of shepherd's pie. While her hair, teeth, and hands were clean, her stained dress was two months too tight.

Thea stared pointedly. "Are you running to the father or away from him?"

"To him." Tears welled in the young woman's eyes. "He's a soldier, and he's sailed for France. We wanted to marry, but…"

But they'd put the cart before the horse and her family had tossed her out rather than suffer a scandal. It was the way of things.

"Where are you going?"

"Ipswich." The tears fell freely now. "But I have…I didn't…"

Thea patted her hand. "None of that. Finish your meal."

While Petra ate, Thea stuffed a small hamper with food and then scrawled a quick note, which she tucked inside with the money Oliver had paid for his meal. It wasn't fair recompense, but it was a start.

She returned to the table as her visitor finished brushing the crumbs from her place setting and stood.

"The coach for the coast will be through at half past." She pressed coins into Petra's hand for the fare. "When you get to Ipswich, go to The Glass Frog and tell Constance I sent you."

Over the past years, Thea had been accepted into a network of innkeepers and maids, each intent on helping as many girls as they could. They were either returning kindness paid to them years earlier or, more likely, making sure another young woman didn't suffer as they had.

"There's a note of introduction in the basket," Thea said. "Don't lose it."

The girl reached to hug her, but thought better of it. Instead, she took Thea's hands in her delicate ones. "Thank you."

As the kitchen door closed, Thea prayed for the girl whose life was about to change forever, regardless of what happened to her soldier lover. She said a second prayer for the unborn child who deserved a safe and long life.

"You're a soft touch," Jenny Snow said from the stove. "Every wayward soul in the county knows to come to The Goat."

"Says the woman who gave her a plate heaped high enough to satisfy a field hand," Thea teased her cook. "You didn't even make her put away the dishes."

"Poor thing would've fallen asleep standing up." Jenny stirred the coals under the stew pot without dirtying her hem. "It was good to see Lord Oliver home, wasn't it?"

Thea didn't answer as she shelved clean dishes. Thea had known Oliver was coming home. Thetford was a small village, and news had spread after his father, the Duke of Rushford, had returned from Canada. She'd prepared herself to see him at church or maybe out shopping. Confronting him in her dining room had been a shock.

For a moment, it had been like every summer he'd returned from Eton. The same thrill had stolen her breath, and fear had warred with excitement. She'd been torn between worry that he'd outgrown her and the need to tell him everything she'd done since their last meeting. She'd wanted to hear everything about his life.

That was impossible. No one could know what she'd done. It was also unnecessary. His life was there for everyone to see in the shape of a little boy with his father's eyes.

"He's been gone, what? Three or four years now?" Jenny asked.

"Six." Six years, three months, and twelve days. If pressed, Thea could probably calculate the hours.

Jenny clucked her tongue. "The years fly faster and faster, don't they?"

"Mm-hmm."

"Those boys were wild as hares when they were younger," Jenny continued. "If they weren't riding, they were running or racing like they couldn't wait for trouble to find them. One year, Lord Garrett lost control of his curricle and ended up in Josephine Bell's chicken coop. Her hens wouldn't lay for a month. Trampled her rose bushes, too. They're still misshapen."

"That was Oliver."

"Are you certain?"

Thea nodded. She would have been in the curricle if Oliver hadn't grown suspicious his older brother would play dirty just to win. She had watched, heart in her throat, as Oliver had crashed. She'd spent weeks afterward at his side, serving as his assistant since his arm had been in a sling. Together they had cared for his injured horses, repaired Mrs. Bell's chicken coop, and had done their best to save her roses.

No one had noticed their attachment then, or at least proscribed any gossip to it. That hadn't come until later. It had taken Thea years to thwart it. Now, with one exchange in her dining room, tongues would be wagging again.

"His little boy sure is a darling thing," Jenny said.

Pain sliced through Thea. Simon, small for his age with midnight black curls no doubt inherited from his mother. The little boy was living proof Oliver had moved on.

She'd barely been able to stand there without screaming, but they'd had a curious audience. Besides, the child wasn't responsible for the tide of grief she swam in every day.

"Thea? Are you ill?"

She was used to the question, though she thought she'd become adept at masking her desolation. Oliver had always made it impossible to hide. Damn him. "I'm fine. Just tired of being on my feet today."

"Would you like me to drop by your mother's?" Jenny untied her still-white apron. "Save you the trip?"

Her mother would never let her forget it. "No, but thank you. The worst of the rain has passed, and the air will do me good." She needed to gather her thoughts and get her rioting emotions under control.

"I'll be happy to wait and go with you. My William always used to say…"

All Jenny's conversations inevitably turned to her late husband. Indeed, most widows' did, helping them form a sisterhood of grief Thea had avoided by insisting her courtship and marriage had been too short—that she'd barely felt married.

John Lawson came in through the back door, bringing the smells of summer and stable with him. "Your horse is hitched,

Missus." He shook the wet from his coat as he scuffed his feet against the rug. Checking his boots, he did it again and again until the soles were clean. "You need to get started."

The old Scotsman had looked out for Thea like a daughter from the moment he'd hired on. He fussed if she lifted too much, if she was out in the weather, or out too late. He insisted she stay upstairs and out of sight in the evenings when the crowd got too rowdy, even hiring his own staff of local boys to work nights and do chores.

"You cluck like a mother hen," Jenny said as she got her cloak. "And you needn't worry. I'm going most of the way with her."

"I'll be a while yet. You shouldn't wait, or you'll be walking in the dark." She shooed Jenny out the door and prodded John to follow her. "Matter of fact...John can make sure you get home safely."

"Missus..." Despite the wary tone, John's lips quirked in a grin.

"Thank me tomorrow," Thea whispered. John had quietly pursued Jenny for two years, though the widow appeared oblivious. The least Thea could do was play matchmaker.

"You'll be back tonight?" John asked.

"Yes." She closed the lid on the stocked hamper. "And yes, I have my pistol with me."

"Good, because I doubt that horse could outrun much."

"He'll do just fine." She defended her beloved, though plodding, horse. "Hurry or Jenny will walk off without you."

Alone in the kitchen, Thea tied her cloak at her neck and counted to thirty to make sure John and Jenny were gone. She lifted the basket and a bouquet of flowers she'd cut before the rain and made her way to the stable and her waiting gig.

"Hello, Neptune," she murmured as she slid her hand under the horse's wavy mane and along his strong neck. It had taken a week of badgering, and double the payment, to rescue the animal from the butcher. The undertaker had sold him simply because he'd found a prettier bay gelding.

The scent of hay and horse made Thea's nose itch. As always, the smell reminded her of Oliver. The damp air seeping through her clothes chilled her even as her memories smoldered. A stormy night. The boy she'd loved. The beginning and the end of so many chapters in her life.

How the hell am I supposed to be across the ocean from you, Thee?

He'd done just fine, hadn't he?

CHAPTER TWO

T HOUGH NEPTUNE WOULDN'T have won races even in his younger days, he made short work of the trip to Thetford. Smacks and slaps in puddles gave way to clattering, sharp strikes against cobblestones as they crossed the bridge. Trees surrendered to buildings, and worn footpaths turned to shadowy alleys.

Thea stopped at the churchyard first. After looping the reins around the top of the iron fence surrounding the cemetery, she gave the horse a slice of apple to keep him happy. She carried the bouquet to the grave under the large oak tree in the corner nearest the church.

"Hello, Father." She ignored the wet and knelt to place new flowers at the base of the marker. *James Aaron Fowler. A good man, gone too soon*, the stone read. He had been, and he was.

Her mother liked to say that, had he had more time, the family would have been in better condition. But Thea understood the truth. Her father had possessed a kind heart and a lousy sense of business. They would have always been poor at his death.

Poor in pocket, but rich in spirit, dear girl.

Right. Spirit. His widow was a bitter shut-in, and his youngest daughter followed the fancy like it was a religion. His oldest daughter was a liar, amongst other things.

"Oliver is home," Thea whispered. Father always liked to keep up with his pupils. "Canada has been good for him, I think, though he looks tired." She chuckled without humor. "Don't we all?" Taking a deep breath, she confessed the truth to the one person she trusted with her secrets. "He's still the most handsome man I've ever seen."

Every marriage-minded debutante had chased the Hawkins lordlings with abandon. Garrett had been the ultimate prize. Tall and gregarious, but English-pale with a bend toward unhealthy habits, he'd soaked up the attention and encouraged the chase that came with his inheritance. Once he'd finished school, he'd begun spending a great deal of time in London, where he'd adapted to a life of ease and debauchery.

Oliver, however, had been the elusive prey. Sable hair, changeling eyes, and a quicksilver smile had combined with coloring inherited from his Spanish grandmother. Rather than haunting ballrooms and gaming hells, he'd spent most of his youth active and working. From all appearances, he was still doing it. He was broader and more muscular than when he'd left. More confident.

Thea rubbed her thumb across her fingers, still feeling his touch. He was callused. Harder.

His voice was the same, though. Every rich syllable reminded her of cinnamon sugar cookies, summers of Spanish lessons with his grandmother, and every sleepy promise he'd made in the dark.

"Mrs. Smith?"

She raised her eyes and met Mary Carver's shy smile. Thea wanted to ignore the woman, to stay with her memories, but it had taken months and the illness of her daughter for the young mother to start a conversation.

Thea stood and walked to the gate rather than making Mary come into the graveyard. The closer she drew, the tighter her heart squeezed at the sight of the little girl, happy and safe in her mother's arms. "Hello, Mary. How are Annie's ears?"

"So much better, thank you. Those drops were just the thing." Mary was short and had been dainty before Annie's arrival. Now her clean, tightly woven cloak barely met in front of her as she leaned in to whisper. "It's just as well, too. Doctor Anderson is busy tending to the duke. My sister, Patsy, was in his office with her son this morning when Lionel rushed in, without a hat even, to fetch him."

As if the years hadn't passed, Thea's first thought was of Oliver and what he could be walking into.

Well, whatever it was, he could handle it without her. Just like she could handle life without him.

Annie fussed in her mother's arms, her cheeks turning from healthy pink to angry red as she reached for Thea. Annie quieted as she explored a new person. Tiny fingers tugged Thea's cloak, struggling to untie it. Small feet bounced against her ribs. Baby smells, baby sounds. The child's weight and warmth were both comfort and torture.

"Is Mr. Fletcher coming back this week?" Mary asked.

Thea picked a flower from the hedge and tickled Annie's nose with it. "He should be here tomorrow for a few days, just to check on us."

"Someone that handsome, checking on me. I'd find a way to keep him for more than a few days."

Thea had long given up fighting the hopeful, well-meaning gossip about her and Drake Fletcher, the man everyone knew as the owner of The Galloping Goat. The women thought she should be married and settled, and under normal circumstances, the attention of a wealthy businessman wasn't anything to ignore.

But there wasn't anything normal about her life. She gently pried her locket out of Annie's grasp.

Mary reached for her daughter. "No you don't, missy," she scolded. "You leave Mrs. Smith's jewelry alone." Her gaze softened. "I'm only joking, ma'am. You and Mr. Fletcher, how you grieve, is none of my concern. I don't know what I'd do if anything happened to my Sam."

Next to the pretty young farm wife, Thea felt too tall, too thin, and too hard all the way 'round. She hoped Mary and Sam

Carver had a long and happy life ahead of them with half a dozen children and that loss would never touch their lives.

"No offense taken, Mary." She curved a hand around Annie's head and let the fine hair tickle her fingers for one last moment before handing the baby back to her mother. "You'd better start home before it rains again. Let me know if you need anything at all."

After their goodbyes, Thea climbed into her gig and urged Neptune forward, around the corner and across the cobblestone common at the center of town. Around a second corner and down a cramped lane, she stopped in front of a narrow, gray stone building. The shades in the tall upper windows were crooked, leaving the impression that the building was angry at her.

It could just get in line. It wasn't Thea's fault the jovial printer on the bottom floor had gone out of business last month and left the grouchy widow upstairs as the sole tenant. She was no more responsible for a decline in business than she was her mother's mood.

She opened the door and tightened her grip on the basket as she drew in a steadying breath. Though her relationship with her mother had never been easy, over the last few years it had teetered between disappointment and grudging acceptance, if not of her then of her help.

Laughter and the scent of roasted chicken floated down the stairs. Thea was torn between relief and dread when she recognized her sister's voice. Mother would be easier to manage with Millie here, but Millie was always difficult to handle.

Her mother's small apartment was crowded with furniture too large to be useful and too shabby to be comfortable. Books and papers teetered in stacks on every surface; some lay in neglected piles on the floor. Her sister swept her into a heavily perfumed embrace and pressed two coins into her palm.

"We were worried you'd run into trouble on the road," Millie said, not sounding worried at all.

When they'd been younger, blonde, curvy, and outgoing Millie had been chased by every gentleman in the county. She'd gone to London instead. Now she was too soft, except for her calculating gaze and the fingers pressing coins into Thea's palm.

"I had to tend to the supper crowd." Thea pocketed Millie's share of their mother's expenses and went to the kitchen to unpack what she'd brought. It wouldn't compare to the feast Millie had undoubtedly supplied, but after the treats had spoiled, their mother would depend on these simpler provisions. "Some of us have to work every day."

"Don't be so prim. Your face will freeze that way," her sister said. "I can't help it that my clients pay more handsome sums than yours."

Thea had visited Millie's London dress shop once, years ago. The few clients she'd had were working class, middle class at best. None of them would pay well enough for this food, not to mention Millie's dress or shoes. Even her hat.

Thea selected a few choice berries from a bowl on the table and popped them into her mouth, letting their sweetness dilute the harsh words on her tongue.

"I've eaten already." She brushed her lips across her mother's cool cheek. "Hello, Mother."

You must promise, Thea. Promise you'll look after her.

The coins in her pocket shifted, a physical reminder of the vow she'd made to her father. Keeping that promise meant keeping too many secrets and telling too many lies. It meant coming back to a place with too many memories.

"You're late," her mother snapped. Some things never changed.

Thea bit her tongue. Again. If arguing with her mother solved anything, they'd have made their peace years ago. That never changed either. "I stopped at the churchyard on the way."

"The Rushford coach went through the square not half an hour ago. Sarah Dalton came to tell me she saw the new earl inside, lording himself over everyone. Did you see him?"

There was no sense in lying. Despite her better impulses, Thea spread a thin layer of butter over a thick slice of bread and enjoyed eating something that she hadn't made.

"He stopped at the inn for a meal." Thea kept her tone neutral as she took her customary seat at the table, nearest the kitchen. "We said hello."

Her mother slapped the table. "How could you feed him after what he did to you?"

"Because his money spends just like anyone else's. And he didn't do anything to me."

"He ruined you. I want you to stay away from him."

"I ruined myself, Mother." Thea repeated the oft-used argument. Oliver Hawkins had broken her heart, but she'd been a willing participant.

"And with it your sister's prospects. Rather than being married to a respectable gentleman with a family, she's in *trade*."

Millie was not in trade any more than Thea was a duchess. The money in Thea's pocket didn't come from a High Street dress shop that catered to the *ton*. It came from a horse race, or a whist hand, or a boxing match.

Be kind, Thea. Your mother only knows one way.

Her father had always believed the best of everyone. He had put the *gentle* in gentleman. Thea worked every day to live up to his example. Today that meant keeping her thoughts about her sister's *trade* behind her teeth.

"I don't think you'll have to worry about seeing him. It's only a visit, and he's going to be busy with the consequences of Garrett's death."

"The duke has taken ill as well," Millie said as she sat. "It was the talk of the market, how Doctor Anderson had been at Felton House all day."

Poor Oliver. Home less than a day and already entrenched in drama and gossip.

"That family is cursed. Serves them right for what they did to—"

Pain and anger stormed through Thea's chest. It was her turn to strike the table. "No one deserves loss, Mother."

Just like no one earned favor. Thea had given up trying years ago.

"We have no home because of that family, and you have no prospects because of that boy. They need to pay however God sees fit."

"God would never take a child to punish a parent," Thea snapped. "And prospects aren't the prize they're lauded to be."

"Hear, hear," Millie said as she raised her glass. "Still, Thea, with Oliver home…"

Thea choked down the bite of bread and considered her movements, careful not to let her knife clatter against the china her mother only used on Fridays. "He means nothing to me, nor I to him." She stood and gathered her things.

"You're leaving?" Her mother's question had an edge like a blade. No doubt she suspected some sort of illicit liaison. Things in Thetford never changed.

"I have work to do." Thea didn't bother to kiss her again. She was beginning to wonder why she tormented herself by visiting at all. "I'm going home."

ROLLING THROUGH THE sea of grasses in the middle of nowhere, too far from Thetford to turn around and too close to Felton House for comfort, Oliver shared the last biscuit with Simon. Grains of cinnamon and sugar dissolved on his tongue, making him feel more welcome than he had all day.

"Those were good," the little boy said as he brushed his hands on his trousers.

"*Abuela* Lita made them for me all the time. She taught Thea, Mrs. Smith, to make them."

"Ab-Ab." Simon squinted up at him. "Huh?"

"Abuela." Oliver enunciated each syllable as he peeled a nectarine. "My *grandmère.*"

"Will my *grandmère* make biscuits?"

Not bloody likely. He surrendered a section of fruit. "I'm sure all your favorite foods will be in the kitchen."

"There's your tree," Emmett called out as they passed an ancient oak, its knots twisting the trunk until it looked painful. It had always been the point of no return. Things had to go back in their appropriate places.

He put Simon on his feet. "Straighten your clothes."

Oliver followed his own instructions, silently cursing the butterflies in his stomach as he tied his cravat. He ran his fingers through his hair, smoothing it down. Simon did the same, but all the boy did was make his curls a wilder mess. Oliver took over making his son presentable.

"Will she like me?"

The question broke Oliver's heart. His mother hadn't even liked her own children. Rather than lying to reassure them both, he looked his son in the eyes.

"I would never bring you somewhere scary, Simon. This is your home, but if she were mean I wouldn't let you come. All right?"

Simon broke out into a fit of laughter. "Your tie is floppy, Papa."

The giggles worsened on Oliver's next attempt. Soon he was failing on purpose. They were both laughing as the carriage stopped.

Oliver shoved the cravat in his pocket as he opened the door. Simon clambered down the steps and stood on the path, craning his neck up and then in either direction. To the four-year-old used to city life in Quebec, the house probably looked like a palace.

With its dark stone walls and narrow windows, Oliver thought it resembled a prison.

The front door opened, and another long-time servant rushed out to greet them. "Thank heaven you're home, Oliver, er, Lord

Elveden."

"Hello, Lionel." The wild look in the butler's eyes concerned Oliver on more than one level. He focused on the primary one. "Let me introduce my son, Simon."

Simon grinned and stuck out his hand. "Hello."

"It's a pleasure to meet you." Lionel greeted the little boy with a quick bow and a quicker smile before leaning close enough to whisper. "We should hurry. There's been an accident."

The words sent a chill down Oliver's spine. He lifted Simon into his arms before hurrying inside. Servants peered from around doors and over the upstairs railing, peeking into the cavernous hall much like Simon did when he snuck out of bed.

His mother, Lady Madeleine, the Duchess of Rushford, was at the foot of the stairs, in yards of black with a handkerchief clutched in one hand. The other was stretched out to him, trembling. "Oliver, dearest. Thank God you're home."

Dearest? That was carrying it a bit far, and probably solely for the servants. Still, he kissed the cheek she offered. "Hello, Mother." Careful not to muss her skirts, he stepped back as quickly as possible. "This is Simon."

"Hello, *Abuela*," Simon chirped.

For a fleeting moment, the grieving mask dropped and his mother's lips thinned. There, in her flashing eyes, was the woman Oliver was used to. He stiffened his shoulders and tightened his hold on his son.

"Did I say it wrong?" Simon asked, his voice watery.

"You said it perfectly," he assured the tired little boy. "But remember what we practiced?"

Simon nodded, but his smile was gone. *"Bonjour, Grandmère. Ravi de vous rencontrer,"* he whispered as he dropped his head to Oliver's shoulder.

"Et toi, Simon." She beckoned a young woman to her side. The girl was as silent and blank as a shadow. "This is Alice. She's your nurse. Go upstairs now so I can talk to your papa."

Alice was too young, too slim, and too pale. Under normal

circumstances, Oliver would never leave her in charge of his son, but he needed to get to the bottom of whatever drama was brewing. He bent double and put Simon on the stairs.

"I have to talk to your grandmother, Si. Please go with Alice and get ready for bed. I'll be in as soon as I can. We'll explore tomorrow."

"Yes, Papa."

The little boy walked away, his curiosity dampened by one conversation and the oppressive state of this house. Oliver never should have corrected him, never should have brought him here. This whole trip had been a mistake.

"You should have asked before you hired a nurse," Oliver muttered under his breath.

"And you should have hired one years ago." His mother started upstairs, leaving him no choice but to follow. "You've taught him Spanish?"

The sneer on the last word set Oliver's teeth on edge. It was best she hadn't met them at the coast. He couldn't imagine being trapped with her for the entire trip. "No. I was telling a story and he picked up on a word. He wanted to impress you." He took the stairs two at a time. "What happened to Garrett?"

"Not now."

They neared the mysterious suite of rooms his parents occupied. Someone exited the bedroom, but it wasn't his father. The black bag made Oliver's mouth go dry.

"Your Grace, the duke is resting comfortably now," the doctor said. "I'll leave him in peace and come back in the morning."

"No," his mother snapped. "If anything should happen, I want you here."

Oliver stepped forward and extended his hand. "Oliver Hawkins, sir. What's happened to my father?"

"Doctor Anderson, your lordship. Apoplexy, it appears. This morning."

How many times was death going to shape his life by surprise? "Will he recover?"

"It's too early to tell, sir. He's confined to bed. There's significant weakness and his speech is garbled."

The man had the harried look of someone who had been working far too long for one day. "Thank you for all you've done, doctor. Please go home and rest." He ignored his mother's outraged gasp. "We'll send for you if he worsens in the night. Otherwise, we'll see you tomorrow."

Once they were alone, she wheeled on him. "How dare—"

"He was exhausted, Mother. So am I."

"I suppose that's why you didn't introduce yourself properly. Elveden, Oliver. You must remember."

"I've been Oliver Hawkins for thirty years. I've been Elveden for half a day." He put his hand on the door latch. "I'm going to say hello to Father before I go check on Simon. Do you want to come in?"

She shrank away, as if eager to escape. "I'll go arrange for your baggage."

It wouldn't take long. He and Simon shared a trunk and a single bag.

Once she was gone, Oliver opened the door and slipped into his father's room. Heavy blue velvet drapes shrouded the windows, and a low fire warmed the room while it cast shadows on the far wall. Oliver sat in the bedside chair and stared at his sleeping father.

His face was heavily lined and jowly. His gray hair stuck up in unruly tufts against the pillow. He looked nothing like the robust man who'd visited Quebec two months earlier.

The old man opened his eyes and blinked to focus. His stare widened, and his mouth worked, but the words were unrecognizable. Tears glistened in his eyes.

Oliver clasped a limp hand and cleared his throat. "Don't worry, Father. I'll take care of everything."

AFTER SITTING WITH the duke and calming his agitation until he slept, Oliver walked through the halls, carrying a candlestick and reacquainting himself with his home. It had always been easy to find his way out of the nursery, but it was now impossible to find his way back in. The change in wallpaper finally indicated the right direction.

He opened the door at the end of the hall and stood on the threshold taking in the moonlit room full of small furniture and the outdated, fragile toys. It smelled of dust, mold, and age.

"Papa?"

He sat on the edge of Simon's bed. "I'm sorry I took so long. Your grandfather is sick, so I had to help."

"Is he better?"

"He will be. How do you like your room?"

"It's a baby's room."

It was, especially for a child who had spent his life with adults. "We'll fix it."

"It's scary here."

Oliver had to agree. Even his room was more imposing than he'd remembered. "Why don't I sleep in here with you?"

Without waiting on an answer, he rooted through the closet and returned with stale linens for a pallet on the floor. He stripped to his shirt, trousers, and socks. Using his coat as a pillow, he wriggled against the cold, hard floor and sneezed as dust tickled his nose. "Goodnight, Simon. I love you."

"I love you, too."

Oliver stared at the ceiling and listened to his son sleep while he shaped the shadows into his late wife's face. *You'd be proud of our boy, Julia. He's a great traveler, and he's curious about everything. He has a quick mind.*

Had her hair swept away from her brow like that? His memories were fading like the patterns on this childish wallpaper. *He already speaks French better than I, although that wouldn't take much, and he's showing an interest in Spanish. I might teach him just to upset Mother.*

Her laughter whispered into his ear. She'd never failed to make him smile, and now she was alone in Canada. In the ground. *They needed me to come back. What was I supposed to do? Simon doesn't have anyone but Richard and me. I wanted him to know my family, to see his heritage. Life is too tenuous. You taught me that, ma lutin.*

He talked to Julia's hazy ghost until his eyes drooped closed, which was too quickly. *I miss you. I swear I do.*

And then, fool that he was, he dreamt of another woman.

CHAPTER THREE

The NEXT MORNING, intent on living up to at least one promise from yesterday, Oliver wandered through the house exploring. Simon sat on his shoulders, serving as lookout.

"Is that you, Papa?"

Oliver looked up at the first painting in the short line of family portraits. "No. That's *mi abuelo*, Edward. My *grandpère*."

"Edward. Like me."

"And me, and your *grandpère*. Edward began life with little but his wits and his honor." Oliver recited the story Lita had told throughout his childhood. "And he served the king so well that he was rewarded with Felton House and a title—Lord Felton. Eventually, he became the Earl of Elveden and then, finally, the Duke of Rushford."

"Elveden. That's your new name."

"It's a town down the road," Oliver said.

"Are there elves there?"

The boy was obsessed with fairies and elves, but Oliver was content to let him believe in magic for a while longer yet. It was, amazingly enough, easier to explain. "Not that I know of."

"Oh. He looks like you."

Simon wriggled on his perch, testing Oliver's reflexes and his muscles. He'd only get one more year, maybe two, of carrying his son this way. He already missed it.

"Lita always said he did."

As a child, Oliver had charged down this hall, barely glancing on his way outside. Now he met the kind gaze of the man who could pass for his twin and wished he'd been able to meet his grandfather. He wanted a chance to talk about Quebec and how daunting it was to face a life that would end with a portrait on this wall. "Let's go see what's for breakfast."

The Felton House kitchen had always been his favorite place. A crackling fire was counterpoint to bacon simmering on the stove. The scent of baking bread mingled with brewing coffee. Hazel, the family cook for as long as he could remember, was bustling across the room.

"Don't know why I have to be here this early," she muttered as he snuck up behind her. "No one will eat until almost noon, and them scones will be hard as rocks. What then?"

"I could probably break another window or two with them," Oliver said.

She whirled on him, spoon at the ready, her eyes wide and a hand over her heart. He danced out of reach, bouncing Simon on his shoulders as they laughed in harmony. "Hello, Hazel."

She held her arms wide, and he walked in for a warm, hard hug. Hazel smacked him with the spoon while Simon clung to his hair for balance.

The older woman backed away first. Tears clung to her lashes as she looked over his head. "Who's this fella?"

Oliver swallowed the lump in his throat and lifted Simon from his shoulders. "This is my son, Simon."

"*Bonjour*, Hazel." The little boy bowed at the waist and offered his hand, and the cook melted into a puddle.

She managed to curtsey first. "Pleased to meet you, Lord—"

"Just Simon," Oliver whispered.

"Of course. Simon." She dabbed her eyes and waved for a newcomer to join their group. "Look who's here, Fred."

The groundskeeper hugged him, too. "It's good to see you home, lad. I was just about to go to the hen house. Simon, would you like to come gather eggs?"

The chance of a new adventure brought a sparkle to the boy's eyes. "Can I, Papa?"

"You may. But do exactly as Fred says."

Oliver watched them leave, smiling as Simon chattered endlessly and Fred nodded in apparent agreement. This should make up for last night's gaffe.

"Your mother would have a fit if she saw that," Hazel said from behind him. "Which is why you did it, I s'pose."

"Yes, ma'am." Oliver snatched a warm scone from the tray and poured a cup of coffee. "What isn't everyone telling me? Starting with Garrett."

"You know how he hated to lose," she said. "They were out at a party and, according to Emmett, Garrett accused Lord Sterling of cheating. Ended in a duel, barely light enough to see."

Oliver remembered Pierce Cavendish, Lord Sterling, from Eton. The man was a crack shot with a short fuse and an almost shorter stature, but he was generally honest. "Was Sterling cheating?"

"Rumor has it that Garrett was the dishonest one, and he cried foul before he could get caught." She kept her back to him while she worked. "Some say Garrett knew the man's wife too well for polite conversation."

Damn. Of course Garret would leave a mess. "And Father?"

"Your mum went on a right tear after Garrett's death. She's been wearing a hole in the floor, and the duke has been hiding in his library. When he was quiet too long yesterday, Lionel went in and found him on the floor."

The door opened.

"But was gray, had long ears, and ate grass," Simon chirped, a wide smile on his face. Fred was laughing so hard the eggs clacked together in the basket.

Oliver's cheeks heated to the point he thought apoplexy might be contagious. "Simon. We've talked about sharing Uncle Richard's rhymes."

"But Fred asked."

"I did, sir," Fred choked, swiping tears from his face.

"Biscuits." Simon scampered onto a stool so he could see the tray coming out of the oven. "Papa never makes biscuits for breakfast."

Hazel stared over the little boy's head, her eyes wide. "Your papa cooks your breakfast?"

"Uh-huh. And *Oncle* Richard and I do the dishes before we go to work."

Oliver squelched the urge to quiet Simon's story. It was the truth, and he didn't want the boy to think he couldn't be open about the life they lived. The one Oliver had chosen for them. He squared his shoulders and winked at his son. "Go with Fred and wash up. And no rhymes."

Once he was alone with Hazel, he went to the cook, put his hands on her shoulders, and ducked to look her in the eye. "You raised me well, *Tante*. He and I are fine. Better than most. I just don't want him to think we're odd. Not yet."

Unshed tears pooled in her eyes as she put a hand to his cheek. "My poor boy."

Four years of worrying about someone else, of being mother and father and grieving when no one was looking, swamped him. Oliver dropped his head to the woman's shoulder and closed his eyes as she comforted him.

Simon's chatter grew louder, and Oliver straightened as he wiped his face. Hazel turned away and blotted her eyes with the corner of her apron.

"Where did this hamper come from?" she asked as she seized on the first distraction.

"Mrs. Smith left it for us," Simon offered.

Hazel's eyebrows arched, and Oliver reconsidered his parenting techniques. Sometimes, secrets were best.

"You've seen Thea, then?" she asked as she packed the basket. "How was it?"

Awkward, tense, stilted. "Very much how I'd expected."

Oliver made sure Simon was occupied with Fred. "Where is her husband?"

"He sailed for India and never returned. Lost at sea. They'd been married just over a month."

A month? When his mother's letter had arrived, Thea had already been widowed. If he'd climbed on the first ship for home—

No. He watched Simon across the kitchen, straightening the hearth under Fred's guidance. Life hadn't turned out how he'd planned, but he'd loved Julia, and Simon was everything that mattered. They had a good life, even if it was improvised.

"Come, Simon," he said as he stood and gathered the hamper Hazel had packed. "Let's explore outside."

They walked from the house and down the lane. The farther they went, the easier it was for Oliver to breathe. Fog still blanketed the valleys, recalling memories of playing soldier. He and Garrett had roared through the mist and tumbled on the lawn until they were soaked.

Yesterday, Garrett's death had simply been another bit of bad news from home, already weeks old before he'd learned of it. Now it was an unchangeable reality that caused a keen ache. Garrett had behaved as though he was favored and protected by God himself, and he'd fought using every unfair advantage he'd had. But he'd also had a hearty laugh, a stout hug, and a quick wit.

"What's over here?" Simon ran ahead and around the corner.

Oliver detoured from his memories and quickened his pace to reach Simon at the stables.

To one side was the coach they had arrived in. Matte paint patches showed stark against the lacquered black exterior. The door latch glinted in the sunshine, but it was tarnished and dull closer to the wood frame.

Inside, the upholstery was faded by years of trips to town and worn thin in places from numerous occupants. New nails in the trim were easy to spot, as was the thin line of blood caked and dried around their heads.

He'd carted his son in the same carriage that had borne Garrett's bloody body. Oliver wouldn't blame Emmett for the state of the carriage. He'd barely recognized the gray-haired, stooped man as the family's coachman. Grooms seemed to be few and far between.

Still, he wondered why they hadn't sent another coach for him. He swept his gaze down the row. A farm cart, his dusty curricle, and an ancient gig waited. The coach with etched glass windows that had been Emmett's pride and joy six years earlier was missing.

Chuffing and stamping caught his attention and familiar noses came into view over the stall doors. "Oh my God." Oliver half-jogged into the stables. "Simon, come here."

Two gray geldings tossed their heads in greeting until he scratched them between the eyes, reaching up under their black forelocks and smiling when they nudged against his pockets, searching for treats. Though they still acted like ponies, white hair threaded through their manes and light patches dotted their coats.

"Mars and Mercury." He'd expected them to be sold long ago. "Hello, gentlemen. I'm home."

Simon inched closer, making it more difficult to explore. Still, at the end of the row, past the draft animals, a giant black horse snorted and pawed his bedding as though he was still angry at being left behind.

Oliver lifted Simon so he could see the animal. "This is Jupiter. I rode him in every race with your uncle Garrett, even leapt a few hedges. Frightened Fred half to death."

He'd been Simon's age when he'd received his first horse. It would have been a luxury in Quebec, but they had an empty stall here and plenty of space to ride. And horses generally lived a long time. It might help the boy pass the time while they were here. "Would you like a horse?"

Simon's eyes widened as he stared at Jupiter, and Oliver knew it wasn't with excitement. How on earth could the boy not like horses? All children did, didn't they?

"Not like him," Oliver said as he put Simon down. "A pony." A small, fat, slow pony.

"I'll think about it," Simon whispered. "Can we go now?"

Oliver picked up their breakfast, and they continued on their way. Bird songs split the cool, sweet air as sunshine banished the fog. He answered Simon's questions about outbuildings and roofs visible on the horizon, sometimes making up stories for buildings he didn't remember. They crested a small rise, and below them on the right was the dower house, *Casa de Lita*.

How many mornings had he stood here and watched smoke curl from his grandmother's chimney? How many times had he tumbled down the dew-slick grass covering this hill in his hurry to get to her? Now, he walked slowly, keeping a steadying hand on Simon as they approached the empty house.

The gate shrieked on its hinges, and the sight beyond its peeling facade brought a bitter curse up his tongue. The garden was a riot of decay and neglect. Ruined fruit from shapeless trees littered the ground. Limbs, branches, and dead leaves had killed the groundcover in places, and rogue vines wove through the shrubbery and climbed the trellises and arbors, strangling Lita's prized roses. It would have made her weep.

Keeping Simon's hand, Oliver made his way through the overgrown morass and inspected the house. Peppery thyme planted between paving stones brought back memories, food and otherwise. Lita had always known he was coming to visit, no matter how quiet he'd been. It had taken far too many childhood summers to realize the plants had betrayed him.

The roof was intact, the doors and windows were secure, and through the filthy glass he could see the shrouded furniture, artwork and mirrors. He kept waiting for Lita to walk down the hall and scold him for lurking at her window. He could almost feel her hard hug.

Estoy en casa, Abuela. Ven a conocer mi hijo. She would have adored Simon. They could have sat in her kitchen, telling stories of Canada for days.

"Can we eat now, Papa?"

Oliver turned away from the house, intending to leave and find another picnic spot, but the gate to the lower garden caught his attention. The roses there, striped like peppermint candies, had been Lita's favorites, and they were blooming in abundance. Wading through the sea of weeds, Oliver reached the arbor and stared beyond it. The verge and trees were trimmed and neat, as were the hedges and shrubbery. He and Simon walked through. The flowers were healthy and well-manicured, buried and mulched for the season. "Who on earth ..."

"Maybe it's a fairy," Simon offered.

A twig snapped nearby. Oliver left his son near the gate and hurried to the tree line. The patterns created by sun and shadow made it difficult to distinguish shapes for a moment. Just as he was ready to surrender, another twig cracked.

There on the far side—that was a bonnet. A plain straw one that blended into the surroundings. The brown dress helped camouflage her as she moved quickly, like someone intimately familiar with this forest.

It had to be Thea. Oliver caught her name on his tongue and swallowed it. Her husband's death changed little between them.

"Perhaps it is a fairy. Should we build her a house?"

When Simon didn't answer, Oliver looked over his shoulder half expecting to see someone spiriting the boy away. Instead, Simon was sitting in the sunshine next to the open hamper, eating a biscuit.

Oliver sat and rummaged through what Hazel had packed, certain it was more than sweets. "Have you had eggs yet?"

"Umm ..."

"Did you at least save some biscuits for me?"

They ate surrounded by flowers, herbs, and fresh air while Oliver shared stories of his *abuela* and tried to remember the name of each plant.

Freshly turned earth and sunshine brought back memories of playing here away from his mother's harsh judgment. He'd picnicked out here, much like now. It had been their refuge—his and Thea's. The care she'd given the plants indicated it might still be hers.

I'll take care of Lita's garden, Oliver.

At least, Thea had kept that promise.

"Look, Papa." Simon giggled. "Ants."

Sighing, Oliver scooped as many pests and as much dirt as possible back into the hole Simon had dug. He moved the hamper, too. Hazel would paddle them both if they brought ants back to her kitchen. "Let's find the makings for a fairy house."

They toiled all morning, carving a doorway and windows into a large section of bark that had fallen from a dying tree, adding a spot for a chimney, settling it in a stump full of violets, and making walls from twigs.

The sun climbed higher, and Oliver squinted into the glare. It was close to mid-day, and dark clouds gathered over the top of the hill. It was going to rain. Again. Even if it didn't, he had things to do. Simply considering the list of chores exhausted him, but there was nothing for it. Until his father recovered, Oliver was in charge.

"Let's go, son." He stood and lifted Simon to his shoulders. "We'll come back tomorrow."

Thea emerged from the forest, her heart pounding as if she'd run home. She very nearly had.

She should have known Oliver would go to Lita's house as soon as was practical. It had been a haven for him, for both of them, as children, and it was natural he would want to share it with Simon.

Deep down, it was possible she had known. Maybe that's what had drawn her to the lower garden this morning for last minute weeding and harvesting herbs that would otherwise go to waste.

The overgrown upper garden always broke her heart, but it had been allowed to go fallow while she'd been gone. Now there was more to do than she could manage. She also couldn't tend it without being seen from Felton House. At least Oliver could enjoy part—

It wasn't for him. It was for Lita. Oliver's grandmother had provided a sanctuary for Thea. The least she could do was make sure those memories survived.

She slowed to remove her bonnet and noticed someone outside the inn's kitchen door. The dark braids belonged to her newest and youngest maid.

"Hello, Polly. Is something amiss?" The girl should be inside doing chores in the guest rooms.

The young maid stared over her shoulder toward the kitchen door, fidgeting from foot to foot.

"Polly."

Thea regretted her sharp tone when the girl turned back, her cheeks flushed and her eyes sparkling with tears. Something had frightened her, and a scolding wouldn't help. Though Polly was far too timid for her own good.

"Mr. Fletcher's here." The awed tone was one children reserved for Father Christmas or God Almighty. "He's in the kitchen inspectin' things."

"Was he harsh with you?" Thea asked.

"No, ma'am. He was nice, not like my—not like at home." Polly's eyes welled again. "What if he thinks I'm not good enough and turns me out?"

"Here now." Thea dropped her bonnet and herb basket and knelt in front of the young girl. "None of that. He won't turn you out. I won't let him."

"But Mrs. Snow says he owns the whole place and can do anything he wants. She didn't even toss him out of her kitchen."

"Yes, well." Thea worked to control her grin. "He put me in

charge of The Goat, and he trusts my opinion. Don't you worry. But if he makes you nervous, stay out here until we leave the kitchen. Then go back to work upstairs. Straighten the linens, dust, and sweep the hearth, then open the windows to air the rooms. All right?"

"Yes, Missus. Thank you."

In the kitchen, a silent Jenny swept back and forth between the hearth and the stove. Drake Fletcher sat at the table toying with a coffee mug.

His hat and gloves lay on the table, and the light from the windows glanced off the dark blue jacket stretched across his shoulders. Bright buttons and trim stood out on his navy and green waistcoat.

"Mr. Fletcher," Thea said as she closed the door. "It's so nice to see you."

Drake winked. "Mrs. Smith. Shall we go to the office?" He unfolded himself from the chair to his full height and carried his cup to the sink.

"I'll take care of that, sir," Jenny said. "You shouldn't—"

"I shouldn't leave a mess for you, Mrs. Snow." He picked up his case. "Thank you for the coffee."

Thea went through the great room in front of him, walking quickly and trying not to feel like he was chasing her as his footsteps rang from the walls. Her office was tucked beneath the stairs. Drake followed her in and closed the door behind him.

She loved this space. It was small, but she'd painted the walls a light color, and her meager collection of books lined the shelves against the short wall at the lowest edge of the slanted ceiling. A bright rug covered the floor under the desk, and a window the size of a parchment square looked out on the rear garden and the forest beyond.

Thea sat behind her desk on a chair she'd rescued from a refuse pile and recovered in needlepoint. She flexed her neck and shoulders.

"Why are you working as a gardener?" Drake asked as

shucked off his jacket and sat in a side chair across from her. His neatly tied yellow-gold cravat kept his collar tight, and the white shirt contrasted with his cinder black hair.

"Because I enjoy it, and I needed to replenish my herbs. There has been an increase in childhood illnesses." Her favorite maid, Rachel, had a sick child, but Drake didn't need to know that. Thea had promised not to divulge the young woman's past.

He rested his ankle on the opposite knee. "Polly's new."

"Ivy at Willow's End sent her on the coach from Norwich," Thea explained as she opened the strongbox under her desk and handed over the profits from the past two weeks. "Her father had *sold* her, Drake. Like a horse. She's terrified you'll send her packing."

"That's my job, is it not? To act the part of the terrifying master who sweeps in periodically." He lifted a ledger from his satchel and opened it in his lap.

It was his job. As far as everyone knew, he was the owner of The Goat and a benefactor who loaned funds to village businesses that had fallen on hard times.

But The Goat's owner was the woman serving them supper. For just over two years, Thea had operated a successful business and loaned money to half of Thetford without anyone learning the truth. It was yet another layer of secrets to her life, as necessary as all the others.

"You can't afford many more loans," Drake warned. "They aren't paying off. So far all we have is a handful of extensions."

"I believe that's about to change." She refused to elaborate because it was nothing more than intuition. While Oliver couldn't put all things right, he would settle his family's accounts. Thea was certain of it.

"All right, but we need a strategy in case they change slower than you expect." He ran his eyes across the account book. "I'd like to put five hundred pounds in the new Barnham ironworks. It's a solid bet for a good return. Is that acceptable to you?"

Everyone in Thetford had been agog over the new rail station and the promise of a train. While Thea hated the noise, she understood the benefit to the economy. Progress would come from goods delivered; growth would come from needing more goods. Trains needed rails to deliver on both fronts. "Good idea. Thank you. What else?"

They continued their meeting in that fashion until Drake stashed his ledger and notes. "Tavie sends her love. She's looking forward to seeing you at the next meeting."

Maybe seeing Aunt Tavie and getting on with life as it was now would help Thea put her past in perspective. But thinking about London made her eager for space and air. Thea stood.

Drake stared at her now empty chair, his lips curling in as much of a smile as he ever allowed. "What happened in that chair?"

"What do you mean?" She looked at her handiwork, expecting to see a spill or a tear.

"It looks like you tortured someone with nails and then put fabric over it."

"They're roses." Thea swatted his shoulder. "I'll find a maid to make up your room."

"Ask Polly to do it." He followed her from the office. "I'll see if I can put her at ease."

CHAPTER FOUR

T HEY WERE HEMORRHAGING cash.

Oliver rubbed his neck as he studied the list of figures and the scrawled explanations for each expense. He could understand the kitchen budget, but how did anyone spend seventy-five pounds on clothing in a single month, every month?

Dwindling rents and income compounded the situation. Those had never been large, but they had been sufficient when managed well. That had been the case until the last few years when the writing in the ledger changed. Unless Oliver missed his guess, Garrett had been placed in charge in the hopes he would rise to the occasion. Father had implied as much when he'd come to Quebec.

Clothing, boots, hats, horses, liquor, cash draws. Garrett and Mother had bled them almost dry. There was barely enough cash to pay for mill equipment and shipping charges.

Given the piles of paper splayed across the desk and the near-empty bottle of brandy, Father had been holed up in here trying to decipher the mess. It had been enough to drive him to a fit. Oliver rested his head on his hand and closed his eyes. He knew the feeling.

"Papa, look."

"Not now, Si."

It would take constant oversight to right this. Years of his life stuck in this room battling a tide of payables. Otherwise, Simon would inherit nothing but a headache.

"Papa." Simon added an insistent tug on his shirtsleeve in a plea for attention.

He couldn't borrow it; everything was entailed. He could write Richard for it, but that would take six months. Six more months. "I said not now."

The words cracked back at him from walls that were closing in. Walls that appeared opulent until he looked closely and saw chipped paint and the outlines of missing artwork.

The loud sniffle was next. "I'm sorry," Simon warbled.

Oliver ran both hands through his hair. *Mierda.* He'd been here two days, and he'd already made his little boy cry. Over money, of all things.

He dropped to the floor and used his sleeve to dry Simon's tears. "I'm sorry I was sharp with you. I'm trying to figure out a very difficult puzzle, and I forgot what was important."

Like a little boy in a strange place with no playmates. A child who probably needed a nap. God knew he'd like to take one. Instead, Oliver focused on the worm nuzzling his son's finger. "What have you there?"

"Fred says it's a cat-pillow and it will turn into a butt-fly."

Swallowing his laughter but shaking all the same, Oliver held out his hand and caught the creature as it fell, content to let it tickle his palm as it explored. "It's a caterpillar." He enunciated slowly. "And it's going to become a butterfly."

"When?" Simon peered closely, as if expecting the magic to occur immediately.

The whole thing reminded Oliver of studying biology in the vicarage library and begrudging Thea every correct answer. They'd placed caterpillars in jars with twigs and leaves and waited for nature. "It will take a while yet. Would you like to watch it happen?"

All it took was one excited nod, and they were off to the kitchen to wheedle a jar from Hazel and filch an awl from the stables before asking for Fred's help in gathering the tastiest leaves. When they were finished, Simon had the best housed, best fed caterpillar in the county.

"Can I name him?" he asked as they trudged up the path toward the house.

The duchess walked out, leading a visitor.

"Certainly," Oliver said while keeping an eye on the women. "What were you considering?"

Given his mother's stony expression, this caller wasn't a friend. She wore a fashionable bright blue coat and a matching lace-trimmed bonnet dangled from her fingers, which were covered by elaborately decorated gloves. Yellow-blonde hair was curled and pinned in an overdone style the bonnet would crush in seconds.

"Spot," Simon declared. "'Cause he has them."

When the younger woman turned, Oliver recognized Millicent Fowler, Thea's younger sister.

He'd always seen bits of Thea in Millie, especially their chins. Everyone else had always drawn a distinction between the sisters. Millie was the pretty one, and Thea was the smart one. Oliver thought that was unfair to both. To him, Thea's intelligence shined through her eyes and her wild red curls and freckles were authentic. To him, she had been beautiful.

In turn, Millie wasn't stupid. She hadn't been as bookish as Thea, but she chose to watch people instead. She knew what they wanted before they asked. She also knew what they wanted to hear.

She'd been so similar to Garrett that they should have been siblings. Just like he and Thea...well, thank God they weren't related.

"Good choice," Oliver said to his son as they neared the doorway.

"I'll have your payment." His mother's tone was icy.

"And I'll have your dresses, Your Grace," Millie replied.

More dresses. Out of respect, Oliver searched for a way to

rationalize the spending. After all, he knew better than most that people handled grief and pain in different ways. However, the duchess needed to find a better outlet.

Surrendering the sunshine of the garden for the shadows of the house, Oliver joined the women at the door. "Hello, Millie."

"Lord Elveden." She glanced down. "And who's this?"

"I'm Simon Hawkins." The little boy extended his hand. "It's nice to meet you, Miss."

"A son?" Millie raised an eyebrow and glanced sideways at his mother. "And an heir. How marvelous."

As much as Thea had been his confidante, and more, Millie had always made Oliver uneasy. If Thea disliked you, she told you so—and why. Millie's words always slid across his skin like oil, and her smile made him wonder when the knife would appear.

"Miss Fowler just finished my fitting," his mother said.

"I see. May we visit for a moment, Mother?" He beckoned a groom forward. "Dale will help with your gig, Miss Millicent. Please give your mother my regards."

He really did try not to sneer the last words.

His mother spun on her heel and returned to the house without as much as a backward glance. Oliver followed, intent on preventing her escape.

"Simon, go upstairs to Alice," his mother commanded.

Oliver tightened his grip on the boy's shoulder, just enough to reassure him and keep him in place. "Simon, your *grandmère* and I need to speak alone. Would you like to continue playing outside?"

His smile was bright, and his nod bounced Spot in his jar.

"Then please go see Fred and ask if you can help him weed."

Once Simon was safely in the sunshine, Oliver led his mother into the library. "He's used to adult company. He doesn't have to leave the room for every conversation."

"He doesn't have to be involved in all of them either." She frowned. "You're in your shirtsleeves."

He waved the end of his black neck cloth, his concession to mourning clothes. "And my jacket is in reach in case of company." Considering Garrett's death and Father's illness, it was a safe bet no one other than her dressmaker would visit. "The doctor said Father was resting well."

"He is." She glanced toward the desk. "Are you finding everything in order?"

"No. Did Garrett sell what's missing or did he lose it gambling?" He rolled his eyes at her practiced blank stare and pointed to the opposite end of the room. "The landscape that used to hang on that wall, the newest carriage, his horses."

"Gambling," she finally admitted.

"Yet you kept spending." He hefted a stack of bills. "We have to cut expenses."

"I've cut all of them I can."

"No. You and Garrett simply didn't pay them." This is why their man of business and their solicitor had quit and why servants were difficult to find. "No more dresses."

"You can't do that."

"You already have more new clothes than all the women in Thetford combined, and if I have to choose between your closet and mill equipment, I will choose the latter."

"Of course you will," she said. "There are expectations, Oliver. Which is why I wanted to talk with you."

Odd. He thought he'd forced this conversation.

"We received several supper invitations in anticipation of your arrival," she continued. "Given the circumstances, the hosts have all agreed to gather for a quiet dinner at one house. Lord and Lady Chitester have offered to host us."

His brother's death, his father's illness, were circumstances.

She stared at the stack of ledgers and piles of papers. "I think you should go with a smile on your face."

Ah-ha. "Should I bother to dress or simply go naked with a rose between my teeth?"

"Do be serious. We need money, and you have a son who

needs a mother. They have funds and daughters who want a title. It's how things are done."

"My son has a mother." Oliver gripped the desk to keep his hands from shaking. "And there are ways to make money other than to whore myself out to a woman who wants to be a countess."

"You might actually like one of the girls, you know."

Like wasn't love. He knew the difference.

"Do this for me." She stood and walked to the door, then paused with her hand on the knob. "At some point, whether you like it or not, you are going to be the Duke of Rushford, and the families here need to overcome Garrett's scandal. Try. That's all I'm asking."

She looked small and pale in her black dress, and the shadows under her eyes had darkened since yesterday. She still had her handkerchief clutched in her hand.

Oliver's responsibility to his family meant all his family.

And the servants, livestock, tenants, houses, fencing, roof repairs…

Oliver walked to the window and watched Simon in the garden, Spot's jar glinting in the sunshine. His little boy didn't need a mother, but he needed a family. A future.

Dinner didn't mean marriage. The same fathers who were willing to barter their daughters for a title ran businesses and built reputations. Perhaps he could court them instead.

THEA SAT IN the dining room, all tables empty but the one she occupied with Lady Chitester.

"I do hope you can help." The lady pleated her glove, finger to finger, then smoothed it out and began again. "With my cook's child taken ill, I'm quite at a loss as to this party. If we were in London, it would be easy, but here…I'm uncertain as to whom to ask."

"Is Gemma's daughter seriously ill?" Thea asked.

"No, thank goodness. She's such a darling little thing. But I can't possibly ask Gemma to care for the child and plan a dinner at the same time, especially on this short of a notice. You come so highly recommended. Can you help?"

The lady's concern over her cook's young daughter guaranteed Thea's cooperation, despite the time frame. "With only two days' notice, the menu will have to be simple, but the food will be good."

Lady Chitester's shoulders dropped as she smiled. "Augustus, Lord Chitester, has been grousing about this meal since the duchess asked us, er, since we decided..."

"I was curious as to who recommended me." Thea was careful to smooth her face and her smile. "I'll be happy to help. If you'd like to review the menu, I can—"

"I trust you, Mrs. Smith. His lordship compliments the food here every time we return from London. Select what you need and send the bills to us." The lady stood and offered her hand. "Thank you. This will relieve much of my stress and allow me to focus on Amelia."

Amelia Chitester. Pretty, smart, kind-hearted, marriageable Amelia. Dinner for fourteen, arranged by the duchess but foisted onto another hostess due to the mourning period. The duchess was wife shopping for Oliver. And her message was clear—Thea was the help.

As if she'd have the man. Even offered on one of the silver trays laid across the Chitesters' table, with an apple between his pretty teeth and burnt sugar glazing his caramel skin. Even if she immediately recalled his favorite foods.

She saw Lady Chitester into the care of the family coachman and then returned to the kitchen. Jenny was waiting.

"You took it, didn't you?" She didn't even wait for a reply. "You'll work yourself into the ground for no reason other than politeness."

The fee for this dinner could go to expanding the garden, perhaps making it less necessary to go to the dower cottage for apothecary herbs. While Thea would miss the home and its garden full of memories, it was for the best. Oliver could care for it now.

"Gemma's daughter is ill. You know she would stretch herself too thin rather than disappoint her mistress."

"Exactly. *Her* mistress. She's not the first cook to have to work when her child is—"

"I'm doing this, Jenny. Thank you for your concern."

The older woman shook her head and sighed. "What's on your menu?"

Eel soup, mock turtle soup, veal, oyster pâté, fatty chicken, gooseberries. She listed every dish Oliver had complained about in the past. "I haven't decided, but I think we need to focus on what we're serving this evening."

They fell into a pattern that had been honed over the past two years of cooking the food that had made The Goat's reputation. Thick hearty stew paired with flaky crusted bread, herb roasted fowl and mutton combined with root vegetables, sausage, and potatoes, sweet yet simple puddings.

"You could do a spring soup," Jenny said. "Pair it with a nice cod."

"Trout," Thea said, allowing her mind to follow Jenny's to the Chitesters' menu as she made a pastry for a fruit tart. "Lord Chitester likes wilder fare." So did Oliver, but she wouldn't think about that.

"Then venison, certainly. And quail," Jenny said.

"Ham and mutton, too." Thea tallied her list. She'd have to take a wagon to the butcher's.

"And goose. We're going to have a busy few days." Jenny slid the tart into the oven and then wiped her hands on her apron. She didn't leave so much as a fruit smudge.

"We?"

"You don't think I'm going to let you go alone, do you? I've heard Oakdale Manor's kitchens are as large as a house. Besides, this is a lot of food for you to manage with a strange staff."

It was, and Thea blessed Jenny for volunteering. But there was one thing she needed to do alone. She untied her apron and lifted it over her head. "I'm short on cooking herbs. Do you have everything in hand?"

"I do, but be back by dusk or John will come searching for you. He's always terrified when you cross the woods on your own, much less onto Felton's grounds. He thinks the duchess has a cell over there just waiting on you."

She probably did. "After two years, I think I'm safe. And I stay out of sight of the main house." Thea peered out the window at the bright, cloudless sky. She'd forgo her cloak and bonnet today. It would be nice to get some air, to feel the sun. "I won't be gone long."

After stopping by the stable to retrieve her gardening tools and a basket, Thea made her way into the forest. The faint path was as much hers as anyone else's, worn by almost daily trips to tend Lita's garden.

The shadows shifting across the moss and stone covered ground tempted Thea to stop and look skyward. Blinding sunlight warmed her cheeks, and she shaded her eyes to watch the leaves dance in the breeze as they formed a shifting ceiling in varied tones of green. Ravens called to one another as they wheeled through the sky, escaping smaller songbirds anxious to protect their nests.

She found a moment's satisfaction when the little birds won, and shared their triumph as they circled in a quick victory celebration before returning to their young.

No one understood her ease here, surrounded by giant trees and forest creatures, and she couldn't explain it without divulging too much of her history. Just like she couldn't explain the painful yet comforting pull toward the dower cottage on the other end of this path.

As Thea got deeper into the wood, she noticed ties around

certain trees. At first it appeared random, but then she realized most shared characteristics in size. Others were dead or dying, and a few stood near small gatherings of saplings. Her heart squeezed when she recognized one larger maple that had served as a sanctuary when she needed one the most. She snipped the tie and shoved it into her pocket before moving on.

At the edge of the clearing, she cast a wary eye for Felton House staff before slipping under the arbor at the lowest point in the garden. It wasn't really poaching, she consoled herself. Everything grew back, and no one used it anyway. Hazel had plenty of herbs in her kitchen garden near the house.

Still she worked quickly, selecting herbs and rubbing their leaves between her fingers. Each scent hinted how they could be used in dishes to make Lady Chitester's meal memorable. Lemon balm and dill for fish, rosemary for soup, thyme for duck, mint for puddings. Every serving would be a beautiful mix for the senses.

She hoped the Duchess of Rushford choked on it.

"Thea?"

She inhaled a bit of rosemary, which burned her nose before lodging deep in her throat. Flowers and herbs wobbled as her eyes filled with tears and she struggled for breath. The herb tickled with every ragged inhale.

A large, warm hand pressed into her back between her shoulder blades, stroking in a slow circle. "Hush," Oliver said. "Calm. Deep breath. In. Out. In …"

Thea quieted as she followed his rumbled instructions. Once she was no longer gagging, he wrapped one hand around her shoulder and offered her a flask with the other. The tepid water relieved her scratched throat.

"My apologies," he said. "I didn't mean to startle you."

She looked into his twinkling eyes and faint smirk. "Liar."

Despite the harsh word, laughter rumbled from him, deep and rich. "Right, then." He offered her his handkerchief. "I didn't expect to see you here."

Thea dried her eyes. The cloth smelled of citrus, cinnamon, and sweat. The latter called her attention to his damp skin, his exposed forearms and his glistening neck. His hair was wet at the roots and near his collar, but the breeze caught the top and ruffled it into a mess. He swept one gloved hand over it, but only succeeded in mixing dirt and grass through the strands.

Her fingers twitched with the urge to straighten him. Instead, she lifted her shears and snipped several stems of mint from a large, unruly mass. "I thought you would be working."

"I am." He sat next to her and lifted the spade from her basket. "These have held up well."

The tools were some of her most prized possessions. The handles were shaped to her hand and lacquered until they slid like silk against her skin. Despite years of wear, her initials were still visible in the hilts. Oliver had given them to her for her sixteenth birthday, delivered them with a proud smile on his face and stained nails visible under bandages on almost every finger.

"They have. What have you accomplished so far?" She inched away, cutting several leaves from a bay plant while she scolded herself. If she'd stop asking questions, he'd leave her alone.

"Simon and I marked trees for cutting."

That explained the rags around the trees. Suddenly, there seemed to be a large number chosen. "Are you going to mow down the entire forest?"

"No." He used the spade to lift a weed from between geraniums. "Thinning the old growth will allow the younger trees to thrive and ensure the forest lasts for several more years. Richard has been experimenting with transplanting seedlings. I might try that as well."

"Richard?" Thea moved away again, cursing her curiosity and her stubborn tongue when he followed.

"Richard Ferrand, my business partner." He cleared his throat. "My brother-in-law."

And that was what her curiosity got her—a reminder of his wife. The one the duchess had chosen for him, that he'd hidden until it was too late to fight for him. And now, here they were again. The duchess selecting his wife while Thea watched from the kitchen. "Where's Simon now?"

"I put him down for a nap and left him under Nurse Alice's watchful eye." He shuddered. "Mother hired her, and I swear she reminds me of a familiar. Like an owl, or maybe a bat."

"Yet you left him there," she teased, goaded by his incorrigible imagination.

"I did. I left him under the care of a bewitched creature so I could look at ledgers until my eyes crossed."

She eyed his sweaty, dirty shirt.

"I'm taking a break to clean out Lita's house. The shrouds over the furniture bother me." He tossed another weed over his shoulder. "And I was thinking Simon could play in there out of the sun while I work on clearing out the upper garden."

"You are the only man I know who would rather be a farmer than a duke."

"Perhaps because I'm not a duke," he snapped. "And I wish people would stop trying to kill off my father."

She'd forgotten his quick temper and the way hers always rose to meet it. When they'd been children, it had been fine to rail at him. Now it was a different story. Innkeepers did not shriek at earls.

She gathered her tools and closed the lid on her basket, intending to leave.

"You are still prickly." He grabbed her hand, keeping her on her knees beside him. "I'm sorry I lost my temper. It's just…not what I'd planned." His touch gentled as he twined his fingers through hers. "Life seldom is, I think."

The sun shifted behind them, casting him into shadow and allowing Thea to see the hollowness in his gaze. "What's happened?"

"Apoplexy. He's incapacitated, and he's not improving." He stared into the forest like an animal searching for an escape route. "I wish I'd never come back."

Thea shoved this second, stinging barb away, and refused to be baited. He had been her friend far longer, and far more often, than he'd been her lover. He'd comforted her over her father's sudden death. She could do the same for him.

That was the only reason she sat quietly, holding his hand.

"Why only this garden?" he asked after a moment. "Why not both of them?"

"I harvest the herbs from time to time. I didn't think it would matter." His slight smile and quick shake of his head gave her courage to admit more. "The hill hides me from the main house."

"You shouldn't have to hide."

His statement recalled earlier times and proved how long he'd been gone, but it warmed her heart in an alarming way and made her far too aware of how close they were sitting. She pulled free and hid behind the friendship she'd spent years cultivating. "You only want my help clearing that jungle."

He put his palm over his heart and swayed in mock injury. "Such a mercenary view." Still laughing, he stood and offered his hand. "But since you're here, come show me which ones are weeds. Everything looks the same."

CHAPTER FIVE

OAKDALE MANOR WAS as different from Felton House as possible. Not cavernous or ostentatious, it was full of books and trinkets from European tours, with fires in every room. It put Oliver instantly at ease.

He couldn't say the same about the women in attendance—at least not all of them. Two debutantes and their mamas, dressed in sedate finery, watched him like they were foxes and he was dinner. The others—Lady Chitester and her daughter Amelia—seemed friendly.

"Elveden?"

The question was timed with his mother's bony finger and sharp nail jabbing his outer thigh. Right. He was Elveden. "I'm sorry, what?"

"Bored, are you?" Lord Grimes drawled over the rim of his port glass.

"Not at all. Simply tired. Simon and I had an eventful day out." In truth, his muscles ached from working in Lita's house and garden.

"It's such a novel notion," tittered Susannah Grimes, whose fine blonde hair resembled her father's. "Being out with a child."

"I don't consider it novel at all," Oliver said, glaring at his mother when she poked him again. "Simon is used to being with me. He's not had a nurse since he was on solid food."

"Though we've hired a governess to look after him once he and the earl are better settled." His mother returned his glare. "She's with Simon now."

"How old is he?" Amelia Chitester asked. "I've seen him with you in town, but only from a distance. It's difficult to guess."

"He's four. We celebrated his birthday aboard ship." Oliver held back the story of Simon's party, attended by weathered sailors who had been delighted to dote on a child.

"That's a lovely age," Amelia replied, smiling. "I remember when my youngest brother was four and full of questions. Simon looks like a very happy boy."

"His mother was French?" asked Margaret Gerard. She'd said little all evening, and Oliver was glad of it. Her voice was entirely too nasal. And she stared the hardest.

"His mother's family is French. They settled in Canada after the war. His uncle, Richard, is still there."

"And your grandmother was Spanish."

"She was." He hoped his gritted teeth resembled a smile. He disliked these people who wanted a title he didn't yet have, though they thought his blood, and Simon's, was somehow tainted. All because they couldn't trace their lineage to William the Conqueror, or whoever was popular now.

Oliver turned back to his host. "I'm sorry, Augustus. What were you asking earlier?"

"Your opinion on the increasing number of highway robberies and outright theft. Thetford used to be an escape from the ills of London, and now they seem to have followed us."

"There is less money in the village, less honest work for good pay," Oliver said. He'd spent a great deal of time this week observing the changes in his childhood home. He was, in part, responsible for fixing it. Or would be at some point. "The farmers do not have the money to buy necessities, which means they overwork their lands to support their families. That, in turn, means smaller yields, and less money, which means slower commerce. To fix it, I believe, will require trade. New businesses, alternative farming tactics, and new markets."

Everyone was staring at him as though he'd grown a second head. Since this was the reason he'd agreed to this silly excursion, Oliver ignored them and continued. "That's why Father asked me home. To start a lumber mill. The forest has suffered from neglect, and wood, properly handled, will sell anywhere. For ships, barrels, carts, even homes and furnishings."

"And you'd hire the villagers?" Amelia asked. "Pay them a wage?"

Her light green eyes hinted at intelligence her friends didn't share or appreciate. Oliver smiled and nodded. "They, in turn, will support the shops, which will improve those wages, and everyone will benefit eventually."

"And in the meantime?" Lady Gerard asked. She was glowering at his mother, and the duchess was, in turn, stunned. It was the same expression she'd worn every time he'd spoken in public as a child.

"I was simply thinking of a larger jail," Lord Grimes said.

"And jailed people produce no wages at all," Oliver reasoned. "You'll have more jails than shops, full of people who resent you for taking what they have rather than helping them better their lives. Which I'm fairly certain will lead to more theft."

"It isn't our place to provide welfare for the entire village," his mother snapped.

Which is the exact argument she'd used when she'd persuaded Father to evict Thea's family from the vicarage before her father's grave had settled.

"Their wellbeing, their success, is tied directly to ours, Mother." As the footmen appeared with trays of sweets, he sat back in his chair and dipped his head to his hostess. "Lady Chitester, I have monopolized your party with business matters. I apologize and offer you congratulations on a lovely meal."

"Thank you, sir. I was quite worried when my regular cook was called away to nurse a sick child—"

"It is so inconvenient when staff have children," Lady Grimes said to no one in particular, though several nodded in agreement. The Chitesters were not among them.

Oliver bit into a sugar-crusted biscuit, and it melted on his tongue. Still warm from the oven, it tasted of butter and lime.

Thea had spent hours in Lita's kitchen learning to make these. He'd eaten buckets of them in varied stages of burnt, teased her about cracking his teeth, puckered when she'd added too much lime juice.

He reconsidered their meal, the dishes and their flavors. The herbs he'd smelled had reminded him of their recent afternoon in the dower garden. Now he suspected why.

He stood, refusing to look at his mother. "Excuse me for a moment."

Once in the hallway, he followed his nose down a dark passage, turned, and almost plowed into a footman. "Kitchen?" Oliver nodded as the man pointed down the stairs. "Thank you."

By now the stream of servants was almost constant, as was the chatter and the laughter. Heat curled around him, alternately welcoming and suffocating. Standing aside and out of the way, he leaned against the doorway and watched as Thea directed traffic through the kitchen with calm, practiced ease. The room was awash with smells of roasted meat, fresh bread, salt, sugar, and cheese.

"Yes, I'm certain. Pull that off the bone and separate it," she ordered, smiling. "We'll leave enough for the family, but you're to take the rest home."

Her gaze met his, and she froze. The rest of the staff followed suit, leaving him feeling like an interloper. All because of a title.

Well, the devil could take their expectations. The Earl of Elveden might not belong below stairs, but Oliver Hawkins had never felt out of place in a kitchen.

"I came to pay my compliments," he said as he walked to the group, acknowledging each quick bow and every nervous curtsey, until he reached Thea. He plucked a biscuit from the tray and popped it in his mouth. "These are perfect."

"Thank you, sir." Despite the apron and her plain dress, regardless of her heat-tinted pink skin and the sweat-curled hair escaping from her cap, she was regal. She belonged at the table upstairs, not in here.

"Thank you for your time this evening, and for a delicious dinner." He met each staff member's wide-eyed stare. "You've been called away from your families for this, and I appreciate it. Have a good evening and safe travels home."

He walked away, smiling as the whispers faded and the work resumed. He'd put one foot in the shadowy hallway when skirts rustled behind him.

"*Mono?*"

Monkey, because he was always up a tree. Smiling, both at the nickname and her use of the language he loved, he stepped into a dark doorway and brought Thea with him. "*Si?*"

"*Amarilla senorita esquemasa mandar el chicho la escuela,*" Thea said.

Disappointment lanced through him. In the past, they'd used Spanish and shadows to scheme and discuss each other; now it was only gossip about other people. Oliver focused on her words and the translation, and his frown deepened. Susanna Grimes wanted to ship Simon off to school.

"*Y Margarita se dedicaba a Garrett.*"

And Margaret Gerard had been engaged to Garrett. She was after the title no matter who held it.

"*Amelia es agradable.*"

Amelia was nice. Nothing bad to report there. Although how Thea knew anything to report was beyond him. "*Cómo sabes esto?*"

"*Hablaron en el pasillo, y sus francés es horrible.*"

His French was horrible because he hated it. French was for romance and spies. For business. Spanish was for secrets, for family. "*Gracias.*"

"*De nada.*"

But it wasn't nothing. Those women had felt free enough to talk in front of her because of her position. They'd assumed she didn't know French, that she was deaf as well as mute, because she worked for a living. How would they have behaved if they'd seen him in Canada, covered in mud with sawdust in his hair, smiling like Simon on Christmas morning?

How would they react if they knew the woman they ignored was a gentleman's daughter, educated better than them, with twice their manners?

Thea had known all that once, but something had happened after he'd left. Something kept her tied to this village, below stairs in the dark. A fine copper curl at her temple caught the light from the kitchen, tempting his finger. For the first few months in Quebec, he'd awakened every morning expecting to see her hair on the pillow beside him, catching the sunlight before anything else in the room.

Something had made her choose someone else. Oliver stroked his thumb across her cheekbone, marveling at how soft her skin still was. The need to know carved a hole through his ribs.

Her eyes, the color of mink, widened and her lips parted. He wondered if they were as sweet as he remembered, if she'd let him find out. He leaned forward, and she backed away.

Not yet. Smiling, he lifted her hand to his lips. Went lower, guided by his nose, to her knuckles where lime juice made his mouth water. Keeping his eyes on hers, he flicked his tongue across her skin.

Thea sucked in a breath that robbed him of air. His skin was too tight, and the sweat had nothing to do with kitchen fires. She pulled her hand, and he held on for dear life.

"Lord Elveden?" Amelia Chitester called from the stairs. "The duchess is growing concerned."

He was holding nothing but shadow, staring at the spot where Thea had been. On the other side of the wall, her instructions to the kitchen staff were full of authority and experience, but her stammer told Oliver she was faltering for footing.

That made two of them.

Amelia approached, her dress reflecting yellow and bronze as she neared the kitchen. "Are you well?"

"Yes." How many times did Thea have to run away from him before he got the point? They could reminisce in the sunshine and talk about weeds, but nothing more. "I was inquiring about the biscuits. They're quite unique."

"If you'd like, I can have the remaining ones boxed for you."

"No." Hearing his sharp voice, seeing Amelia's raised eyebrow, Oliver looked for a way to soften the word. "Simon would eat them all."

"Just so." She smiled up at him. She really was quite pretty. "Give me a moment," she said as she walked into the kitchen.

"Mrs. Smith. I wanted to thank you for stepping in at the last minute. It was a wonderful meal. We are so glad Her Grace suggested you."

He should have guessed his mother was behind this. Little wonder she was concerned about his disappearance.

"It was my pleasure to help," Thea said. "I hope Dottie recovers quickly."

"As do I. She's such a sweet child. Good night."

Amelia stepped back into the hallway, and Oliver offered her his arm. Together they went up the stairs, back toward the dining room and the insufferable party.

He let Amelia enter without him and counted to ten as he straightened his jacket. Entering the room, he was immediately confronted by Augustus Chitester, who pulled him aside.

"This plan you have for the mill, you'll need ready cash."

Oliver followed Augustus's gaze to Amelia. She deserved better. Oliver knew because he'd had better. "Seems a cheap trade, Augustus. I'd get all the benefits. All she'd get is a drafty house."

The older man's shock faded to a bemused smile, and he clapped a meaty hand on Oliver's shoulder. "You are a good man, Elveden. Good man." He walked away shaking his head.

Oliver's relief didn't last. The other fathers were now eyeballing him, looking to each other to see who would move first. Downing his drink, he strode across the room, bowed to their hostess, and offered his mother his arm. "We should take our leave. The way home is, as you say, dangerous at night, and I should get Her Grace back in time to say goodnight to the duke."

There was no way she could argue with that, so Oliver led her to the carriage and handed her inside before he followed Emmett to the top. Standing on the ladder, he met the coachman's wide eyes. "Don't worry, I'm not riding up here. Are you armed?"

"Yes, sir." Emmett handed him a pistol. "That's my extra." He lifted a box from the seat. "Mrs. Smith left a treat for the youngster. I'll take it to the kitchen when we get home."

Though he was unsure whether it was safe for him to be close to his mother and armed, Oliver returned to the carriage. Stony silence filled the space until they passed through Oakdale's gate.

"You cannot mean to go into trade," his mother said.

"I mean to do whatever is necessary to make sure Simon has an inheritance other than a ruined forest, a drafty house, and a closet full of dresses. We have a perfectly suited building sitting empty, and the equipment is on its way."

"You have no right—"

"I have every right, as you keep reminding me." She'd even offered the previous earl's fiancée as a wife. "But while we're on the subject, how could you suggest Thea as a cook for tonight?"

"Because she's a cook. No matter what you thought when you were younger, she has always been little more than a servant."

"Her father was a gentleman. Her uncle was a baron."

"Her father was a poor gentleman who didn't see fit to set aside a dowry for his daughters or to provide a home for his family outside our generosity."

Laughable, that.

"And you'll be a duke."

Also laughable, and slightly terrifying.

"She married someone else, as did you. And now you have a place in society to maintain, as does she. It's high time you both remembered what those places are."

Oliver ground his teeth together, stifling his argument. Anything he said would sound petulant and obstinate. He never should have come back. Hang the inheritance. He had plenty for Simon already.

For the rest of the short trip to Felton House, he plotted his escape. Emmett would take them anywhere he asked. They'd get Simon and head for Ipswich, catch the first ship for anywhere that wasn't here.

At the end of the lane, the house was lit as though for a party, raising the hair on Oliver's arms. A glimpse of Dr. Anderson's carriage sent his spine straight as a shiver trickled down it.

The coach stopped, and Oliver was out before Emmett could reach them. Fred, Hazel, and Lionel spilled through the open front door, the light making a halo of Lionel's wild hair.

The duchess's muffled sob had Oliver looking over his shoulder and into her teary eyes. He was losing a father, but she was losing a husband. He'd lost a wife. Gone through the agony alone.

He helped his mother down and wrapped his arm around her waist, almost lifting her as she stumbled against him.

"The doctor is up with him," Lionel said. "You should hurry."

CHAPTER SIX

THE CHURCH WAS full. Regular parishioners rubbed shoulders and elbows with holiday-only visitors, who jostled for space with those who'd never darkened the doorway. They'd all come to pay respects to the old duke and the new, all while looking very much like crows scavenging for corn after the harvest.

For all but those on the front rows, Reverend Carson's words were lost in the scratchy rasp of fabric and heavy shuffle of nervous feet. It didn't matter. Those in the front rows needed the words more than anyone else.

Thea shifted to her left, inching closer to her mother, to avoid Drake's knees and feet as he made room for the fidgety farmer on his other side. "Sorry," Drake muttered as he dropped his arm behind her, sliding it along the pew. "I'd swear this fellow is sitting on an ant hill."

Whispers hissed behind them, his action temporarily distracting token mourners from their prayer books, but Thea couldn't be bothered with their gossip today. There were too many memories of other funerals crowding her thoughts, those with Oliver to comfort her and those without him.

At her father's service, he'd sat behind her in a silent show of support. He'd been the first person to meet her gaze when the service had ended; his hand had been the first to reach for her.

Now, their places were reversed, but they were separated by

a throng of people, and Amelia Chitester sat behind him.

Reverend Carson continued with his eulogy, listing all the duke's accomplishments and reminding Thea that the older man had always been kind to her. Slightly dismissive, yes, and altogether bemused by the gangly red-headed girl always in his son's shadow, but that was the way with older men who were busy working. Or so her mother had said. He'd at least never been actively cruel, and any harm he'd caused had been to serve the greater good of keeping peace in his family.

As the sermon continued, Simon looked over his shoulder. His glance became a wide-eyed stare as he surveyed the crowd. He recognized her and craned his neck to keep eye contact. His wide smile was infectious, and Thea had to tighten her fingers into a fist to keep from returning his wave.

Oliver lowered his head, drawing Simon's attention with a whisper even as he coaxed the boy to face forward. That he still managed a smile despite everything happening around them brought tears to Thea's eyes. She rubbed her thumb across the face of her locket, letting the engraved pattern serve as a reminder of everything she'd lost.

Then, like his son, Oliver's gaze lingered on her. One hot tear slid down her nose, then another, as she wrapped her arm around her waist and pressed it into her shaking ribs. Her mother's sharp elbow had nothing to do with a request for space.

"Thea?" Drake whispered. "Are you well?"

She closed her eyes and inhaled. Counted to three, exhaled. When she opened her eyes, Oliver was once again paying attention to the sermon, which was ending. "I'm fine."

After the benediction, the building seemed to groan as every-one stood. A crowd gathered at the front, surrounding the grieving family—the now dowager duchess, the new duke, and his impish little boy who was now an earl. The mourners around Thea filed out, allowing her a good deep breath.

"Thank God." Drake stretched his legs and stood.

"I can't believe someone took our pew," her mother groused.

"You'd think the queen had died. All these people eager for a seat and a view."

Which is why, Thea supposed, her mother was so bitter about losing their customary spot at the front of the church. "It's a good thing we aren't up there," she reasoned. "We'd never get to leave."

Drake covered his laughter with a cough. The crowd had thinned enough for daylight to reach inside the church. It bounced against the mahogany coffin and slid along the communion rail; it spotlighted Oliver as he spoke to Amelia Chitester, his hand over hers where it rested on his arm.

"Come, Thea." Her mother thumped her cane against the floor, making her presence heard if not seen. "I want to leave."

Drake helped them both into Thea's gig and then left for the inn. As they pulled away from the churchyard, Thea kept her gaze on Neptune's right ear.

"There will be a wedding soon," her mother stated flatly. "It's all over the village that the duchess is practically throwing the Chitester girl at him."

"I know." Every night when she closed her eyes, Thea heard their voices echoing down the kitchen hallway the night of the party.

"She has a fine education," her mother said. "And her family is well situated."

Like his last wife. But neither of them was as well-off as Thea was now, and she had the finest education her father had been able to manage. What did it matter that she couldn't draw? Or sew?

And what did it matter at all? Oliver Hawkins was not her goal. Not any longer. He'd made his choice, and she'd lived with it. Nothing could change what had passed between them or erase the past six years.

"Men like him never marry—"

"Women like me." She reined Neptune to a halt and felt a pang of pity as he tossed his head in protest of the rough treatment. "I understood that then, and I understand it now. There is no need to repeat it."

"Given your behavior, I think there is. I've often wondered what brought you back here. You cannot still hold out hope."

"Of course I can't." Thea climbed down and went to help her mother from the carriage, pandering to her charade that she was old and feeble. Hope had died long ago, and Thea had often cursed the pull that had urged her home. The promise she'd made her father warred with memories, good and bad, that lingered around every corner.

In the end, the fields and forest had haunted her in smoky, grimy London, as had what she'd left behind.

"If you tell him, we'll be a laughingstock." Her mother snatched Thea's forearm in a hard grasp. "Even more so than when you left. Our reputation here will be lost."

Thea opened the door and followed her mother up the stairs. "Social standing isn't everything." She'd let that argument sway her before, and she would always be paying the price for it.

"It is when you have nothing else." Her mother wound her way through the crowded living room to her rocker by the window. She removed her bonnet and discarded her shawl, but stayed in her black crepe as she brushed the lace curtains aside to stare out the window at the empty lane.

It was too dark in here, too close. Taking matters into her own hands, Thea joined her only long enough to lift the window and allow fresh air and life into the house.

"It might rain," her mother complained.

"And it might not." Thea went into the kitchen and checked the larder to make sure the food was lasting. There was too much of it.

"Are you eating?" she asked as she quartered an ignored apple as a treat for Neptune.

"When I'm hungry."

Though Mother had groused about the window, the breeze lifted Thea's hair as she passed through on her way to the living room. She hoisted the nearest pile of papers. "Perhaps Reverend Carson would like some of Father's sermon notes."

"He has our house, isn't that enough?" Her mother glared over her shoulder. "Put those down. Don't go snooping in things that are none of your business. And come close this window."

Thea gathered her things and grasped her mother's hand, releasing it before she clung in a demand to be obeyed. "Close it yourself, Mother. I'll see you tomorrow afternoon."

She returned to the street and scratched Neptune's forehead as he chewed his apple. "I'm sorry, old boy. She gets under my skin." He stared at her with large dark eyes until she confessed. "You're right. It's more than that, but I won't solve it on the street talking to you. Let's get home, shall we?"

As they made the circle around her mother's block and then into the commons and around the fountain, Neptune's hoof beats clattered against the stones that jostled Thea in her seat. The village was quiet otherwise, closed out of respect for the duke's passing.

Her reflection danced through a succession of darkened shop windows. Straight posture, crisp bonnet, nicely painted gig with good springs on the seat and a fine, healthy horse. Nothing squeaked or wobbled. She'd come a long way from the girl who'd walked out of town in the middle of the night all those years ago.

The churchyard was empty now and the doors were closed to allow the building a chance to rest before Sunday services. As Thea passed by, a massive black gelding tossed his head and danced away as much as his tied reins would let him.

Jupiter. If he was here, Oliver was, too.

Thea pulled Neptune to a halt and stepped down, ignoring the butterflies in her belly as she secured her solid steed as far from the racehorse as possible, as though his wildness was contagious. She split the last of the apple between them, careful to keep her palm flat as Jupiter greedily snatched his treat.

Once in the cemetery, she slid her fingers along her father's grave marker as she passed by. He'd be proud of her for providing comfort in the face of everything else, for eschewing gossip in favor of friendship.

At least, that's what she'd tell him if he were here. It's what she'd always told him. Until now, it had never occurred to her that he might not have believed it.

Trees and sunshine created patterns of light and shadow over every surface. Oliver was sitting on the bench facing his family's mausoleum, his shoulders curved and his elbows resting on his knees. His black coat was stretched taut across his back.

"I have spent my life dreading this place." He spoke without looking at her. "And now I have a reservation." He pointed at the window, an oak shaped from stained glass. "Just below there."

Thea perched next to him on the bench, a shiver going up her spine. "Not for a while yet."

He cast her a sideways glance. "I used to be certain of that, but I went into Julia's room a father and came out as both parents. I sailed from Canada a businessman and landed an earl. And I walked into my father's room a son and came out a duke. No fanfare, no warning. Someday, Simon will do the same."

Thea swallowed the words scaling her throat and sat beside him in silence. She wouldn't double his pain today, and she wouldn't leave him to grieve alone. There was nothing worse.

"When he came to visit in Quebec, it was the first time…he saw me successful. And he adored Simon. It was easy to agree to a visit. We had a plan to do something together. Now it's just me and Mother." He scraped his hand through his hair. "She wants me to marry. Says Simon needs a mother."

"He has a mother," Thea said, refusing to be proud when he nodded in clear agreement. "But people have married for less, Ol."

"Would you?"

The quiet question had too much weight to be rhetorical. Thea met his gaze and shook her head, knowing he was implying she'd married for more and struggling to keep the conversation on topic. "Simon deserves better."

He listed sideways slightly and nudged her with his elbow. "But imagine the look on her face."

Despite herself and their surroundings, Thea laughed quietly and elbowed him in return, playing along with the joke. "That is no reason to marry at all."

"At least we would eat well. Your cooking skills have grown significantly."

"What did you expect? Toad in a Hole?"

"There is nothing dishonorable about a good batch of Toad in a Hole." His smile warmed her more than the sunshine, making her glad she'd stopped to help him through at least one moment of his grief. "I would've liked to see Lady Gerard's face with that dish in front of her."

Her laughter grew, encouraged by his, until they were both giggling. "I wouldn't have done that to Lady Chitester," Thea said. "They really are quite nice."

"Too nice for Mother's schemes." He stood and offered his hand. "Speaking of that, I've left Simon with her for far too long today."

They ambled through the silent, stone garden.

"Once all this is over, I'm never wearing black again," he said.

"It isn't my favorite color." She swept her fingers, once again, over her father's marker.

"Wasn't it odd? Mourning someone when you should have still been on your honeymoon?"

Thea faltered, tightening her grasp on his arm. "Oliver—"

"I always thought it was strange, celebrating my anniversaries alone." He helped her through the gate and into her gig. "Thank you for stopping."

Deep sadness once again lurked in his eyes. Thea watched her hand, sure it belonged to someone else, until his strong jaw warmed her palm through her thin glove. "Make the life you want. Your father would want that more than anything. He always did."

Touching him like this, she could feel the words building on his tongue. The tightness in her chest doubled, as though she was under the gig instead of in it. She dropped her hand. "Goodbye."

Though she could feel his gaze on her back, she didn't turn. Once over the bridge, she increased her speed and pushed her bonnet to her shoulders, allowing the sun and wind to dry her tears and swallow her words as she chided herself for reaching for him, for touching him and laughing with him, for stopping at all. As always, there would be a price to pay for doing the right thing.

And she wasn't even sure this was *right*.

No matter the past, Oliver deserved the whole truth about what had happened after he'd sailed. On the other hand, Thea knew better than most that the past was of little use to the present or to the future. It affected everything, but fostered little. Certainly not hope.

Hope had sustained Oliver for as long as she could remember. All of his schemes for adventure, his wild plans, had been built around making his own way. He'd always planned for his own life.

All of that was in danger here, including his hopes for his son. Simon would be better served if he were far from his grandmother's influence.

The best thing would be for the mill to be completed before Oliver grew resigned to staying. He could return to Canada and resume his life. He wouldn't be the first duke to serve by proxy.

All she had to do was keep a secret she'd been keeping for years.

She handed the reins to a stable hand and hurried across the garden. Best to put this plan in action before she changed her mind. The deceit she was planning had already begun to weigh on her.

In the kitchen, she caught Drake's eye and silently beckoned him to follow. He did so almost without a sound. Once they were safely behind the door to her office, she whirled about, putting her desk at her back and facing the only other man in her life she trusted.

"I need your help." Her words were rushed, and she could feel the heat building under her skin. God help her, but she was excited. She remembered this feeling. Years ago, all those schemes with the boy she'd loved…

Drake arched an eyebrow. "Do I have to shoot someone?"

A wry smile shaped her lips as she shook her head. "The Duke of Rushford is going back to Canada, and we're going to help him."

CHAPTER SEVEN

T HEA CURLED THE pillow under her head and pressed her eyes closed. It had been a busy week since the duke's funeral—she'd made sure of it. Her body was exhausted, but her brain wouldn't let her sleep. Instead, it cataloged her stinging fingertips, as though she'd never pricked them while sewing. The snoring guest down the hall grated on her nerves as though he were her first.

Oliver had snored.

She put her forearm over her eyes, and the roses and lemongrass she used in her nightly bath competed with the faint vinegar and lavender scents on the sheets. Sheets she'd sewn, washed countless times, and put on every bed at The Goat. These had been used so often that the sturdy cotton had become threadbare silk, cool against her toes as she stretched her foot to the other side of the mattress.

A tear slipped down her temple and slid into her hairline.

Her mother was right. Oliver Hawkins had ruined her. He'd given her hope and snatched it away.

And she wished, to heaven and back, that she could hate him.

A pounding knock on her bedroom door jerked her nerves taut. She snatched a dagger from the table and stalked across the room just as the visitor knocked again, louder and longer this time. At this rate, they'd wake the entire inn.

"What is it?" she groused as she swung the door wide.

Rachel, her favorite maid, stood there with wide eyes, clutching her child to her shoulder. "I'm sorry to bother you, Missus, but Hannah is worse," the girl said through her tears. "I don't know what to do."

Her skin prickling, Thea reached for the toddler and unwrapped the blanket. Hannah shivered and whimpered. The child had a raging fever, and between coughs, every breath rattled and wheezed.

"Should I send for Doctor Anderson?" Rachel asked.

Bitter memories flooded in, and Thea gritted her teeth to keep them bottled inside. Doctor Anderson meant well, but she knew what he would prescribe. She wrapped Hannah's blanket tight and handed the child back to her mother.

"Go downstairs by the fire while I get dressed. I'll be down quickly."

Rachel did as commanded, and Thea dressed while she mentally inventoried her herbs and remedies. Damn. She was out of elder flowers after the winter.

But they'd just come on the tree in the dower garden. She looked out her window at the full moon in the clear starry sky. She'd have to rush, but she could do it. And she could gather pine needles on the way. Steaming them would help Hannah cough.

Thea put on her sturdiest shoes and raced downstairs where Rachel was waiting, silent and pale with her child in her arms. Rattling wheezes filled the room. Rachel should have asked for help much sooner.

Thea combined the herbs she had and started the kettle before making a poultice using mustard seed and pepper. "Rachel, listen to me." She wrapped the medication around Hannah's chest. "I have to go out and get something I need. I'll hurry, but you're going to have to do a few things on your own." She dabbed peppermint oil on the toddler's nostrils. "When the kettle boils, pour it over the herbs and make Hannah drink the tea. It can cool slightly, but it needs to be as hot as she can take it. Do you understand?"

When there was no answer, she shook the young mother's shoulders until her eyes focused. Rachel's chin trembled, but she nodded.

"Good girl. Once her cough isn't dry, swat her on the back. Not gentle." Thea demonstrated, hitting Rachel on the leg. "Like this. It will help empty her lungs. And wipe her down with cool water to help with the fever."

Drake strode downstairs, disheveled and bleary eyed. "What the devil—" He saw Rachel next to the fire and straightened. "Sorry. What can I do?"

Thea repeated the instructions and told him where she was going.

"I'll go," he said. "What do you need?"

"You won't know how to find it." Thea tied her cloak around her neck and shoved a basket up her arm before grasping her pistol. "Make sure Rachel eats something. Keep a kettle on." She glanced over her shoulder and then back into his worried gaze. "If I'm not back in an hour, send for the doctor."

Thea closed the door and the dark settled in. Her pounding pulse drowned out the customary night sounds. She let her eyes adjust before flying from the porch and toward the tree line, lifting her skirts as high as manageable. Once into the trees, she tripped over a shadowy root and tumbled to the ground. Forcing herself to stay still and quiet, she waited until the amorphous shadows became individual trees and the path snaked out in front of her, glowing dimly in the moonlight. This time, her steps were more considered though her pace was no slower.

She reached the dower garden breathless and sweaty. Keeping her cloak close to her body, hoping it made her look like a shadow, she slipped inside the garden and to the elder tree in the corner. Working quickly, she snipped as many flowers as her basket would hold.

An orange glow on the horizon stopped her breath. It couldn't be dawn, could it? Had she miscalculated that poorly?

No. The path took less than an hour at a walk, and she'd at least halved it by running. And that was the wrong direction for sunrise. It was a fire. Quite a large one. What could be—

A twig snapped nearby, and Thea froze like a rabbit. *Not now. Worry after it later. The luncheon visitors will be full of gossip.*

She returned to the forest and to her run, stopping only to strip pine needles from the closest, thinnest branches. Halfway home, someone stepped across the path.

"Well, this is better than payment, I think," he said.

He'd probably be huge and menacing in daylight, and that effect was only heightened in the darkness. Thea spun on her heel, hoping to disappear but only smacking into another man who smelled of smoke and sweat.

"Here now," he purred. "What's your hurry, love?"

Despite the fear tightly balled in her stomach, Thea squared her shoulders. "I'm on an errand for an ill friend. Move aside."

"Hear that, mate? She sounds right ladylike. As though she's better'n us even though we're all wanderin' around in the dark." His hand closed over her arm. "What's in the basket, girl? Did you find our money out on your walk?"

"They're herbs, you daft lout." Thea hoped her tone was sufficient to bluff them. "Get out of my way."

"Maybe we should search you, just in case," the larger man said as his chest pressed against her shoulders.

Thea shoved her pistol into the gut of the man facing her.

"Blimey," he shrieked as he stumbled aside.

She took a step, felt the jerk as they scrambled for her cloak, and twisted free. Veering from the path, she zigzagged between trees until the shadows enveloped her and she found a trunk larger than she was. Pulling her hood low, she listened to her pursuers crash through the woods.

"Ah, don't matter none anyway. Find the coins."

"And all you know is they're in a hollow log halfway to the road. All these logs look hollow in the dark. I say we find the chit and keep her until the sun comes up and it's easier to search.

Then we can have both."

Behind her, something crashed through the forest. Thea suppressed the urge to scream and run. Would they find her, or would a wild animal attack her before they could manage it? As the threat came closer, and closer still, Thea's resolve weakened. Sucking in a deep breath, she gathered her skirts and took a step.

A large hand grasped her arm and another covered her mouth, muffling her scream. Smoke filled her nose, and ashes and grit scratched her teeth. Dropping her basket, she flailed for freedom, kicking her captor's shins as she struggled for a grip on her pistol.

"*Silencio, Pepinilla,*" he grunted in her ear.

Pickles.

Thea sagged against Oliver, too relieved to protest the childish nickname and then too aware of the strong arms holding her and the broad chest pressed against her back. She made herself straighten and pull free of the hand curving around her waist.

Another chorus of cracks and snaps had her aiming her pistol to her left, vaguely aware that he was aiming the other direction. She recognized Jupiter's shape and raised her hand just as Oliver's shot deafened her. Screeches and shouts faded as the men fled.

Oliver cursed, loud and long. He hated to miss.

Hard fingers gripped her shoulders, and her head whipped backward, bobbling on her neck.

"What in the hell were you thinking?" he shouted. "Do you know how close I came to shooting you? If it hadn't been for the bloody basket—"

The basket. The sick little girl waiting on her. If everything had been scattered in the fight, the delay would be all her fault. Thea dropped to her knees and righted the hamper, grateful to find the lid had stayed closed.

"What in God's name are you doing down there?" Oliver hauled her back to her feet. "Or out here in the dark for that matter? Have you gone off your head?"

"I needed elder flowers from the dower garden," she said as

she took a step away from him. "Thank you for your—"

He grabbed her. "Bugger all, you stubborn woman. I am going to shoot you."

She pulled her arm, increasing her fight when his grip tightened. "I don't have time for this. There's a sick child waiting on me."

Though he didn't let her go, his hold gentled. "I'll take you." He whistled, and Jupiter ambled forward, his head down. Oliver bent double, obviously intending to give her a leg up.

"You don't have to—" The look on his face quelled her argument. She lifted her skirts, stepped into his hand, and tried not to wobble as he lifted her. Or to blush when he swore. Of course she'd gained weight in six years. Who didn't?

Hooking her knee around the pommel, Thea arranged her cloak as best she could while keeping her grip on her basket. Oliver nudged her foot from the stirrup, and she stared at the tree in front of them as he swung up behind her and into the saddle. Jupiter danced beneath them.

"Lean back, Thee. He'll throw us otherwise."

Once she was settled, he urged Jupiter forward, weaving carefully through the trees.

"I can walk faster than this," she complained. Anything to keep from thinking about all of him pressing against all of her.

"I'm not going to run him through the trees in the dark like some daft innkeeper," Oliver grumbled back. "We'll speed up when we get to the road. Where in bloody hell did you get a pistol?"

"It was a gift from…someone who worried about me being alone."

"Then perhaps he shouldn't have left you that way."

It was on the tip of her tongue to remind him *he* had done the same, but that would be ungrateful after the last few moments. Besides, she needed to fight a larger battle than her own indignation.

Her nose wrinkled at the smell of smoke. One of her attackers

had smelled the same. They'd been running; he'd been chasing…
"Did those two have something to do with the fire?"

"They put a torch to the building I intended to use for my mill."

"You should be pursuing them," she scolded. "Not ferrying me."

"They aren't important. Neither is the building." As they climbed an embankment, he anchored her to him. "The equipment wasn't in place yet, so finding a new location will set me back a day or two, that's all." They ducked a low hanging limb and reached the road. Oliver took her in one hand and the reins in the other. "Hold on."

As they trotted, then cantered, Thea wrapped her free arm around his waist and tightened her knee around the pommel. She'd have bruises on her backside in the morning, but it was worth it.

Oliver delivered her to the inn's back door and dismounted. His large hands clasped her waist, and this time, she saw the grimace when he helped her down. Once on solid ground, she pulled his hands free and lifted them. One was fine. The other was blistered. Pus and blood had seeped onto his cuff.

"Come in the house. Let me tend that."

They walked into the bright, chaotic kitchen. Hannah was wailing in misery, drowning out the screeching kettle, and Rachel was close to sobbing. Drake sagged in relief. "Thank God."

"I had a bit of trouble. His Grace was kind enough to help me."

She looked over her shoulder. Oliver was covered in soot and sweat. His eyes were unfocused and his blinks were slowing. "First room at the top of the stairs," she ordered. "I'll be up in a moment."

As he trudged up the stairs, Thea let herself stare for a few seconds before going to work. Adding the elder flowers to a bowl, she doused them in hot water and then put the pine needles in a tea kettle. She handed the latter to Drake. "Take this upstairs to the back room and put it over the fire. Hannah needs to sit with it close by and breathe the steam." She lifted the steeping bowl and nodded for Rachel to follow. "It's good that she's crying, Rachel. Her lungs are better. We'll keep feeding her tea until she's quiet, then we'll see if she can eat."

Once they were upstairs, Drake took Hannah in his arms. "Lie down and rest," he commanded Rachel. "I have her. We're going to drink tea until she's sleepy." When Rachel dithered, he guided her to the bed. "I have five brothers. This isn't the first sick child I've held."

With his free hand, he pulled a nightshirt from his bag. "I think your duke needs this."

Thea shook her head. The man never ceased to amaze her. She left him to care for Hannah while she returned to Oliver.

He opened the door and stood aside, looking dirtier than when he'd come up, his face creased with pain. Refusing to think about anything other than the present and his injury, she strode into his room and filled a basin with hot water before putting the kettle near the fire. "Can you strip and bathe?"

When he nodded, she dropped the night shirt on the bed and turned to leave. She could be brisk and businesslike. She had to be. "Open the door when you're finished."

Thea kept moving lest she dwell on thoughts of Oliver naked under her roof. She went to the stable and woke two of John's lads who slept in the loft. After setting one to work to care for Jupiter, she sent the other to Felton House with a message for Hazel. Next was a stop in the garden to gather fresh herbs, and last was to get the whiskey from her bedroom. By the time she returned upstairs, her heart was thudding. After kicking the laundry into the hallway, she closed the bedroom door.

Oliver was sitting next to the fire, bare from his knees down with his toes curling in the rug. His hair was dark from his bath and the shirt was bright against his skin. The firelight, though, turned his eyes to molten gold.

In her dreams, he'd stayed the boy she'd loved—flirtatious,

impulsive, and too charming for words. Fit, but thin in a way most girls, including her, had considered stylish.

He wasn't that boy any longer. His shoulders were thicker, his chest was broader and dusted with hair that tempted her fingers. And his eyes were soaked in an understanding few could grasp. It broke her heart, but it also made her ache in spots she had willed herself to forget.

Cursing her trembling fingers, Thea arranged her workspace and then offered him a glass of whiskey.

He cocked one eyebrow. "Is this going to hurt?"

"Not if I do it correctly." She lifted his hand toward the light. "But whiskey is a better sedative than chamomile tea."

He downed the drink in one gulp. "Theodora, do you drink before bed?"

"Sometimes," she muttered, willing her skin to stop heating. "And if you call me that again, I'm going peel your skin all the way to your wrist." She swiped a witch hazel soaked cloth across his burn.

"Are you certain you aren't doing that already?" he grunted. "Damn, that stings." He poured another drink. "I can't go home tipsy in a nightshirt. Hazel would never forgive me."

"You're exhausted. You'd probably go to sleep, topple from Jupiter, and break your neck." She surveyed the blistered skin, keeping a light hold on his long, callused fingers. "I've already sent someone to Felton House so Hazel will know you're safe here." She lifted the cloth, cueing him to another stinging swipe, and waited until his fingers tightened on hers.

Once that step was completed, she squeezed an aloe spike and used the juice to soothe the sting. "Better?" When he nodded, she continued, layering fresh comfrey leaves over his damaged skin.

"Whose shirt is this? The fellow from downstairs?"

"His name is Drake Fletcher." Calendula leaves were next. She wouldn't think about how warm he was. He poured a third drink, and she moved the bottle out of his reach.

"Don't worry. I only get foxed on Simon's birthday." His smile was as dry and brittle as leftover lavender. "Who is he?"

Yarrow leaves were last. She was almost done, and then she'd be safe in her room away from his sinful voice and the shadowy stubble across his jaw. "You can introduce yourself at breakfast in the morning. Ask him then."

"I'm asking you."

"He owns The Goat," Thea said as she wound a thin bandage from his knuckles to his wrist.

She hated the lie, but it was necessary. Every lie in her life was necessary. And they were necessary because of him. So she deceived him just like she did everyone else. He was, after all, just another villager. Except with a title.

And except that his free hand was heavy on her waist and his touch soaked through the fabric, warmer than the fire. His bandaged wrist was thick in her grasp, her only anchor as she fell past his thick lashes and into his deep, golden eyes.

His lips were dry and supple against hers and, as they parted, his breath teased her until her nipples pebbled and all her skin ached to feel him. Six years fell away, and they were back at The Owl, saying goodbye the only way they'd known how.

Oliver's sharp inhale robbed her of breath and set her backward. The shock and grief in his gaze stole her warmth. They weren't those people any longer. Too much had happened, too much hung in the balance. She shouldn't be here, letting yearning drown the past.

Thea gathered her supplies, filling her hands to keep from touching him. Distance. She needed distance. "Goodnight, Your Grace." She forced the words past the ones she yearned to say. "Your laundry will be ready in the morning."

He held the door for her, his lips in such a tight line they were white on the edges. "Goodnight, Mrs. Smith. Thank you for your assistance."

OLIVER WOKE WITH the sun in his eyes.

Simon.

Sitting upright, he listened for his son, and instead, heard everything else. Clattering dishes, people in the next room, creaking floorboards. Right. He was at the inn, and Simon was safe with Hazel.

And the mill was most likely a pile of ashes and blackened timber by now. At least the equipment was secure. No one had died. He lifted his hand and flexed his fingers, watched the bandage move as the burn pained him less than he'd expected. Thea had done excellent work.

The thought of her doubled every emotion as he stared at the empty bed. It had been a tumultuous evening. From exhaustion to panic, despair to anger, dry-mouthed fear as he recognized Thea in his sights at the last moment. Frustration had built from the moment he'd touched her in the shadows through having to sit still and let her tend him, her hair copper in the firelight. Her intense focus and her quiet voice had made him forget how many years, how many events, had passed.

Which was why he'd kissed her and then felt like a traitor as her breath had warmed him from the inside out. It had been like a spring thaw, and it had continued rushing through him long after she'd left the room.

Washing as best he could with one hand, Oliver dressed and straightened his hair. His sleeves smelled faintly of vinegar. As had his sheets. Pickles. Damn.

At first, he'd teased Thea about her erratic stitching and pricked fingers because he'd been glad to find something she did poorly. But then it had hit a tender spot only she could reach, like a pebble in his boot that grew until he'd begun sniffing the air like a hungry dog. He'd filched her handkerchiefs and hair ribbons and carried them to Eton, spent nights planning…

Well, he'd planned all sorts of things that had never come to pass because she'd been fickle. His fickle Pickles. He snorted humorlessly at his rhyme as he left the room.

Downstairs in the kitchen, an unfamiliar woman bustled about the room tending to breakfast. Drake Fletcher sat at the table sipping coffee. He looked up when the bottom riser squeaked.

"Rushford," he drawled.

Perfectly groomed, cleaned and pressed, the businessman looked more like a duke than Oliver ever would. And try as he might, and he had tried, Oliver couldn't forget the man's arm around Thea as he'd comforted her at the funeral, or that she'd known where he kept his spare nightshirts. He nodded and took an opposing chair, resisting the urge to scratch his day-old beard. "Fletcher. How is Hannah this morning?"

"Much better. Her fever broke in the night, so she's finally sleeping. Coffee?" he asked, even as he stood and reached for a cup.

The kitchen had fallen quiet, and Oliver looked up into the cook's wide eyes. "Hello."

"Jenny Snow," Fletcher said as he went to the stove, "may I present the Duke of Rushford."

The woman curtsied quickly. "We won't have anything fancy, sir. No one told me to expect you, too."

"What you have smells wonderful," Oliver assured her as he accepted coffee from Fletcher. "Thank you."

"Thea is out front checking on guests after last night," his host said as he reclaimed his seat. "She'll be back in a moment."

Jenny set a plate in front of each of them. "I've told a lad to take breakfast to Rachel, Mr. Fletcher."

Not *Mrs. Fletcher*. Oliver looked over his shoulder toward the dining room, wondering what sort of establishment Fletcher ran that allowed him free rein with young women in the middle of the night, and what exactly he expected from Thea when she wasn't busy running through the woods alone in the dark.

"Rachel is a maid here," Drake said once they were alone

again. "And, no, Hannah isn't mine. Thea would hang me by my balls in the courtyard for that." He took a bite of eggs. "I hope we didn't disturb you overmuch."

Oliver savored his bacon before shaking his head. "Simon was a colicky baby. His uncle and I spent several sleepless nights walking the floor while he screamed himself hoarse." He had, in fact, worried the boy would die. Or that he would. Or that Richard would kill them both. "Thea says you own the inn. Don't you mind her turning it into a hospital?"

"You know Thea." Fletcher smirked. "Do you think she'd care whether I minded?"

Thea never heeded what other people wanted, what they promised. "Why didn't she just send for Doctor Anderson?"

"She doesn't like doctors, especially for coughs and fevers." Fletcher placed his fork on the table with a precision that would have made a schoolmaster proud. "Forgive me for being forward," he said. "But the duke's—your late father's—plans for a lumber mill have been the talk of the village, and I understand the building you intended to use burned to the ground overnight."

Oliver had forgotten how quickly gossip traveled in Thetford. "I'll begin searching for a new location today."

"I know of a suitable building, close to the river and the new rail line." Fletcher glanced past him to the door and then refocused. "It's for sale, but the owner won't sell to you. He had some, er, dealings with your late brother." His gaze flitted off again. "A duel, I believe."

Sterling. Damn it to hell.

"He'll sell to me," Fletcher continued, his words running together as though he was on a timetable. "If you're interested."

The longer Oliver listened, the more he liked this man. He was very much like Richard. "Go on."

"My business—the other part of my business—is representing a group of investors. They trust me, and a few others, to find worthwhile enterprises which need assistance."

Fletcher's furtive tone and carefully chosen words made Oliver suspicious. "Honest investors?"

"Completely. You'll need a sponsor, and you'll have to travel to London to meet them. They're scheduled to convene in a fortnight. They'll want to review your finances and see a business plan, all that."

Careful not to blink, Oliver considered the pile of debts and ledgers on his desk. "And they'll leave me to run the mill as I see fit?"

"They'll only be as involved as you'd like." He looked up and straightened. "Hello, Thea."

"Gentlemen." Her voice was hoarse from lack of sleep, and her hair was styled more simply than usual. When she turned from the stove with a cup of coffee, the shadows under her eyes were disconcerting. "How is your hand, Ol—sir?"

"Remarkably painless," Oliver replied, refusing to be needled by her formality. "You'll have to show me what you used."

"I've just invited His Grace to London," Fletcher said.

"Really?"

The disapproval in the word was jarring. Her frown was worse. Oliver glanced between them, trying to gauge Fletcher's reaction and wondering if he'd misjudged the man and the offer. "I've not agreed yet."

Unaffected, the other man stood and carried his plate to the sink. "I'll go up and check on Rachel and Hannah." Turning, he dipped his head. "We'll talk soon."

Jenny had also abandoned her post, leaving him and Thea alone in the kitchen. Silence stretched. Just as Oliver was about to break it, she stepped in front of him, lifted his hand, and began unwrapping the bandage with brisk efficiency. Before she could rip the poultice away, he pulled free.

"Why are you angry?"

"I'm not." She reached for his hand.

"Liar." He kept away from her. "You're tending me much the way you sew."

She stalked to her cabinet and returned with a handful of fragrant leaves, more bandages, and a bottle he suspected she'd like to douse him in. That thought was confirmed when she dropped everything on the table in a clatter. "It's my day off, and I'm eager to get on with it." She motioned for his hand and rolled her eyes when he didn't obey. "I promise not to hurt you."

He only half surrendered, putting his fingers in hers but keeping his arm stiff. True to her word, she teased the poultice free, followed by the soggy, wilted leaves. The burn was milder than he'd expected. It let him think about other things, like kissing her again.

"What are you going to do with a whole Saturday in front of you?" he asked. Her irritated gaze flew to his. "It's conversation, Thea. I'm not going to sit here in meek silence just to keep from upsetting you."

"I'm going to Brandon," she muttered as she cleaned his wound. At least she was careful. "It's on the other side of—"

It was his turn to be irritated. He wasn't a stranger. Not to this country and not to her. "I bloody well know where Brandon is. What's there?"

"Someone who expects me." She slapped a pungent, stiff leaf across his hand and pressed it into the burn.

"Damn."

"Sorry." She said it like she'd bumped into a passerby on the street.

He waited for her to soften again. "Should I avoid business dealings with Fletcher?"

She shook her head, keeping her eyes on her work. "Drake is honest, as are his associates. It's just…do you not have money of your own?"

"I have cartloads of it in Canada, but there would be a delay getting it, not to mention the imposition on Richard." She patted a clean cloth across his burn and her skirts brushed his uninjured fingers, teasing him with memories of last night and of all the years before. "The equipment will arrive any day, and it will soon be too late to fell trees." Another frown from his nurse. "It's not wise to thin a forest and leave saplings unprotected in cold weather." He kept the rest of his fears to himself.

"Which means you'd have to extend your stay," she whispered.

How was it that, after six years and marriage to another man, she could still hear what he didn't say? "My stay may be extended whether I like it or not."

"You could hire a proxy."

"I could." She was wrapping a clean bandage around his hand now, and the movement transfixed him. Around his palm and across the poultice, then again, loop his thumb, around his wrist, again, and back, retracing the path. Her touch was light and delicate. "I don't want you in Lita's garden past sunset."

"I'm not making soup," she said as she gathered her supplies and carried them back to the cupboard. "People don't take ill on schedule."

"Then send someone else. Have you any idea—"

"That's impossible. It's useless to describe a plant and have any certainty of results. And you needn't worry—"

"Someone should." Why didn't anyone else look after her? She was too thin and too pale, except for the hollows under her eyes, and those were so incredibly sad. As though she'd seen the worst of the world, the part he'd vowed to protect her from.

"You work far too much and wander the woods in the middle of the night. You also stayed up too late doing *my* laundry." She wasn't his servant. She wasn't supposed to be a servant at all. He strode to her. "Did he leave you with nothing but a pistol?"

Color flushed her cheekbones and anger flashed in her dark eyes, hardening them like fine mahogany. "My life is none of your concern, Your Grace."

He leaned closer. *"Nunca me llame de nuevo. Ya sabes que odio."* He didn't know which he hated most—the title or that she was calling him by it on purpose, putting distance between them the way few things would. As though she were the damaged party in this, left adrift in a far-off country with no dreams to work toward.

He straightened and blindly put coins on the table, hoping it settled his bill for the night. "Thank you for your help. Tell Fletcher I'll be in touch."

CHAPTER EIGHT

"I T'S BEEN TWO days, Thea. Are you ever going to speak to me?" Drake asked as they stood on the street corner and waited for a hay wagon to pass.

Thea took his arm and stepped into road. "I'm sure I'll have to eventually."

"You asked me to help him."

"That doesn't mean I expected to be his business partner." She needed to stay as far from Oliver as possible.

"Since Rushford's return, the villagers' fortunes are improving, and all talk centers on his mill. I believe it is a solid investment for you and the rest of the group."

Drat and damn. The man was too astute. "I do not need his money." She shook her reticule to emphasize her point. "Elias Ford was able to repay his loan in full. If everyone else follows suit, that's enough."

"Rubbish." He strolled beside her. "You won't build significant wealth by loaning money to wainwrights, farriers, and blacksmiths."

"I've done fine," she snapped.

"You have, but if these businesses no longer need loans, how are we going to replace your interest income? Do you want to tend The Goat forever?"

"What would be wrong with that?" It was a reasonable question, though her lower back was already providing an answer.

"Most people hope to spend their later years working less, not more."

"Later years?" she chided. "I'm barely thirty. I hardly think—"

"That is exactly my point. You should have the hope of a more leisurely life." Drake thumped his walking stick on the pavement and turned to face her. "Why are you fighting me on this? Do you want to work yourself to death?"

Right now, she wanted to get away from this street corner. A family down the way was known for their rambunctious red-headed children and, judging by the racket, they were playing outside this morning. Thea tugged on Drake's arm. "Never mind. Let's continue—"

"No, not until this is sorted. Why are you so against it? He strikes me as an honest man. Am I wrong in that assumption?"

"No." He wasn't wrong. Oliver was reckless, impulsive, and stubborn. Single-minded, charming beyond measure. Short-sighted but well-intentioned. Her life was in shambles because of those traits, but it was all personal. In business, he'd proven, time and again, to be a genius. A hard-working one, but a genius nonetheless.

The noise from down the street increased, cheering and jib-ing. "Tommy! Go get the ball, y'clod."

The ball in question, lumpy and more stitches than hide, rolled drunkenly to Thea's feet. A little boy, Tommy no doubt, ran close behind. As he neared them, his pace slowed and his eyes widened. "It didn't hit ya, did it?"

"And if it did?" Drake asked, his voice icy.

If possible, Tommy's eyes popped wider. His chin trembled.

Thea whacked her man of business on the shoulder. "Behave yourself." Kneeling, she retrieved the ball and held it out. "We're fine. Here. I think your mates are anxious to continue the game."

Tommy grinned as he lifted the ball from her fingers. He was missing a front tooth, though the replacement was already poking through his gum. That would make him almost six. His hair was the color of port wine and his pale complexion was reddened by the sun and play. Thea's lungs tightened.

"Thank you, Missus."

His eyes, the color of cornflowers—the *wrong* color—were her salvation. Still, she stopped her hand before it reached his hair. "You're welcome, lad. Watch the ball until it reaches your hand. You won't miss catching it that way."

He gave her one last ragged grin and ran away, careening awkwardly the way little boys do, until he rounded a corner and vanished from sight.

Drake helped her stand and cleared his throat. "Shall we go, then?"

They walked on in silence, around the corner and down three doors, until Drake stopped and stared in a window. "I'm just going to duck in here for a moment. Come along?"

It was a toy store. Thea shook her head. She had absolutely no business in there.

"They need a proper ball," Drake whispered. "Why don't you wait on me in the sweets shop? I'll take it to them before I collect you."

Thea walked to the other side of the street, her heels clicking on the cobblestones, and through the door of Murphy's Candy Shoppe. The bell clanged, much louder than when she'd been a child barely able to reach the latch and this had been one of her favorite haunts.

The shop hadn't changed. It smelled of sweet and bitter, of baking bread and fresh cream. Peppermints sat next to lemon drops, which filled the bin next to cinnamon chips. The glass jars atop the counter were stocked with licorice, lollipops, and taffy. Tray after tray of chocolate, in every form, filled one case. Biscuits and pastries waited in another.

When she'd returned home, two years past, Murphy's had been one of her first stops. She'd stood here, hoped for magic, and left in tears. Now she only came once a year, not staying to chat with Mrs. Murphy even though the older woman always asked.

Because, much like today, mothers and children too young to be in school sat enjoying treats under candy-striped curtains.

But unlike those other visits, a father stood in front of the cases, one hand guiding his son while the other clutched his hat and gloves in a white-knuckled grip. It shouldn't surprise her that Oliver was here, and it shouldn't make her heart lighter.

"Thea." Mrs. Murphy greeted her with a grin and a wave. After all these years, it was still impossible to tell if the white in her hair was age or flour. "I didn't expect to see you until April. Come in, dear."

Left with the alternatives of the toy store and a gaggle of red-headed children or wandering the streets alone, Thea shored up her courage and stepped to the case.

"Hello, Mrs. Smith," Simon said as he shifted the jar in his arms. "How are you today?"

He looked every inch a little boy, but he sounded like an old man. "I'm well, Simon. Thank you. Are you having fun in town?"

"It's better now."

"Sweets make everything better," Oliver drawled. He glanced sideways and nodded. "Thea."

"Hello." She made herself smile at the shopkeeper. "A dozen chocolate biscuits, please, Lizzie."

"Which are those?" Simon asked as he hurried to the case, the leaves in his jar bouncing wildly. He pushed his nose to the display, watching intently as Mrs. Murphy got a take-away box.

"Be careful, Si," Oliver said. "Don't leave a mess."

"It's not the first time I've cleaned a Hawkins boy's finger-prints from those bins," Mrs. Murphy scolded gently. "Tea or coffee?"

"Tea, with mostly milk for him. Or all milk if you have it to spare." Oliver glanced in Thea's direction. "Bring a kettle, please."

Thea's lungs tightened at the olive branch she knew she should ignore. "Plate the biscuits, please."

Simon stabbed the glass, pointing at biscuits covered in icing sugar. "Those look yummy."

Thea knelt next to him. "They only *look* yummy. All the sugar is on the outside."

Oliver came to eye level on the other side. "They're messy, and they taste like sawdust."

The little boy's grimace suggested he knew sawdust from first-hand experience. Oliver's eye-roll and nod confirmed it. Thea covered her laughter with a cough. "The chocolate ones are the best."

"Trust her, son. Thea knows her biscuits." Oliver stood and urged him away from the case. "What else would you like?"

Simon took her hand and pulled her with him, and Thea's knees wobbled as all the air left the room. She eased her hand free and then put it behind her and out of reach. Walking beside him, she kept the child firmly between her and Oliver as they answered every question about the candies on display.

"Those." Simon pointed at peppermint sticks.

"Plain or chocolate dipped?" asked Mrs. Murphy.

He looked up, waiting on a suggestion. *Chocolate*, Thea mouthed.

"Chocolate ones, please. And some of that." He indicated the taffy.

"The purple ones," Oliver suggested. "And you might as well have a few caramels."

"And licorice," Thea added.

"Not the black. The red." He winked, his smile quirking with contained laughter. The only time they'd had black licorice, they'd spent five minutes trying to wash the taste from the whips. He looked down the jars. "I don't suppose…"

"I made Oliver's earlier in the week and hid them for you," Mrs. Murphy said. "I'll bring them. Anything else?"

"Lemon drops," Oliver said quietly. "Oh, and fruit. We should have fruit. Whatever you have on hand."

They walked to a vacant table and sat opposite each other, careful to stay well separated and conscious of prying eyes. Simon sat next to his father and carefully put his jar on the table, turning it just so toward the window.

"That's Spot," Oliver explained. "We're waiting on him to turn into a butterfly."

While Thea poured tea, he pulled a list and pencil from his jacket pocket and put it on the table in front of Simon. "Find an I. Remember what it looks like?"

"Like an H, but turned on its side." Simon studied the list and finally pointed. "There?"

"*Muy bien.* Mark through that one. Careful, don't break the tip."

He put everything away and picked up his cup. He smiled and nodded to her when he found she'd made it to his liking—a splash of milk and three sugars. "Thank you for remembering how I take it. We've just left Ivory's Harness Shop."

Payment would be a relief to Claude Ivory, who'd been fretting about repaying her. But still, Oliver was paying bills in person? Most peers left that for their men of business.

"Our solicitor had more regular clients to attend to," he explained as he lifted a biscuit. "Why are you in town today?"

"Business." Thea looked out the window, both relieved and irritated not to see Drake headed to her rescue.

"Seeing you both in here brings back so many memories," Mrs. Murphy said as she approached their table with a sweets-laden tray. "Does my heart good to see my children home." She dabbed her eyes smiled at Simon, who was already reaching for a peppermint. "To see new little ones."

Thea set her cup in her saucer and moved her trembling fingers to her lap. It was normal for long-time residents to consider this a friendly reunion. She hoped they looked friendly. Just friendly. She glanced over her shoulder to make sure the other women were busy with their children.

Oliver was watching them too. Rather than worried, he looked wistful.

"Are those nurses like Alice?" Simon asked.

"I don't think they're nurses," Oliver answered. "They look

more like mothers."

"Oh. Where are the fathers?"

"At work, I suppose." Oliver shifted in his chair and toyed with his teaspoon.

"All by themselves?"

"Yes."

Thea watched father and son, her heart squeezing tight and then expanding, over and over until it cracked. A father who answered all his son's questions honestly, who only got foxed on the boy's birthday. A little boy who talked very much like a thirty-year-old, who thought women were nurses and children went to work with their fathers.

All she'd known was that Oliver's wife had died, and even that had come as second or third-hand gossip when she'd returned home. It had already been old news. Now, however, she was certain the woman had died in the cruelest way imaginable. Thea covered his hand with hers. *"Lo siento, Mono."*

He put them palm to palm and lightly closed his fingers around her hand. *"Yo también."*

Widower and widow. Thea kept her smile in place but slid her hand free and tried not to think about how cold it was.

"You have a candy named for you, Papa?"

"I do." Oliver popped a chocolate dipped cinnamon chip into his mouth and waggled his eyebrows. "Because Mrs. Murphy likes me better."

"Because you snuck into her kitchen and made them your-self," Thea corrected.

Oliver lifted a finger to his lips. "As if he needs any ideas."

Sure enough, Simon was already dipping his peppermint stick in his glass and lifting it, watching the milk run to his fingers.

"You're making a mess," Oliver sighed as he attempted a clean-up. Despite the grumbling, his eyes twinkled. "Is it good?"

"It makes the milk tingly."

"Maybe we should feed peppermint to cows," Oliver teased. He was still grinning when he lifted his gaze to hers. "You only come here on your birthday?"

She nodded and put a lemon drop on her tongue, which involuntarily curled around the sour candy. Her watering mouth prevented her from telling the entire sad story. How the sight of happy children flayed the skin from her flesh. How Murphy's simply wasn't the same without him.

"I'd come here every day." Simon swung his legs under the table, his shoes brushing her skirt. "I had my birthday on the ship. The sailors sang the best song."

Oliver spluttered his tea. "Which you will not sing in public," he warned between wheezing coughs.

Thea dissolved into laughter and it felt warm and tingly, like Simon's peppermint milk. It had been years since she'd felt this way. The reasons why pressed on her tongue and her conscience. She scrambled for a distraction, any distraction.

"Was it your fifth birthday? Or your sixth?" If it was his sixth, they could talk about the looming adventures of school.

His mouth full of candy, Simon held up his fingers. She counted them carefully.

Four.

A wife who'd died before her first anniversary, a mother who'd died in childbirth, four years ago.

Not six. Four.

The bell clanged, and Drake stepped inside, removing his hat as he ducked under the transom. He smiled broadly but stayed near the door.

Oliver looked over his shoulder and nodded a greeting. When he turned back, his face was shuttered. "Simon and I could see you home."

The group of mothers and children walked past the table, and the women's stares were too prolonged. News of their reunion would spread across town by breakfast. As would the breakdown she felt rippling across her bones. "I should get back, and I don't want to interrupt your treat. Please enjoy the biscuits."

He frowned when she opened the latch on her reticule, and it deepened when she put coins on the table. She shook her head and stopped him from pushing them back to her. Drake was studying the planks in the floor, his shoulders shaking with laughter.

Irritated by far too many things to count, Thea stood and swished her skirts to straighten them. "Good day, Oliver. Simon. Thank you for the sweets and the tea."

She was halfway to the door when Oliver's long fingers closed over her wrist to stop her. Not here. She couldn't do this now.

"You forgot your gloves." He held them out and curved his hand over hers when she took them. "It was good to see you, Thee."

With the knot growing in her throat, all she could do was nod. Calling on years of practice, she kept her spine straight and her chin level as she took Drake's arm and left the shop. She didn't look back as he helped her into the gig, choosing instead to tighten her fingers around her gloves.

The lump in her palm made her scalp prickle. If he'd returned her payment …

Thea slowly opened her fingers and saw the packet of lemon drops tucked inside her left glove. A childhood trick from long ago—Oliver had hidden the candy everywhere for her to find. She'd found one last package in her sewing basket after he'd sailed for Canada.

She stole one final glance at Murphy's window. Simon was making his peppermint sticks duel, but Oliver was watching her. He lifted his fingers in a clandestine wave. Her hand lifted of its own will.

And then Drake pulled away and the villagers separated them. Some were smiling and waving, others were looking over their shoulders to see what had captivated her.

A lie. She'd believed a horrible, cold-hearted lie. *Stop. Turn around.* The words were on the tip of her tongue when the Chitester carriage stopped in front of the candy shop and Amelia stepped down.

Whether his wife, his Julia, had been waiting for Oliver's arrival in Quebec didn't matter, Thea decided. He'd never sent word, never asked her to join him. Too much had happened since then, and too much was at stake now. It was too late.

"What is it?" Drake asked.

Thea faced forward and slid the candy into her pocket. "Nothing. Let's go."

∽

"WOULD YOU LIKE to drive up the lane to the stables?" Oliver asked. That had, after all, been how Emmett had hooked him on driving, and racing, and freedom in general at about Simon's age.

Simon shook his head and tightened his hold on Spot's jar, securing it to his knees. Clearly, freedom didn't interest Simon.

They left the curricle with a groom and trudged toward the house, both slowing their pace as the shadows stretched toward them. Simon's small hand slid into Oliver's.

"Can I stay outside with Fred?"

All right then, horse-related freedom didn't interest him. Sunshine and dirt did. That was good enough for now. "Do exactly as he says and don't be a nuisance."

Oliver watched his boy scamper away, wishing he could go along. He'd even trim holly hedges. Anything to put off this confrontation.

You can do this, Julia's ghost whispered. This time, Thea joined her. *Live the life you want.*

His mother was easy to find. She was in her drawing room, an ink blot on the otherwise sunny room. She looked up from her easel and, as she wiped the charcoal from her fingers, Oliver wondered if she was the only duchess who used her drawing room to draw.

The question was merely a tactic to stall the argument he'd

been dreading since Saturday, when he'd awoken at Thea's inn. He closed the door and dragged a chair opposite her before staring into her disapproving frown.

"How is your hand?"

Oliver blinked. That wasn't what he'd expected. "Better, thank you. We should talk about the fire. The impact of losing the building."

"I'm sorry. I know that enterprise meant a great deal to you and your father."

"We're going to keep moving forward." He shifted in his chair, bracing himself. "We're selling the houses in Bath and in London."

"No."

"I don't recall the last time you were in Bath," he reasoned. "It's ridiculous to keep a house and a staff there. The same with London."

"London is necessary. The Season is—"

"None of my concern." He raised a finger to interrupt her. "I'm not on the marriage market, and Simon won't be for almost twenty years. The house can't stay empty until then."

"You'll need it for lords."

Damn. Cooped up in a room arguing with a bunch of titled layabouts and no way to get out of it. "Fine. For lords, but the rest of the year we'll rent it, and we're still selling the Bath house."

"We can't let other people live in our house, use our things." Her eyes narrowed. "This is punishment, isn't it?"

"No, I'm trying to—"

"You have always preferred other people over me and then blamed me for their choices."

"Mother—"

"Your grandmother chose to leave this house and live on the edge of the woods, and you considered that my fault."

"Because you treated her as an afterthought," Oliver snapped. "She wasn't English, wasn't proper, wasn't consumed by—"

"And that girl didn't get what she wanted. Couldn't use your standing and your name to pull herself from poverty, so she married someone else. And you blame me because I'm the one who told you."

Good news from town. Thea Fowler has married. He'd almost heard her smile in the brief sentences. "You disliked her."

"I disapproved. You had a duty to—"

"I needed a respectable career and a proper home, and you didn't care how I got it as long as I didn't marry her."

"And you found someone who made you happy, who gave you a son." She sniffed and dabbed her eyes, though Oliver wasn't sure he saw tears. "I would've liked to have known her, but I'm certain you've found some way to blame me for that as well."

He rubbed his aching head. Dear God, no wonder his father had given her anything she wanted. He walked to the window and shoved his hand in his pocket, clicking the beads in Julia's rosary through his fingers, digging his thumbnail into each knot as a reminder to stay calm.

A splash drew his attention. The courtyard fountain stood just to his left. Simon was using the narrow wall as a tightrope. One leg of his trousers was wet to his knee. "Si. Get down from there."

"But—" The little boy thought better of his argument. "Yes, sir."

Oliver reached the cross in the rosary. After tracing the shape, imagining he could feel the engraved roses and thorns bite his thumb, Oliver clicked past it and let a cool jet bead soothe his skin. He faced his mother and forced their conversation back on topic. "I am not punishing you by restricting your spending. We don't have it to spend."

"So you'll make us live in last year's styles and take us into trade? If we could just go to London for a Season," she wheedled. "You'd see the benefits of society. I could—"

"Enough, Mother. No." He stepped into the courtyard, bolstered by the sun on his shoulders, and refused to consider it running away. "Settling accounts in town has put me behind schedule today. Simon and I will be home for supper."

He slowed once gravel crunched under his boots and the breeze cooled his skin, but he didn't smile until he reached the fountain.

"Come along, *hijo*. Let's go to work."

IT WAS COWARDLY, and he knew it, but Oliver kept working until it was too dark to see and Simon was grouchy from both hunger and exhaustion. They ate a quiet dinner of leftovers alone in the kitchen and, after putting Simon to bed, Oliver went to the library to work on ledgers.

It was a return to their normal life, or as close as he could get, and it also served to keep his mother at a distance. She never crossed the imaginary battle line drawn by the library door.

Once he was certain everything was thoroughly accounted for, Oliver slung a pack over his shoulder and vanished into the woods, taking Thea's path to the inn. He walked through the front door, noting the change from bright dining room to shadowy tavern. The respectable luncheon crowd had given way to a rowdier din of working men who'd stopped for a pint. Boys in clean but plain clothes now served drinks and food.

Drake Fletcher was waiting at a corner table, the chair across from him vacant. Oliver had dressed for this meeting, and his cravat was strangling him, but Fletcher *still* looked better. Even in the bleeding middle of the night.

Ignoring the pint set in front of him, Oliver risked a glance around the room, both hoping to see Thea and dreading the sight of her. He didn't want her to see him with his hat in his hand. He shouldn't want to see her at all.

"She's upstairs," Fletcher said. "John, the barman, insists she's too refined for this crowd. He exiles her upstairs to practice her sewing. Not that it will help much."

For an employer, he knew a great deal about Thea and her habits, and it made Oliver uneasy on several levels. He picked the most practical one.

"You live here?"

"I live in London, but business frequently takes me to the coast." Fletcher set his tankard on the table without a sound. "I stop by on my way to and from town."

"Were you at Eton?" Maybe they knew some of the same people, or at least shared an experience.

One dark, fine brow arched. "I was educated abroad."

He was irritated, but that feeling went both ways. Oliver rested one ankle on the opposite knee. "Fletcher, I like to know who I'm partnering with. I don't believe these are extraordinary questions."

"When you put it like that." The other man adjusted his posture, shifting so one elbow rested on the back of his chair while the fingers of his other hand traced the tankard's curved handle, down to the table, up to the rim, then back. "I grew up on the coast, I was educated abroad, and my background is in shipping."

"Shipping? Did you know Captain Smith, then?" It was *not* a practical question, but Oliver couldn't help himself.

"Xavier?" He shook his head. "I met Thea well after his death. Octavia introduced us."

Thea's Aunt Octavia had ventured out of London to visit her family exactly once in Oliver's memory. He didn't recall much except that Thea had become much more interested in mathematics afterward.

"Good enough?" Fletcher asked, smirking.

Oliver refused to be rushed or agitated. All he had to go on was the association with Thea's favorite aunt and Thea's own faith in the man and his mysterious partners. Faith she hadn't had in *him*. However fickle her heart might be, her brains were always in the right spot. Besides, he had damn few options. He reached across the table. "Just so, Drake. Thank you."

The handshake was firm and swift, just the sort you'd like from a partner. Much the same as Richard had given him all those years ago.

"My pleasure." Drake's smile widened as he accepted the ledgers. "Oliver."

CHAPTER NINE

"THE USHERS WILL assist you for communion," Reverend Carson said as he descended the steps from the pulpit to the rail.

Beginning with the back row, the congregants moved in an orderly fashion to receive sacrament, and Thea's disquiet increased. As a child, communion had been her favorite part of Sunday service, a chance to have forgiveness in exchange for her promise to do better in the week to come. But now she lied to God just as she did to everyone else.

Still, when the ushers reached the front row, she stood and helped her mother, who had grown feebler with every peal of the church bell, into the aisle. It was always the same, stand behind her while she faced Lady Rushford in a tense standoff, then endure the glare of the lady herself. However, today, as she stepped into place, Oliver and Simon fell in behind her.

"Will he be okay?" Simon whispered. "No one will take him?"

"He'll be fine," Oliver replied. "Hush."

Taking her place as far away from the battling matrons as possible, Thea knelt at the rail and hoped Oliver would stay with his mother. She should have known better. She also should have predicted the congregation's whispers as he and Simon knelt beside her.

Without looking, she knew he faced forward and refused to

acknowledge the speculation just as she did, though her neck crawled. Thea lifted her black shawl to her shoulders, using it both as a barrier and a reminder and ignoring the guilt that flooded her.

These same parishioners who shook her hand every Sunday had spent months staring after her and then years gossiping about her hasty departure. They'd been the first to hear of her elopement with Captain Smith and the first to visit upon her return. They'd said all the right words of condolence over her husband's death while glancing into every corner in search of something they'd never find.

A small hand touched her arm as they waited for the vicar to reach them. "Hello, Mrs. Smith."

Ignoring the wails of her heart and her conscience, she looked down at the little boy's smile and found her voice. "Hello, Simon."

"Shh," Oliver said as he glanced sideways.

"You look very pretty today."

"Simon. Hush." Oliver was blushing worse than she'd ever seen him, at least in public. As though he'd never misbehaved in church.

Between her memories and the weight of everyone's stares, Thea grew reckless. She tilted lower and put her head next to Simon's, dared to inhale the scent of the little boy. "Thank you. So do you."

He giggled, and her heart broke wide. She'd cry later, probably wake on a soggy pillow with scratchy eyes and a hoarse voice, but it was worth it. When both her mother and Lady Rushford gasped in frustration, it only spurred her on. "Did you make Spot wear a tie to church?"

"Papa said we need to find—"

"Simon," Oliver hissed, turning fully to face them and glare. Too late he realized Reverend Carson was standing in front of him, offering a communion wafer. "Bugger all."

Barely concealing his laugh, Reverend Carson dropped one

wafer and retrieved another. Oliver, now purple, accepted it meekly and kept an eye on his son to make sure he did the same.

As Thea's turn came, she focused on the vicar's smile and the weight of the wafer against her tongue. The wine followed, bitter and sweet at once. Repentance, forgiveness, sacrifice. Heat crawled up her skin, and it was all she could do to stay in place for prayer.

Heavenly Father, thank you for Aunt Tavie and for my inn. Forgive me for the lies that keep me safe, that prevent my exile into poverty and disgrace, and allow my independence. I can't repent, but I hope you understand why. The child next to her radiated heat and happiness as he fidgeted on his knees, and tears welled in Thea's throat and up, threatening to claw their way out of her. *Forgive me.*

Keeping her eyes lowered, she scurried back to her side of the church.

After the closing hymn, her mother wrapped an iron claw around her arm. "You caused a scene with that boy," she hissed. The lace on her cap trembled. "People will talk."

They would talk regardless. Thea was tiring of living up, or down, to what everyone expected. Life had been different in Brandon and with Tavie in London. Why had she ever come home?

"He isn't yours."

The barb stung so sharp, sunk so deep, Thea expected to see blood spreading across her dress. She raised her eyes to her mother's pitiless frown and fought the urge to run. Running, after all, had gotten her into this mess. She'd just have to wait for the tirade to pass.

"You are a selfish girl."

She willed her eyes not to roll. It went this way every time her mother was angry.

"I don't know why I expected differently. You've never considered what people would think. Leaving in the middle—"

"Mrs. Fowler." Oliver stepped between them. "Forgive me for interrupting, but I hadn't had a chance to say hello. It's nice to see you haven't changed after all these years."

His voice was cold and his posture rigid as he bent to her hand.

"*Hrumpf.*" Her mother snatched her fingers from his and stomped away, relying heavily on her cane for balance. More heavily than when she'd arrived.

She bumped into a scowling duchess, and they each backed to their separate sides of the aisle.

Oliver barked a dry laugh. "Alley cats to the end, hissing and scratching over the same small territory. Your mother is still in mourning?"

"Her black has nothing to do with mourning." Thea walked down the aisle toward the safety of the outdoors, careful to keep her hands in full view and their shadows separate. "By the time our third vicar left, citing his wife's health, Mother's curse on the vicarage had become all but fact. Rather than being embarrassed, she imagines herself as some sort of church gypsy."

There was no space visible between their shadows. She sidestepped and answered the question she knew was coming. "We've had eight vicars in six years. She's a legend."

"I see." The tight words shook with restraint.

"Don't laugh, Oliver. It isn't amusing."

"Oh, but I owe you after that debacle at the rail."

Ahead of them, Simon wove through the crowd in the churchyard, speaking with everyone as Spot's jar glinted in the sunshine. "He's rather irresistible."

"All children are," Oliver said as he stepped forward to speak to the vicar.

Not all children. Thea knew full well that some were easy to ignore. Just as some people were easier to forget. Oliver, in fact, picked and chose. And here she was, laughing with him, waiting at his elbow, as though the last six years hadn't happened.

As the men talked, Thea skirted around them and down the steps to the cemetery gate. Under the shadow of the trees, it was barely possible to pick out her mother's shape next to her father's grave. Bitter thoughts added to Thea's worsening mood, and she fought them back. It was Sunday, the traditional day of fresh starts. Maybe her mother didn't only visit when there was a crowd to see her. Maybe church services made her think fondly of the husband she alternately called a saint and a near-sighted do-gooder.

Thea let the sunshine soak into her shoulders and chest, hoping it would warm her heart. She'd learned about being judged harshly, seen how bitterness took its toll. She didn't want to live that way.

A challenge to that vow appeared as Simon scampered toward her, his father in tow. Childish chatter mingled with Oliver's deep, quiet voice. What he was saying didn't matter as much as the slow and gentle pattern. He was a doting father to a little boy who knew he was loved. She had always known…

As they drew closer, she rooted her feet into place and reminded herself to smile.

Simon reached her first and lifted the basket she'd left them during their first visit to the inn. "Papa says we have to give this back."

Careful not to touch him for fear of grabbing hold and hanging on, she grasped the handles and slid them up her opposite arm. "Thank you."

He took the jar from his father's hands. "Spot needs more leafs. Do you want to help?"

"Leaves, Si." Oliver's smile was half-embarrassment, half-indulgent. "And I'd like to talk to Mrs. Smith for a minute. She can watch you from here."

"Yes, sir." Simon went to the closest tree, plucking leaves from low-hanging branches and carefully opening the lid to drop them in.

"That bug will suffocate before he has a chance to make a cocoon." Oliver shoved his hands in his pockets, never taking his eye off the boy. "A hat. That's what I said he needed for church. A hat."

Thea pleated her skirt between her fingers. Awkward silence stretched, but she couldn't make herself walk away. "I'm sorry if I encouraged him to misbehave."

"Not your fault. I do it all the time, so I shouldn't be surprised when he does exactly as he pleases." He put his hand on her nervous fingers. "Besides which, he was right. You are pretty."

Those three words were the alchemy that reversed the clock. Instead of the insomniac innkeeper with aching feet and a broken heart, she was now the teenager who had followed him everywhere. Dangerous magic, this. She shifted out of his reach.

"Did Drake mention my visit last week?" he asked.

She limited her response to a nod. They'd spoken of little else, and her dreams had been full of their schemes and her worries. Even now the words climbed the trellis of her tongue. Church…Sunday…confession…forgiveness. Thea tore her gaze from Oliver's and stole a glance around the churchyard. Lady Rushford glared back, out of earshot but still a threat.

A threat that was based on a lie wasn't much of a threat, though, was it?

"How is your hand?"

He flexed his fingers and winced. "Hazel has been kind enough to help me bind it, but she doesn't have your expertise." He leaned close enough she could smell the cinnamon in his cologne. "*¿por qué no va a visitar y me muestras?*"

Visit? Just the thought of driving through the gate and up to Felton House made her sweat. "I can describe the herbs you'll need."

"I've been told descriptions of herbs are unreliable." He winked, his smile widening. "We're working in Lita's garden today. *Encuéntrame ahí.*"

Simon ran up to them, sloshing Spot in his jar. "We have a fairy that takes care of it, and Papa and I are building her a house."

A fairy. It had been a long time since anyone had considered her magical.

"Thea," her mother called. "Come take me home."

Oliver squeezed her fingers, and Thea looked down, fumbling for an excuse, resenting the need while still being relieved for the interruption. His boots caught her attention. The highly polished hessians he'd always hated started just below his knees.

He wasn't her Oliver anymore. Despite the call of her past, because of it, this man and this boy could not be in her future.

"M'lord," Emmett said. "Her Grace is ready to leave."

Imagine the look on her face. Thea didn't have to imagine. The duchess was all but snarling from the carriage doorway. For once in her life, the woman should have to worry about something.

Strengthening her resolve, Thea looked into Oliver's eyes. Her chores wouldn't take that long today. She could be in the garden by mid-afternoon. *"Sí. Después de las tareas."*

A CRACKING TWIG alerted Oliver to approaching prey. Crouching on the other side of the thicket, he marked each soft step and waited until the last possible moment. Then he lunged around the corner and tackled his son to the ground. "Got you."

Except he wasn't holding a giggling four-year-old.

His first clue was the delicate cotton dress crushed between him and the dirt. The second was the smell of lemon and roses instead of sweaty boy. The third... God help him, but the third were curves that fit his hands like she was made for him.

Thea stared up at him, wide-eyed and close enough he could see the blonde dusting her brows and lashes and the freckles sprinkled across the bridge of her nose. The flush in her cheeks matched her pink lips, which were parted just enough to allow her tongue to sweep across them.

Heat curled up from his toes, melting his muscles. Six years faded to nothing, sunshine faded to firelight, clothes vanished altogether. In a long-fought battle, guilt rushed forward to mortar the spaces in the wall he kept his memories behind.

"You aren't Simon."

The blush crept to her hairline as she shook her head, mussing a straw bonnet that had already seen better days, and pressed her hands to his chest. With his heart pounding, it took several seconds to realize she was pushing him away.

Their legs tangled, tormenting Oliver with a moment of intimate friction before he helped Thea to her feet. Rather than being irritated by the distance between them, he was grateful for the chance to compose himself. Why was it so difficult to remember this woman had broken his heart?

"We were playing hide—"

She snatched his hand in a hard grip, her eyes widening as she looked past him. "Dear God."

He followed her panicked stare, higher and higher up a tree, until he saw Simon against the trunk, sitting on a branch and waving, smiling widely.

"I won!"

"You did." Oliver's smile was frozen on his face. *"Bueno."*

He was too high and still in his shoes. Getting down would be treacherous. It was always the most challenging part of climbing trees. As if to prove the point, Simon slid off the branch and reached with his feet for the one below, much like getting out of a chair, and lost his balance.

"Papa!" His cry warbled as he flailed for a handhold.

Oliver's breath stopped. After squeezing Thea's hand in silent reassurance as well as a plea for bravery, he freed himself and tugged off his boots. All the while he smiled up at the boy and focused on calming his voice. It wouldn't do to scare him.

"I'll be right there," he said as he peeled off his stockings. "Wait on me."

Wincing as rocks bit into his toes, Oliver pulled his shirttails loose and strode to the tree. Bark scratched his fingers as he tested the largest low branch. Reaching upward for the next one, he climbed. The crack was still echoing as he dangled, his feet swinging and his shoulders stretching.

Thea, thankfully, stayed quiet.

Widening his grip and rolling into a ball, he put his feet on the branch before swinging upward. Gripping the rough bark with his toes, he pushed forward and up, grasping a limb with one hand and the tree trunk with the other. He looked over his shoulder and winked at Thea. "Nothing to it."

The rest of the climb was easy. Simon wasn't high enough to frighten a thirty-year-old veteran tree climber, unless that man was his father.

Oliver stopped on the branch below, putting him almost level with his son's pale face and wide eyes. "Ready to come down?" When Simon nodded, Oliver reversed his grip on the branch and carefully turned. "Put your arms around my neck and wrap your legs across my tummy."

Despite the strangling hold, the weight of the little body and the breath in his ear were comforting. Oliver crouched, grabbed the branch, found his balance with the extra weight, and dropped. It became a rhythm. Crouch, grasp, balance, drop. Crouch, grasp... By the time they reached the ground, Simon was giggling. Which was dangerous.

Oliver knelt in front of the boy. Using his best fatherly scowl, he rested his trembling hands on two tiny, very breakable, shoulders. "You do not climb trees unless I'm with you."

"But Papa—"

"No." Oliver tightened his grip and shook Simon to hammer the point home. He'd intended to be gentle, but the boy's trembling chin indicated he'd failed. He gritted his teeth, determined not to be derailed. "Not without me, *hijo*."

Fat tears rolled down Simon's cheeks. "I'm sorry."

Now was the time for a hug, and Oliver gave in. Gathering his son in his arms, he breathed easily for the first time since he'd tackled Thea to the ground.

She was standing apart from them, pale under her hideous bonnet, her eyes glassy and her fingers covering the lips that had distracted him in the first place. He hoped he'd been better at masking his fear.

"Go assure Thea you're none the worse for your adventure." He backed away and wiped Simon's face. "If you cry, she won't believe you weren't afraid."

"Hello, Thea," Simon said as he walked to their guest. "Don't be worried. I'm fine."

"Good." She knelt beside him. "Because I've brought you a present."

"You have?" The boy peered into her basket, tears forgotten, and their conversation faded to an unintelligible mutter.

Oliver sat on the ground and struggled into his stockings and boots as he stared up at his son's perch, counted the branches he could have struck falling to the ground, estimated the distance he would have plummeted. Pushing his hair back from his brow, he let his exhale shake through him. *How the hell am I going to get him to adulthood alone, Julia?*

"Look, Papa." Simon ran back holding up a small piece of hollow branch, worn smooth of its bark and weathered soft and gray. "Thea found it for the fairy house."

"Really?" Oliver plucked it up and peered through it. "Is she going to spy on Fred for us?"

"No, silly. It's a chinbly."

"Chimney," Oliver corrected carefully. "Good, because the nights are still chilly. We wouldn't want our fairy catching cold."

Which she would probably do if they stayed on the bare ground much longer. He stood and reached out his hand, braced himself for the tingles that sparked to his elbow when she touched him, and congratulated himself when she was the first to pull away.

As he walked with Simon toward the garden, Oliver looked back to where Thea was hesitating. She stood half in the shadows as if arguing against her better judgment.

It had been that way since they'd first met in the vicarage study. She'd been on the edge of the room, tall for a girl, with impossibly bright hair, holding a book that was thicker than she was.

As children, they'd competed and fought. As adolescents, they'd read and debated. He'd gone off to Eton and come home content to do little else but walk with her and discuss everything they'd learned and seen while they'd been apart.

He beckoned her forward. "You can't lecture me on medicinal herbs from there."

CHAPTER TEN

ONCE THEY WERE inside the gate, Simon ran to the corner and knelt in front of the fairy house, intent on construction.

"The violets in that stump were a nice touch," Oliver said as he tucked Thea's hand into his elbow. It brought her close enough her skirts brushed his trousers. He shortened his steps, slowed them, content to be outdoors with the sun on his hair. "That is the ugliest bonnet I've seen in recent memory."

"No one gardens it their best bonnets." She pointed to a pre-historic looking plant tucked into a pot in a corner. "That's aloe. After you clean your burn, break off a section and dab it over the wound."

"Usually garden bonnets are old, not spectacularly ugly." He pointed toward another plant hiding under a shade tree next to a bench. "What's that one? The one with the gray looking leaves."

"It's a brunnera," she stopped and pointed toward a sunnier spot. "That one there—"

"It's a marigold." The bitter smelling, stiff flowers were his least favorite in any garden. But that memory gave him pause, and he lifted his hand to sniff the bandage. "Marigold leaves?"

Her smile brightened. "Yes. Calendula." She said the word much like he corrected Simon. "It will stave off infection. One of the maids at the inn gave me the bonnet as a thank you gift. I believe it was her first attempt." She nudged him away from the shade and into the sun, toward another plant in a freshly mulched bed. "This is comfrey. Use it as well to help your skin knit quickly."

Oliver nodded, but it was lost on her as she walked across the garden, focused on her lesson. She stopped in front of a small rock garden and tall yellow flowers covered in bees that were too nectar-drunk to move.

"Yarrow," Thea pronounced. "It will help with any bleeding. Can you remember those? Aloe, marigold, comfrey, and yarrow." She chanted it like a rhyme, pointing at each flower until, smiling, he repeated it with her. Then she gathered her skirt and turned, clearly intent on leaving.

"Why don't you rest in the shade for a moment?" he asked as he took her hand and wrestled to keep it on his arm. "So far, I've knocked you over, frightened you, and made you walk around in the sun." By the time he had finished, they were back at the bench under the tree. He swept his hand toward it and waited.

She sighed and shook her head.

"A moment, that's all. Stay out and enjoy a day with no rain."

He refused to gloat when she sat, perched so close to the edge that she risked missing the bench and so near the arm that the plants covered her hand. He took a spot in the middle, giving her space, but not as much as she wanted, and far too little to be polite.

It shouldn't be this way. She wanted to leave, and by rights, he should want her to go. But each time he saw her, the need for her increased. He couldn't be on this damned island without her.

Thea untied her bonnet and set it between them. He lifted it and inspected it before setting it away, removing the flimsy barrier. "Let's hope the maid improved her millinery skills."

"She makes hats in Suffolk now, so I think she's learned quite well." She shook her head, obviously irritated by his confusion. "Honestly, Oliver. Maids don't have to stay maids. If they can learn a skill and make a living, why shouldn't they?"

"No reason, I suppose. I just thought...aren't all women

eager to marry? The women Richard and I hired to care for Simon seemed to be."

Her eyes twinkled. "They were eager to marry *you*."

"Well, yes. I suppose I was one of those pitiful creatures one would want to care for."

"You have never been pitiful in your life."

"You didn't see me when Simon was an infant." He watched his son play in the sunshine. "I was terrified I'd break him or neglect his brain in some way. That he'd be deficient."

Thea's hand covered his lightly and quickly. "He's a fine boy."

"Who almost broke his neck in a tumble from a tree. I'm lucky you saw him up there."

"I wouldn't have if you hadn't put me on my back."

A blush crept across her cheeks even as the heat climbed his neck and ears.

"I am sorry about that." But he couldn't be, really. Not when he craved feeling her against him again. Heat returned, deeper this time, licking his muscles and urging him to move, making him war between being a man and a gentleman. "How on earth can he climb like a squirrel but be afraid of horses?"

When she stayed quiet, he glanced and saw her frown. "It's true, Thea. I've offered him a pony, and he'd rather have a caterpillar."

She angled her body, facing him on the bench. "Has he ever seen a pony? Not a horse, Ol. A pony."

"Of course. Just last week he was staring at the wooden one in Ivory's harness shop like it was going to carry him to hell."

She rested her elbow on the back of the bench and wagged her finger. "That model is a miniature of Jupiter who, I believe, did try to bear you to hell more than once." In scolding him, she had closed the distance and left the dutiful nurse, the frightened girl, behind. "Take Simon out to Greenlee's and let him see one of those fat, hairy beasts that live for little else than sweet clover and a child their size. Let him pick one for himself."

"Perhaps you're right. His uncle Richard does tend to hare about on the wildest—"

"Oliver Hawkins." She swatted his shoulder. "Most of the village houses are surrounded by hedges and walls to keep you and Garrett from tearing through their gardens."

"That was Garrett. Mostly." He caught her hand before she could pull away. He'd wanted to be close to her, but damned if it didn't make him ache. "Thea—"

"Thea," Simon squealed as he ran through the garden toward them. "Look what I found. Papa says it's a tree egg." He held up an acorn.

"I've never said the words *tree egg*," Oliver grumbled. "I said a tree would hatch out of it and then get bigger. And you should say Mrs. Smith."

"You don't," Simon said as he examined his treasure. "I wonder what sort of tree it is."

"Maybe it will be fuzzy like a chick," Thea teased, winking.

"There's no such thing."

There was no better sound than his son giggling while he played, unless it was Thea giggling with him.

"Yes there is," she said. "Pussy willows are fuzzy in the spring, and oaks are fuzzy in the fall." She tilted her head. "But maybe you're right. Maybe it will be a chick covered in bark."

They made a lovely picture, surrounded by summer plants, cast in afternoon shadow, heads together as they studied the tiny nut.

"You are both far too silly for words," Oliver said as he got to his feet. "Bid Thea farewell and go in for your nap." He used his practiced glare to quell any argument from either of them. He wanted Thea to himself.

Simon threw his arms around her neck as though he was leaving for China rather than bed. Thea hesitated, looking much like she'd been doused in cold water, before she carefully returned the embrace.

"Sleep well, Si." Her words were garbled by his stranglehold.

She pried his arms free, her eyes far too bright. "I'll go."

Oliver lifted Simon into one arm and extended his other to her. He wanted to know what brought tears to her eyes. "Come up to the house for a moment."

Despite her skeptical stare, she came along and left the ugly bonnet behind. The sun glinted off her hair as she kept her posture straight and her head high, reminding Oliver of the figurehead decorating a ship's bow.

She paused as they passed through the rose arbor. "What happened to the morning glory that had woven through the hedges?"

"Is that what it was?" He shrugged "I tore it out. It seemed too plain to be a flower."

She pulled free when he reached the threshold, and he let her. At least she was closer than she'd been in the church yard this morning. Worrying she'd run when his back was turned, he strode into the cottage's living room and put Simon on the sofa they'd both beaten clean earlier in the week. They'd pretended it was a giant whale out to sink their ship.

The boy put the acorn on his pillow, and Oliver moved it to the table next to Spot's jar. All he needed was the child to roll over and put out his eye.

"But Papa, what if—"

"It won't turn into a tree while you nap, Si. As a matter of fact, it won't do it at all if you stare at it too long."

"Oh." Simon wigged onto his stomach and tapped the terrarium. "I saw lots of worms outside. Could I go get one? Maybe Spot is lonely."

Four-year-old children shouldn't know the meaning of the word *lonely*. They should be surrounded by friends and playmates and two parents, and large families that doled out hugs as often as English rain. "Spot isn't lonely. I promise. Now—"

"Can I have a drink of water?"

"No."

"How about a biscuit?"

"No." Oliver raked a hand through his hair. This was taking too long. "I'll bring you a biscuit in five minutes. But only if you close your eyes and stay in bed." One of these days, this trick would stop working. He prayed it wasn't today.

Simon snuggled into the pillow and pulled the blanket to his chin. "I love you, Papa."

"I love you too, *hijo*." Oliver kissed his forehead. "Now close your eyes."

He walked out of the room and hurried back outside, glad that there hadn't been a long discussion about naps. But he still hadn't been fast enough.

Thea had disappeared, leaving nothing but her ugly bonnet behind.

SHE NEVER SHOULD have gone.

Something crashed through the underbrush, and Thea spun on her heel, ready to do battle and finding only squirrels as opponents. She should have known better. Oliver would never leave Simon alone.

Thank God, because she couldn't have resisted much longer. She turned toward home and quickened her steps, ignoring the pull that had drawn her to the garden in the first place, denying the urge to go back and tell him in agonizing detail what he'd left behind. For the first time in years, the truth could be her safety.

And, as always, it would be her downfall.

What had she been thinking? Thea's vision blurred. It was impossible to fight the duchess, not without leaving her conscience behind. She hadn't been raised that way, it was just—

She kicked a rock from the path. She'd lied for so long she'd begun lying to herself. It was just *Oliver*. As she'd rushed through her Sunday chores, she'd thought of little else but him in the sunshine whispering secret invitations, or his grimace when he'd flexed his hand under the bandage.

It had been easy to convince herself it would be a simple trip. That, since everything he needed to know was in the well-tended lower garden, she could teach a quick lesson, be seen long enough to goad his mother, and leave. She'd even rehearsed on her walk over, though the trip had been quicker than expected.

She'd been breathless when she'd arrived, and it had only worsened when Oliver had knocked her flat. It wasn't just his weight against hers. It was the way his eyes had darkened to green, making him look like a creature from the forest he loved, and the way his tongue had darted across lips in a clear indication of his thoughts.

Or hers. She would have kissed him herself if she hadn't seen Simon up that tree, which had set off another breathless fit. The afternoon had been full of them. Every time Simon giggled or Oliver's callused fingers claimed hers. It had been impossible to turn her back on the torture of watching Oliver as a father.

Hijo. Son. Thea swiped angrily at her tears. His son. Not hers.

Never hers. Because in his rosy life full of a wife and children, she was a morning glory, too plain and wild—too common—to be wanted for anything permanent.

It was like scratching a scab. A moment of relief followed by an incredible mess and days of pain, leaving a gaping hole. Wrapping her fingers around her locket, Thea renewed her vow to stay well clear of Oliver and Simon. A scar was easy to hide, a weeping wound was not.

At the edge of the forest, she kept an eye on the inn's kitchen door while she straightened her skirts and her spine. Reaching for the strings of her bonnet, she touched her chin instead. "Damnation." She'd left it behind.

Well, she wasn't going back for it. Maybe no one would notice. As she stepped into the clearing and through the gate, a loud roar of laughter rang out. Thea quickened her pace. The dining room had been empty when she'd left. It was Sunday, and they were shorthanded.

She walked through the door and barreled into John, who was wide-eyed.

"Thank God you're home, Missus. Jenny and I are doing our best, but it's a mess."

A raucous cheer from the front room drowned out the rest of his sentence, and the large man visibly cringed. "A large fancy crowd has stopped over to celebrate a boxing win, and they ain't movin' on."

Thankful for the distraction, Thea tied an apron around her waist. "Start rationing the ale. That will deter some of them. I'll make vegetable stew and scones to sober everyone up."

"Scones are already in the oven," Jenny said as she came into the kitchen, her hands full of pottery shards. "One of those louts hurled his mug across the room to make a point."

"You shouldn't be out there." As he talked, John walked into the pantry and back, his arms full of produce. "Stay back here where it's safer. If one of those—"

"You can't serve ale and meals at the same time, and they're calmer when you're behind the bar." Jenny picked up a knife and a potato. "Go on back. We'll handle this."

"What about rooms?" Thea sliced the top from a carrot and tossed it into the bucket she kept to feed the hogs penned behind the stable. "Should we get them ready?"

"I wouldn't let this crowd stay, Missus. They're trouble." Another roar came up, and he looked over his shoulder. "I'm wading back in there and shortening the draughts."

Taking her place next to Jenny, Thea focused on the carrot and kept her fingers clear of the knife. When she reached the end, she scraped it into a bowl and blindly reached for another. A potato this time. The toasty smell of baked bread filled the kitchen even as the heat raised sweat on the back of her neck. She traded a chopped potato for a handful of string beans.

The bowl was full now, so she carried it to the fire and dumped it into the cauldron of simmering broth.

"The scones should be done," Jenny said from behind her.

"Can you check?"

They were. Thea snatched two pads waiting nearby and lifted the baking stone out of the oven. She batted her eyelashes as she stepped away, grimacing as the heat singed her fingers.

Jenny came behind her and put a second tray in the oven, and they returned to their spots at the worktable, wordlessly selecting vegetables and taking up their knives.

Her fingers ached. Her feet hurt. The stiffness in her shoulders climbed up her neck to the top of her head. "After today," Thea vowed, "I'm not cooking, or chopping, anything for the next three days."

"Well, then, here's hoping business is slow," Jenny replied.

Right, because she was a gentry daughter who had nothing to worry about but catching a wealthy husband with a title. And plenty of time to scheme about how to separate that husband from an inconvenient child.

Titles had always been out of her grasp, but now husbands were as well. It wasn't fair to marry someone and keep a lie between them, or to make them party to that lie. And children? The ache in her body doubled. She'd have to be content caring for other people's children.

Cheese. They needed cheese. Thea retrieved the block of cheddar from the pantry and uncovered it.

Her life spread out before her, day after day of endless meals for people who never stayed, night after night of laying her aching muscles in a cold, empty bed. A lifetime of hiding and lying. She viciously sliced a piece of cheddar from the block.

That was the life Drake warned her about, the one he swore riskier investments would protect her from. Not that the lumber mill was a risk. Business-wise, Oliver was a solid gamble. He'd never endanger his family's finances and he'd give everything he had to succeed.

Everything else about Oliver, however, was a risk. To her heart. To her future.

"How much of that cheese are you going to slice?" Jenny

asked. "It'll dry out if we don't serve it, and I'm not sure we should waste second helpings on this lot."

"Right." Thea plucked a few apples from the bin and deftly chopped them first into quarters, then eighths. There were two options with Oliver—keep the truth from him and hasten his return to Canada or tell him everything and deal with the consequences.

She rolled her shoulders and her muscles screamed down her spine to her hips. He'd fight her to make things right, she knew that.

John carried a load of dirty dishes to the sink, sweat dotting his brow, and she imagined Oliver in his place. Working until he was bent and gray, even on a Sunday full of sunshine. She wouldn't doom him to this. She'd push him away first. Watch him lose his will to fight his mother until he gave in and married someone chosen by his family.

At least Amelia Chitester was pleasant and intelligent. She would make a fine duchess, she'd be kind to Simon, and Oliver would move forward, contented. He'd done just fine at that before, hadn't he?

He'd hate her. But it was better than—

"Are you crying?" Jenny asked.

"Onions," Thea muttered as she swiped the corner of her apron across her eyes. She couldn't live like that, crying for the moon for the rest of her life. Her best bet was to help him succeed and send him back, happy and none the wiser. And if he took Amelia with him, well then, so much the better.

"You're not slicing onions. Are you well?"

"I'm fine." Keeping her back to the astute cook, Thea retrieved as many bowls and plates as she could find. Scones, apples, and cheese went on every serving. "We're lucky you were out this way."

"Yes, well, um…I stopped by after services to look in on John. I'd made too much…pie, and it wasn't going to keep."

Thea looked over her shoulder. The flush across Jenny's

cheeks could be blamed on the stove, but the stammered details could not. "I see."

After a moment, Jenny dissolved into giggles. "You don't *see* anything, Thea." She tossed a towel across the kitchen and it floated into Thea's hands. "Nothing but two lonely people keeping each other company."

She ladled stew into the bowls and grasped two. Thea followed suit, and they swept into the dining room under John's watchful eye. Although Thea thought he watched Jenny a bit closer. The teasing thought died on her tongue when she heard a familiar laugh.

"Millicent." She slapped the plate onto the table in front of her sister, heedless of stew sloshing onto the plate.

"Hello." Millie tipped her head back, leaning against a man's shoulder and giving him an ample view of her cleavage. "Freddie, have you met my sister?"

The man grasped Thea's hand and wrestled to keep hold until he bestowed a kiss that lasted too long. "It's a pleasure. Millie has told me so much about you."

"Could you come into the kitchen?" Thea asked Millie as she wiped her hand on her apron.

Millie shook her head and then tilted on the bench. "Celebrating." Her words were slurred, but Thea suspected her grip on Freddie had little to do with balance. "Thought we'd stop in. Have a room for family?"

"No. Full up," Thea lied, and didn't bother to apologize. "You might try The Owl."

"The Owl's fallen down-at-the-heels in the past year or so," Freddie said.

Though she'd never admit to actively ruining their business, Thea couldn't help a smile. "That's what happens when you cater to rowdier crowds and people bent on mischief."

"Ooh, look at Missus High and Mighty, staring down her nose at fun. How long do you think your respectable friends would stay if they knew—"

"Eat your dinner, Millie," Freddie commanded. "There's no profit in embarrassing your sister in her place of business."

Millie smiled slyly and sidled back under his arm. "You're right, love. No sense at all." She batted her eyes and nibbled on a piece of cheese. "Sorry, Thea, I'll be good."

Eager to be away from them, Thea returned to the kitchen and scurried back, staying well clear of Millie's corner. After several trips, everyone who wanted food, or needed it to help sober them, had something to eat and fresh coffee as a substitute for ale.

"There's no meat in this stew," a burly man grumbled. "And the ale's gone dry. What's going on?"

A few of his cronies grumbled in agreement, and Thea's frayed temper snapped.

"What's going on is that you lot have run us out of ale and meat, and everything but what's in front of you. You'll eat what you get and move along."

"Well, that's a fine how d'ya do," someone groused from a corner. "In London, they always got plenty, and they always welcome a crowd."

Thea stared at the man's empty bowl and clean plate. She'd wager his cup was empty as well. "Then you are welcome to pay your tab and move your ungrateful arse along to London."

With that, she marched away. This would not be the rest of her life. Drake was right. If it was successful, Oliver's mill would change the village's fortunes, and she'd gamble right along with him. He owed her that much.

CHAPTER ELEVEN

"EXCUSE ME." OLIVER brushed past an onlooker. "Please."
The lady swept her hand down her arm, and her gaze down her nose, as she untangled the fringe edging her shawl from the rough, thick rope in his hands. "Do watch where you…" She finally looked into his eyes. "Your Grace. My apologies."

If there was one benefit to having a title, it was the way people got out of his way while he was working. Nodding stiffly, he tightened his grip on Simon's hand and continued their trek to the train.

The large engine, glossy black against the green verge, its brass work gleaming in the late morning light, belched steam and rumbled, complaining about Oliver's delay in unloading his cargo. It was eager to be on its way.

He understood that feeling. Eager to start, eager to finish, anxious to escape this crowd of formal observers. They were all staring, frowning, as though they'd expected to see the mill arrive fully formed rather than in wooden crates.

Simon wriggled from his grasp and charged headlong down the embankment to reach the tracks, clinging to Spot's jar. Oliver rushed to keep up, grinning as gravity pulled him forward, tilting his center of balance and pulling his feet forward faster than he'd intended to go. Slightly out of control.

Dwarfed by the train, the steamy mist swirling around his

knees, he stared into the crowded car. Gears, belts, wheels, saws—every thick-walled crate was carefully labeled.

"Where do we start, Your Grace?"

By not calling me that. The words sat on Oliver's tongue. He knew speaking them, asking to be just like everyone else, would be more shocking than seeing him greet the train this morning. He turned to Hamish, the mountainous village lad he'd hired thirty minutes earlier as hourly labor to help unload the equipment. "Do you think you could manage *Mr. Hawkins?*"

"For a shilling an hour, I'd call you Mary." The young man blushed. "Sir."

Oliver barked a laugh and clapped the young man on the shoulder. "Mr. Hawkins'll do, Hamish. Let's begin with the smaller crates." He put Simon on the low wall between the tracks and the depot. "You stay there."

"I want to help."

The whine in the little boy's voice was the warning bell of boredom. Oliver snatched the pulley from the wall and handed both it and the rope to Simon. "All right. Thread the rope onto this, keep it in the grooves so the wheel spins, and pull it through until the front edge is as tall as you are. Understand?"

Simon nodded and grasped the end of the rope, which was as thick as his forearm.

Certain the child was busy for a while, Oliver pulled himself into the train car and shoved the first small crate toward the door and Hamish's waiting hands.

Then another, and another.

It was hot, difficult labor, but straining muscles and sweaty clothes were Oliver's reward for weeks of managing and waiting, of watching the weather and staring at columns of figures. This he understood; this gave him a sense of purpose few things did.

He hadn't felt this good since Sunday in the garden with Thea, next to her on the bench in the sunshine, talking as though the years hadn't passed. But the minute he'd turned his back, she'd fled. Again.

She was impossible to understand, as was the push-pull she inspired. He should be relived to be free of her. Instead, he caught himself hoping to see her—in the forest that separated their homes, on the road, in the crowd here.

"Mr. Hawkins?" Hamish shouldered a crate. "I have a few mates who could use the money. They'd make short work of this."

The stack of crates in the freight wagon was sizable, and Oliver's back muscles spasmed as he stood. "Are they your size?"

"I'm the runt of the litter," Hamish said over his shoulder as he strode toward the wagon. "They're hard workers, and their mother is one of the best cooks in the county. They could bring lunch."

The mention of food made Oliver's stomach rumble and, predictably, brought his thoughts back to Thea. He pushed them aside and focused on the problem at hand. He hated to lose time while Hamish located his friends, but they needed the help. "Good idea. Try to hurry."

The young man grinned as he mopped his sweaty brow with a ragged kerchief. "Not necessary." He pointed to his left, where three men hulked on the embankment. They were moving before Hamish lowered his hand.

Introductions were short and to the point. The three were brothers—Daniel, Thomas, and Matthew—and they each agreed to the same pay as Hamish. Daniel joined Oliver in the train car. Thomas and Matthew stayed on the ground and, together with Hamish, carted containers to the wagon.

Soon the only crates left were too large to lift. Oliver put his shoulder to one corner of a large box and heaved; nothing moved but his boots as they slid against the planks of the car. At least Daniel's corner didn't move either.

Oliver stood and stretched his work-stiffened joints. "Lunch, I think."

"Thank God," Daniel sighed before swinging to the ground.

The meal was a feast of meat pies, cold chicken, cheese, fruit, and cakes. Flasks of cider washed everything down and reinvigorated Oliver's lagging spirit. Despite working with his hands every day, it had been years since he'd done this much back-breaking labor. He and Richard had done it for their first mill, and they'd helped with the second. After that, they'd been able to hire a knowledgeable crew.

He looked overhead, wondering where they were going to use the pulley to finish unloading. And then curious as to how they were ever going to load stacks of lumber for shipping. Thetford's depot still smelled of paint. It wasn't prepared to be an efficient freight station, though it didn't seem to lack laborers.

"How was it that the four of you were available this morning?" he asked his first employees.

Hamish shrugged. "We're available every morning now that planting's through."

Daniel nodded. "Have to admit, Mr. Hawkins, we were glad you needed us. The spring money's about to run out."

"Why not go down to Ipswich and work the docks?" Oliver asked. It always stunned him, how young men would rather scrabble for a living at home rather than venture further afield.

"Can't speak for Hamish," Daniel said. "But we couldn't all leave Mum, and we couldn't decide who should go and who should stay."

"And I'd rather stay here where I can see blue sky," Hamish said. "City's not for me."

"Me neither," Oliver agreed as he watched a puff of a cloud skate across the sky. As much as he hated English rain, he loved the countryside in the sunshine. Everything was brighter, richly-colored. Like Canada, but tamer. For the first time in his memory, the domesticity didn't make him itch.

He also saw these young men differently. They were no longer nosy men with nothing better to do. These were men who had *nothing* to do.

A shadow stretched from behind them, and Simon tipped his head backward. "Hello. Who are you?"

Oliver glanced over his shoulder. "Simon, this is Drake Fletcher. He's a friend of The—Mrs. Smith's, and he's our partner."

"Like Uncle Richard?" Simon grinned, happy for the bit of familiarity. "So he's Uncle Drake?"

He and Richard had managed to get Simon to almost school age without discussing Julia. It seemed traitorous at times, but it was easier than explaining how he did, and didn't, have a mother. They worked together, they lived together, and they shared Simon. That had always been enough for the boy. However, this question revealed an obstacle Oliver would have to hurdle sometime soon.

It also needled him because he didn't know exactly how Fletcher fit anywhere, especially with Thea. He was always at the inn, always at her elbow. Always dressed to the teeth and unruffled. Was he only her employer?

"He's Mr. Fletcher to you." Oliver saw the brewing argument on both sides and put his foot down. "Until you begin shaving every day." Then he focused on Fletcher. "How can we help you?" Partners or not, Thea or not, he didn't like to be managed.

"Just riding by and saw the crates. Thought I'd stop and say hello." Fletcher, unperturbed, motioned toward the wagon with a gloved hand. "What's left?"

"The largest saws and the engine itself." Oliver wagged the pulley. "We need to work out a way to lift those crates with just this and no cross beam."

"Don't need to lift it." Daniel pointed to a large elm tree. "We can use that for leverage and move the wagon close enough to more or less slide the crates in." He took the pulley, stared hard at the center hole, and then nodded. "Going to the wainwright's."

The other three went to work getting the wagon in place. For the first time all day, Oliver had nothing to do. He rather liked it.

Daniel returned from the wainwright, a large smooth spindle in one hand and a sledgehammer in the other. Matthew came for the pulley, which Oliver surrendered without a word. The brothers and Hamish went to work as one unit, measuring distance and angle, pounding the spindle into the ground, notching the pulley where a wheel would normally go.

Drake stripped out of his coat and turned up his cuffs. "You're going to need an extra hand."

They took their spots on the rope with Hamish as the anchor. The three brothers braced their feet wide and waited for the crate to teeter on the edge of the train car. They caught it like it was a pillow falling from a bed.

Oliver sunk his heels into the soft dirt and pulled his elbows tighter into his ribs, ignoring his shaking arms as they pulled a second crate forward.

"Engine's next," Daniel called.

"Doesn't that have wheels?" Drake whispered.

"It does." Oliver dropped the rope and went to his crew. "Break the crate open and assemble the engine. We'll roll it down."

Drake motioned him aside. "Where are you going to store all this to keep it safe?" He waited for a moment. "Because I have a suggestion. You'll have to charm an innkeeper, though."

Oliver shook his head. Using Thea as a hiding spot was not a good idea.

"There are young men sleeping in the barn loft, and people come and go all day," Drake argued. "Plus, that barn is practically empty in the summer and it's convenient to the road when you're ready to assemble everything. No one will look there."

He was wrong. The person most likely behind the sabotage attempt, who had arranged for arsonists and God only knew what else, would look to Thea first. Oliver knew it in his bones, though he couldn't voice it. To do so would mean the end of his rapidly dwindling family and failing at one of his main reasons for coming back—for staying at all.

"Let's go for a walk."

Oliver left Daniel in charge of assembly, gathered Simon, and the three of them made short work to Sterling's vacant building.

They couldn't store it here, but they might be able to use a nearby spot. However, everything was either open to the air, rickety, or impossible to secure.

Damn.

"You know," he said to Fletcher as they continued their exploration. "That depot's not set up well for freight. Incoming or outgoing."

"Agreed," Drake said. The calculating gleam in his eye was familiar. "Think I'll take Daniel to Ipswich for a business discussion. See if he's interested in something other than farming."

They'd reached a narrow alley off the center of town, and Oliver stared up at the printer's sign over the darkened windows. "I'd been hoping to print employment advertisements, perhaps a few reward posters."

"They closed several months ago."

Oliver had to look down his nose to see the speaker. Thea's mother was standing in front of him, leaning on her cane with Millie at her side. "Thank you, ma'am. How are you?"

"Tired, old, and poor." She didn't move aside. "Everyone's all atwitter about how you're going to turn the fortunes of the village, but I know the truth. All you'll do is disappoint them."

Really? She was going to lecture him on disappointment? The woman had hated him all his life, and time hadn't helped. Thea marrying someone else hadn't healed whatever imagined slight. Regardless, she had married, her mother had wasted no words in explaining the reasoning, and he'd be damned if she got to stand here and upbraid him as though he were Simon's age. "Mrs. Fowler—"

She scowled over his shoulder. "Mr. Fletcher. I hope your presence doesn't mean my daughter is involved in this scheme."

They weren't alone and no one deserved to know his past, least of all Fletcher. Oliver ground his teeth together, crushing his retort.

"Come, Mother," Millie said. "I'm sure this has little to do with us." She focused her gaze on Simon. "Hello again."

"Hello."

Oliver stepped between them, a shiver of parental warning going down his spine as he nodded a greeting. "Millie."

The women walked on. Once they were alone, Oliver turned to Drake. "Let's get on the way to the inn."

THE ROWDY EVENING crowd was in full swing. Laughter, bawdy songs, and shouting floated up through the floor. Mugs thudded dully against table-tops in time with music or in staccato demand for refills. For the thousandth night in a row, Thea wondered at John's belief that a set of stairs and wooden planks would separate her from a rowdy crowd and allow her a good night's sleep.

Right now, all it was doing was keeping her out of her office. She stared at the ledgers splayed open across her bed, both amazed and proud that Oliver had surrendered such an accurate accounting of his family's business. Proud because he kept books much the way she did—the way her father had taught them. Amazed because he'd admitted something most men of his class would go to great lengths to hide.

The Rushfords were poor. Not by Thetford villager standards, no. They still had their lands and houses, but their cash was far short of what they needed. He'd never have enough capital for the mill.

She ran her finger down the line of figures, tracking the decline of the family's fortune, which had been far more modest than most believed. She went faster with each row, darting her eyes along the line. Reaching the end of the page, she did it again, not believing what she'd seen. But there it was in black and white.

Seventy-five pounds to Miss Fowler's Ladies' Finery, Millie's London shop, paid at the first of each month. When other payments lagged, or stopped altogether, this one continued.

Of course, it was nothing for a duchess to spend regular money on a seamstress. Seventy-five pounds was excessive for one woman without a daughter to support through a Season, but it wouldn't be unheard of. Lady Rushford did like to dress in the latest fashions.

However, she would never knowingly buy from Millie. And no seamstress, no matter their skill, could produce that number of dresses each month for years. Five years, to be exact. It was too much of a coincidence.

Bile soured on the back of Thea's tongue. Millie was blackmailing the Duchess of Rushford with the only piece of gossip that could threaten her carefully crafted life and the hold she wanted over Oliver.

Shock gave way to a giggle at the irony. The Rushfords were impoverished all so the Duchess could cover her lies, and their money had gone to support Thea's mother, who would've just as soon burned it.

Despite the delicious thrill, Thea's scheme was in grave danger. Without capital, Oliver would never get a loan, not even from a non-traditional source. Without the loan, he couldn't start the mill. Without an operational mill, he wouldn't return to Canada.

Worse, there would be no industrial revolution in Thetford. Everyone in the village would lose hope. They'd lose their faith in him. He'd be a failure.

Because of lies and secrets. Because of her family. Because of her.

Thea abandoned the row of damning figures in favor of pacing her room, the short distance only serving to increase her agitation. She rubbed her dressing gown's velvet tie through her fingers and considered her meager options.

The truth dangled in front of her like a loose thread. She could pull it and let everything unravel. However, it would most likely take her livelihood with it. And her income and investment were now doubly necessary.

As she passed her window, movement near the stable caught her attention. By moonlight, all she could make out were shadows, but they were carrying things into the stable rather than out. The first hint of their purpose came into view behind a team of two draft horses. The engine was as recognizable by shape as the two men in front of the team.

They couldn't store it here. Oliver wouldn't be able to resist checking on its safety, and if the duchess found him here, everything would crumble.

She was downstairs and to the door, her hand on the latch, when it opened from the other side. Drake entered first, his palm raised in a request for patience and solidarity. Oliver followed on his heels, head down slightly but not enough to hide one raised brow and the teeth worrying his bottom lip.

At that moment, she hated everything about this situation. The ruse Drake represented and her past with Oliver were bars in the worst kind of prison—familiar and comforting, but always slightly threatening.

"It's temporary," Drake said. "We'll store it just long enough to secure Sterling's building. Nowhere else is suitable."

"Do I need to remind you that he needs Sterling's building because his was burned to the ground?"

"Do I need to remind you that I'm standing next to you?" Oliver snapped. "Honestly, Thea. Do you think I'd do this if I had any other option?"

She was well-aware of being outside his consideration. She was, once again, nothing more than convenient. She kept her focus on Drake. "Do I get a vote?"

He held her gaze. "The mill cannot operate without equipment, Thea."

The words were pregnant with meaning. She'd given him a task and now she was complicating it. His frustration was sharpened by the exhaustion visible in his sagging shoulders. He was more unkempt than she'd ever seen him. Oliver was worse. He looked like a dock hand rather than a duke. "Have you eaten?"

"Not since luncheon," Drake said.

She stepped past them and to the oven. "I have shepherd's pie, but not enough for the six of you."

"The others went home to check on their families."

Water splashed in the sink as the two of them washed up. Chairs squealed and scratched as they were dragged across the floor. Thea dished up two hearty helpings of meat and potatoes and carried them to the table as Drake returned from the great room with tankards of ale. She put the bread and butter between them.

Oliver looked up at her, his eyes soft the way she'd always remembered them. "Thank you for this."

"It's just leftover dinner, Ol. Nothing else."

She forced herself to take a seat on Drake's side of the table. The men shoveled their food, barely tasting it. As utensils scraped on pottery, she retrieved the tart she'd hidden away on the sideboard.

Oliver speared a cherry with his fork. "Simon will be sorry he missed this. I sent him home with Emmett."

"Which reminds me," Drake said. "How did the old man know just when to arrive?"

"Magic." Oliver slid his gaze to hers, his lips curved in a wry grin.

Thea hid her smile behind her hand. It was the magic of Hazel, who had always known exactly how long Oliver could be away without needing food, a nap, or a scolding. The outside limit for a child Simon's age was approximately four hours, perhaps a bit longer if he was fed and slightly coddled.

Drake pushed his plate away. "Thea, I can understand your concern, but this makes sense. There is always someone here, and John's lads can ward off any trespasser."

"Most of them are just boys. They'd be no match for anyone bent on mischief."

"Not one-on-one, but they'd be formidable as a group."

He was right. Damn. She looked from him to Oliver. "You'll have to stay away." When he bristled, she resisted reaching for his hand to convince him. She needed to teach him to rely on her brain, not the shorthand they'd developed as children. "Anyone searching for your hiding place would follow you straight to it. You shouldn't be seen here."

Oliver nodded.

Drake tossed his napkin on the table and stood. "I'll go tell John." He took the tankards with him.

Squelching her disappointment at being traded for a steam engine, Thea carried the dishes to the sink and reached for the pump handle. Instead of cold metal, she touched warm skin and thick knuckles.

"I'll do this," Oliver said. "You get the kettle."

She added hot water, careful to miss his fingers.

He refused to give up his spot. "You dry."

"You've worked all day."

"So have you." He elbowed her aside. "This isn't the first time I've done dishes in the middle of the night, Thee." He picked up the dishcloth and slipped his hands into the water. "We ran into your mother and Millie in town."

Thea could guess how that had gone without her to moderate. Still, there was more to worry about than his feelings. "With Simon?"

His nod tightened her lungs. She shoved her hands into the sink and snatched his fingers. "Keep him away from Millie."

"I will."

They were shoulder to shoulder, elbow to elbow, hip to hip, and almost eye to eye. His fingers curled around hers, softening, pulling, threatening her balance. The water helped her slide free of him, but she had to force herself to step away.

She worked next to him in silence, careful not to touch him again. Even when they were finished, he didn't move. "What color was that robe originally?"

"Brown." She touched the lapels, which years of wear had

finally softened. She'd hated it from the moment she'd bought it. Drab and cheap, it had been all she could afford and all that had fit her. So the first time it had ripped, she'd patched it with a piece from her favorite dress, which had been worn to rags.

Oliver's finger unerringly found that piece, tracing the faded lawn fabric so softly she didn't feel the touch. "I remember this dress," he whispered before moving to another nearby scrap, carefully stitched to cover a threadbare elbow. "And this one."

She'd long ago earned enough to replace the dressing gown with another fancier one. Instead, she'd kept this one and used it as a diary, eventually almost totally covering the ugliness. Now she wouldn't trade it for anything.

It had nothing to do with Oliver's raspy voice or his traveling finger. It didn't.

"This ribbon." He touched the frayed pink grosgrain edging the purple velvet circling her wrist.

"You teased me mercilessly about them."

"They clashed with your hair."

She lifted the other arm, displaying a mismatched cuff trimmed with green satin and needlework. "And I lost one, so now everything clashes."

"What's this one?"

His touch on the soft knit above the green satin cuff branded her. She pulled her arm away and tucked it behind her. "It's a horse."

"It looks like a gravy stain." He grinned, a mischievous twinkle in his eye. "Your stitching really is awful."

"As are your compliments."

Like this, it was easy to forget *what* he was in favor of *who* he was. She'd trusted him most of her life with every secret she'd had. Except for two, both of which he deserved to know. Maybe she could start with the smaller one first.

"About the mill. What if you took on more investors? Smaller amounts?"

"Like whom?"

"I have funds—"

"No. I won't take your money." He held up his hand to stop her protest. "This isn't playing truant to fish or running a curricle through a chicken house. This is risky, and I won't endanger your savings."

"But I can help. If you'll just—"

"No, Thea. I appreciate the offer, but I need more than a lady's pin money."

So much for trust and honesty. So much for partnerships. He'd never see her as anything other than the poor, foolish village girl she'd been.

"I see." She stacked the plates and carried them to the shelf. Anything to get away from the temptation that was Oliver Hawkins.

He, however, wasn't done tormenting her. His warmth soaked through her ratty, patchwork robe as he stood behind her. "I suppose I am unused to complimenting women." He tugged one of the curls she'd tied back. "I like your hair like this. It's how I remember it."

Dear God, this was too much. "Ol—"

"Let me finish." His breath heated her ear. "I won't put you in danger, Theodora."

The kiss on her cheek was so light she could've imagined it. "Goodnight."

The word was still curling through her ear as the door clicked closed. Thea hung her head and put one hand over her racing heart. The other dropped into her pocket, searching for her handkerchief.

Instead, she found a lumpy paper envelope.

Lemon drops.

CHAPTER TWELVE

"**D**O I HAVE to stay here?"

The question was as surly as a four-year-old could make it, and Oliver understood why. He remembered how it had felt to wander the house with only servants for company—and he'd wanted to be here.

"I can help," Simon insisted. "Uncle Richard always lets me."

Richard did. Hell, Oliver did as well. It was easy to let the boy play at helping when it was as simple as pointing at a tool or giving him a ledger sheet and a pencil for scribbling make believe entries. However, Oliver had spent the week repairing roofs, cleaning reeds from muck-filled ponds, and restoring field irrigation. Just yesterday, he'd helped rebuild a wall to keep the Standring family's sheep from wandering off. His toes were still cold from hours atop the hillocks in the gale.

It was impossible to do that work and keep an eye on a child, and it was irresponsible to ask a tenant's wife to sit with him. Not to mention the risk of illness or injury. Still…Oliver's first and best responsibility was as a father, not a duke.

He sat at the breakfast table and faced his scowling little boy. "Why don't we have a day with just us? We'll flag more trees this morning and then do something fun this afternoon."

Simon's pout faded. "No lessons? Can I help Fred until it's time to go?"

"You may go ask Fred if he'd like your help, and you must do exactly as he says."

Simon most likely missed the last words. He was already halfway out the door, as though he expected to be snatched back inside at the last moment.

"He reminds me of you," Hazel said from her post at the worktop. She was kneading bread dough, and puffs of flour fogged the air, ghostly in the sunshine.

Finished with his coffee and satisfied with his job as a father, Oliver gathered his and Simon's dishes. While washing up, he inhaled the sweet scent of yeast, flour, butter, and eggs. "He looks like his mother."

"But he acts like you. Always afraid he's going to miss something or be forgotten upstairs." She slapped the dough into a smooth, round loaf. "Always busy. Like you. You're working too hard, lad."

"I don't have a choice right now, *Tante*. Garrett broke too many long-standing promises to our tenants. Until I can get the mill going, they're going to doubt my every intention."

Truthfully, helping them increased Oliver's worry as much as it eased his conscience. The families who depended on him needed more than patched roofs and good irrigation. Many of their needs required money they didn't have and couldn't find. He barely had enough to keep Hazel in flour.

The forest with its trees marked for cutting was a vow to those families and to himself. Change was coming, but it now hinged on equipment hidden in a stable and equally mysterious financing.

"What happens when you leave?" Hazel asked without looking at him. "When they've learned to trust you only to watch you head for the coast?"

He'd asked himself that, late in the night when his doubts and suspicions kept him awake. "The mill will take on its own life. I'll find a strong, independent manager who understands its importance. And I'll hire an intelligent proxy to vote in lords."

"It won't be the same."

"I won't stay gone so long this time." He knew the promise was shallow. He'd now forever be torn between two sides of the world. Never quite settled. Much like before.

The only thing he could do now was not disappoint Simon. He dried his hands and kissed her cheek. "I need to tell Alice she has a holiday. Thank you for breakfast."

As he left the kitchen, the downstairs bell rang. The cheerful, not quite musical jangle had always been rare, but since his homecoming, it had been unheard. Unless, of course, it was an impatient creditor, a tenant needing assistance, or a seamstress. As much as he loathed that idea, at least it would keep him away from the dour nursery.

Lionel met him in the hallway, carrying a coat and cravat. "Her Grace has requested that you join her in the drawing room to entertain guests."

He couldn't possibly entertain. There was too much to worry after, too much to do. He was weary from it, and despite the sunshine gleaming through the windows, he was cold to his marrow. "Who?"

"Lady Chitester and her daughter, Lady Amelia." Lionel hesitated and then stepped closer. "She asked Emmett to take them an invitation yesterday."

Mierda. Since she hadn't mentioned it, Oliver had hoped his mother had given up her marriage schemes. He should have known better. His luck in England was always bad. "Thank you, Lionel."

Oliver faced the mirror by the door and tied the black cravat as loosely as possible before taking the coat. As soon as their mourning period was over, he was burning this coat and dancing around the flames like one of the heathen islanders the sailors had recounted in tales for Simon.

Outside the drawing room doorway, he paused and put on the polite smile Julia had taught him to use whenever parties had become too trying. *Think of yourself in the woods, love.*

What waited on the other side of the door wasn't a shady glen. His mother was on the sofa, angled so she could see him arrive. While she chatted with Lady Chitester, they'd left Amelia alone on a small settee. All the other chairs had been moved to the edges of the room.

"Dearest." His mother held out her hand. "Lady Chitester and Amelia have been kind enough to call."

"Mother." He inclined his head and clasped her fingertips before turning to the other ladies, who had obviously searched for the most plain, subdued dresses in their closets. "Lady Chitester, Lady Amelia. It's good of you both to visit and help take Mother's mind from her grief. If you'll excuse me—"

"Stay." His mother remembered, somewhat late, to make herself smile. "Trees don't run, Your Grace. They'll still be waiting after our guests leave."

Trapped much like Spot in his jar, Oliver bowed lower. "Of course. My apologies." He smiled at their guests. "I tend to be single-minded. I'll ring for tea." He suspected Hazel was already on her way, but it gave him an excuse to stand near the fire.

Unlike the study with its missing art and piles of ledgers, this room remained much as he'd always remembered it. Dainty chintz-covered furniture was draped in frills and lace. A needle-work basket rested between an over-stuffed chair and the hearth, though he'd never seen his mother with a needle. A half-finished landscape rested on an easel. It was the garden and, judging by the colors on the canvas and the matching flowers outside, the paint was probably still wet.

"I didn't know you painted."

The women stared at him, and a flush built under his mother's skin. He'd no doubt embarrassed her. Again.

"I'm sorry to interrupt," he said as he walked to the easel. "But this is lovely, Mother."

"It is, Your Grace." Amelia joined him. "You've caught the light beautifully. Even the wind tossing some of the taller blooms."

The blush built higher, and his mother's smile deepened to the first real expression Oliver had seen in days. Perhaps ever. "Thank you. I've never been good at gardening, but I love the color in summer."

"You've done this one as well, haven't you?" Lady Chitester asked from an opposite wall, where she was admiring a spare, gray winter landscape. From the angle, Oliver guessed that it had been done in an upstairs bedroom.

"I did." The duchess took Amelia's arm and they walked together, their skirts whispering against the carpet. "Three winters past, when the heavy snows came, during the influenza outbreak. We were shut up in the house for weeks." She touched her handkerchief to the corner of her eye. "Garrett and I spent one morning looking out every upstairs window to find a suitable view and good light. Then he carried everything upstairs for me."

Three years ago, it had been so frigid in Quebec that the mill equipment had seized. Oliver had carried Simon in a sling under his coat while they'd stoked furnaces to dry snow-soaked wood. Then he and Richard had gone home, decorated for Christmas because all children deserved a tradition, and had fallen into their beds, too exhausted to move.

That seemed a distant memory now, here in the English summer staring at a sea of flowers. Keeping one eye on the women across the room, Oliver stepped behind his mother's desk. From this spot, in her high-back chair covered in richly hued embroidery, his mother could see the entire perfection of the room, including the gridded shadow of the garden doors slanting across the floor.

Her desk was a masterwork as well. A pen in a perfect shade of robin's egg blue, a seal with wax of the same color, a blotter that looked as though she'd never written anything. Her monogrammed stationery stood waiting in a rack; page after page of dainty Rs imposed over the family's crest faced him. Oliver lifted a page from the middle and, careful not to crease it, flipped it over so that it faced the door rather than the windows. He then ran his finger along the top edge of the stack to make sure everything was level.

"M'lord?" the duchess called sharply. "Why don't you take Lady Amelia for a turn in the garden?"

The heat built under his collar, singeing its way to his ears. It worsened when he saw Amelia's blush. The thin line of her mouth, though, hinted this was no flirtatious Miss. Perhaps the shared irritation could be their savior. Oliver stepped to her side and offered his arm. "Single-minded, as I said. Would you like some air?"

"Thank you, sir." She put her hand on his arm yet kept her fingers flat on his sleeve.

He led her into the sunshine, careful to keep away from the roses so the thorns wouldn't catch her skirts.

That was a lie. He kept clear of the roses because they reminded him of Thea.

Six years ago, he'd boarded the ship for Canada in a cloak that smelled of lemon and roses. That first evening, pitching to and fro in his small cabin, he'd realized it wasn't just his cloak. His clothes, his skin—even his hair—had carried her scent. It had comforted him then. Later, it had turned to torment.

Julia had once bragged to her friends that he didn't bring her anything as pedestrian as roses, that he was more creative with flowers than most men. Guilty over the praise, he'd finally told her he was allergic to them.

He'd lied to his wife.

And here he was, lying again.

Once they'd turned on the path and were out of sight of the house, Amelia removed her hand and put distance between them. In the sunshine, the gray silk in her dress bloomed in an iridescent sheen of pink and blue.

"I should apologize," he began.

"I am so sorry," she said at the same time.

They shared a brief, awkward laugh. "May I claim a host's right and go first?" he asked.

When she nodded, he stepped aside and urged her to continue their walk. "It was kind of you and your mother to visit and to be respectful of our mourning attire."

"You don't think I look fetching in gray?" Amelia's question dissolved into a snort of laughter. "Don't look so embarrassed, sir. No one looks fine in gray. We weren't quite sure what to wear on such short notice. It was a shock to receive—"

It was Oliver's turn to laugh when she looked as though she wanted to swallow her tongue. "Please. I'm aware Mother invited you. I regret that she's once again entwined you in her schemes."

"And I'm sorry to be foisted upon you like a one-eyed spinster with a wooden leg."

Damn. That impression would never do. "My apolo—"

"Oh please. All this regret only makes everything more awkward. I'm aware that I'm pretty, just as I'm aware that you couldn't be interested in me even if I were willing to be auctioned off like a prized heifer."

"Wise girl," he said as he took her hand, placed it on his elbow, and put his fingers over hers. They walked in companionable silence for another turn around a hedge. "Is it that obvious?"

"Most dukes wouldn't know where the kitchen was in a house, much less risk being seen with a cook in a shadowy hallway."

Or doing her dishes, searching for an excuse to touch her, and kissing her goodnight. If he focused hard enough, he could still feel her skin against his lips. "She isn't a cook."

Amelia's smile quirked upward, along with her eyebrows. "Obvious, Your Grace."

At the end of the path, they turned back toward the house. The dread in Oliver's bones vanished when he heard Simon laugh. The child was still outside with Fred, by the sound of it.

"I can reach the drawing room unsupervised," Amelia whispered. "Why don't you make a run for it?"

He could easily vanish through a hedge, but that would be

rude, not to mention childish. And he wasn't a child anymore. "Nonsense." He kept her at his side and continued their walk, though he quickened their pace.

Returning to the house, he ushered Amelia into the drawing room and winked as he bowed low. "Thank you for your company, Miss Chitester. Ladies, if you'll excuse me. Work calls."

"ARE YOU SURE you wish to do this?"

Thea took a deep breath and counted to five. It wouldn't do to snap at her mother's landlord. After all, the man put up with the constant stream of complaints from his only tenant, and Mother's situation here kept her from living at the inn.

"I'm certain," she said as she pushed the coins across the table.

"This is a great deal of money, Mrs. Smith. I can't help but think you'll need it."

It was the same discussion she'd had with Drake last week after Oliver had left. They'd spent an entire evening holed up in her office reviewing ledgers and accounts, budgeting and segregating cash. He'd begged her to wait, to not be rash. The delay had only solidified her resolve.

Taking note that the landlord was eyeing the money with the glee children reserved for sweets, Thea stood. "I've been able to save quite a bit of money living at The Goat, so this isn't a hardship. I'd prefer to pre-pay Mother's rent and eliminate the worry for everyone concerned."

"Well, then." He scooped up the coins and deposited them into a strongbox much like hers before walking her to the door. "You needn't worry about that any longer."

"And you'll not accept payment from my sister? Nothing. If Mother needs anything, please contact me. I'd consider it a personal favor—as would Mr. Fletcher." After all, *Mr. Fletcher* had loaned him the funds to repair the building's roof.

"Certainly."

"Thank you, sir."

She was already halfway up the stairs when the door closed behind her, and she didn't slow as she swept into the apartment. "Mother?"

"It's not necessary to raise your voice." She was sitting in her chair in the corner, doing nothing but watching time pass. "The walls are so thin I could hear you coming up the stairs."

Thea carried the basket of supplies into the kitchen. "I saw Elizabeth Whitman at the market. She said they'd invited you to help at the church."

"They wanted me to help repair the needlework for the kneelers."

"That would be marvelous. The old ones are getting quite threadbare."

"Why should I give anything else to that place?" Her mother banged her cane on the floor for emphasis. "What has it ever done for me but take my husband and throw me out as if I were worthless?"

"Service isn't a repayment for rewards," Thea reminded her. It was a lesson her father had repeated to them every time they'd grumbled about their responsibilities.

"Don't preach to me like I'm a child." Another crashing thump echoed. "I saw Mr. Fletcher with that Hawkins boy again this week. You'd best be well clear of any scheme of his."

"If I can't preach, neither can you." Thea dropped the cupboard door closed. "And I have no say over what Drake does with his money or his time."

"That's not what I've heard. People say he spends too much time with you under the same roof."

"I'm far too busy to listen to gossip," Thea said. "As are Drake and Oliver. *People* will just have to find someone else to snipe about." As though that would happen. Tales and whispers had followed her most of her life, some true and some half-true. Some were outright lies.

"You should have stayed in London. You could have worked with Millie and shared in her success."

Two years ago, when Thea had arrived in London, she'd gone to find her sister's shop. Instead, she'd discovered the deception Millie had perpetrated—a storefront with a fancy sign and dresses in the window, an apartment upstairs, but no clients, no orders, and a hired seamstress for anything that needed done, which were most often Millie's clothes.

Two years ago, Thea had seen nothing wrong with keeping that secret. There were so many in her life already. At least Millie had kept up with her share of their mother's expenses, and her mother had one daughter to be proud of.

Thea knew better now, but years of complicity tied her tongue. "My stitches aren't fine enough."

"Because you spent more time chasing after that boy. I should have put my foot down when your father insisted on taking over your education."

Yes, because she could have drawn her way out of starvation. "I'm thankful every day that Father taught me something useful."

"And you'd rather use it to be a servant rather than help your family."

You're a disgrace to your family. You've brought shame to your family. You're no longer a member of this family.

"Odd," Thea said. "I thought that's what I was doing." She swept to the door, heedless of the stack of papers that toppled in her wake.

"You're leaving?"

The guilt-laced question had lost its effectiveness with inconsistency and overuse. "I'll see you on Sunday."

Thea left the house and sucked in a gulp of fresh air tinged with baked goods and manure as she climbed into her gig. Once Neptune had crossed the bridge and the village was behind them, she shoved her bonnet back and let the sun warm her hair. It served to banish her foul mood, but it didn't keep her worries at bay.

The first was Oliver. He was always first lately, but now it was doubled. Extracting her mother from Millie's schemes was the best for everyone, but it limited the amount of cash available for investment in the mill. Backing out now was impossible. She was his only hope. Besides, she had a lot to prove. To his mother, hers, and him. To herself as well. She was not a helpless girl any longer.

Drake, and his concern over her *obsession* to overextend her cash reserves, was her second greatest worry. Blackmail, he'd said, was one thing. Impoverishment was quite another. But she wasn't impoverished. Not anymore. She'd set aside enough for the inn's expenses and payroll, and the inn itself was a source of income. Not to mention the remainder of her loans, which would surely pay off soon. Oliver would never let his family stay in debt.

Which had led to Drake's other argument—that the money was coming from the same pocket, so what did it matter? Other than the crime, obviously. Though one simple explanation would clear his confusion, she couldn't bring herself to do it.

She needed to tell Oliver first. He deserved the truth, and it was the easiest way out. However, now she was faced with not just his safety and independence, and not just hers or her staff's. Now it was her mother's. Every time she turned a corner in this deceitful maze, she faced a new hedgerow higher than the last.

Damn the duchess and her lies. Damn Millie and her greed.

Rounding the final bend in the road, she slowed Neptune in anticipation of the sharper turn into the lane that led to her now crowded stable. A too-familiar coach waited in front of the inn. No. Not today. She wasn't prepared for another duel of words with Lady Rushford.

However, it wasn't the duchess. Laughter on the breeze was her first clue. Jenny and John were between the coach and the house, keeping a watchful eye on Simon as he pursued the barn cat. If Simon was here, his father wouldn't be far behind.

Thea tightened her grip on the reins. If she couldn't deal with his mother, she certainly couldn't deal with Oliver. Not now. However, as she stopped in the lane, he left the shadow of the coach and came to her side, hand outstretched.

She didn't need his help, couldn't take it. It was too late for it anyway. She kept hold of the reins. "No, Oliver."

He kept his hand extended. "What harm can possibly come from me helping you?"

If he only knew. "Simon needs to take care with the cat. He's the best mouser I have."

"And you don't want him tamed?" he teased.

"I don't want the boy clawed to ribbons."

Following her stare, Oliver glanced over his shoulder. "Leave the creature be, Si."

The brief break gave her a chance to compose herself. When he looked back, she could ignore the charm that seeped from his pores. "You aren't supposed to be here."

"I'm not supposed to be here without reason," he countered. "I'm following your advice and taking Simon to Greenlee's to look at ponies. We'd like you to come with us."

He wasn't playing fair, and he knew it. She could tell from his smile. "No, but thank you. I have chores to finish before the dinner crowd arrives."

"The girls and I can handle them," Jenny said as she and John walked closer. "We've already done the laundry."

"And one of the new lads needs to work for his board. The boy eats enough for two grown men," John said as he wrapped his fingers around Neptune's halter. "He's going to help with the floors after he finishes mucking stalls. I'll get him to groom this old chap."

Thea gritted her teeth. Oliver had made them accomplices to his scheme, and they'd pitched in without any thought of the consequences or her wishes. In the middle of them, all smiling, she was trapped by good manners. After handing the reins to John, she grasped Oliver's fingers and stepped down from the gig.

CHAPTER THIRTEEN

"ND THEN WHAT happened?" Simon asked, his eyes bright. "Feathers flew everywhere." Oliver threw his arms wide as he narrated, as much to get a giggle from his son as to get a reaction from their passenger. "They dangled from the horses' ears and stuck on the thorny roses that were tangled in the wheels. And the chickens were lumbering about and squawking so that I couldn't hear myself think."

"But you won the race, didn't you?"

"I did not. Your…Garrett bested me that time."

Thea glanced sideways, allowing Oliver to see one arched eyebrow. Yes, he'd left out several things. Like a broken arm and worry over his horses. That he'd gotten into a roaring fight with Garrett because he'd cheated to win, and because, except for last minute intuition, Thea had been beside Oliver in the curricle.

And that Garrett was Simon's uncle.

She had always been his conscience. Even when he'd been across an ocean, married to someone else, he'd heard Thea's voice in his head when he'd made decisions.

It was comforting and annoying at the same time.

Just like now. She was close enough to smell, and her penchant for hats let him see the sunshine and shadows cross her face. But she was staring out the window as if she hadn't seen the view every day for thirty years.

It hadn't been Oliver's intention to ask her along for the afternoon, but Simon had begged to stop. Oliver had given into his son and the sizzle in his veins, which had built when she'd refused to go.

A bump in the road jostled the coach and swayed the curtains, letting in sunlight that glanced off a frayed hem he'd missed during his inspection. Oliver pulled his penknife from his pocket and trimmed the thread. At least the coach was clean—he'd made sure of that before he put Simon in it again.

Emmett had been horrified to see Oliver up to his elbows in soapy water. Oliver had been embarrassed that his mother had fired Emmett's apprentice, leaving the aging servant to manage back-breaking work alone.

Another bump, and his boots collided with Thea's, leaving a smudge on her skirt as she jerked her feet against the seat box. The crack echoed through the coach.

Like she didn't want him to touch her. Like she was afraid.

He looked past the flush in her skin that could have been anger or embarrassment, or something deeper that warmed his insides in response. Were her knuckles white for a reason other than determination? Were her eyes glassy?

Reluctance was one thing. Fear was quite another.

"*¿Por qué tienes miedo de mí?*" he murmured, fighting the cold trickle down his spine. Thea had been many things in his life, but she'd never been afraid of him.

Her level gaze met his as her posture shifted and her shoulders squared, reminding him of her barn cat. "I'm not. Your legs are too long."

"I've not grown taller in six years,"

She avoided another swipe of his feet. "You've also not grown less vexing."

There was *his* Thea—the girl he'd sparred with since they were eight years old, the woman who'd driven him to distraction and broken his heart.

And had made it thump against his ribs for the first time in four years.

He levered himself upright and swung to join her on her seat, forcing her to move to avoid being sat on. Across from them Simon continued to stare out the window as Spot's jar reflected the sunlight. The seat next to him was still dented, waiting for Oliver to return.

To go back to a place where Thea's skirts didn't brush his fingers, where her body heat didn't warm him through his shirtsleeve.

"What are you doing?" Her voice was sharp, but she didn't move.

"Solving a problem." To prove his point, he stretched his legs to their full length and wiggled his feet. "Now we both have plenty of room and you can relax."

Now she did shrink away, toward the corner of the coach, and Oliver missed her immediately. He might have always missed her.

It was a traitorous thought, but he couldn't stop it. It was honest, and he was tired of being anything less.

"Go back—"

As it always had, her determination spurred his. "I'm not carrying you to prison, Thee. It's a few hours in the country. With ponies." She'd always shared his weakness for horses. They could start over there.

"I have work to do."

"This isn't the first time we've played truants."

"And it was always a bad idea."

The breeze through the coach carried her rosy scent across his nose. It was impossible to think of anything but kissing her. Given the way her throat flexed as she stared up at him, she was thinking the same thing. "It was never a bad idea."

"I'm not a school girl any longer. I have a business to run."

"It will be there at the end of the day, and the rest of the staff can survive without your constant supervision."

He'd turn around if she insisted, though it might kill a part of his spirit he'd overlooked for too long.

It might have been his imagination, but her shoulders dropped slightly. He was winning.

"*¿Por que me estas haciendo esto?*" she whispered as she glanced toward Simon.

The movement reminded Oliver of their audience and how easily children repeated things at the worst possible times. The switch to Spanish told him they were moving past pleasantries in a coach on a sunny afternoon.

What was he doing to her? He just wanted to see her relax, to catch a glimpse of the carefree girl he'd known. "*Porque eres mi mejor amiga y yo te has perdido.*"

The admission brought a sliver of guilt with it. It was one thing to know he missed her, quite another to say it aloud. He'd been happy. If Julia had lived, he would still be married to her without regret. But she wasn't alive. And Thea's husband wasn't either.

"*Extrañas a la chica que conociste, Oliver. No puedes vivir en el pasado.*"

"Then stop keeping me there," he snapped. Closing his eyes, he drew a deep breath and exhaled slowly. Everything about this place conspired to keep it in the past, to remind him of what he'd lost, what he was losing. "No matter what happened between us," he said in a softer voice, "no matter our choices, you *are* my friend—at least I'm yours."

And, yes, that was a lie. He wanted more than that. But he had to start somewhere. One day at a time. Oliver wrapped his fingers around hers, giving warmth but applying no pressure. "*Un día, Pepinilla. Dame un día.*"

The coach slowed, then stopped. Sunshine flooded through the windows, and a small, faint whinny drifted in on the breeze. Simon's eyes widened just before he craned his head out the window.

Oliver exited first and lifted Simon to the ground before handing over Spot's jar. Then he offered his hand to Thea, and his pulse quickened as her fingers curved against his and she stepped to his side. The sky was blue and the air smelled of hay and stables. Ponies made their way to the paddock, some lumbering, some at a trot, all drawn by the promise of carrots and affection.

Thea's hat hid her eyes, but he could see her smile.

One day. He had an afternoon to convince her to abandon their past.

ANOTHER LIFETIME AGO, Thea had fantasized about this. A little boy and his father, sunshine and ponies. Now it was a reminder of everything she'd wanted and lost.

I've missed you. Those words had sealed her fate. When he'd never sent for her, she'd surrendered the hope that he'd loved her—but then she'd had him *that* way for a small interval. What she'd missed most was talking with him while they'd wandered through the woods, sharing adventures, laughing. She'd missed *him*.

And now she had one day to last for the rest of her life.

"You've been smirking for the past thirty minutes."

"Why shouldn't I?" Oliver said as he stretched his face to the sun. "It's a beautiful day, Simon is having a wonderful time, and you've quit fighting me over keeping your hand."

She had. Because it helped stifle the pain inflicted by everything he was enjoying. And because Oliver's heat soaked through her clothes and past her skin, making her warm for the first time in years. Part of that was probably due to his insistence that she leave her hat in the coach. "No one likes a poor winner, Ol."

"As though you aren't gloating every time Simon finds a new pony to pet."

"Well, you must admit, I was right," she said as she elbowed him in the ribs.

He nudged in reply. "I'll admit nothing. But I'm going to

blame you for my carrot debt to Greenlee. You're feeding as many hungry mouths as Simon."

"They look lonely with just us as company." As irresistible as the creatures were, she was fantasizing about selecting a mount for a boy who didn't exist. In the end, it had always been little more than a dream.

"They'll make up for it on Saturday. The paddock will be a riot of children ignoring their parents, their grubby hands full of treats."

"Speaking of, why are you and Simon free this afternoon?" she asked as Simon ran back to them, his dark hair almost blue in the sunshine and his cheeks rosy.

"We finished marking trees for cutting, and we were at loose ends," Oliver said as he doled out carrots.

"And we didn't want to go back home in case *grandmère* still had visitors." Simon counted his treasure and ran ahead again.

"Visitors?" Thea asked, willing her anxiety lower. She'd counted on the mourning period to keep Millie at bay.

"She invited Lady Chitester and Amelia to visit," Oliver muttered.

"I see." Thea pulled on her hand. She would have preferred blackmail to matchmaking.

Oliver tightened his grip. "I have no interest in Amelia Chitester."

"And you decided to prove that to your mother by being seen with me." The battle for her hand became a restrained tug of war. This would never do. The saboteurs would burn her stables. The duchess would think the worst.

"I'm not going to spend a rare good afternoon by arguing with you about my mother," Oliver grated. "And if you didn't notice, there is no one around to carry gossip back to her. I am out with you because I prefer to spend my afternoon with a prickly caterpillar."

She yanked so hard on her hand that when she regained her freedom, she almost lost her balance. "Me? A caterpillar? How totally flattering, *sir.*"

"What else would you call it, *madam?*" He faced her, his fists planted on his waist. "You spend every day hiding behind your chores and responsibilities, closed off in that inn on the outskirts of everything. Yet you never manage to build a cocoon."

"You're a fine one to talk." Thea pointed a finger at his chest only to withdraw it when it trembled as much as her voice. "You hide behind a four-year old boy."

"What?" The color was high on his cheeks, and his eyes were almost gold.

"He goes everywhere with you, a ready excuse for anything you'd like to escape. Rather than playing with children his own age, his friends are two thirty-year-old men and a *bug.* He should be in school, or at least at lessons, learning—"

"He learns quite well."

"What *you* like, as you like it," Thea persisted. "What are you going to do when he wants out of the jar?"

"And what would you know about raising anything other than your ferocious barn cat?"

More than you think. The words were on the tip of her tongue, but the sob building in her throat choked all sound. She spun on her heel and walked away.

As much as she hated Millie for using secrets to manipulate, Thea wouldn't confess out of anger or frustration. Oliver didn't deserve to have the truth hurled at him. Drawing air into her lungs as deeply as she could manage, she wrapped her fingers around her locket and willed her bones to stop shaking.

A small hand slipped into hers, and she looked down into Simon's huge smile and heartbreaking hazel eyes.

"Would you like to meet my new pony?"

Oliver was talking with Mr. Greenlee near the paddock, and Thea considered keeping her distance. But it had taken courage for Simon to consider a pony, much less choose one. "Certainly. Lead the way."

They stopped in front of a piebald gelding, almost as wide as he was tall, who gave up a search for carrots so Simon could stroke his nose. Kneeling, Thea removed her glove and slipped her hand under the pony's coarse mane. "He's a fine mount, Si. What are you going to name him?"

The little boy tilted his head first one way, then the other, then he nodded. "Spot."

"You already have a Spot," Oliver said as he joined them, kneeling on the other side of the boy. Though his tone was casual, he refused to look at anything but the horse, and the muscles in his jaw were bunched to the size of a peach pit. "Won't you get them confused?"

"No," Simon said. "This one's bigger than the other."

"Just so." Oliver's smile, his stare, focused on his son. "I'll put in an order for a saddle and tack, and when it's done, we can start riding less—"

"No," Simon said, shaking his head until his short curls bounced. "I don't want to ride him."

"You have to—"

"I won't." The little boy shouted and stepped away until he was nearer to Thea. She shrank back. Oliver had made it clear that Simon was none of her concern.

"Simon Edward Hawkins," Oliver grated. "That is quite enough."

"You can't make me," Simon wailed as he turned into Thea and threw his arms around her neck, his wet cheek buried so tightly she could feel his lashes.

Oliver's color went to a dangerous mahogany, and his mouth drew into a decidedly angry line as he reached for his son.

Thea put up a hand in a silent request for stillness. She kept it upraised until Oliver nodded, but his eyes remained wary. Frightened.

Keeping her gaze locked on his, she stroked Simon's hair, then his back. "You like your new pony, don't you?"

Sniffling loudly, Simon nodded.

"And you like to feed him?" Another nod. "And pet him?"

Another. "And you'd like your papa to show you how to groom him?" A final nod. "Then why don't you want to ride him, darling?"

Simon's reply was garbled by tears and sniffles, and he was still talking into her neck. She gently pried him away from her shoulder and dried his tears. "Your papa isn't angry with you, I promise. He and I had a disagreement. Can you take a deep breath and tell me why you don't want to ride Spot?"

The small, shaky inhale ended on a hiccup. "I would-wouldn't wa-want someone t-to put a sad-dle on m-me."

Oliver's shoulders drooped as he dragged his hand down his face. The resulting expression made him look twenty years older. He stroked his fingers through the boy's hair. "Si?"

He crawled from her lap into his father's, and Oliver cradled him close. Their heads bent together, their conversation was limited to hoarse, shaky rumbles, and sniffled, childish replies. After several minutes, Simon wrapped his arms around Oliver's neck.

Tears filled Thea's eyes. This was a family moment, and she was an outsider who did not wish to be. She needed to leave. She shouldn't have come at all.

Oliver's hand covered hers, stilling her mid-rise. His fingers trembled, and his stare was a mixture of sadness, chagrin, and relief. "Please don't go."

Once she was settled, he tossed his hair out of his eyes and eased Simon away. His smile brightened, and she recognized the tactic of a parent trying to put their child at ease.

"Do you know how you like to help me when I'm working?" Oliver asked. "Ponies are like that, too. Their job is to carry people places or pull carts, and they are happiest when they do that. The animals in your story ran away from home because their people didn't think they could work anymore, not because the people made them work."

Oliver winked at Thea. "Uncle Richard and Simon have been reading *The Bremen Town Musicians* at bedtime."

She hid her smile. "I see."

Simon stared past her and into the paddock. "Do you think Spot sings?"

"I'm not sure," Oliver said. "But did you see Thea's horse today? He looks like a fine singer."

"Oh Neptune is," she agreed. "When he thinks no one is listening, he sings hymns in a lovely baritone. I've caught him once or twice."

As Mr. Greenlee tied Spot to the carriage, Oliver and Thea told stories about Neptune until Simon was a mass of giggles and questions. He insisted on sitting nearest the back window, faced backward so he could make sure Spot trotted along.

"You and I have never fought like that," Oliver whispered.

"We always fought like that. Sometimes, it's the only way to make you pay attention." Holding her breath, she put her hand over his. "But I was wrong to question your judgment as a parent. You have been both mother and father, and it isn't—couldn't have been—easy. You've done it well."

"Thank you." The shadows made his lashes appear longer and thicker. Despite his slow, tired blinks and his loose-muscled stance, his smile was wide and bright.

"What are you going to do with Spot the Larger when you leave?" she asked.

"Take him with us, I suppose. Or convince Simon there's a pony cousin in Canada who needs a home."

Outside, the shadows stretched longer and longer as the sun slid toward the far horizon. Birds went quiet, and night bugs began to sing. After a few moments, heat and exhaustion loosened her muscles and she sagged against the seat. The thump and bump of the carriage, the clip-clop of hooves, and the squeak of the axle all worked to lull her eyes closed.

Oliver gently pressed her head to his shoulder. Keeping his arm around her, he rested his cheek against her scalp. "I'm sorry too."

In her dreams, past fantasies and memories mixed with present recollections and wishes. When a warm little boy crawled into her lap, she tightened her grasp and cuddled him closer until his coarse curls brushed her chin.

Her eyes flew open and she crawled back against the tufted upholstery, trying to escape. "Take him."

Oliver knelt in front of her and slid his arms along hers, jolting her nerves. "What's wrong?"

"Take him." She fought her reaction, using years' old tactics to deflect the pain. She couldn't lose control now. "He shouldn't sleep here. I might drop him."

Oliver's fingers grazed her breasts—the side of one, underneath the other.

"Sorry," he murmured, his breath warming her neck. That, combined with his touch, stole her breath and locked her muscles. He tugged on the boy between them. "Let go, Thee."

Without standing, Oliver twisted and settled Simon across from them. After covering the boy with a coat, he reclaimed his seat. Thea inched away. She was too raw. His touch was a temptation and a torment.

"It was an accident," he grumbled.

"Of course it was." She wished her shaky breaths were the result of panic instead of attraction.

The coach rounded a sharp curve in the road, sliding her across the seat until she rested against him, hip to hip. Oliver closed his hand around her shoulder, anchoring her in place. His thumb brushed her collar bone—forward, back, forward back. "This is not."

His touch hypnotized her, relaxing her until she once again dropped her head to his shoulder. His breath stirred her hair the moment before he pressed a soft kiss to it.

"Neither was that, *mi mariposa*."

She recognized the spot in the road. Almost home. Earlier today, she'd wanted nothing more, but now she couldn't remember why. Every cell in her body was aware of him, much the way she imagined a butterfly was aware of the breeze on its wet wings when it first awakened to a different life.

But she wasn't ready to fly just yet. "Oliver?"

In the darkening coach, he was little more than a shadow, growing larger until he blocked the feeble moonlight in the window.

Oliver's lips closed over hers, tasting, clinging, softly sharing breath. His tongue traced her bottom lip. Back, forth, dipping just inside and repeating the action until she opened her mouth and let it slide against hers.

She pulled away to catch her breath. "You taste like carrots."

"You smell like sunshine." He nuzzled her neck, then her ear, scratching his whiskers across her jaw before setting his mouth against her cheek. His hot, moist breath tempted her to turn into him.

His teeth scraped her lips as he pulled her closer until his body heat soaked through her clothes. She kissed him in return, shoving her fingers into his thick hair and shuddering as his groan rattled down her spine.

She needed to stop this. She needed to tell him.

In a minute.

In a minute.

"*Ahem.* Your Grace?"

The coach had stopped. Emmett was holding the door, his eyes averted as he fought a smile. Beyond him, Thea recognized her gate and front garden.

"Oops," Oliver whispered before clearing his throat. "Give us a moment please, Emmett."

"Certainly, sir. I'll tend to the beastie."

Oliver stepped down from the carriage and offered her his hand, using the other to pull his jacket closed.

"Are you cold?" she asked.

"Not exactly." His blush crept to his hairline, but his smile was his unique blend of boyish and sinful.

Six years melted away and she remembered the feel of him against her body, in her hand. Heat rushed upward to her ears, but there was still plenty to flow lower. "Oh," she squeaked. "Goodnight."

As she rushed by, he caught her hand and kissed her fingers. *"Dulces sueños."*

She stood at the door and watched the coach disappear. Oliver's taste—mint and carrots—was heavy on her tongue, and her clothes smelled of cinnamon. Her tears bit into the spots chafed by his whiskers, and the burn was echoed in her conscience.

Her dreams would not be sweet.

CHAPTER FOURTEEN

"HELLO, MRS. SMITH."

"Hello, Martin." Thea untied her cloak and delivered it to Tavie's butler. "How have you been?"

"Well, thank you. You look beautiful, as usual."

Every time Thea crossed this threshold, it was impossible not to think of the first time. Three years earlier, she'd practically fallen into Martin's arms when he opened the door in the middle of the night.

"Thank you." Then she'd been in a third-hand black crepe. Now she was in bespoke silk, beige with a bright blue stripe. Her wool cloak matched the blue, as did the ribbon flowers on her hat. She handed that to Martin and then removed her gloves before checking her reflection.

A totally poised woman stared back at her, nothing like the girl years earlier, and nothing like the nervous wreck she was inside. So much hinged on today.

"Has Drake arrived?"

"Not yet," Martin replied as he hung her cloak and hat in line with all the others. "I'm sure he'll be along soon. It's not like him to be late."

The moths fluttering against Thea's ribs doubled in both size and number. Drake was meeting with Lord Sterling this morning to discuss the purchase of the mill building. It was a tight schedule, but Sterling had dragged his feet until the last minute. Without a price, their proposal was incomplete.

"Your aunt is waiting." Martin opened the ballroom door.

Why on earth would I need a ballroom? Tavie had always asked. *I have no daughter to come out. No, darling. I need a boardroom.*

A large round table sat in the middle of the room, shaped like a *C* to allow for ingress and egress. The center was currently full of ladies, dressed in every color of the rainbow. Ignoring that they sounded like her chickens, and that some even looked like her chickens, Thea greeted everyone on her way to Tavie.

Her aunt, always formidable, was even more so when in her element. In a yellow day dress, which somehow didn't clash with her fading red hair, next to a sideboard almost sagging under the weight of food, she could have actually been hosting a tea.

Leaving her group in mid-conversation, Tavie swooped in and kissed Thea on both cheeks. "You look lovely, dear. How are you feeling?"

"Slightly terrified." Thea scanned the back of the room where the businessmen were standing in much more somber circles, hoping Drake and Oliver had come in without Martin's knowledge. Even though Martin knew everything that went on in the house.

"Nonsense. You have no reason to be." Tavie tapped Thea's shoulder with her fan. "Sit up straight, don't stammer, and make a logical argument. You're among friends, and if you can make them money, so much the better."

"But—"

"They'll approve it or they won't, dear. But that's up to them." It was the same advice Tavie had given when she'd sponsored Thea's purchase of The Goat.

The door opened, and Drake and Oliver walked into the room. They hovered on the edge of the crowd, suspended between both groups.

Tavie raised her spectacles to her nose and stared across the room. "That's the Hawkins boy? My. Was he always that pleasant to stare at?"

"Yes." Thea stamped on her jealousy as the women stole glances at the newcomers. Drake always drew attention, but now it had doubled. "He's also quite intelligent and accomplished. He has a sound head for business, and his plan—"

"Do calm down." Tavie patted her arm. "I've gone over it all with Drake. I don't doubt his judgment, and he has every faith in your man."

"He's not mine." Both men's stares fell on her, and both were far too somber. Her moths grew to sparrows.

Oliver's wary gaze swept her from across the room, and then back, taking everything in, both curious and confused.

Tavie's eagle eyes now turned on her as well. "You didn't tell him, did you?"

"I lost my nerve."

"More likely he upset you." Despite her words, Tavie's grin was impish. "You have better sense than any woman here, other than me of course, but this is a large risk. If you're doubting your decision, there's no shame in saying so. Are you certain you wish to do this?"

In his black trousers and hessians, with a bright white shirt under a sedately printed vest and a powder blue topcoat, Oliver looked every inch a duke. But what she remembered was his animated explanation of his business, how knowledgeable he was about every step, and how determined he was to succeed.

"I'm certain." She was just as certain something was wrong. "Excuse me, Tavie."

As she reached Drake, he opened the door and led the way to Tavie's library. It was his favorite room in the house, and it was always set aside for negotiations.

He closed the door, guaranteeing them a few last moments of privacy. "We have a problem."

Sparrows morphed into crows. She looked from him to Oliver. "What's happened?"

"What's going on in here?" Oliver asked, entering the boardroom.

She should have swallowed her anger and told him everything rather than letting her pride take over. "Not now, Oliver." She switched back to Drake. "Tell me everything."

"I was at Rushford's this morning for breakfast and a last-minute review. Sterling surprised us."

"Someone told him Fletcher was involved with my business," Oliver said. "What aren't you telling me?"

They were the only three who knew the specifics of this plan, other than Tavie. Unless…of course he would've said something to his mother. Probably in a fit of pique, because that's how they generally communicated. And the duchess, given a choice, had chosen Sterling and the status quo.

"Is the price much higher than we anticipated?" she asked Drake.

"There isn't a price."

They were staring at anything in the room other than her, like misbehaving little boys. Oh God. Vultures now circled in her stomach. "What happened?"

"I hit him."

"*Mierda.* Oliver—"

"He was insufferable. I could handle the wildly high price, but he insulted Garrett to my face, Thea."

The Hawkins brothers could fight like dogs over the same bone, but they had always been a solid unit against any outside threat. She looked at Drake. "And you just let this happen?"

"I may have held him steady to give Rushford a target." Her unflappable man of business scratched the back of his head and stared out from under his brows. "He really was out of line."

Martin rapped on the door, but didn't come in. It was their five-minute warning. The meeting was about to begin. She had no idea what to do.

"To hell with Sterling. I'll build my own mill." Oliver brushed his fringe from his eyes and gave the same smile he'd used to reassure Simon. "It wouldn't be the first time."

"Our last estimate was high due to Sterling's expected demand," Drake said. "We could add a few hundred pounds as a cushion."

The room fell quiet. Thea ran the figures in her head, as she knew Drake was doing.

Martin knocked again. They were out of time. Drake opened the door. "In for a penny."

Oliver offered her his arm. She took it and her doubts vanished. She'd known this man her whole life. He'd broken her heart, but he was a genius. He could do this. And if he could, she could.

"Oliver, this is a lending circle. We pool our money and our resources, and we're able to help those who can't obtain financing elsewhere, either because of gender or lack of resources."

"We?"

"Tavie was my sponsor." She sucked in a deep breath. "Now I'm yours."

"What does that mean?"

Martin opened the boardroom door just as Tavie clapped her hands sharply, stopping all conversation. "The quarterly meeting of the London Ladies Charity Circle is called to order," she trilled. "Everyone take your seats."

OLIVER LET THEA lead him to the head of the table, which sat where most people would stage a quadrille or a waltz. Now, however, everyone took seats that appeared assigned in a proscribed male-female pattern. Or perhaps female-male since Thea's aunt Octavia sat in the first position. Thea broke the line, putting Oliver between her and Drake. Given that he and Richard often sat with Simon between them, Oliver wasn't as relieved as he would have been.

"Let the record show everyone is present," Octavia said, her voice bouncing from the chandelier and into the far corners of the room. "We'll begin with old business. Lady Carlton's ball raised over five-hundred pounds for the church's Wayward Children's Home, which is enough to support them for almost two years if their rolls don't increase dramatically. Congratulations on the success, Mary."

Oliver tapped his fingers on his knee. He'd thought he was meeting investors, not a charity circle. It was honorable, yes, but he had serious business to discuss.

Their chairman allowed a brief smattering of applause before she called the meeting back to order. "We should consider a new beneficiary for our next endeavor."

"I would like us to consider a project in Kent."

The speaker was a lovely young woman in the middle of the table to Oliver's right. Her trembling voice was just above a whisper, and each woman facing her smiled and nodded in encouragement.

Having once been a new member of several organizations, Oliver sympathized with the woman's discomfort. However, he barely resisted the urge to clear his throat. They needed to conclude their agenda and leave the room. Why wasn't this done over tea? That's how they did it in the village. Wasn't it?

"It's a home for unwed mothers," the woman continued, her voice gathering strength. "They're taken in and taught a skill to support themselves."

"What happens to their children?" Thea asked. "Are they taken away?"

"Only if the mother wishes it, and then the adopting families are chosen carefully. Otherwise, the goal is to keep them from poverty and to reduce the rolls in the Wayward Children's Homes."

"What is your plan, Celeste?"

"Card parties, with the profits going to charity. It needn't be one large event, and it wouldn't even have to be in London. Those of us who live outside of town could participate and perhaps gain larger attendance and contributions."

Octavia glanced around the table. "Do I have a motion?"

"So moved," said a portly, sedate woman on the other side of the room.

Thea took his hand and squeezed slightly, her fingers brushing his trousers and teasing his thigh. Lust heated Oliver's blood, stealing his breath and clouding his vision. Thea's tightened grip help clear it, and when he looked at her, he was amazed to find her at ease in this bizarre world. She was his lifeline in this place that was both familiar and not. He laced his fingers through hers only to have her pull away.

"Seriously, Ol," she hissed. "Pay attention. Would a party like that work at home?"

Home had a nice ring to it. But rather than being romantic, he focused on her question and recalled the ill-fated dinner party. Matrons and daughters on the country marriage mart, men eager to flaunt their wealth. The Season in London was ending. Everyone would be going to the country for house parties and shooting. "Yes. I think so."

"Seconded," Thea said.

The plan passed unanimously. Celeste sat back, her pale skin flushed with pride.

"Well done, Lady Clayton." Octavia clapped her hands. "On to business reports."

Finally.

But no one left the room. Beginning to Octavia's left, woman after woman gave reports that sounded very much like a banking record. Each member glanced over the sheets in front of them, clearly following along. Oliver's brain itched, warning him his world was about to shift.

Sure enough, when they reached Thea, she straightened in her chair. "The Galloping Goat's profits are in front of you, and you'll notice they are steadily increasing. You'll also notice there is a line for loan income. Times in Thetford have been difficult, and I've loaned small amounts at a competitive rate to village businesses to keep them from closing. Those have begun paying off."

She had loaned. Not Fletcher. *I have funds.*

"Bloody hell," Oliver breathed. To his left, Drake choked back a laugh.

"That is largely due to the new Duke of Rushford's commitment to restoring his family's fortune and reputation, and with those the health of the village economy," Thea continued. "The largest part of his plan is the construction and operation of a timber mill on his property. I propose a loan, which I will sponsor."

"Why do you need *our* money, Your Grace?" a woman asked from the end of the table.

Our money, she said. Nontraditional investors, Fletcher had said. Oliver looked to him, and then to Thea. Both nodded. Drake's was encouraging, Thea's was more like permission. And now Oliver felt more like Celeste Clayton than he'd considered possible.

"My family's fortunes are…lacking due to prior mismanagement and overspending," Oliver said, refusing to weasel his words. "I assume you have my financial statement in front of you. While I have the reserves, they are tied up in Canadian investments, and I would prefer, if possible, to leave them there for the benefit of that business and, ultimately, my son."

"Will he not also inherit your title and any monies here?"

"Certainly, he will be entitled to whatever I have, and my conservation of his inheritance doesn't spring from a lack of faith. The timber there belonged, in part, to his late mother. By rights, the money is his."

"Can you elaborate on your plan?" another lady asked.

"I'd be happy to, madam." And he did, explaining every step to their satisfaction. Each lady alternately nodded and whispered to the man at her elbow.

"Your Grace, I'm Eliza Sheridan," the lady at the end of the table stated. "Would you be interested in selling your remnants—

sawdust, shavings, and pulp—at a bulk discount?"

"For what purpose?" Oliver asked, genuinely interested in her intentions.

"Paper," the lady answered. "They are making paper on the continent using wood pulp rather than rags. I'd like to try it."

"What if I gave you the pulp in exchange for a share in *your* mill?" He looked at Drake, wishing someone had explained the rules for this topsy-turvy meeting. "Can I do that?"

Laughter filled the room as Drake shrugged and nodded.

"Yes, well, you two can discuss side business later," Tavie decreed. "At the moment, we have the duke's petition for funding, sponsored by Thea Smith. The amount requested is three thousand pounds."

"The amount is large because there is no longer a suitable building in Thetford," Drake explained. "We will be constructing the facility. The remaining funds will be used to pay for labor costs and supplies until the mill turns a profit, which it should do quickly."

"Why is there a line item for security?" asked Mrs. Sheridan's man, who had the look of a barn owl.

"We have had several instances of interference, more a nuisance than anything else," Oliver replied. "Those will be resolved upon my return to Thetford."

"The guard is merely to protect your investment," Drake added. "We take that responsibility quite seriously."

"You are asking for a great deal of money," the woman at the end of the table stated. "Your home has been in Canada for the past six years, all your lands are entailed, and you have no other collateral. What guarantee do we have, other than your word?"

"You have mine." Thea's voice rang back from the walls, and the ladies' eyes widened. She cleared her throat and continued in a quieter tone. "I will guarantee the debt with a mortgage on The Galloping Goat."

Her inn, for Oliver felt certain now that it was hers and not Fletcher's. She'd hidden it from him for some reason he was determined to discover. It had allowed her to help the village when he couldn't, to help herself when no one else had done so.

I have funds.

"No," Oliver snapped. "I won't take—"

"All in favor?" Tavie crowed.

"Aye."

And it was done, leaving Oliver to feel like the fox in a room full of hounds. It wasn't lessened when Mrs. Sheridan swept across the floor, her man following in her wake, to discuss wood pulp and paper.

Drake came to Oliver's shoulder. "Be on your toes, Rushford. She's a ruthless negotiator, and he's no softer. I'll step in when you need me."

Thea walked away in a swirl of cream and blue, her red hair turned to bronze in the sunlight slanting through the windows. Their glances met and clashed as Drake made formal introductions. Oliver smiled and nodded when all he wanted to do was charge across the room and demand answers.

He shook the owlish man's hand.

And, in that brief moment, Thea vanished from sight like the imaginary creatures he'd never believed existed.

CHAPTER FIFTEEN

THE CROWD ON the street eventually required Thea to slow her pace, and their noise kept her pounding pulse inside, banging against her ribs. But no amount of noise or foul air could stop her smile. She'd done it—managed to get Oliver his loan, carried on the work of the Circle to help others in need, and shown herself to be every bit the manager Tavie had praised her for becoming.

She wished she'd been able to do it *with* Oliver instead of despite him, that he could share her success. The look on his face had confirmed her fears. He was angry, and he'd stay angry for a long time. But in the end, it didn't matter. He'd finish his mill and be on his way back to Canada. He and Simon would be safe, and the village would have a future.

And that would have to be enough.

Thea turned the corner into the market she'd frequented during the year she'd lived with Tavie. Visiting her favorite shops, she purchased herbal books, fabric, and spices and gave instructions for delivery to Tavie's home before the morning. After buying a supply of balsam oil, she stopped for an ice and watched the people pass. Courting couples mixed with young families, children ran ahead or pressed their noses to shop windows.

No matter how proud she was of herself for today, for the business she'd built from the ashes of her life, there would always be a barb, a sting, under her ribs. Some days it was a prick, like a thorn. Other times it coursed through her blood, singeing her until she was raw. Today, she felt like her skin was new.

An elderly couple stopped at the flower cart on the corner. The husband waited by his wife's side, laughing with the vendor as she considered each selection. And, when he paid for them and delivered the flowers into her hands, she acted like it was a total surprise and kissed him, right there on the street.

"Young love," Tavie had once said, *"holds no candle to old love."* She'd said it to comfort Thea, to assure her that someone else would come along, that she'd forget her ill-fated loss. But she'd said it without knowing the entire story.

Eyes stinging, Thea turned away from the sweet scene and caught her reflection in the glass.

Old love.

With a sigh, she finished her treat and went back to her mission. The afternoon was passing too quickly, and she needed to return to Tavie's and face Oliver. She had to deal with Millie first.

Miss Fowler's Ladies' Finery sat on the edge of the fashionable addresses. A freshly painted sign stood out from whitewashed walls, and dresses of the latest mode stood in the windows, their full skirts starched until they resembled meringue.

As Thea crossed the threshold, a tinkling bell announced her arrival. A very prim young lady emerged from behind a curtain.

"May I help you, ma'am?"

"I'd like to see your mistress, please."

"Miss Fowler is upstairs in a private fitting. I can help with whatever you need."

"If I wanted a dress, I'm certain you could," Thea said as kindly as possible. "But I don't. I need to see your mistress at once."

The young woman nodded before disappearing. The ceiling creaked overhead, and Thea used her time to explore. Despite the posh rug quieting her steps, no matter the tasteful paper on the walls and elegant full-length mirrors, there were no other shoppers. No fabric was displayed.

"May I help you?"

In an apron, with a tape dangling around her neck and a cushion bristling with pins in her hand, Millie looked every inch the dressmaker. "Oh. It's you. Hello."

"Hello. We need to talk. Privately."

Millie shrugged, but led the way into a tearoom clearly staged for visitors.

"What are you playing at?" Thea asked as soon as they were alone.

"Playing? I'm not sure what you mean," Millie said as she divested herself of her disguise. "I own a dress shop. I make dresses."

Thea swiped her fingers across the table and raised her dust-covered glove. "For who, Millie? Tavie would have helped you with a proper shop."

"*Tavie* helped me get a job as an apprentice."

That was a rule of the Circle. You had to be trained in the business you operated. Thea had come to them with housekeeper and cook experience, and innkeeper wasn't a tall step. "It was only for a year. If you'd proven—"

"Do you know what that life is like? There were nine of us crammed in an attic like rats, three to a bed. It was so cold I couldn't hold a needle. I worked until all hours of the night in poor lighting, and still my stitches weren't fine enough. They were never going to be." She shifted in the chair and smoothed her skirts, looking every inch like a lady having a proper conversation. "And I made barely enough to live on, much less to send home."

"Why didn't you say anything?"

"To whom? Mother had her bragging rights, Tavie was convinced her way was best, and you'd bought into the whole *sweat of your brow* theory of repentance."

Thea's blood simmered, heating her skin and curling her muscles, bringing her spine straight. "I was working myself to death."

"You had the perfect opportunity to pull yourself from the kitchen to the parlor, and to take me with you, but you never used it." Her smile curved in a cold arc. "So I did."

Thea frowned. She'd buried the secret, *her* secret, so deep only she could reach it. There wasn't a reason for the duchess to fear exposure.

"Honestly," Millie sighed. "And they call you the smart one. She's not afraid of *that*. She's afraid of *them*. The old duke. Oliver. Garrett told me once at a race when we shared a few pints." She leaned forward, her eyes sparkling. "If they'd learned what she'd done to you, she'd have been shuffled to some obscure property with a pittance of an allowance. She'll pay *anything* to keep that from happening."

Opportunity. Gossip. Money.

Her son was none of those things. "How dare you."

"Spare me the lecture. That witch owed Mother a stipend, and you didn't care where the money came from as long as I paid my share."

Millie had always had an entitled streak, but this was a shock. They hadn't been raised to be selfish, much less greedy. "How can you live with yourself?"

"I live quite well, actually. Freddie says I'm a natural with horses, and I'm learning to gamble properly. I apparently have the face for cards."

She'd always had the uncanny ability to bluff her way out of anything, even music lessons. This was completely different. "You will not use my son for your personal gain. I don't care what you do or where you get your money, but you will cease blackmailing Lady Rushford or I'll go to the authorities."

"Maybe I'll just blackmail you. Oliver's return does mean you have the larger secret now, doesn't it, *Mrs. Smith*?"

No matter what she could accomplish, she was doomed to be confined to a box someone else had put her in and she'd been too frightened to escape. But Millie wasn't the only one who knew how to bluff. "You can try, but I've spent all my ready cash to pay Mother ahead for the year, and I've just mortgaged myself to my eyeballs. I'm not sure what you could get other than satisfaction."

"Millicent? We really must leave." Freddie stopped in the doorway, and his calculating smile was a companion to Millie's. "Hello, Thea. This is a pleasant surprise."

Thea stood and nodded. "I'll take my leave. Safe travels to Surrey." She met her sister's cold, hard glare. "We'll talk again, Millie."

WHERE THE DEVIL was she?

Oliver opened his watch to check the time and then resumed his pacing. Thea had been gone for hours now. After turning his fortunes around, and his life on its head, she'd decided to go for a walk. In London. Alone.

"She can take care of herself," Drake said from his post near the hearth. "She spent a year living with Tavie, you know?"

No, he didn't. She never told him anything relevant to what had happened while he'd been gone. "Just because she's familiar, doesn't mean—"

The front bell interrupted him, and he strode to the library door, hoping to see Thea but finding a delivery man instead. The footman added the box to a growing pile of packages also waiting on her arrival.

Rather than explaining herself, she'd gone shopping.

"Did you really say *pin money?*" Drake asked, his smile widening when Oliver refused to answer. "No wonder she was irritated."

"She wasn't totally honest with me. Come to think of it, neither were you." He helped himself to Tavie's whiskey. He'd earned it. As an afterthought, he poured Drake a draught and set it on the mantel. "How does this work exactly?"

"Exactly?" Drake shrugged out of his coat and draped it over the nearest chair. Hooking a finger in his neck cloth, he loosened the knot. "They are a group of incredibly smart, determined women who were tired of being told they couldn't do something."

"You help them?"

"No. They help themselves. Their sweat, their savings, their skill." Drake rolled his sleeves to his elbows. "I'm the right face, a name on a dotted line."

Remembering the exchange in the meeting, Drake's neat summary, Oliver shook his head. "You're more than that."

The other man's smile curved to a wry arc. "I've always had a talent with numbers." He retrieved his drink and lifted the glass in a toast. "And a gift for people."

Everything about this made Oliver nervous. No one did anything for free. "What do you receive in exchange?"

"A salary. We have a contract."

"That she can't enforce in court." How could Thea get involved in something this risky? "What's to keep you from—"

"Loyalty," Drake said. "Tavie gave me a chance when no one else would."

That made no sense. A smart, capable man of business, properly apprenticed and trained, could have all the clients he wanted. Unless...*lived abroad, background in shipping.* "You're a privateer."

Drake sauntered to the bar. "I was. Now I'm a respectable businessman." He poured a drink. "And before you ask, the same loyalty is extended to Thea. I admire her."

Oliver tipped his glass, hoping the mouthful of whiskey would wash the bitter taste from his tongue. He'd thought his rival a worthless dead man, not a pirate standing at Thea's shoulder and whispering in her ear. Still, when Drake offered, Oliver joined him in another drink.

"She's smart, determined, and kindhearted." Drake slouched against the wall behind him. "She's come quite a distance in the last three years." His gaze was level, his shoulders relaxed. "We're friends, Oliver. Nothing more."

The outer door opened and closed, and heels clicked on the tile. Oliver strode to the library door. Thea was surveying her pile of packages while handing her hat and cloak to the footman. Her sunrise-colored hair was in braids and curls that made his fingers twitch with the urge to muss her.

"Where have you been?"

Her golden brows arched as she swept her hand across the pile of purchases.

"Do you realize what time it is?"

She stared at the glass in his hand. "I'd guess it's at least two drinks past six." Her shoulder brushed his chest as she walked into the room, trailing the scents of the city, but underneath was the quiet, sweet smell that was hers alone.

Drake had vanished. "Fletcher was here."

"He's good at disappearing," she said as she sat on the sofa and smoothed her skirts.

"I'd expect nothing less from a pirate."

She sighed, as if disappointed in *him*. "He's not a pirate." The corner of her mouth hitched. "He's a smuggler."

She'd worn that look every time she'd bested him in school.

"Do you have any idea what you've done?" he asked as he paced the room. "This isn't a lark, Theodora. You have an agreement you can't enforce if he walks away with everything. You have no assurance—"

"And I had that before?"

She looked very much like the woman who'd kissed him just a week earlier, but this Thea harkened back to their childhood arguments. It was evident in the tilt of her chin and the angle of her shoulders, in her calculating gaze. Under other circumstances, Oliver would have welcomed the change. "What possessed you to do this?"

"I didn't rob a bank, Oliver. What *I've done* is support myself the only way I knew how that wasn't on my back." She rolled her eyes. "Don't look so shocked."

Damn her worthless husband. Oliver hoped he was rotting on the bottom of the sea. He pressed the heels of his hands against his temples. "You lied to me. To *me*."

"Don't take it personally. I lie to everyone. It's a necessary sacrifice for no longer being a willing victim in my own poverty."

"Which is exactly why I didn't—don't—want your money."

"It isn't my money." Her smile hitched again, a bitter shadow of happiness. "It's theirs."

"That is *shite* logic, and you know it. You manipulated me and backed me into a corner to prove you could do it."

She leapt to her feet. "And I got you what you wanted."

"What if I fail? You'll lose everything."

"It won't be the first time."

The break in her voice caught him, and her unshed tears sucked the wind from his argument. She backed away and turned, and he let her go. He was ten times a coward, but he couldn't watch her cry. He hoped Smith had been swallowed by a whale.

"I never would have put you in this position."

She looked over her shoulder, frowning as she dashed a tear away. "What?"

"I went to Quebec to—"

"To escape," she snapped. "And you fell off the ship into the arms of a timber heiress."

He was to her in two long strides. "Julia scrapped next to me and her brother for years to build something from nothing. She loved me enough to scrape me together after you married some lout who couldn't see fit to take care of you. And I loved her for all of it."

Thea's tears fell unhindered now, coursing down her cheeks. "Get out." She gripped the back of the chair, her white-knuckled hands trembling.

He'd finally reached through all the tough talk and posturing and found her. Now he could help her see things as they were. "Thee—"

"Leave," she shouted as she backed away. "Leave. Me. Alone."

CHAPTER SIXTEEN

THE COACH STOPPED in front of Felton House at dusk, and Oliver climbed out. His boots thudded on the stone drive, resonating to his knees and doubling his exhaustion from being cooped up all day.

Emmett hadn't even let him ride up top for fear of losing yet another Duke of Rushford. Which was fine because Oliver didn't want to make small talk. Instead, he'd stared at the seat Thea had occupied to and from Greenlee's and listened to his own breathing.

He'd tried to fix things. He'd stopped at Tavie's this morning to fetch Thea, hoping to have a more rational conversation in the light of the day while they traveled. But she and Drake had left in the middle of the night. The butler's stony gaze told Oliver all he needed to know. She had been in a state, and the blame had been placed at his feet.

That was unfair, to his thinking. All he'd done was straighten out her misconceptions. Of course, he could have left off insulting her dead husband, but she'd struck a nerve.

The coach clattered off toward the stables, leaving him with the breeze at his back as he faced the imposing walls of his childhood home. So many years ago, he and Garrett had played in the garden pretending the house was a castle guarded by a dragon.

They probably hadn't been far off.

Gathering his courage, he strode toward the door, intent on winning a battle he'd begun long ago. But it opened before he could reach it, and Hazel scurried out.

"Thank God you're home. Simon's missing."

An icy hand gripped Oliver's heart, and he defied his wobbling knees to shoulder past her into the house. He never should have left the boy here alone. "How long?"

"Since sometime this morning. We think."

He wheeled on her. "You think? What the devil does that mean? I left him with you because I trusted you to keep him safe, and you *think*—"

Fred came from behind the stairs and put a protective hand on Hazel's shoulder. "Watch your tone, lad."

Oliver tossed his hat into a corner and ran a hand through his hair. The cook's tears gutted him. "I'm sorry, *Tante*. It's not your fault. I know better." He wrapped her in a hug and swallowed hard as she shook against him. "Tell me what happened."

"He's had a rough few days with Alice." Hazel wiped her eyes. "It ended this morning with a row like I'd never seen."

Simon? His Simon? The boy was never cross. At least not for long.

"You shouldn't be shocked," Fred said, half smiling. "The young lord is yours without a doubt. They got into a dandy tussle about him going down to the dower garden to check on his fairy, and Miss Alice locked him in the nursery to do his lessons. Wouldn't let us take him lunch. When we opened the door, he was gone."

The nursery was on the second floor. "How did he get out?"

"I think he climbed down the trellis," Fred said. "We're lucky he didn't break his neck."

"Alice," Oliver thundered.

His voice was still echoing when the nurse appeared, spine erect and chin high. "Your lordship?"

"Where is my son?"

"He is hiding from his punishment. When he gets cold and hungry, he'll reappear."

"He is four, in a strange country." With a penchant for daredevil antics. What if he'd climbed another tree?

"He kicked me, sir. He is willful and spoiled. And he—"

"He is *mine*." Oliver spun from her and looked across the top landing, saw his mother staring down at him, her lips in a hard line, but no evidence of his little boy.

"Simon!" His shout boomed back at him, hollow and harsh.

And there wasn't an answer.

"Get Emmett and the grooms to help, and Lionel," he instructed Fred. "Split up. Some in every direction. Hazel, you and the maids search from attic to cellar." He shoved a finger at Alice. "Except you. You will never go near him again." He glared up at his mother. He'd have it out with her once things were righted.

And they would be righted.

The house sprung to life, doors opening and closing, each maid gently calling for the little boy. Every unanswered call scratched Oliver's already raw skin, and he bolted for the safety of the open air.

It didn't help. Simon's name was a chorus on the breeze, leaving Oliver to spin in a circle, straining to hear a giggle or a cry.

Nothing.

He couldn't just sit here. Where would the boy go?

Outside. Adventure. It was a place to start.

Through the garden maze to the large oak, to the chicken house, down to the stable and in the pony's stall. Oliver went to the orchard and, heart in his throat, Julia's rosary was wrapped tightly through his fingers as he checked the base of every tree.

Fred came around the corner, his pale face illuminated by a lantern.

"Did you check Lita's house?" Oliver croaked. He already guessed the answer.

"It was the first place we looked. Couldn't find him anywhere."

Where is he, Julia? Can you see him?

The first stars lit the sky. Behind Fred, lanterns bobbed across the grounds and candles bounced across every window. Oliver shivered under his jacket, but the tremble had nothing to do with the cold.

On the horizon, the velvet night sky met the dark, greedy fingers of the forest. Full of wolves and snakes, rivers and holes to tumble into, highwaymen for Simon to chat with—all about Canada and sailors, his caterpillar, his *grandmère* the duchess, and his father the new duke.

Unless…

Once, long ago, Simon had been worried about being scolded for some now unremarkable offense and had hidden in his favorite place—under Oliver's desk—until calmer tones had lured him out.

Oliver sprinted to *Casa de Lita* and through the gate, his heart keeping time with his thudding steps. Taking a deep breath, he slowly opened the door, just like coming home at the end of the day. "Si?"

"Papa?"

Oliver's knees finally gave way as he opened his arms for the little shadow barreling toward him. Pulling Simon close, he buried his nose in the boy's hair.

"Thank God," Fred whispered behind them. "I'll go tell everyone he's found."

Oliver nodded, still unsure of his voice.

"Am I in trouble?" Simon asked.

"We're going to have a long talk about running away, and you're going to apologize to Hazel for scaring her." Oliver shifted so he could look the boy in the eye. "And the next time Fred calls for you, you answer him. *¿Comprende, hijo?*"

"Alice was mean to me."

Vaguely aware that someone had slid a picnic basket inside the door, Oliver walked Simon to the hearth so they could start a fire. "Tell me what happened."

Every detailed story lightened his heart. Despite the troubles with Alice, Simon had still managed to have a few adventures. By the time they got to the row, they were eating sandwiches and using their sleeves as napkins like proper boys would do.

"I wanted to come check on the fairy," Simon said. "And *she* told me that fairies were made up."

Oliver cringed. "She did?"

Simon nodded, his short curls bobbing. "And I told her she was wrong because you and *Oncle* Richard said they were real. And she said you lied to me. So I kicked her."

Oliver coughed as he choked on his sandwich, and then kept his hand over his mouth to hide his smile. "I see."

Simon beamed up at him. Not a good thing.

"Si, you shouldn't kick girls. Or anyone, really. Not unless they're trying to hurt you."

"But she hurt my feelings."

"Feelings are different." Oliver rubbed his chest. Sometimes, feelings were worse, but the boy didn't need to know that yet.

"I like it here better than at *Grandmère's* house."

Oliver scanned the small room with its carefully chosen furniture. Lita was everywhere, even in the art on the walls. Oliver half-expected her to come out of the kitchen and scold them for staying up too late and leaving crumbs on her carpet.

"Would you like to live here?" he asked Simon. "Never go back up to the big house unless it's to visit?"

"Can we?"

"We can do anything we want," Oliver said. "Why don't you crawl up on the sofa and sleep for tonight, like you do when you take a nap? Tomorrow we'll sort out our beds and our rooms."

Simon lay on the sofa, staring at Spot in his jar. Oliver didn't even want to know how the boy climbed down a trellis with the caterpillar.

"Papa? I've been thinking."

"About what?" Oliver stretched out on the floor and bunched

a musty pillow under his head. *Please God, no mice, or fleas, or lice, or lizards. I'll happily sneeze all night so long as nothing crawls in my ears.*

Simon leaned over the sofa to stare down at him. "I don't think Spot likes his jar. If we're going to live here, maybe I could put him in the garden and the fairy could take care of him. I think he'd like that better."

It took a few seconds for words to form. The little demon was full of surprises, as though he'd aged several years in two days. "Whatever you think, son." He took a deep breath. "Would you like to go to school? Not with Alice. A proper school in the village with the other boys."

"Would I have to leave you?"

"Just during the day." Oliver swallowed hard. "You'd be home every night. I promise."

"All right." His little head disappeared over the edge of the sofa, and the cushions shifted as he burrowed under a blanket. "Goodnight, Papa. I love you."

Oliver batted the dust away and sneezed. "Love you too."

After two nights of travel, the quiet here was jarring. He would swear he even heard Spot chewing on leaves in his jar. A few brief minutes later, Simon's snores were mostly whistles. The fire popped, sending sparks up the chimney as its flames cast shadows on the walls, lengthening everything to twice their normal sizes.

Recollections filled the quiet. Spanish lessons, music, dancing, laughter. He and Thea had sat here and discussed everything from schoolwork to theology. They'd debated and argued, sometimes they'd even agreed.

When anyone else had been watching, she'd been the perfect pastor's daughter—mild, helpful, always in the background. But when they were alone, she had been fierce. Her brilliant mind and razor-sharp logic had kept him on his toes as much as her freckles and curls had distracted him.

And while he'd been distracted, he'd fallen in love. He

would've sworn she had, too. She'd once trusted him with everything, but something had changed.

He stared at the wall, at the giant reflection of Spot's jar and a caterpillar large enough to devour a man. Turning his back on the horrific imagining, he closed his eyes. Simon was right. Wild things didn't belong in jars.

THE NEXT MORNING, with a scratchy beard, bleary eyes, and rumpled clothes, Oliver walked Simon up to the house and watched carefully as he made his penance to every servant he'd worried the day before. Then they took a bath, which was basically rendered useless when the little boy went out to help Fred in the garden.

Lionel was waiting on the stairs. "Shall I pack your things?"

"I would appreciate it. We'll be moving to the dower house for the duration of our visit."

The butler walked next to him, hands behind his back. "We were all hoping you would stay, lad."

He had to be the only duke in England whose staff treated him like their own child. If pressed, he'd have to admit that he'd missed them more than his blood kin. He would miss them again. He might never see them again. They'd age and die, and the news would be old before it reached him in Quebec.

But, after the meeting looming at the bottom of the stairs, he would likely never be welcome, or comfortable, here again. "In a few months, you will all be tired of my shenanigans and ready to see us go." He clapped the older man on the shoulder. "I have to meet with Mother. Is she in her drawing room?"

"She is. I'll have a maid carry your bags down and dust while she's there. If you'd like, I can send someone down every morning to help."

"Once will be plenty," Oliver said. "The girls have enough to do up here. Simon and I are used to taking care of ourselves."

Assured that at least Lionel would follow his wishes, Oliver finished his dreaded trek to the drawing room. He caught himself tidying his appearance and stopped. He was a grown man, a duke for God's sake, not a truant child. He rapped on the door and entered the room without permission.

The duchess was sitting with Alice on the sofa, and both women turned to him.

"Your Grace," his mother began. "I believe you owe Alice—"

"I owe Alice nothing but two weeks' severance and a letter of recommendation." He glared into the young woman's pale, pinched face. "Which I can barely write after she left my son to climb down a trellis because he was frightened and hungry."

"She is in charge of the child's education."

"His name is Simon, and I am in charge of anything related to him. Including his schooling, which he will be receiving from Reverend Carson beginning next week."

"You cannot send him to village school." His mother sneered the last two words. "That isn't fit—"

"Careful, Mother," Oliver drawled as he helped himself to coffee. He stared over the top of his cup, daring her to remember his education.

"You were different." She waved a hand in dismissal. "You were headstrong."

"I was second," he challenged.

Her gaze met his and then skittered away, and he saw a chance for a concession. "I'm content to pay Alice a reduced wage, plus room and board, to stay on as your companion. If you are both agreeable, of course."

Alice might have actually smiled. "Thank you, sir."

He dipped his chin. "Would you leave us, please? Mother and I need to visit."

Once they were alone, his mother faced him and folded her hands serenely. "That was kind of you, but I'll thank you not to discuss my perceived failings in front of the staff."

As though everyone under the roof didn't already know. But there was no need to wave a kerchief in front of a bull. He nodded.

"Simon is well?"

"Yes, thank you. We'll be staying in the dower cottage for the remainder of our time here. I think it will make all of us happier."

She dipped her chin in acknowledgment. Damn. Why did this feel like a business negotiation? He toyed with the dainty curve in the cup's handle. "Did you burn our own building to keep the mill from proceeding?"

She reared back, her eyes wide. "How dare you suggest such a thing."

Ignoring her bluster, Oliver kept an eye on her fingers. He'd learned ages ago that she could control everything but her hands. Though she still sat quietly, her knuckles were white. She was afraid.

"No one outside this house knew the details, Mother." He stretched his legs to their full length, acting more nonchalant than he felt. "And I'm fairly certain you tipped my hand to Sterling so he'd raise the price on his property."

"Sterling *killed* your brother," she snarled, her knuckles even whiter. One hand gripped the other so tightly, her fingers looked nigh on to breaking. "You have no right to accuse me of that."

He rested his elbow on the chair arm, his chin on knuckles, and waited in silence.

"You're dividing this family over your obsession with this project. We should be relying on one another in our grief. Instead, you're poisoning everyone with your suspicions."

"And you're paying people to stand in the way of progress, which only makes me work harder for it. Speaking of which, we begin construction this week."

"Where?"

He set his cup on the serving tray, careful not to let it clatter. "You'll know when you hear the saws."

CHAPTER SEVENTEEN

"**M**OTHER?"

Thea tapped on the door and stopped to listen, half-hoping her mother had forgone her routine trip to the milliners and would answer, delaying the search she was compelled to do.

"After you married some lout..."

Oliver's words stirred unease in her stomach, a sickness she'd fought all during the trip home. It was one thing to suspect she'd believed a lie, quite another to hear it plainly. And something altogether worse to suspect he'd been deceived as well, and by whom.

That thought made her straighten her spine. She wasn't a child, or a disgraceful daughter, anymore. She let herself in her mother's rooms and stood in the doorway, surveying the jumble of papers and books obscuring her father's desk. Thank God her mother never threw anything away.

But where to start?

"Mother?" Might as well make sure she was alone.

When no one answered, Thea scanned the piles closest to the door. These had more recent dates, so Thea lifted her skirts and waded forward, careful not to topple anything as she went back in time. With each stack, she relived a parallel story—the events in Thetford versus the memories of the life she'd created in

Brandon. Marriage announcements compared to the nights she'd gone to bed exhausted and aching. Country dances coincided with washing floors and counting the days until Saturday.

After a careful search, she narrowed her focus to two stacks next to a dusty armchair. Halfway down the second pile was a yellowed envelope with a broken seal. Sloppily poured green wax, the oak cut into it so sharply that the paper was visible in spots.

The Rushford family crest. Oliver's preferred color.

Thea's fingers shook as she slid the letter free and unfolded it.

Oliver's penmanship had never been neat, mostly likely a casualty of his reluctance to sit still. These words, however, scrawled worse than she'd remembered.

Darling Thea…

She dropped to the arm of the chair, fighting to breathe as she focused on the letter's date. Stinging tears blurred the edges.

When he'd written this, she'd been the size of a whale. Her feet had ached from water weight and standing all day at a kitchen bench. Her hands had been raw from dishwater. She'd given up praying in favor of using pillows to muffle her sobs.

"What are you doing?" The question cracked through the room. "You have no business looking through my things."

Thea met her mother's hard stare and lifted the page. "This letter is mine. How could you?"

"You were gone when it arrived." Her mother busied herself by dropping her basket and removing her cloak. "I forgot it was there."

"You opened it." Thea was torn between screaming and weeping, faced with a truth too horrible to believe. "You wrote him, didn't you?" When no answer came, rage burbled through her blood. "Answer me, Mother."

"You were gone," she repeated. "It was clear word had reached him, and I didn't deny it."

"You confirmed it." Oliver's opinions, his marriage to Julia— it was the only explanation.

"I told him you'd found a husband, which is what I'd hoped you'd be bright enough to do. How was I to know you were content to—"

"To wait on the man I loved?" Thea swept her hand behind her. "I sat in this chair, hopeless, while you forced me to live *your* lie, and all the time you knew—"

"That you'd been in Brandon telling your own lies?" her mother snapped. "That you had so little faith in his loyalty that you didn't board the first ship for Canada? I did what I had to do to save this family's reputation. Something you have cared very little about since the moment you met that boy."

The argument melted away the years, but Thea was no longer a heartbroken girl too exhausted to fight. "All I wanted was to be his wife."

"You couldn't wait to turn your back on your family, whether it was Brandon, London, or Canada. Even now, you have no sympathy that I'm exiled to these rooms with nothing."

Any sympathy had vanished the moment Thea had opened the page still in her hand. She shook it as evidence. "We deserved the truth, Mother."

"Then tell him." Her mother's eyes narrowed. "If you dare."

Thea's blood went cold. It was easy to be daring when it was just her, just business. The risks had been easier to ignore when she'd been younger. Now, however, she knew what she was losing. Again.

"You are already in each other's pockets again," her mother continued. "It wouldn't surprise me if—"

"How long am I going to have to do penance before you deem me absolved? You are no more God than you are a gypsy, Mother."

"How dare you take that tone with me? I will not stand by again while you shame what is left of this family."

Shame was a matter of perspective. Thea hadn't felt it before because she'd been young and in love. With one obvious exception, she didn't feel it now. "I'm tired of shouldering the blame for everything that's happened to you." She swept through the piles of paper, keeping a tight hold on Oliver's letter and heedless of the mess she left in her wake. "Goodbye, Mother."

LOST IN WHAT she'd learned, in her mother's hateful words, Thea ended up on the road to Brandon without conscious choice. No matter how many Saturdays she made the trip in a gig, she remembered trudging this route in the darkness, puddles soaking through her shoes and the wind slicing through her ill-fitting cloak while she'd struggled with her case, weighted down with everything she valued in life.

Those valuables, books and gardening tools, had been useless as she'd carved a life here. One that welcomed her back each Saturday, though it was just as fragile as the identity she'd built in London or the one she'd crafted in Thetford.

Every street held a memory. She'd been hopeless at times, exhausted at others, but she'd also been happy. Friendship and laughter. Sticky fingers in hers, red hair that smelled like sunshine.

She urged Neptune along the road and over the bridge. The Crowned Lion was busy, as usual, and Thea winced in empathy for the kitchen staff even though she no longer knew them.

Mrs. Wood, the innkeeper and Thea's first employer, waved from the doorway. "Come visit, love."

"Another time," Thea promised. "I don't have long today."

It wasn't a lie. It wasn't Saturday, so she didn't have all day to chat with old acquaintances. And, given her last argument with Oliver, it felt traitorous to do so.

Traitor. The word had whispered through her brain since he'd left Tavie's library. Every decision she'd made since she'd stumbled over that bridge had separated her from her old life and put her on a path she couldn't escape. And, in some ways, didn't wish to.

Caught in nostalgia, Thea circled the green and drove in the long shadow of Ebberley Hall. The home, like the people within it, didn't deserve the shiver that rippled under her skin. Some events simply left cold spots.

But the people in Brandon had always been warm. Like the thin, neatly dressed couple walking alongside the road. Thea reined Neptune to a halt and stepped down to say hello.

Edna Malloy greeted her the same no matter how often their paths crossed. Her tight hugs always lasted just a moment too long, her last breaths almost shuddering before Thea could step away.

"It's good to see you, Edna." She looked over the woman's shoulder. "Samuel."

"Lass. You're early this week. Is everything all right?"

"It is, thank you. Are you both well?"

"We're fine, love." Edna patted Thea's hand, and the lace-edged handkerchief tickled her wrist. "Just fine."

Not for the first time, Thea considered the irony of people who couldn't speak of shared experiences, yet the experience lay under every word they traded. In twenty years, she and the Malloys would probably exchange the exact same words, and the same subtext would be there.

I'm sorry. I tried. It wasn't your fault.

Samuel put his hand on his wife's back, urging her forward. For months after that horrible winter, Thea had thought him distant and emotionless. Now she understood that some emotions ran too deep. "We'll see you soon, lass. Safe travels."

"Soon, yes. Thank you." But they would always meet on the road. She'd never revisited their home, just past the Hall. "Best get home before it rains."

Back in the gig, Thea watched over her shoulder until the Malloys turned the corner for home. She could still see the small stone house with the large garden, chickens that missed being chased, a cat in need of stroking, the small, warm room near the kitchen.

"Come up, Neptune." She urged the horse forward, around the green, to the church yard.

It was easy to find the grave with its maple sapling straight and true, promising years of shade and color, hopefully the same shade as its sire. Kneeling where she always sat, Thea plucked the few weeds that had grown since her last visit.

"You're early this week."

She shaded her eyes to meet the kind smile of Reverend Allen, who had been her vicar here. "Hello, sir."

"Sir," he sighed as he sat beside her, cross-legged. "I forget that vicars' daughters are always so formal. Is everything all right?"

This was one of the largest problems about having a schedule, other than the itch that built when she missed a visit. If she came too often, everyone worried she was cracking. Granted, the vicar had more reason to think that than others. "I'm fine." Thea went back to work, searching for weeds in the flowers, shriveled leaves, signs of disease or drought. Answers. "When I was younger, my father explained repentance as the promise that you would stop doing whatever you were sorry for doing in the first place."

"Generally speaking, yes."

She plucked her gardening shears from her basket, sharing this moment with Oliver the only way she was allowed. The tools sank into the well-worked earth, digging up a layer of rich mulch she'd spread years ago. "And without repentance you can't have forgiveness."

"Again, generally speaking." Reverend Allen plucked a pansy that had strayed from its boundary. "What does your current vicar say?"

"He's new." Thea exchanged the garden shears for linseed oil and a rag that had previously been a blanket. The wood marker glowed from its last treatment, but the persistent English rain ruined things all the time. "What if you aren't sorry? Or what if you are, but you can't stop? If it isn't your doing?"

"Not your doing?"

"If someone lied. Not you, but it affects you and ties you up in it. But it isn't your wrong to fix. And telling the truth would hurt someone—people." Thea inched away from him to clean the back of the marker and check the sapling.

"*Tell him, if you dare.*" Confess. Break his heart.

Break hers.

"More than one person," she hedged. "And telling the truth wouldn't solve anything."

"You're justifying a sin, Thea."

She'd done nothing but justify sins since Oliver had carried her into The Pewter Owl six years ago. She glanced over the top of the marker, terrified to meet the vicar's gaze. She shouldn't have. He was laughing at her. "You aren't helping."

"All right." Reverend Allen changed his position, stretching out to lean against a nearby tree. "I would say, with all respect to your father, that he should have discussed grace as well as repentance. Because grace says God understands the circumstances and has already forgiven you."

"Even if I lied?"

Reverend Allen shook his head, laughing again. "You just said you didn't."

"If I lied about something else. For a very good reason." Which is why she'd come here, to him. "And I know I'm justifying again."

"Did you harm someone with your lie?"

"Not intentionally. I didn't know it was even a possibility until recently." Until two days ago in a London library. "But the truth will harm more people."

"And the lie hurts only you?"

If Oliver went back to Canada none the wiser, if she carried her secret alone… She was used to doing that. "Yes."

"No." Reverend Allen wagged the pansy at her. "A lie never hurts only one person, no matter its purpose or the justification.

From your earlier example, you know that already."

That wasn't the answer she'd wanted, but she hadn't expected more. She'd always been too willful to be one of God's favorites.

"Don't look at me like that. God's forgiven you. I absolve you. But that's not what you need."

She moved back to the front of the marker, cleaning the carved letters last. There had never been any question about her son's name. Her Jamey, the grandson her father had never seen. The son who'd never seen his father. There were times she felt him snuggled against her, and others she wondered if she'd imagined the whole thing. In the spring, when all the leaves were green, she almost forgot the shade of his hair. Then again, she saw him everywhere.

She sat back on her heels and rubbed her thumb across her locket, burnishing it. She'd lost her family; she'd lost Jamey. Confessing that would mean losing her business. She'd lose Oliver, which was more painful than she cared to admit. "The truth won't bring him back."

"The lie didn't kill him," Reverend Allen countered.

Under the layers of lies in her life, there was one truth. Like the pea under a pile of mattresses meant as a test for a princess. Or a duchess. Or even a frightened girl trying her best to do the right thing. Her lie hadn't killed anyone.

But she had.

CHAPTER EIGHTEEN

"**J**UST A BIT more. Toward me. Come ahead. Another inch." Oliver grunted as he put his shoulder into the wheel, and it slotted on the axle like a puzzle piece. "There."

He stepped back and relished his tired muscles as he surveyed the almost assembled saw. Between the fire in the steam engine and the unseasonably warm day, the mill was suffocating. Even the air filtering through the canvas walls, making the temporary structure breathe like a living thing, was thick on his tongue. "Everyone take a half an hour to cool off and rest, then we'll install the belt and do a trial run."

As his small crew made for fresh air and cold water, Oliver pulled his kerchief from his pocket and wiped it from his brow to his neck. Grit and salt flavored his parched lips, but it wouldn't do for him to be first in line for water. Besides, he had work to do.

He opened the only real door in the mill—the one to his office—and stopped to stare. At Thea. Behind his desk. Looking over his books. "How did you get in here?"

"I slipped in while everyone was working." She looked up from the ledger. "Drake explained, didn't he? That while he was in Ipswich, I'd have to—"

"Check on me? Yes. He explained." Oliver fell into the nearest chair, dropped his head backward, and closed his eyes. He immediately missed the sight of her.

Green lawn, dove gray shawl. Her hair was a mass of braids and curls, though the curls were probably due to the moisture in the air. The same air that trapped her scent in the space. Roses and lemons mixed with new wood planks and grease.

Grit dried on his skin and exhaustion settled through his muscles and into his bones. Would he ever see her when he wasn't a mess in one way or another?

Her pen scratched across the page. Checking his figures, just as she'd done when they were younger. "Is it the situation you loathe, or me?"

For the last two weeks, they'd been on opposite sides of the forest, separated by oceans of responsibilities and hard feelings. Fletcher had been frugal with details—a trait Oliver had cursed as much as his inability to refrain from asking questions.

"I would resent anyone sent to manage me as though I were a spendthrift," he said without opening his eyes. "Do you need help making sense of things?"

"Why is the mill half finished?"

"Because lumber is expensive." He turned his head and opened one eye, bracing against her intense stare. She looked very much at home in his chair. In his office. In his life. "I'm counting on it."

"Rubbish," she said. "I made sure you had plenty to build what we originally discussed. You have a line of credit you've barely touched."

His teeth on edge, Oliver pushed himself upright and propped his elbows on the chair. "I didn't know I was locked into a course once I took your money."

Thea dropped her pen into the inkwell. "Maybe I wouldn't have loaned it if I'd known you were going to operate in a tent."

"I won't be manipulated. Not by Mother, and not by you."

"What?"

The question was cold, and her brown eyes went shallow and flat. It was a familiar warning, but he ignored it. "She threatens them with power and influence, and you, Theodora, you *save* them with benevolent half-truths."

"I wish I'd never told you my full name. Out of all the things you forgot, why couldn't you—"

"I didn't forget anything," he snapped, stung by her assumption. "Especially that look. You wore it every time you bested me at lessons."

"That's ridiculous."

Anyone else in this village could think her the dutiful vicar's daughter. Oliver knew better. He'd always known. "This is about you being the smartest person in the room."

"This is about keeping them afloat until their fortunes changed. Because your mother—" She bit off the sentence and pushed away from the desk.

He pursued her across the room, trying to keep his temper in check and his voice level. It was one thing to argue with her, quite another to be overheard. Or, worse, caught. "Because my mother didn't see fit to pay our bills." He stopped too close, blocking her retreat. "Tell me there isn't some satisfaction in that. In fixing her mess."

"Only because they needed—"

"Bloody rubbish." He poked a finger at her nose. "This is about them coming to *you*."

"And why not?" She faced off against him and pulled her face into a disapproving frown. "Poor Thea," she sing-songed in a mocking falsetto. "Chased after her lord, and he sent her home with the mail."

His stomach dropped. "What?"

"Always knew that wouldn't end well," she continued, imitating another tormentor. "Set her sights too high. No dowry. No position. No prospects. Doubt even a village lad would have her after this. She'll end up in a workhouse, no doubt. Or worse."

The bitter words, the hard planes of her face, rocked him back on his heels.

"It never occurred to any of them that I had feelings or a brain. All that mattered was what I didn't have. So you'll forgive me if I take a little justice from this entire situation." She stepped around him and snatched her hat from the corner of his desk. "And if all you're going to do is lecture me about things beyond your understanding, then you can deal with Drake from now on. To hell with it."

Oliver didn't realize he'd reached for her until his fingers closed around hers, tethering them together in the stifling air and the sunlight filtering through the canvas roof.

"I shouldn't have told you like that," she said after a moment.

"I'm glad you told me at all." He shifted to face her. He needed to look her in the eyes for his next words. "I'm sorry. I never considered the consequences."

"You weren't the only one involved," she sighed, but kept his hand. "Where's Simon?"

"School. I put him in Reverend Carson's youngest class. Today was his first day." Oliver rolled his eyes at Thea's mocking smile. "Don't gloat, Thee."

She held up two fingers, measuring a small distance. "Just a little."

The shared joke, her genuine smile, drew him closer even as he released her. "The canvas is temporary. The men we hire will be inexperienced, so their first planks will be practice. We'll use them for construction."

"Have you hired everyone?" she asked as she dropped her hat back to the desk.

"They're queuing up tomorrow. I would very much like your help in the selection."

"Certainly. I'll just don breeches and a fake mustache."

He knew it was a futile request. He wasn't hiring household staff, and she wasn't his wife. Still… "I don't know the villagers as you do, and I would appreciate your input. What if I brought you a list?"

Thea nodded, hesitant at first, then stronger. More decisive. Oliver wasn't sure if her uncertainty was due to becoming more involved in his business or at seeing him again. "I expect you to rule out anyone who was cruel to you."

"Oliver…"

Her grim expression told him everything she wouldn't say. She didn't want his help in vengeance. She might even get perverse satisfaction from being a benefactor to her tormentors. Too bad. Now that he was here, that he was aware, this was his responsibility. "Promise me, Thea."

"On one condition." She held out a slip of paper. "You have to—please hire these three."

He glanced briefly at the list before setting it on his desk. "I'll look out for them tomorrow."

She shook her head. "They won't queue up with everyone else."

Employees who expected special treatment were almost always a problem. "What makes them different from everyone else?"

"They're boys. Tim Bell's the oldest at nine."

"You want me to hire children?" No. He wouldn't do that. He'd seen too many accidents, too many hopeless faces at cotton mill doorways.

"I'd like you to help these boys earn a wage. Their fathers are gone—either dead or adventuring—and they're the sole support for their families."

"At nine?"

Her eyes went as fiery as her hair and her chin tilted at a stubborn angle. "Their mothers can't work, Oliver. Not at anything that will pay a wage. Tim's mother took in washing until this past winter when she fell ill. The other two families are in worse shape than them."

"I'm not giving children sharp tools and having them gallop around the woods while trees fall whichever way." Never mind that, at times, he'd been accused of doing just that with Simon.

"There has to be something they can do."

Damn. He hated it when she looked at him like that—certain he could, and would, do whatever she wanted. But it had been a long time since his heart had swelled like this. Working with her made his blood sing. "I can't promise, but I'll try."

"Thank you."

Her touch was light and quick, but he swore he heard the sweat on his skin sizzle.

"Your—Mr. Hawkins?" Hamish called as he rapped on the door. "We've managed to get the belts on."

They'd been in here too long. Oliver automatically put Thea behind him in case the young foreman opened the door. "I'll be out in a moment."

"I'll go," she whispered.

To his embarrassment, she went to the edge of the tent and lifted her hem, clearly intending to slither under the canvas. So much worse than the mail coach.

He wrapped his fingers around her elbow and winced as he dirtied her shawl. "Wait. If the belts are on correctly, we're going to test the saws and cut our first plank. I'll leave the door cracked open."

"I'll leave as soon as—"

Oliver shook his head. This was a triumph for them both, and it wasn't the same if they didn't share it. "Stay and watch. Please."

THEA KNEW THE smartest thing was to walk away. Well, the smartest thing would have been not to come at all. She could have sent word for him to come to the inn or waited for Drake's return. She knew Oliver wasn't wasting his funds.

She'd suspected he wasn't using them at all. Which is why she'd come.

That, and she'd missed him. She'd wanted to see the progress she'd heard through the trees, to see him work. It was a perverse impulse that had become a distraction. And standing here, spying through a crack in the door as he walked away, wasn't helping.

It wasn't just his broad shoulders or his confident stride.

It was the way he was welcomed by the men he'd hired. Any other time, these men would defer to his title. Now they were laughing and joking as they all worked together.

It was the smile she could hear in his words. Oliver was always happiest outside, whether it was work or play. He'd never heeded rank—said it was something no one could garner or control. His grandfather had earned the title; after that, it had been a matter of birth and death. Oliver had preferred to earn the respect he was given, the living he made.

And he'd done just that, with a few recent exceptions that he could neither right nor control. Those were two things she could help repair, whether or not he wanted it.

He was proud. And stubborn. And arrogant. Far too charming, and much too smart. It was an incredibly vexing combination.

And Thea loved him all the same.

It's what had kept her away, kept her pestering Drake with questions until he'd told her to come herself, that he was tired of being the go-between. It's what rooted her to the floor now, watching through the door like a child eager to be included.

At the saw, Oliver tested the belts and connections before nodding and clapping the nearest man on the shoulder. He then led the crew through loading a log onto the table and coaching them to engage the engine.

Heat and deafening noise filled the tent as the saw spun to life, slow at first, then faster and faster.

Oliver climbed onto the table and grasped the rope overhead as he placed one foot on the log while the men bracketed it tightly. Then, to Thea's horror, Oliver stayed put as the table moved forward and the saw bit into the wood.

Heart in her throat, one hand tightly gripping the door, she watched him ride the length of the cut. As the plank fell free, he raised his eyes—not to the cheering men waiting on him, but to the door. To her.

Triumphant. Powerful. Elemental in a way she didn't recall. Dangerous feelings flooded her heart, dragging suspicious heat and heaviness to her muscles and other places she'd been able to ignore until he'd returned.

He leapt to the ground and was surrounded by his men in a celebration that couldn't include her. Rather than feel out of place, Thea took the chance to slip away, forcing herself not to return the stare she could feel as surely as if Oliver had touched her.

But she wanted to…and she wanted him to.

Cursing her foolishness, she made for the forest, not stopping until she was well into the shade and facing a fresh tree stump perfect for sitting.

It had been an ash, given its remaining bark, and an old one at that. A quick scan of the rings marked it as almost her age.

Thirty-two. Old. It had survived every storm that had threatened it. And now it was gone, out of the way to make room for something new, destined to be a table or a work bench—something everyone overlooked until they needed it.

Thea drew in a deep breath, but the comforting scent of the forest had been replaced by sawdust. The steam engine had frightened the birds away. All she felt was hot, dirty, and heavy with regrets and secrets.

So she went farther in, seeking the cool shade under larger trees. Birdsong coaxed her deeper. Ferns caught her skirts, and moss coated old, round rocks. When she stopped to get her bearings, a breeze, slightly cooler than before, lifted the fine hair along her nape as a whisper reached her ears.

A smile split Thea's face as she picked up her pace, hurrying forward until she emerged at the edge of a pool, the terminus of a stream and a waterfall. She'd first seen this place at age eight when she and Oliver had run away from school on a day much like this one. Since then, it had become a favorite spot. It was isolated. Safe.

Tempting.

Thea sat on a boulder and removed her shoes and stockings. As she wiggled her toes against the cool, spongy moss, she undid her hair and strained to hear anything other than water and songbirds. Certain she was alone, she removed her clothing one layer at a time, sighing with relief when the breeze touched her bare skin.

As much as she'd anticipated the cool swim, the water still stole her breath.

"Just jump in, Thea. It's too hot to dither."

"Turn your back."

"The-a."

"I'm in my chemise. Turn. Around."

Sucking in a deep breath, she stepped in up to her knees and waded forward until the water was to her shoulders.

"See? Isn't that better?"

Thea ducked her head to drown the memory, and the world went silent except for her own breathing and the thud of her heart. Those never stopped. Ever. Even now her lungs were burning, urging her to kick to the surface.

"This place seemed like the ocean when we were eight."

Thea whirled and planted her feet on the pebbled bottom, pushing upright until she remembered she was naked. "What are you doing?"

Oliver paused, his shirt already to his shoulders, leaving his abdomen bare. His boots were already off. "Swimming."

She kicked backward, closer to the falls. "You can't come in here."

"I own it," he said as he tossed his shirt next to her clothes. "You're the one trespassing."

He'd never brought up their differences before, and it made her feel more exposed. Heat flooded her cheeks. "Give me a moment's privacy, and I'll—"

"Don't be so prickly." He unfastened his trousers and pushed them lower.

"Oliver," Thea shrieked. "Don't you have any modesty?"

"Says the naked woman in my pond watching me undress." His grin was the wicked one she remembered. Her favorite, but now tinged with a masculinity that did funny things to her insides.

Or maybe it was all his muscles.

Oliver quirked an eyebrow, and Thea had no choice but to turn around and wait until she heard the splash.

"Are you in?" she called over her shoulder.

"Don't trust me?" Laughter coated his question, not to mention the relief she'd felt earlier at finally being cool and clean.

That sound made her certain she was safe from further temptation. "Not on your life."

Her laughter faded as she turned. She should have been prepared for the sight of him—sleek, wet, and bare.

She wasn't. "The rock is still the boundary," she said, hoping her voice wasn't as shaky as it felt.

"Then switch with me. I want the falls on my side." He swam to a safe distance, parallel to her. "It's only fair, Thee. I'm dirtier."

She waded to the far side of the pool, trusting the water and the distance to keep her hidden. "You'll say anything to get that side."

"You don't go near the falls. It's a waste for you to have them," he called back as he made his way to the cascading water.

Like everything else here, the stream toppling from above had seemed much larger when she'd been a child. Then she'd been worried about drowning while standing up or getting trapped underwater.

Oliver had convinced her to do it once, promising to keep her safe and goading her until she'd given in. The water had robbed her of her senses and her breath, threatened to push her off her feet.

Much like now, as he lifted his face to scrub it clean and shook the water from his hair. He stood taller, exposing more and more of his back, then his waist, and then—

Thea spun away and ducked under the water, counting to ten

before she resurfaced. Thankfully, Oliver was decent again—or at least concealed. His smile had nothing to do with decency.

"I've never seen you speechless for this long. I may have to go naked more often."

I've seen you naked before. The words, the memories, sent a dangerous shiver of heat down her spine. Best not to recall that night. "That would be dangerous around saws and axes, wouldn't it?"

His laughter rolled across the water and scaled the trees behind her. Thea swam for the safety of their boundary marker, which was still large enough to shield her. Mostly.

Oliver joined her, staying firmly on his side. "What did you think?"

Her giggle burbled out before she could stop it.

"The saw, Thea."

"It was impressive." She rolled her eyes at his thick, deep chuckle. "I miss the larger trees, though. The forest isn't the same without them."

"Things change," he murmured. "Sometimes for the better."

And sometimes not. "How is your mother adjusting to your plan?"

"She visited Gregory yesterday and had a long talk about his business and his family."

Saul Gregory was the village blacksmith. He had a son in Reverend Carson's school, and his daughter was planning her wedding to his apprentice. Without a blacksmith, the mill's tools would be useless by the end of the week.

His feet appeared on the edge of vision, idly swishing through the water. "I've offered Gregory double pay and absolute secrecy to work at the mill after dark. It appears you'll get your wish."

He had no idea what she wished for. Not any longer. And his feet were changing her wishes by the moment. It was time to go. "I'm glad I could help."

"Are you that eager for me to leave?"

Yes. He and Simon needed to be free of the duchess. Thea

didn't want to share her secrets. She didn't want to ruin their lives.

No. It was so nice to not be alone. "Tell me about Canada."

"What would you like to know?"

Over the years, she'd imagined him there. "Where do you live?"

"I own a home. It's not large, but it's big enough that I can't hear Richard snoring at the other end of the hall. It has lots of windows, so it's full of sunshine. There's no fussy wallpaper. All the flowers are outside in the garden, and you can see everything from the porches. One wraps around the lower level, and another around the upper."

A house for a family, which is what he'd had. What he'd always wanted. No wonder he'd been happy.

"Is it surrounded by the forest?"

"No. It's in the city. I have a few trees in the garden, though. Simon's swing hangs from the largest."

She hadn't imagined Quebec as a city. It was just a dot on a map, like so many other places she'd never seen. "I always pictured you living in a wood."

"It's not particularly safe to live in the forest. There are small tribes of savages that roam through it. While they're friendly most of the time, they are unpredictable. And then there are the animals."

"Wolves?" That's what they saw the most here, lurking in the shadows or leering from their dens.

"Yes, but there are others I'd never seen. There are moose that have legs twice as long as mine and antlers shaped like the boat we used to take out on the river, and almost as big. Elk, which are like deer, but much larger, and their call—their *bugle*— is terrifying the first time you hear it. But not as terrifying as the cats—cougars. They look like the lions we saw at the zoological exhibition, without the mane."

The exhibition had made her cry. The animals had looked pathetic behind bars, pacing in their tiny cages. She'd imagined them in the wild. "Really?"

"The most amazing are the bears. Huge brown monsters that can stand on their back legs and tower over you. Their feet are the size of two hooves set adjacent and their claws are as thick as your pruning shears. They are kings of the forest."

A shiver went down her spine. "And all of this is where you work? Are you in danger?"

"It's worth it, Thea. The trees themselves are mammoth, but the mountains loom over them, sharp enough to slice your fingers and so tall that they're covered in snow even in the height of summer. The air tastes like spring water."

She swept her gaze across the gentle hills that brought her peace and saw them as he must. "This must be disappointing."

"It used to chafe, that it never changed. But it does, like that field of heather."

Even with the slight breeze, a nearby hill turned from gray-green to silver, and then back again.

"It's pretty in an ancient way," Oliver continued. "I didn't think I'd missed it, but there are times I can't stop staring."

"It was like that when I returned," she said. "I liked the convenience of London, but the dirt and noise were unbearable."

"Did you go straight there from the coast?"

"Yes." The lie tightened Thea's throat, and she shivered as a cloud passed overhead. "I have to go."

She pushed away from the boulder and swam until the water was too shallow for anything but wading. Old pebbles, worn smooth and round, massaged her feet as she refused to look behind her.

But that meant looking at their clothes scattered together in intimate disarray, nudging his boot away from her chemise so she could use it to dry spots the breeze couldn't reach. Water slapped against the shore, proof that Oliver was headed for another trip to the falls and that he could change his surroundings with the wave of his hand.

A shadow loomed, too low to be another cloud. "Thea?"

She froze, torn between which parts of herself to cover. Finally choosing her backside, she tied her chemise around her waist and brought her wet hair forward over her breasts. "You're supposed to keep your back turned."

"We made that rule when we were children." He brushed his shirt down her spine, drying the trickle of water sliding toward her waist. "We aren't children any longer."

He hadn't reached for any other clothing, and thinking of him naked made Thea feel decidedly adult. "Still, a gentleman would—"

"I'm a duke, not a gentleman."

Of course he wasn't. She could marry a gentleman. "Ol..."

"Aren't you tired, Thea?"

He was close enough that his heat warmed her back and water dripped from his hair onto her shoulder. Her shiver had nothing to do with the temperature difference.

"We work for the same things, but not together." His callused fingers brushed her waist just above the lace already tormenting her. "We circle one other, but don't touch." His whisper traveled through her ear and curled deep in her stomach. "Because God knows I'm tired," he continued in a gravelly tone that scratched her everywhere at one. "I'm tired of grieving. Of waking, eating, working, sleeping, celebrating. Everything. Alone."

She had one last chance to stop this, to talk sense into her rebellious body and treacherous heart. "It can't be that way, Oliver. Not now."

He brushed his nose along the curve of her shoulder. "The differences between us are as imaginary as that boundary you drew in the water when we were eight."

"Too much has happened." There was so much she needed to tell him. He was close enough now that she could feel him against her.

"The past is as flimsy as your chemise." He tugged the garment to prove his point. "It shouldn't keep you from being what you always should have been.”

Thea told her feet not to move, but they did anyway, turning her to face him. One look at his flushed skin and heavy-lidded, dark green eyes and she was lost. She swayed forward, and he caught her.

“Mine.”

His whispered growl brushed across her lips, but he didn't kiss her. It was up to Thea to close the distance between them.

And she did.

CHAPTER NINETEEN

THE MOMENT SHE pressed her lips to his, Thea's world tilted and toppled. The moss was soft on her back, and the sun was bright against her eyelids, but everything else was Oliver. His tongue in her mouth, his hands on her skin, his hard body against hers.

"God, I need you," he rasped.

She got a glimpse of his passion-glazed eyes before he swept his mouth along the side of her neck, sampling her as though he was starving. It was almost as intoxicating as sliding her hands across his shoulders and feeling his muscles work, his chest hair brushing her nipples. "I've been with you."

His hair tickled her ear as he shook his head. "We talk about things that don't matter and all the while I'm imagining you like this. Remembering what you felt like, what you sounded like."

His palm covered her nipple, drawing it tight and sending heat through her body, pulling a groan from her.

"Better than I imagined," he purred as he closed his lips over the puckered flesh. "I don't want a business partner, Thea."

She shifted to make room for him between her legs. His thighs were like tree trunks, and his erection prodded her stomach, tormenting and tickling her at the same time. "This is decidedly unbusiness-like," she giggled.

His eyes twinkled as he loomed over her. Her Oliver. The

one who'd always made her lighter, wilder, than she was. And there was a name for wild women who had sex with dukes in the woods. She'd heard it before.

"Don't," he whispered as he brushed his fingers along her jaw. "You aren't my mistress."

"Don't let the past keep you from being what you were meant to be." A dangerous rebellion bubbled over Thea's ribs and traveled through her blood. She wanted this man, and nothing else mattered. Leaning up, she pressed an open kiss to his salty-sweet neck, flicking her tongue and reveling in his muffled curse. "I am, and I don't care."

He knotted his fingers in her hair and gently tugged her away. His eyes still blazed, but his mouth was a grim, determined line. "I do, and you're not."

She couldn't be anything else, and she didn't want to be without him any longer. Kings had mistresses. Dukes could, too. Even in Thetford. No one would be shocked if it happened.

"You're the woman I'm going to marry."

He said it right before he kissed her, leaving her feeling like standing under the falls, so it took a moment for the statement to register. By then he'd returned to her breasts, licking one nipple until she was writhing beneath him. She fought to get free, but he shook her off.

"Oliver," she panted, trying to get her reactions under control. "No. I can't…"

"You certainly can." He slid his hand between her legs, finding the achiest, neediest parts of her. "You can do anything."

"I can't be a duchess." Her words were thick with want and frustration, and her pulse thudded in her ears. "Just…"

"I don't want a duchess, Thee," he whispered against her stomach. "I want a wife."

He filled her, first one finger, then two, teasing her until her toes were curled against the moss and her body was balanced on her shoulders, reaching for something, someone, she'd missed for six years.

And then he stopped, withdrawing his hand and circling his fingers around her opening, applying more pressure every time he reached the apex. "Marry me, Thea."

Tossing her head from side to side, Thea clamped a hand over her mouth to keep her wail inside as Oliver replaced his fingers with his tongue, then his teeth. Over and over again, licking and tasting, he urged her to a pinnacle only to withdraw and send her crashing back to earth. Pushing her higher each time while his body weighted her to the earth.

She was crumbling to pieces.

Oliver came over her, stroking his shaft through her wetness and swearing under his breath. "Please, Thea," he rasped. "Say yes. I'll give you everything you need. I swear it."

It was unbearable torment, being this close and not having him. Feeling only so much when she wanted everything he offered.

"Yes." Her scream echoed through the trees and sent the songbirds scattering overhead. She pulled Oliver down to her and wrapped her heels around his waist, pulling him tight and kissing his full lips, tasting her on his tongue. It was decadent and perfect, and everything she wanted. "Yes, yes. Please, Oliver. Please."

He eased into her slowly, sucking in a sharp breath as his fingers dug into her hips. "Christ."

Heat bloomed through Thea, sending sparks from head to toe, rippling through her muscles.

Oliver's fiery gaze locked on hers as he withdrew and returned, deeper and harder, rocking against her and stoking the fire until it was out of her control. All she could do was rake her nails down his arms, searching for a handhold as sensation robbed her of everything but spiraling pleasure.

He scooped her up and buried her face against his neck as his strokes grew shorter and more desperate. As his muscles shook, a growl began deep in his chest and rumbled upward, shivering against her breasts as his fingers shook on her hips. His shout was deafening, and the moment he stilled, Thea wanted to do it again.

OLIVER CRADLED THEA closer and put his free hand on his chest, relieved to feel his heart returning to normal and inordinately proud that it had almost flown from his chest in the first place. But it was Thea's screams of pleasure that would keep him smiling until they could be together again.

Permanently this time. It wasn't anything he'd planned, but it felt right. Her hair tickled his nose, and her breath teased his skin. *She* felt right.

Except that her shoulders were rigid for someone who'd just had incredible sex. He wasn't even sure his knees would work yet. Was she worried?

"You'll love Canada."

She propped her head on one hand, and her tangled curls cascaded to her elbow. His shirt, her makeshift blanket, slid low across her breasts. "You blackmailed me, Oliver. It doesn't count."

It wasn't the words as much as her sad smile that sent chills over his exposed skin. For the first time, he wondered if their memories differed. He mimicked her position so he could look in her eyes—so she could see his. "I have always thought we both wanted…this."

"I wouldn't change a thing that has happened between us."

That was good, but something still bothered him. "Was Smith at least kind to you?"

"Oliver."

He ignored her warning. This was important. And it grew more urgent the longer she took to answer. She was thinking too hard.

Her nod was a hollow victory. Either she was lying, or Smith was a saint. The thought of her with another man had driven Oliver into a bottle and kept him there until Julia had pulled him out.

Thea's delicate jaw shaped his palm, her curls teased his fingers, and those pretty pink lips parted for him. Soft with surprise for a moment, they firmed, then slanted. Her breath teased his skin.

Oliver curved his fingers around her waist and pulled her close. Her tongue was sweet against his, better than even lime biscuits. Strong and agile, it tempted him deeper and closer until her breasts were flat against him and her spine bowed under his fingers.

And then her hands were on him, her nails digging into his shoulders, holding him still when he might have backed away. Might have, hell. He wasn't backing away from anything. Never again.

Her mouth was sweet, her skin was heaven, honey against his tongue as her throat flexed with each soft groan. Her hip gave under his fingers as he lifted her knee and made room for himself between her legs. Responsibilities and titles fell away. There wasn't anything but them. Her. Him.

Thea tugged him to claim a ravenous kiss, one hand on his hip and the other knotted in his hair. Her fingertips brushed his nape and, of all their touches, this simple one undid him.

He brushed his thumb across her nipple, and her whimper and wiggle at the friction encouraged him to do it again. And again. Oliver slid his thigh against her center, tormenting them both, until her eyes glazed over.

Need and nerves made it difficult to talk. "Do you want to marry me, Thea?"

Her nod sent relief over him in a warm wave that fizzed to his toes as he slid inside her. "Then we will," he rasped. "And we'll go home to Canada." He gritted his teeth, resisting the sweet pull of her body and the urge to lose himself inside her. "We'll be Mr. and Mrs. Hawkins, and we'll do whatever we want." Tears slid from the corners of her eyes, and he stopped them at her hairline, erasing the salt from her skin. "I need you, Thea. Say yes. Please."

She stared at him for a long few seconds before rising up to kiss him, further tightening her muscles. "Yes."

Joy and heat foamed together, dissolving Oliver's control. He pushed her backward and drove inside her, wild with the feeling of her body beneath him and her hands on his skin, her cries in his ears.

When they were both limp and sated, he collapsed against her. "Thank you," he whispered against her ear, startled to still taste her tears.

He rolled to one side and pulled her with him, close enough he could feel her heart hammering against his ribs. "I thought we could host the Circle's charity card party at the main house in a few weeks. We'll make the announcement then."

Once again, she rose up to frown at him. "Your family is still in mourning. You can't—"

"I'm weary of grieving, Thea. I want to move forward, and I don't want to wait six months to do it." He kissed her nose. "And before you object to hosting it, don't. As my betrothed, you need to get acquainted with running the household so you can help me hire a steward."

The sun had shifted behind them, golden now rather than glaring. It made her hair catch fire and served to remind him of the time and his responsibilities. "I need to see you home. Simon will be out of school soon."

Thea's grip on his arm tightened. "We need to talk."

He wasn't going to argue with her about their engagement. She'd said yes. He'd made a promise. And he'd be damned if either of them backed out again.

The look in her eyes, the determined set of her jaw, told him this wouldn't be a quick conversation. He sorted through clothes to find his stockings and her chemise. The delicate fabric teased his fingers. "Tomorrow? I'll come to the inn after work."

She nodded as she exchanged his shirt for her clothing. "Tomorrow then. And you don't need to see me home."

From naked in the forest to newly engaged and walking

home alone in opposite directions? "You're not—"

"I am half an hour from home, at the most, and it's a path I walk frequently." When he would have protested, she put her hand over his. "It's foolish for you to go an hour out of your way, Ol. I'm not a young miss who needs an escort, and Simon will be expecting you."

He considered his options as they finished dressing and finally had to concede. "You'll go straight home?"

"I have to prepare for the dinner crowd," she said as she accepted his help in standing. "I should have been at work already."

As soon as he could manage it, she'd never be a laborer again, even a pretend one. He pressed his lips to her knuckles, not trusting himself to kiss her properly and keep on schedule. *"Hasta mañana, mi Pepinilla."*

Thea pulled free and rubbed her hand over her knuckles. "Tomorrow."

He watched her leave until she was swallowed by the forest, and then he turned in the other direction. Not the wrong one.

A new one.

CHAPTER TWENTY

THE NEXT MORNING, Oliver stood at the fence surrounding the churchyard as Simon ran up the path toward the schoolroom, never glancing backward. He looked taller than yesterday—more a boy and less a child.

Once the door closed, Oliver walked across the square to the market. Fred was already loading goods into the cart.

"I thought it would take you longer," Oliver said as he lifted a sack of potatoes. "Hazel had quite a list."

"The number of stalls shrinks every year."

Fred's explanation drew Oliver's attention to the row of vendors and the villagers milling about with baskets on their arms. When he'd been a child, the market had run the length of the street, on both sides, and even then he'd known it was small. This remnant was pitiful.

"And Hazel's list is always the same," Fred continued as he pushed a bushel of corn into the wagon. "Though she asked for larger amounts this time."

When he climbed into the box, Oliver followed. He knew better than to reach for the reins. Though he itched to guide the draft horse through the crowd; the *duke* behind a work horse would embarrass Fred.

As they passed by the church on the way out, Oliver was disappointed to see the empty yard. It was ridiculous to think they'd be out to play so soon after the bell. It was also inane to have children cooped up inside on a sunny morning. He'd hated that part of school.

He craned to watch, half-hoping Simon would run after them and beg for a rescue. But it never happened, and a bend in the road finally hid the village from view.

"It's not the same without the boy around," Fred said.

It wasn't. "Never looked back this morning. I suppose that's a good thing."

It was also a mixed blessing that he'd left Spot at home. Simon had decided over breakfast that the caterpillar should stay behind from now on. Oliver felt some kinship with the fat, green worm. And for the hundredth time, he wondered if he'd made the right decision.

"We were the same way when we sent you to school," Fred confided. "Wandered around the first day just waiting for the clock to chime. Emmett and I almost got into a row over who'd go get you."

In the end, it had been Emmett and Lita. Oliver had wanted to crawl into a hole when he'd seen the coach at the vicarage gate. All the other children had been walking, either alone or with their parents. It had begun a new battle in his war for independence.

"Best thing your grandmother ever did for you," Fred said.

It had certainly been the wisest. Reverend Fowler had channeled Oliver's rebellious streak into determination and opened his eyes to the world around him, and not just the wider questions. Oliver had learned to be a villager, not a Hawkins. But it hadn't been the best gift from his grandmother.

Lita had given him a home. As had the four, now old, servants who'd never left his family—who had become his family.

"Should I take you to the mill?"

Oliver shook his head. "To the manor."

He'd delayed the conversation with his mother too long. It hadn't been a purposeful decision. Simon had been stuffed with excitement and stories after his first day of school, and the boy deserved to be the center of attention. He also didn't deserve to hear a row between the adults in his life using words he didn't understand.

Jealousy.

Grief.

Wife.

Mother.

As they passed the gnarled tree, Oliver's point of no return, his stomach knotted. He had no doubt he was doing the right thing for all of them. Just like with the mill and the village, it was time for all of them to move forward. To change.

It didn't mean he was looking forward to another fight.

"Would your unease have anything to do with Mrs. Smith?"

Oliver cast a sideways glance and caught Fred's teasing smile. A servant would never ask that—but an uncle would. "Am I that obvious?"

"We watched you grow up with her, lad. No offense to your late wife, but we weren't expecting you to leave Thea behind when you left home."

He'd wriggled his boots deep in the sucking mud as he'd watched the mail coach take her home. Only the dread of ruining her reputation and dragging her off to an unknown, roughneck future had prevented him from chasing after her.

"I won't leave her behind again," Oliver confided. "She's coming with me and Simon when we leave."

Fred's expression grew wistful as he stared out over the draft horse's broad back. "We were hoping you'd change your mind and stay."

"We won't stay gone as long."

It was a hollow promise. The journey took three months, all told. If he came back every year, he'd fail at everything. Every other year might be manageable, depending on the weather and the expense. "I'll hire a reliable estate manager."

Who would protect everything financially but only mitigate

any retribution. And there would be that, Oliver was sure of it. His mother would dismantle everything he'd accomplished, brick by brick.

"It isn't about the estate, lad. The house has come alive with you and Simon here. We knew we'd missed you, but we weren't aware of how much."

He'd missed them, too. Somehow, in his mind, they'd never aged. Coming home to grayer heads had been alarming. If anything happened to them while he was away, it would be old news when he received it. He wouldn't be able to do anything but grieve.

Like with Garrett. And Thea.

"It'll break Hazel's heart to watch the little boy go. She cried for a month after you left, and you were a grown man."

He'd thought of Hazel every morning at breakfast, especially in the early days of taking care of himself. The meal had either been raw scones and burnt bacon, or the other way around.

They turned in at the gate, and the manor house's roof came into view. Oliver planted his feet and straightened his spine. He'd have to think about this later.

"Thank you for telling me, *Tío*. It seems I have a lot to consider."

"Do it after you talk to your mother. She's not going to take this well."

That was an understatement. It might have been what made Oliver stay to help Fred unload the wagon, and torment Hazel by serving himself in her kitchen.

"Is Mother awake?" he asked around a mouthful of tender, perfect scone.

"She's in her sitting room upstairs," Hazel said. "Or she was when I went out to do laundry." She shook a wooden spoon at him. "The next time you go traipsing through the forest, just set fire to your pants. Those grass stains are never going to come out."

Fred's snorted laugh ended on a cough, and heat flooded

Oliver's ears. Better his pants than Thea's backside. "Yes, ma'am."

Sipping his coffee, Oliver climbed the stairs with resolute steps. Halfway up, he realized the main windows were still shuttered, an outward symbol of mourning that threw the entire house into cavernous shadows and unnatural quiet. He knew better than most that grief didn't banish the sun. Sometimes, it was the other way 'round.

"Lionel?" he called as he leaned over the bannister.

"Yes, la—Your Grace?"

"Ask Fred and the grooms to open the shutters, please."

The butler's hesitation was visible, even from the second floor. The duchess had ordered them closed, and the household had always been her domain.

"It's time we had some light," Oliver said. "I'll manage it."

He went to the end of the hall and stopped at the mirror outside his parents' rooms, checking his clothes and the state of his hair. He was stalling now, he realized. It didn't matter what he looked like. His words were more important.

He rapped on her door and waited.

"You may enter."

She was at her easel, her sleeves pinned at her elbows and an apron over her black dress. Even the colors on her palette were muted and drab. She was sitting near the window, which gave her a view of Lita's house, the lane, and the fountain perpendicular to the front door. Nothing happened without her knowing about it.

"Good morning, Mother."

"Simon is at school?" she asked.

"He is."

"All he could talk about yesterday was going to see someone's piglets." She sneered the last word. "And you did nothing but encourage him. It's not wise, Oliver. He's an earl now, not a villager."

"He's a little boy." He'd continue to be one for as long as Oliver could manage it.

Her mouth turned down at the corners. "Regardless, you

shouldn't be out socially yet. We *are* in mourning."

Her windows here were open to the sunshine, just as the drawing room's windows were. She had invited the Chitesters to visit, even arranged a matchmaking dinner party in his honor. Mourning was apparently limited to the front of the house or to things she didn't want to do.

"Life moves forward, Mother." He tightened his fingers around his empty cup. If they were going to argue, they might as well get to the point. "We'll be hosting a charity card party here in two weeks."

Her eyes snapped to his as her brush clattered to the floor. "No." The angry flush across her cheeks added the only color to her features. "Your father—"

"Would not stay locked in a house more than was absolutely necessary, and he would welcome a distraction from grieving." He'd gone riding or walking every day after Lita's death. Careful to keep off public paths, certainly, but he'd still gone out.

"Garrett—"

"Would ignore every custom for a game of cards." Hell, that's what had killed him. "It's not a ball. No music, light food. Not a large crowd. I'm inviting the gentry you've been pushing me to befriend since I arrived." Plus a few people who would shock her sensibilities, but he'd deal with that later.

She rose from her chair. "I will not host an event in this house."

"You are not required to be my hostess." He'd presided over business events in Quebec. This would be no different really. "But you will make an appearance, and you will not wear black."

"Color would be unseemly."

He resisted the peevish urge to remind her that black was a color. "Gray will be acceptable in all circles, Mother. Surely you have a gray dress in your overstuffed closet."

"Why are you doing this?"

They were still on opposite sides of the room. If this was going to work, he needed to cross the divide. She would never do it. He took two deliberate steps forward. "Because I've decided to take your advice and marry."

His mother was practiced enough not to smirk, but he recognized the spark in her eyes. He got the same look when he had the upper hand in a negotiation.

She walked to his side and laid a gentle hand on his arm. "I know it's difficult to give up on a childhood hope, to suffer loss as you have. Your father went through this, as did I. But it was for the best."

Garrett had advised him repeatedly to let Mother have her way and then do as he pleased. Life would be better, he'd said, to take the wife she chose and then keep a mistress who made him happy. The lure of her approval was tempting.

But it wouldn't be fair to anyone, and it wasn't what he wanted.

"You will be in London for weeks at a time," she continued. "There won't be time for trees and a mill. Your business will be influence, and Amelia is the perfect wife to help you succeed. Augustus was one of your father's trusted allies. He'll be a fine guide through your first year in lords."

"I'm marrying Thea."

She flinched as though he'd struck her. "You have a responsibility to this family." Her grip tightened, and her quiet words stung like tree bark flung from a saw. "You are expected to do what is best for everyone and to continue a steady presence for the village. That woman isn't fit to be a duchess. She has no education, no breeding, and no acceptable skills to speak of."

"Her skills as a hostess—"

"She's wholly unprepared to do anything but serve ale to travelers in search of a bed who aren't particular about how it's warmed."

Oliver squelched the childish urge to hurl Thea's financial rescue in his mother's teeth. She couldn't be trusted with such a dangerous secret. "She's managed her own affairs for years and pulled herself from poverty without anyone's help. She's fought for everything she has and managed to keep grace and compassion while doing it."

"And she's slept with you, that Fletcher man she clings to like a leech, and God only knows who else."

"Her husband, perhaps?" He wasn't going to argue about Fletcher. It wasn't worth his breath.

"Oh yes. How could I forget the illustrious Captain Smith?" The jibe was clear. "How could you even consider her fit when you have your choice of a suitable—"

"You have no business judging who is fit. You ruined Garrett's life, you made Father miserable, and you're on your way to driving me mad. I won't have it. Not anymore."

He leaned closer, satisfied to see her cringe. "And you will leave Amelia out of your schemes. She has no more wish to marry me than I do her, and I won't see her trapped in this hell." He wouldn't see anyone shackled to this family. It was poisonous.

"Or you'll banish me to Elba?"

"I'll see you rot in debtor's prison and toast you from the Canadian shoreline with Thea by my side. I am the fucking Duke of Rushford, and this family will by God change."

"Watch your tone, young man. I am still your mother."

She was, God help him, and only some unspoken vow to his father kept Oliver from throttling her. He would prevail in this, and she would see he was right. The mill would cut its first shipment. She'd get used to it and calm down.

And then he'd leave. She'd probably undo it all before his sails vanished over the horizon. Unless he could find a manager with a backbone and a masochistic streak that went the length of it.

She spun away from him in a swirl of satin, a tilt to her mouth that reminded him of Simon in a fit. Or, honestly, of Thea in Tavie's library.

"You think she loves you?" The question was icy, like sleet on horseback.

Of all the questions Oliver had expected, this wasn't one of them. It also wasn't one he could honestly answer. He wanted to say yes, to prove to his mother how wrong she was about Thea. About him.

But, truth be told, Thea had never said the words.

"I have no idea," he confessed. "But she has always had faith in me, and that counts for something."

When she turned, her dark eyes glittered in her hard features. Her smile was cruel and sharp. "Brandon Cemetery. Row 9, Lot 10."

CHAPTER TWENTY-ONE

OLIVER CROSSED THE bridge into Brandon, his perch on Jupiter's back giving him an excellent view of the rocky brook below as he paused to let a shepherd and his flock pass. Shifting in the saddle, Oliver twisted his aching back and rolled his shoulders before stretching his neck, relieving the tension from an hour on horseback.

Damn his mother's taunt and his infernal curiosity. He should be at the mill instead of here. They'd have to make up time tomorrow. Cutting trees might improve his mood. At least he wouldn't be sitting on his aching arse.

Nudging Jupiter in the ribs, he continued into town. The horse's clopping hooves faded to dull thuds as they reached solid ground.

Brandon was smaller than Thetford, and prettier as well. North of the main road to London, it rested in a clearing. Everything centered on a main intersection, the arms of which invaded the forest circling the village. The largest trees still battled, however, their long limbs reaching out to claw the land back. Without the bustle of a main trade thoroughfare, the village still depended mostly on agriculture, though there was one inn that served as a coach stop.

The church was easy to find, near the center of town with a tall white steeple. Neat gardens surrounded the building, and flowering shrubs edged the gate surrounding a cemetery, which lay under a canopy formed by large, old trees.

Oliver dismounted, grimacing as the impact jolted him from his heels to the top of his head. He wrapped his fingers in Jupiter's mane, using the animal for balance as his body adjusted to moving under its own power. It wouldn't do to sway like a drunkard going in for confession.

It also gave him a chance to ignore the cemetery gate looming in front of him. Covered with a leafy trellis, the entrance reminded him of a creature prepared to eat anything and anyone that entered.

Once, years ago, Garrett had dared him to jump from the top of the falls and into the swimming hole. Oliver remembered standing there, staring down, with his muscles quaking and his tongue stuck to the roof of his mouth. This was worse.

Still, he'd jumped and lived to tell the tale. He was older now, used to going places he didn't want and doing the responsible thing. Putting aside the shiver of apprehension crawling down his spine, he stepped inside.

The gate latched with a quiet *snick*, as though it loathed to interrupt the quiet. Bees hovering over the hedges didn't cross the fence, too respectful to sting mourners.

Noise ceased here. No bird songs or squirrel chatter; no greetings from the residents. No laughter. No wives grumbling good morning over chocolate. God, he hated cemeteries.

And he could never remember how to count rows and plots. Did they start from the back? How did they do it in Quebec? Julia was in…a pretty spot close to the fence because she hated to be confined, and not under a tree because she'd loved the sunshine. He'd never paid attention to what row, he just *found* her. Who the hell wandered a cemetery counting graves to find their loved ones?

"Can I help you?"

The question jarred Oliver from his thoughts. The man at his side was thin and tall, almost his height, with neatly trimmed salt-

and-pepper hair. His brown eyes hinted at years of secrets, but their crinkled corners told of many more smiles. His collar clung tightly to his throat, making Oliver gulp in sympathy. "Hello, vicar. I'm…looking for someone."

"Well, you've found me." He offered his hand. "I'm Reverend Allen."

Oliver hoped his palms weren't sweating. "Oliver Hawkins. My, ummm… It's my understanding that Thea—"

The man's face hovered between shock and glee. The greeting grew more enthusiastic, shaking Oliver's arm almost to his shoulder. "It is so nice to finally meet someone from Thea's family."

There wasn't enough air in the entire village to keep Oliver breathing. His muscles seized as his vision tunneled.

Reverend Allen's grasp went from welcoming to comforting, and he added a hand on Oliver's shoulder. "Has something happened to her?"

When words failed him, Oliver shook his head. Then he shook it harder. "She's well, sir."

"Oh good." Honest relief softened the man's smile. "I enjoy our Saturday visits a great deal." He took a step and waited on Oliver to join him. Then another. "Your sister-in-law is a remarkable woman, but I'm sure—"

"Sis-sister-in-law?"

"I'm sorry." The vicar glanced sideways, his brow furrowing. "You're the late captain's brother, are you not?"

How could he connect Smith to Hawkins? Unless…

"Cap-Captain *Hawkins*?"

"Are you well?" The vicar urged him to sit. "You look decidedly pale."

Oliver raked a trembling hand through his hair. He had to piece himself together. "Long ride. Hot day."

"Water, perhaps?"

He stopped the vicar from leaving him alone in this place that was more awful than he'd originally thought. "I'll be fine, but thank you." Gritting his teeth, he forced his knees to hold him.

"Thea never mentioned any family," the vicar said as they continued their walk. *Two, three, four rows.* "Have you been on the continent?"

Oliver coughed to make his voice work. "Canada." *Seven, eight, nine.* They turned left. *One grave.* "How long have you known Thea?"

"Oh, let's see." Reverend Allen tilted his head in thought, as though they were walking in a park instead of a garden full of people. "She arrived shortly after me, so about six years." *Fourth grave, fifth grave, sixth.* "We hated to see her leave, and I know Lord Ebberley and Lady Celeste miss her. The food at the Hall has never been the same." *Seventh, eighth, ninth.* "But no one blamed her."

Tenth.

"I think this is who you're seeking," the vicar murmured.

The grave, shaded by a maple sapling, was covered in forget-me-nots. Carefully tended so they didn't escape their boundaries, the flowers stopped at the base of the wooden marker, just below the engraving. *Dulces sueños, mi hijo.*

A shiver began at the top of Oliver's head and trickled down his spine. It couldn't be. She would have… He wouldn't have… No.

He tore his gaze from the inscription only to land on the neatly carved name. James Edward Hawkins.

The ground gave way, taking Oliver to his knees.

James, after her father.

"*Edward,*" Simon's cheerful voice ricocheted through his brain. "*Like me.*"

"*And like me, and your grandfather.*"

"*Like your older brother, who died at…*" Oliver swiped his eyes and focused on the dates. At three.

A year ago, at that same age, Simon had gone to bed a toddler and awakened as a little boy—a separate person with his own character and personality. He'd been a bundle of frustrated energy, a source of constant worry and entertainment. That loss would've crippled Oliver.

Now it was a phantom pain from a limb he hadn't even known he had. He ran his fingers over the windblown flowers, ruffling them much like he did Simon's hair.

"How?" he rasped.

Revered Allen knelt beside him. "She was a good mother to young Jamey."

Jamey. Lord Jamey. And of course she was a good mother. All those times with Simon, playing with him, soothing him. Too panic-stricken to hold him.

"It always brought a smile to my face to see them at market," Reverend Allen continued. "Her with her basket and him on his stick horse. She'd fashioned it from a mop, if the mane was any indication. He caught a fever right before influenza swept through with the snow. Jamey was one of the first to succumb."

Grief crawled up from Oliver's lungs like an animal, leaving him hollow. Only the vicar's hand on his shoulder kept him anchored.

"Is there anything else you'd like to know, Captain Hawkins?"

THEA JERKED HER hand away from the herbs on her table. A thin line of blood dotted the edge of her index finger.

"You wouldn't cut yourself if you'd stop watching the clock," Jenny teased.

"You're doing just fine dividing your attention between work and me," Thea snapped as she rinsed her hands and dried them on the backside of her apron. She could feel Jenny's stare between her shoulders.

"Are you well? You've been peevish all day."

It had been longer than that, but John's upstairs rule had kept anyone from seeing it. "I'm sorry. I didn't sleep well."

She hadn't slept at all. Every time she'd closed her eyes, her mind and her body had relived yesterday with Oliver. The way he'd felt. Tasted. Sounded.

All the opportunities she'd had to tell him the truth.

That she hadn't even tried.

All day long, she'd jumped in her skin every time the door opened and any time there were footsteps in the hall. Now, he was late, and she wanted to scream at the unfairness that had become her life.

She returned to work, mincing dried yarrow to a fine powder, and recited every sin. Not coming straight home. Going to the mill. Introducing Oliver to the Circle without properly preparing him. Putting everyone at risk. Getting tangled up in his business. Hiding. Running away. Believing the duchess. Her stunning lack of faith in the man she loved.

"Do you want to marry me, Thea?"

Last night, she'd curled around her pillow and admitted she wanted nothing more. It's what she'd wanted since they'd been ten years old.

He'd never forgive her for Jamey. Never understand that she'd thought it best to—

No. She wouldn't lie to herself any longer. She'd been terrified of losing him *again*, so she'd kept the worst secrets from him and started small. She'd tested his faith, but she'd been the one to fail. Now, with yesterday and promises between them, she was going to have to tell him the truth—all of it.

Thea lifted the board and held it over the funnel, scraping every piece into the bottle, working the whiskery pieces from the wood grain to avoid wasting them. Wiggling the cork into place, she shoved it hard with her thumb, which made the cut there leak again.

"Damn," she muttered as she wrapped her apron around the deeper wound and applied pressure to stanch the flow. She'd need to apply a plaster before she went into the dining room to check on the crowd.

Crack.

The door whipped back, banging into the wall and rattling the bottles in her apothecary. Its passing flung her hair into her eyes and whipped her skirts toward the spluttering fire.

Thea flailed for the nearby poker as her squeal melded with Jenny's. She whirled, expecting to fend off a highwayman. Instead, she came face to face with Oliver, and his wild, dark eyes sucked the breath from her. The poker thudded to the floor as he trapped her against the wall.

"What was the last thing I promised you?" he demanded, his words rushed and gravelly.

She clapped a hand over her trembling lips to keep her sob inside, but she couldn't do anything about her tears.

The years fell away. She was back in the cemetery, exhausted from bargaining with God. Snow had soaked through her skirt and stockings, and her tears had frozen to her face as she'd counted the shovels of dirt separating her from her son. Reverend Allen had found her there that night and every night for a week, sat with her while her nails and lips turned blue, argued why she shouldn't just crawl in the grave. Her body had given Jamey life once; maybe it could again.

And now, under the memories, was a swell of relief. She didn't have to lie to Oliver any longer. She hadn't had to tell him at all. She hadn't had to watch his heart break.

Except the man in front of her was broken to pieces, and he'd gone through it alone.

"Ol?" She reached for his shoulder, needing his solid reassurance, needing him to know he wasn't isolated in this fresh grief.

Hissing, he flinched away. Lost to her. Again.

"Rushford," Drake barked.

"Leave us," Oliver shouted back. "This is none of your concern."

"The hell it isn't. Look at me," Drake commanded. "Oliver. Look at me."

He turned just enough to keep one eye on Drake and the

other on her, exposing the angry flush of his neck as it met his collar and his pulse pounding under the skin. Even his hair was trembling.

"Thea?" Drake asked sharply.

"I'm fine." Her wobbly words sounded anything but. She cleared her throat and kept her gaze on the rigid curve of Oliver's jaw. "We need some privacy, please."

"All right," Drake replied. "But if she so much as whimpers, I'll put a knife in your ribs."

Oliver's nod was sharp, and when he turned his full focus to her, Thea knew they were alone once more. "I would have given anything—"

"Answer my question," he growled. "The last thing."

"That you'd send for me," she said. Every night for almost four years she'd repeated them like a prayer, and they'd been as unanswered as her pleas to God to save her innocent little boy.

"And I did," he said, though his lips barely moved.

"I didn't see the letter until a month ago. Mother hid it from me."

"And answered for you," he said. The sad glint in his eyes was quickly snuffed out. "Smith is a lie then?"

"Mother invented him to explain why I'd disappeared." God help her, but it felt good to finally say it, even though he was staring like she'd sprouted a second head. "What was I supposed to do? Confess the entire sordid tale and be branded a whore, if not worse? Have Jamey…" Her voice broke. "Have my little boy tarnished because of my selfishness?"

For years, Thea had seen the ache in the mirror. She'd gotten used to it. But now Oliver's grim expression, like he was holding himself together by will alone, ripped through her.

"The coast?" he asked through tight lips.

"I walked to Brandon." With each word, her shoulders lightened, but she would have kept carrying the burden rather than watch Oliver crumble. "After…I went to Tavie."

"How could you keep my son from me?"

"I tried." She looked into his eyes, hard with anger and doubt, and nodded, hoping to convince him of something he'd never seen. "I went to your mother."

"Why to *her*? Father would have—"

"Village girls don't talk to dukes without their parents, Oliver. You know that. An abandoned pregnant girl—"

"Dammit, I didn't—"

"You weren't here to confirm anything for him," she insisted. "I didn't know where to find you. All you told me was *wait*."

"And you didn't."

Heedless of his distaste, she pushed her hand into his chest to make room for herself. "I was so sick I thought I'd die, and I waited. When he became impossible to hide under any of my dresses, I made new ones while I *waited*. I ran to Brandon and worked in a kitchen until my nails bled while I listened for any news from home, praying you'd come back for us. I gave birth, alone, and I looked into my son's eyes." She thudded her palm against her breastbone. "*Mine.*" Her throat closed around the watery words. "I waited for you until I buried him."

But she'd always hoped; she knew in the way her fingers twitched with the urge to touch him. The way her skin ached for his arms around her. She'd hoped he would learn the truth and understand. That *her* Oliver would comfort her the way he always had.

The haggard and drawn man across from her, his knees stained by grave dirt, was separated from her by an ocean of grief wider than any sea. The vision doubled her tears until she was muffling her sobs for fear Drake would charge into the kitchen intent on murder.

Oliver raked his hands through his hair, left them there as though he'd pull himself bald. "You could've come to me."

"How?" she asked. "Stow away on the first ship to Canada and hope I didn't give birth on the way? Show up on your doorstep with a bag and a baby? She told me you were married."

"How could you believe that of me?" Oliver demanded. "Of

me?"

His hair was wild now, matching the rest of him as he prowled like a wounded animal. She remembered that feeling, late at night, alone in the sea of people that was London, how it had felt to have her normally gay and commanding aunt comfort her. Thea took a step forward, raised her hand to touch him, to soothe his pain. To share it.

He recoiled as though she was going to shove another knife home.

Pain sliced through her. Thea wrapped her arms around her waist and felt the difference. Empty of grief and bereft of hope, she was as brittle as cone flowers in the fall. "How could you think *I* would marry anyone else?"

"After everything we shared, Thea...before...since..." He dropped his gaze. "Yesterday. And you wouldn't tell me the truth about anything. Not until you absolutely had to. Not until I was backed into a corner. Why?"

Dread chilled her gut and crept upward. She couldn't tell him this way, while he was angry and hurt. He'd never understand, never listen to reason.

When she didn't answer, his chin dipped low as he glared at her. "I deserve the truth."

He did. "My silence for your freedom. She promised."

"Mother." His jaw clenched again. "So you mortgaged yourself to your eyeballs to...what? Give me a mill to replace our child?"

She wouldn't keep his answers from him any longer. It would doom her to a life lonelier than she'd thought possible, but maybe she deserved that. "Millie has been blackmailing your mother. You couldn't succeed because—"

"Because no one would tell me the truth. Why couldn't you simply tell me?"

There was nothing simple about this, about them. "I knew when you learned everything, you'd never want to set eyes on me again," she whispered.

"You never intended—" His bleak stare turned to hard amber. "I made you a promise, Theodora."

His lifeless, bitter tone sent a chill down her spine, freezing her objection in her lungs. "It was under false—"

"You may be carrying my child again. I will not make the same mistake twice."

Thea planted both hands in his chest and shoved him backward. It did little but rock him back on his heels, but it gave her some space. "My son—my *life*—are not mistakes." She twisted out of his reach and walked to the door. Threw it open. "Get out of my house, *Your Grace*."

Oliver's boots thudded against the floor, each stride like a nail in a coffin. "We *will* announce our betrothal in two weeks at the card party." He stopped at the threshold, one foot on the back stoop, one in the kitchen. "We *will* marry." His eyes were as cold and hard as the wind on her face. "And then, *Mrs. Smith*, we are leaving this godforsaken island."

CHAPTER TWENTY-TWO

THE NEXT MORNING, Oliver returned his curricle to the stable and took a moment to pitch hay into each horse's stall, ignoring the twinges in his shoulders and back and the thick, sticky cotton lining his mouth and head.

Before Julia had agreed to marry him, she'd made him promise he'd never drink excessively again. He only broke that rule once a year, on Simon's birthday. After his son was asleep in bed, he and Richard would do their level best to drown the double-edged sword of joy and pain. Oliver didn't think she'd begrudge him that.

But last night had been different. It was the first time he'd gotten drunk without Richard, without the excuse of Simon's birthday and the grief over Julia's death. No, last night had been more selfish than that. It had been about lost opportunities, the life he might have had with Thea, knowing Jamey. He'd been grieving for a life that never was.

Which made him the worst sort of traitor. Grieving for one child while the other was asleep in the next room. Mourning Thea instead of Julia. Knowing that if he'd had Thea and Jamey, he wouldn't have had Julia and Simon—that had Julia lived, Thea would have remained in his past.

Halfway through the bottle, he'd realized Simon's birthday aboard ship had been the first time he'd truly celebrated the day for what it was, not what it had been. There had been only laughter and songs. He'd fallen asleep early, in the middle of a silly story—heedless of the ache in his back and totally sober.

Maybe Julia wouldn't begrudge him that either.

Maybe Thea would accept the future she'd shoved back at him. The one she'd never intended to take in the first place. Because she didn't trust him.

Oliver thrust the fork into the hay pile and strode out of the stable. Damn her and who she did and didn't trust. He would right this mess and give her what she deserved, what she always had, before his mother had taken it from her.

Gravel crunched under his boots, seeming to bite through the soles and his socks, and he squinted against sunshine that felt as though God was jabbing glass through his eyes and straight into his brain. The carriage waiting under a tree near the house gave him pause enough to scowl. He pushed his way through the door, and the sunshine glaring against the tile floor made him wish for the gloom his mother preferred.

He followed the faint trails of conversation to the drawing room, irritation and anger building as the voices became clear.

"He should return shortly," his mother was saying. "And then I'll leave you two alone. It shouldn't be unseemly, here in the house."

She was awake ungodly early for someone who'd always kept London hours, even in the country seasons.

"I shouldn't wish to disturb him or cause any discomfort," said Amelia Chitester, who sounded much more uncertain than her last visit here. "Perhaps I should go and—"

"You'll do no such thing. I won't send you home to your parents empty-handed," the duchess insisted. "The servants won't dare gossip, and I would never say a word."

Unless it fit her objectives, which having him alone with an unchaperoned lady of her choosing would certainly do.

Oliver rapped his knuckle on the door frame as he entered the room. "Good morning, ladies. Am I interrupting?"

The question was rhetorical. Amelia looked as though she'd been caught mid-scheme. Perhaps he'd misjudged her.

It wouldn't be the first time he'd done it this week. Hell, even in the last twenty-four hours.

"Oliver." His name was almost lost in the rustle of his mother's skirts. "Amelia has come to call this morning, hoping to catch you before you left for…the day."

"For *work*."

"Yes. Well. If you'll excuse me, I'll retire upstairs and give you two some privacy." She paused at the door and gave their visitor the genuine smile she saved for special occasions. "It was lovely to see you, Amelia. I hope you'll visit more often."

Oliver waited for her to pass before nodding to his mother's guest. "Excuse me for a moment, please."

He caught up with his fleeing parent at the bottom of the stairs and wrapped his fingers around her upper arm, tightening his grip until she stopped and faced him.

"What the bloody hell are you playing at?" he grated.

"Absolutely nothing," she said as she pulled free. "She is here—"

"Unchaperoned, early in the morning, whispering with you in the drawing room. You couldn't even wait a day—"

"Do I look prepared to receive anyone?"

She was dressed in black, as always, but her hair was covered with a cap—still neat but not styled. She was also missing jewelry and cosmetics. It made her appear smaller. Older.

"She arrived on her own, so any chaperone questions should be taken up with her parents, and we were hardly whispering." The illusion of fragility vanished. "As for why she's here, I can only hope the two of you will surrender your pride and see common sense."

He was seeing a lot of things lately, but one thing he would not do was surrender. "We'll talk more later, Mother."

"Is that what we were doing?"

The barb hit his back as he walked back to their guest, who

was pacing in the drawing room.

"I apologize for keeping you waiting, Amelia," he said as he closed the door.

"And I'm sorry for arriving unannounced. I missed you at your cottage and was hoping to catch you here before you left for the mill. But I seem to have interrupted something."

If everyone waited until he and his mother were finished fighting, they'd never have visitors again. "You are caught in a drama, I'm afraid."

"And you're foxed," she teased. "Don't look so affronted. I've seen my share of parties. I hope the drinks were good."

They had been. Drake had gifted him with a bottle of Eamon Brewer, the whiskey they'd shared in Tavie's parlor. Oliver already regretted wasting it. They were in short supply. "What brings you out so early, alone?"

"In light of our last conversation, I've come to you with a proposition."

Before, she'd been forthright and open. Now, she was speaking too fast and she refused to meet his eye. Oliver's stomach lurched before it tumbled. Did all women mean the opposite of what they said? They agreed to marry but didn't intend to. They said they didn't wish to marry, but secretly hoped for a proposal. "I cannot—"

"I'd like to hire you to make barrels," she said, drawing her chin slightly higher. "Or at least to cut the staves so I can take them to a cooper."

The unexpected request melded with his hangover and his lack of food or coffee. Oliver dropped unceremoniously to the corner of his mother's desk, heedless of the mess he might be making. "I'm sorry, what?"

"I have a small section of land that came to me from my mother. It has a stand of mature oak trees, and I'd like them harvested and cut into barrel staves. I can pay you five pounds per tree."

"Five pounds?"

"I think that's fair. A woodsman in Brandon offered a price of seven pounds, but part of that was for travel, and your crew would not have that expense."

In a pink morning dress with a matching pelisse and white gloves, she looked every inch the proper miss, which made her words that much more difficult to grasp. Oliver walked to the mantel and pulled the bell rope. "I need coffee. Would you like tea?"

"Coffee would be fine, thank you."

The footman arrived at the door and left just as soundlessly with Oliver's request for coffee and scones. His return was mercifully quick.

Oliver offered Amelia a chair and then sat opposite. "Why do you need barrels?"

"Do you ask all of your clients about their intentions?" She accepted the coffee he offered and, to his surprise, drank it black.

"I don't," Oliver confessed. "But I've never had a female client, and I wish—"

"To protect me from my wild ideas?"

He smiled in what he hoped was an encouraging manner. Having Thea as a partner had taught him a lesson. "To know the story behind the reason. You have my promise of secrecy."

She regarded him for a long moment as she sipped her coffee. "I need them to make whiskey."

Oliver swallowed a too-large gulp of coffee, and it singed its way toward this gullet. A deep breath and a short cough helped soothe the burn but not the feeling that his world was being tipped on its head. Again.

For her part, Amelia was frowning as though he'd criticized her choice in clothing. "I had hoped you would be more—"

He held up his hand as he sucked in one last, deep breath. "Whiskey?"

"The small batch I've put on the market did quite well, but to maintain an income while the next ages, I'll need to distill gin. That will take all the barrels I currently have. I need more."

"You've already sold product?"

"I have. It's quite good, if I do say so myself." She pulled a small flask from her reticule and poured a dram in an empty cup. "Try it."

Oliver's stomach and head rebelled at the offer, but he didn't want to offend her again. Lifting the cup, he wet his lips and ran his tongue across the sample. It was very good—and sickeningly familiar.

"Dear God. You're Eamon Brewer."

She blushed with pride and tucked the flask back in her bag. As she talked about discoveries, theories, and recipes, Oliver's head spun with problems and possible solutions.

"Amelia," he interrupted. "I cannot possibly use the trees on your entailment."

"You won't help?"

"If I go about cutting trees, it will be impossible to hide. Especially from your father."

"I have no choice." She toyed with her coffee cup. "I cannot afford the supplies and the barrels. I also want to control the quality. And you're quite right. I cannot ask my father for funds."

She'd also need a larger facility as demand increased, which his instincts told him it would do. It would be nearly impossible for her to do alone.

Luckily, he knew just the person to help. He stood and offered his hand. "Do you mind an early morning drive?"

THEA LATCHED THE chicken coop gate and kept a tight grip on the egg basket. The wicker handle bit into her skin, keeping her focused on the tasks at hand. Memories and distress had kept her awake far into the night. Though she was used to that, sunrise had always been a reminder of the line between past and present. Bleak at times, yes, but a call to focus on the day before her and all the days beyond that.

Now, everything was mixed in a miserable stew, and dread lay in her stomach like a lump.

The clop of hooves and the jingle of harness prodded her forward. Breakfast was busy this morning, and new arrivals would mean more food to cook and more work for her already harried staff. She paused when the carriage left the road and took the gravel lane toward the barn—and her.

The horse wasn't familiar, but the driver—in shirt sleeves and suspenders, without a hat or a neck cloth—made her traitorous heart skip to life. It fluttered to a stop when she recognized his passenger.

Oliver had brought Amelia Chitester out for an early drive. Since they were probably in her hack, questions and answers tumbled through Thea's exhausted brain—all of them logical, and each of them leading to an inevitable conclusion. It wouldn't be the first time Oliver had left her in a huff only to realize later that she'd been right all along.

She'd always enjoyed those moments.

As they made their way forward, Amelia's hand tucked into Oliver's arm and her dress, impossibly pink, pressed, and fashionable, Thea straightened her posture and ignored the impulse to smooth her hair and her skirts. Yes, her dress was plain, but it was clean and it wasn't black. Her apron was still crisp and white, given the early hour.

Still, she tightened her grip on her shawl as cold dampness soaked through to her skin and deeper, reaching her joints and locking them into place. There was no option but to watch her future come toward her, cloaked in a beautiful couple who were far too fine for an inn.

"Miss Chitester," Thea said as they stopped. She bobbed a quick curtsey. "Your Grace."

"Thea."

Oliver's voice was tight and sharp, making her name an epithet. It hurt more than if he'd actually sworn at her.

"How can I help you this morning?"

When Oliver remained quiet, she looked to Amelia, who seemed as confused as one of Thea's pesky chickens. The thought of a yellow hen in a pink pelisse stuck in Thea's tired brain until she felt herself smiling.

"I'm as lost as you," said Amelia as she withdrew her arm. "Oliver and I were…discussing something this morning and he asked me to go for a drive. To you, it seems."

Thea looked to Oliver, who had one hand in his trouser pocket and seemed to be staring at everything other than the two of them. He always did that when he was thinking, or rather when he'd charged ahead without considering the necessary steps or the consequences.

He couldn't marry Amelia until he'd cleared her out of the path. Part of that was, undoubtedly, explaining their earlier relationship. It would be an embarrassing conversation for all of them.

Underneath her serviceable dress and drab shawl, and behind the basket she pulled tighter to her waist, her heart wilted. This was why she'd never visited him at Eton and, she knew now, what had kept her from boarding a ship to Canada six years ago. Imagining him moving forward was one thing. Seeing it firsthand left a hole large enough for his steam engine.

She'd be damned if she made this easy for him. *"Di tu pieza."* She combined her invitation to confession with a perfect curtsey.

His gaze snapped to hers. *"Obstinados,"* he grated. *"Nunca vuelvas a hacer una reverencia."*

Stubborn, was she? Thea almost curtsied again just to tweak his temper. Instead, she crossed her arms and waited for the ax to fall.

"Amelia has—"

"Thea?" Drake strode out the kitchen door and across the yard. "Jenny sent me to see about the eggs."

He was also without a coat and hat and, as he reached her side, she could still see soap near his ear. Oliver hissed a curse, and Thea almost joined him. This needed to be over. She thrust the basket at Drake, heedless of the eggs rolling together. Rather than leaving, he cocked an eyebrow at their guests.

Instead of irritating Oliver, the challenge brought light to his eyes as he smiled. "Miss Amelia Chitester, may I present Mr. Drake Fletcher." He swept a hand toward his companion. "Drake, may I present Eamon Brewer."

Thea blinked at the name. She had a bottle of Brewer's in her bedroom.

Whiskey? Amelia Chitester distilled *whiskey*? Thea smothered a smile. She'd thought an inn was scandalous.

Amelia's cheeks went pink and quickly to red. Tears gathered in her eyes. "*Sir!*"

"The devil you say," Drake said at the same time, his smile widening.

Thea sympathized with the other woman's frustration and stepped in before more damage could be done. "Your secret is safe with us, Miss Chitester." When Amelia's suspicions remained, Thea drew in a deep breath. "I own The Goat."

After a moment, the young woman relaxed bit by bit. She looked to Drake as he offered his hand. "And you are?"

"Her man of business," he said, chuckling. "And, for the most part, Oliver's as well."

Thea kept her gaze on Oliver. Though she now understood part of the reason for the visit; Amelia's enterprising nature was another trait that would make her a suitable bride.

He stared back, unblinking. "She needs a sponsor, Thee."

"Would someone explain this to me, please?" Despite the question, Amelia was smiling. "I feel as though I've tumbled downhill for a very long time."

Thea remembered that feeling well. She'd sat in Tavie's drawing room, relieved to hear there were other women who made their own way and their own rules, yet terrified by the enormity of the task in front of her. As he had then, Drake now stepped forward and stood next to Amelia, the egg basket at his feet as he explained the rules for audits, collateral, and business plans.

"Walk with me." Oliver tucked Thea's hand into his elbow. "They don't need us for this discussion."

The silence between them was broken only by the pebbles underfoot and the clucks of her stupidly contented chickens. His fine cotton shirt was soft under her fingers, and it did little to hide the warmth of his skin and the curve of his biceps. She moved her hand, only to rest it on his thick forearm and have his coarse hair continue to tempt her.

"Fletcher said collateral," Oliver said as they neared the barn.

"She'll be fine. She has the experience necessary and the proven success. Money would be an added incentive, but it isn't necessary."

"She has it."

"Her dowry won't be accepted. In fact, it would be best if you held your announcement until—"

"If I held..." He pulled free and turned to face her, half in shadow. "*Mierda.* Is that what you think?"

She began to answer, but he cut her off.

"She offered to pay me to cut trees on her entailment so she could use them for barrel staves. Rather than pay me, she can use the money for the Circle. And may I remind you that I am already betrothed? To you."

She didn't need reminding. Wild swings between joy and hopelessness had haunted her fitful sleep.

"I wanted to know what you used as collateral," he said. "I have my title and my experience. Amelia has her existing business and money. You had what? I assume it wasn't the inn."

Because she had nothing without him? Because her family had always been dependent on his? Thea tilted her chin until she could return his stare. "I had experience and money."

"How did you get the money?"

The question dashed cold water across Thea's skin even as it stoked the heat of her anger and hurt. How dare he take her pride and her effort and make it about him and his family? How dare he think she'd participate in any scheme of Millie's?

"You have your choice of answers. Either I whored myself out to anyone who'd have me, or I bartered my child to your mother, or I saved it." When all he did was stare at her, she gathered her skirts and turned to leave. The tears were thick on her tongue, and she'd be damned if she'd cry in front of him. "Choose whichever you'd like."

Oliver stopped her. "I didn't mean it like that," he said. "Of course you saved it."

It was just his palm against her shoulder. It would be easy enough to break away. It should have been her only goal.

"Don't cry, Thee," he whispered. "I can't bear it. I just…I want to *know*."

Just like she'd wondered about his life in Canada. But it wouldn't help anything to tell him about long hours and extra work, about using leather scraps to block holes in her shoes and the care she'd taken with her only two dresses. "He never wanted for anything."

"But you did." He put a gentle finger under her chin and coaxed her to meet his gaze. "God, Thea. Why? Was this always your plan?"

She hadn't known the inn was an option, but she was tempted to lie and spare him the painful truth. "A pony."

The words were thick liquid on her tongue. Jamey's eyes had lit up the moment he'd seen a horse, and she'd set an impossible goal of buying him one on his fourth birthday. Every month she'd set aside as much as she could, but by the time he was three, she had just enough to buy him a goat.

And then it had turned snowy and cold.

Oliver's sharp inhale shuddered at the end. "How could you believe me capable of marrying anyone else?"

Because he'd done it before and been happy. Now he was dooming them both to rashly made promises.

Drake's sharp whistle caught their attention. Amelia was shading her eyes to gaze at the sun.

"She's been gone too long," Oliver said as he offered his arm. "Augustus will think she's been kidnapped, and Mother will have the banns posted in the church yard."

"We don't have to marry, Ol," Thea whispered in a rush. The walk back wasn't taking as long as she needed. "Please. Just wait a month. If my…if everything goes as it should, we'll know for certain that I'm not increasing. And you can—"

"Two weeks, Thea." They'd reached Drake and Amelia, so he unwound her grip on his forearm and kissed her fingers. The jolt went past her elbow, searing her already frazzled nerves. "I'll send Emmett for you tomorrow so you can come discuss the party menu and arrangements with Hazel and Lionel."

There was no need for a carriage, which would have to take her through the village. She knew her way just fine. Thea tugged her fingers. *"Puedo conducir yo mismo."*

Oliver tightened his hold. *"No caminarás hacia la puerta de la cocina como un sirviente."*

Why did it matter which door she used? He'd been coming and going from the manor's kitchen since he was a child. And she was a servant, more or less. For two more weeks, anyway.

"I will send a carriage every day until you take it." His words were quiet and soft, but his stare was that of a predator with its prey within reach.

Sometimes, the best escape came from playing dead. "Fine. Thank you."

He arched an eyebrow, indicating she hadn't fooled him at all, but he let her go. For now.

Thea refused to return Oliver's farewell just as she ignored Drake's presence until their visitors had turned the corner and were on the way back to town.

"You have soap in your ear," she said, hoping to derail the questions she could sense coming.

"Jenny was afraid you'd hurl eggs at him until he beheaded you. What the devil is going on between you two?"

"Nothing." Nothing unusual anyway. She'd spent most of her

life trying to talk Oliver out of his stubborn insistence on having his own way. "He came to get Amelia—"

"Horse shit, Thea." Drake turned, facing her broadside. "Half of that was about Amelia, the other half was about something entirely different. It's not like you to exclude half the group from a business conversation."

Damn her life that the men surrounding her knew her far too well. Thea stiffened her backbone and her resolve. Recent experience had taught her not every question needed an answer.

CHAPTER TWENTY-THREE

THEA FACED A dining room full of her family and closest friends, comforted that friends outnumbered family. By only one, true, but there was strength in numbers, and she needed all the strength she could borrow.

"I don't understand what could be so important that you had to drag us out here." Her mother swept a searching gaze over the room, no doubt expecting to see a half-naked drunken patron. Her disapproving frown left Thea wondering if she was disappointed to not see one or if she simply didn't like the décor. "It's far too early for respectable women to be out, especially in an open carriage."

Millie, bleary-eyed and sitting beside their mother, had the good sense not to agree.

"We'll be serving lunch soon, and I refuse to lose—to let Mr. Fletcher lose—any business for this discussion. If you'd like, you can stay for shepherd's pie and Toad in a Hole."

She'd put the latter on the menu in a perverse salute to her now-reluctant betrothed.

Drake, seated at the bar to her immediate right, smirked. "Take all the time you need, Mrs. Smith. My money is yours." He nodded to her mother. "And luncheon is on the house."

"That's very kind. Thank you." Thea drew in a deep breath. "The Duke of Rushford is hosting a charity card party ten days hence, and he has asked me to extend an invitation to all of you." She cast a pointed gaze to John and Jenny. "*All* of you."

While the staff looked gobsmacked, Drake's eyes narrowed in calculation—no doubt cataloging questions to ask when they were alone. Her mother's disapproval was obvious from her eyebrows to the shivering lace on her collar.

"Absolutely not. I will not set foot in that house. And neither will any of my family."

"That will be difficult since I'm to be his hostess." Thea ignored the gasps from her audience. "The proceeds are a donation to a charity I heartily approve of, one benefitting unwed mothers and their children."

Millie's attention had sharpened throughout the conversation. Now her gaze was almost lethal.

Their mother's frown deepened. "You cannot host at his home. You are not—"

"We intend to announce our betrothal that evening."

Only Jenny and John reacted with anything that could be called happiness. Drake was slightly smug about the whole thing. Thea just hoped her smile looked happy, or could at least be explained away by nerves. A woman, a smart one anyway, didn't become a duchess without some trepidation.

"What have you done?" her mother asked.

"I've accepted a proposal most single women would give their eye teeth to receive." One no one thought she'd ever get. That he wished he'd never offered, and she regretted taking.

"A widowed housekeeper with no dowry?" Her mother's eyes narrowed. "What have you to offer him?"

A dead son. The possibility of another heir. A business partnership. Buckets of collateral to save a family she'd inadvertently helped bankrupt. A mother to his child.

What was left of her heart?

"He's aware of *everything* I don't have," Thea said, locking eyes with the nemesis that had given birth to her.

"We should be happy, Mother," Millie said as she poured

more tea. "All those fine rooms in the manor, each one larger than your entire apartment. And servants."

"No one will be moving into the manor," Thea snapped. She'd known the Felton House servants all her life. She wasn't subjecting them to her family. And she certainly wasn't living under the same roof as her mother *and* the duchess. No matter how briefly. She wasn't sure she'd be living there at all. "We'll be sailing for Canada before winter."

"Canada," Jenny gasped. "You're leaving?"

"Ol—His Grace is eager to return to his life there, as is Simon."

"And you can't wait to run away," her mother said. "Again."

Drake drew himself straight, frowning in displeasure, and Thea loved him that much more for it. It doubled when he led Jenny and John from the room.

Relief and abandonment churned through Thea as she faced her family. "I am taking the life you stole from me."

"By living in a manor and lording yourself over us?" Millie asked. "Not sharing—"

"We've received quite enough from the duke and his family," Thea said, pleased to see the words hit home.

"We've no such thing," her mother argued. "And now you expect me to celebrate everything we've been cheated out of?"

"I do, because if you didn't, people would talk. I know how much you hate that." Thea put the invitations on the table. "If you'd like to stay for luncheon, please make yourselves comfortable. I'll ask someone to freshen your tea."

"Oooh. La. She already sounds like the mistress of a grand house," Millie taunted.

Rather than continuing the fight, Thea rose and straightened her skirts before leaving the room. She reached the stairs before hard fingers closed tight over her arm. Turning, she faced her sister's thin-lipped anger.

"This explains a great deal of the duchess's recent behavior. If you think you're keeping your money to yourself, you have another thing coming, *sister dear*. I have debts that need paid. If you don't want the entire village to know you've disgraced yourself again…"

As though anyone in Thetford would think differently when the marriage was announced. "You have profited quite enough," Thea grated. "Get out of my dining room."

"Mr. Fletcher—"

"Has rescinded his invitation," Drake said as he shouldered his way out of the kitchen. "Allow me to show you and your mother out, Miss Fowler." He took Millie's arm and kept walking, forcing her to follow. "Thea, why don't you wait in the office?"

Once she was alone in one of the few sanctuaries she had left, a dangerous thought formed in her brain. It was her last hope, and if he agreed, they could be in Gretna Green by supper.

When the door opened, she faced her closest ally. "Drake, would you marry me?"

"After you've announced your betrothal to Oliver?" he half-laughed the question. "Not for all the crown jewels."

"No would have sufficed," Thea said, oddly stung by the utter refusal yet relieved just the same, which gave her more pause than it should have. "Why not?" She wasn't unattractive, and he knew her worth. They both knew what to expect from the other. "It would only be—"

"I like my head and my entrails where they are," he said, a twinkle in his eye. "And I believe Oliver would gladly relieve me of both." He leaned one hip against her desk and crossed his arms.

"He'd get over it," she insisted, but it was half-hearted. He might not kill Drake, but he'd never forgive her. At least they wouldn't be doomed to a life on tenterhooks. "He'd see reason eventually. And you could have an annulment after a month, two at the most."

"Are you…increasing?"

There was something charming about a semi-reformed smuggler who could still blush.

"No. At least I don't think so." Thea fingered her locket, tracing each heavily embossed blossom. She'd been praying every night for her courses to begin, just like she'd done six years earlier. "But I was once. A long time ago."

The confession stole her breath for a moment, and then it all came pouring out of her. The rain, the inn, the coach. The duchess, Jamey, the winter. Her mother. Her sister. All her lies abandoned her, leaving her hollow and leaning against the only friendly shoulder left to her.

"And they say life in the country is boring," Drake drawled as he wrapped her in what Thea could only guess was a brotherly hug.

"Thank you," she muttered as she wiped her eyes.

He handed her his handkerchief, which smelled of mint and sage. "Don't be grateful just yet. I'm quite upset that you kept all this from me. We're supposed to be friends, Thea. Friends don't let each other suffer alone."

"And you've told me everything of your life before?" she asked.

He tucked the handkerchief back into his pocket, careful to put the damp side facing his jacket. "That's different. I'm not suffering."

Yet he wouldn't meet her eyes. "Drake?"

"You won't change the subject that easily, Mrs., er, Miss." He scratched his ear. "Dash it, what am I supposed to call you? Mrs. Smith is easiest, I suppose." The twinkle reappeared. "Until it's Your Grace." When she didn't respond, he sobered. "You deserve to marry the man you love, Thea."

Even if it was so one-sided it threatened to crush her? Even if the man was committed out of sheer stubbornness and guilt?

Maybe it was what she deserved.

OLIVER RESTED HIS foot on the bottom fence rail and draped his forearms over the top one. The rough-hewn timber scratched and poked, but the fence didn't wobble. It didn't surprise him. Nothing about the tidy cottage farm surprised him anymore. There wasn't a hint that the man of the household was nine years old.

"You're payin' too much for that shoat, your—Mr. Hawkins," said Elsie Bell. "For that price, you could almost have two."

"It's supply and demand, Mrs. Bell." Oliver had planned his backward negotiation strategy during the ride here, only halfway listening to Simon's excited chatter about "Pig Saturday." And *demand* was a good word—besides nine-year-old Tim, who was one of the mill's youngest employees, there were at least two younger Bell children, both of whom were playing in the barn with Simon. "I need a healthy pig, and you have one."

The woman fell quiet for a moment, perhaps warring between refusing charity and filling her children's stomachs. Childish giggles traveled on the breeze.

"Tim, crate that pig for his lordship."

As the boy ducked between the fence rails, Oliver delivered payment. "Thank you for holding one back for us."

"'Twas the least I could do, sir. The money Tim's earning at the mill is a blessing, and he says you're a right good boss."

If feeding the younger boys lunch and making them leave work at an early hour made him a good boss, then so be it. But Oliver thought he was escaping too lightly.

The pig seemed to be the only one not happy with the transaction, given its squealing and thrashing about in the crate.

"He ain't used to being boxed up like that," Tim said, sounding very old and very young all at once. "Once you get started home, he'll settle down."

"This isn't my first pig," Oliver confided. He tipped a bucket of Hazel's kitchen scraps, dumping half into the crate. The squealing gave way to happy grunting, and Tim smiled up at him like he was a genius.

Uncertain how long the silence would last, Oliver went into the barn. "Si? It's time to leave for home."

When there wasn't an answer, he followed the fits of giggles and found Simon with the younger Bell children, covered in a pile of gangly puppies. Their giant of a mother looked on with a doggy grin. When Mrs. Bell arrived at the stall, the dog stood, shook the hay from her coat, and reached them in two long steps. She was a fine Wolfhound—and as tall as Simon's pony.

"She showed up a month or so back," Mrs. Bell explained as she scratched the dog's large head. "I kept waiting for a gentleman to claim her, but none ever did. The pups are just weaned."

"Can I have him, Papa?" Simon asked through his laughter as a brown beastie licked him from chin to ear. They both toppled backward into the hay. "He likes me."

One of Oliver's classmates at Eton had brought his Wolfhound to school. The dog had eaten as much as four people and shit as much as five. Fred and Hazel would be unhappy, not to mention the sailors on the return trip to Quebec. Besides, the Felton House budget could only be stretched to accommodate a pig that would be gone after the card party.

Thinking of that event brought up thoughts of Thea. All week, he'd left for work late and come home early in the hopes of catching her in Hazel's kitchen. Every time, he'd missed her. It was as though she hid behind a tree and waited for him to leave, or hid in the cellar until his back was turned. She was perverse enough to do just that.

"Simon, we have to go."

He was bent on seeing her. Talking with her. Hazel reported that she was getting on fine, and Lionel half-loved her already. But second-hand news was dissatisfying...and what had caused their problems in the first place.

"But Papa..."

The rest of the sentence was lost in peals of laughter as puppies and children bounced against one another in something that was a combination of tag, keep-away, and ring-around-the-rosy.

Simon's laughter had always been one of Oliver's favorite sounds. On the best days, it doubled his happiness. On the worst, it made him feel like he'd done one thing right. He'd learned every shade of it, from ticklish fits to mischief-making.

But he'd never heard this kind before. It rolled from him in waves as he played with children his own age and furry balls of energy that loved unconditionally and at first sight. His cheeks were red, and his eyes danced.

Oliver remembered being that way once, when he and Garrett had learned to ride.

He leaned against a post and watched his little boy. All these years, he'd told everyone that he didn't need a nurse, or a governess, or another wife. That he could raise Simon on his own.

And he had. He and Richard had done it, and as a result, Simon had gone to business meetings and lumber camps. He'd learned his numbers and letters from billets, and he could wield a hatchet with enough proficiency that Oliver didn't need to worry.

But he learned between business obligations and travel, and he entertained himself. With the exception of Oliver and Richard, Simon was largely alone. It had never occurred to Oliver that Simon might need a mother or siblings.

Ah-choo. Simon's sneeze shook his entire body. The boy never did anything halfway.

"Excuse me," Tim said, sounding much like a schoolmaster. "You're supposed to say excuse me. That's what my Mam says."

Mrs. Bell's blush reached her ears as she inhaled sharply. "Tim—"

"Please don't scold him," Oliver said. "He's right. And Simon knows better."

Or he would if the reinforcement of polite behavior was more constant than two bachelors could manage.

"'Scuse me," Simon muttered as he wiped his nose on his sleeve.

"And you're supposed to use a handkerchief." Tim pulled a

neatly folded one from his pocket.

Simon wiped his nose and handed it back, making Oliver cringe. Mrs. Bell chuckled under her breath.

"Simon, you're supposed to say *thank you*." Oliver strode into the melee. "And not return something dirty." He exchanged his handkerchief for Tim's. "We'll wash yours and return it. Thank you, Tim."

"Can't I have the puppy?" Simon pleaded, not to Oliver but to Mrs. Bell.

"Simon!"

Now Mrs. Bell laughed outright. "Supply." She pointed to herself. "Demand." She pointed to Simon.

Still, she could get a good price for fine hunting dogs. Oliver opened his mouth to object, but she shook her head.

"I'm no more charitable than you, m'lord."

He'd been had. And in that moment, she reminded him of Thea when they were younger, or in Tavie's ballroom with the Circle. Proud, resilient, and enterprising.

She was a good mother to young Jamey, the vicar in Brandon had said. Of course she had been. She'd always excelled at everything she'd set her mind to. She would have raised her son much like Mrs. Bell had raised her children.

Their mothers can't work, Oliver. Not at anything that will pay a wage, Thea had scolded. *Their fathers are gone—either dead or adventuring.*

They'd walked away without a thought to the consequences, leaving the mothers of their children to make their way however they could. Leaving their sons to take their places.

And, though Tim was a few years older than Jamey would have been, Oliver had no doubt that he was seeing Thea's future had Jamey lived. They would have struggled and survived together.

And alone.

They deserved so much more. Even Tim's missing father deserved to know how well his son was doing.

And Simon deserved to be a little boy, even if that meant a giant puppy.

"Thank you, Mrs. Bell. Can we go now, Simon?"

Simon rushed forward, half-dragging the large puppy over to say goodbye to its mother and to Mrs. Bell, both of whom he hugged violently while promising to take care of the dog and to bring him for frequent visits.

Tim went with them to the cart and secured the dog to the seat. Oliver checked the knot and found it surprisingly tight.

"That'll hurt him," Simon argued. "I can hold him."

"You ain't big enough."

"Aren't," Simon said, a little too smugly for Oliver's taste. "You're supposed to say *aren't*, not *ain't*."

The older boy's cheeks reddened. "Oh. Okay. Have you ever had a dog before?"

Simon shook his head, and Tim began explaining all the responsibilities of feeding and playing. Despite his puffed chest, all his words were gentle and encouraging. Simon hung on each one, his eyes wide as he nodded with reverence. It reminded Oliver of his childhood alternately in Garrett's shadow or his footsteps.

It made him wonder what Jamey would have been like as an older brother. How he and Simon would have gotten on.

How they never would have been alone.

Oliver raked his fingers across his shirt. "Thank you, Tim. We should get on the road before our pig runs out of patience."

"Pinky," Simon chirped as he climbed into the seat next to his dog. "His name is Pinky."

"The dog?" Oliver eyed their newest pet, which looked nothing like his new name.

"You're silly, Papa. The pig. 'Cause he's pink."

"Wonderful," Oliver muttered as he took the reins. If the boy got attached to another animal, they'd have a zoo. "What are you going to name the puppy?"

Simon's eyes lit up. "Sp—"

"Not Spot. Two of them are confusing enough. Think on it

during our drive home."

Halfway back to the village, he pointed the wagon toward the forest and the clearing that served as the entrance for the Roman Road. The ancient shortcut would bring them just above the manor.

A tower once used as a rabbit warren loomed to their left. Thankfully, Simon was too distracted by the pig and his puppy to notice. Oliver didn't fancy discussing hunting parties and hauntings with his imaginative son.

Once past the tree line, and in the cool shade of the forest, they followed the faint trail along a wide ridge and then crossed the bridge over the widest part of the river.

"Could we swim here?" Simon asked.

"Absolutely not. Never swim here, no matter what anyone says." The last thing Oliver needed was Simon's newest friends daring him to cross the swift, icy river, like Garrett had done to him years ago.

They rocked along, the motion lulling everyone to quiet. The puppy heaved a deep sigh and dropped to Simon's feet.

"Simon, don't correct Tim when he talks, please."

"But he corrected me."

"That's different. He corrected your manners because everyone should know to be polite." Oliver wasn't going to lecture about how Simon already knew to be polite. That wasn't the point. "But Tim's not been to school; lots of boys haven't." Jamey wouldn't have gone.

"And you shouldn't point that out. Understand?"

One look told him Simon didn't. He tried again. "You know how, after Christmas, you're not supposed to brag about your presents?"

"Yes, because not everyone gets presents."

"Right, then. School is like a present."

Simon was quiet for a long time. "It's not as fun as a present."

"No," Oliver laughed. "It's not."

"If Tim doesn't go, why do I have to?"

"Because you need to learn all about caterpillars and pigs and puppies, and how to do sums and spell."

"And Tim doesn't?"

That was a question that had no end and no explanation that made Oliver happy. "That's a very good question, *hijo*."

The nickname recalled the marker bordered by flowers, stealing his breath. Today was Saturday. Thea was in Brandon with Jamey. Alone. Oliver wound the reins through his fingers. He was ten kinds of an arse for not going with her, though he wasn't certain she would have welcomed him.

They'd reached a crossroads. One way would take him toward home, and the other would take him toward open countryside and the inn.

The horses' snorted and shook their heads until he loosened his grip and made his turn.

"Why don't we go show Thea your new puppy?"

CHAPTER TWENTY-FOUR

"**D**ON'T CRY, POLLY."

Thea did her best not to snap or sigh, but the young maid just sobbed harder. "But Missus—"

"It was only a dish."

It had, in fact, been the fourth dish this week, which was a new record. The girl was doing no better with her shyness. If anything, she was more timid than when she'd arrived.

"Mr. Fletcher and I have had a talk—"

It was the wrong way to begin. Polly's shoulders shook as she put her head in her hands.

"Polly!" Thea's temper snapped. It had been a long day in a series of them, and she didn't need anyone else's disappointment weighing on her. "Do be quiet and listen. It does not pay to jump to conclusions and make yourself ill in the process."

Once the sobs had subsided to hiccups, and their girl had dried her tears, Thea began again.

"What would you think of helping Mrs. Snow in the kitchen?"

To her credit, Polly considered the idea carefully before nodding.

"Good. You'll help with the rooms and in the kitchen, but you won't be serving any longer."

"Shall I start straight away?" Polly wrung her hands as she looked toward the hallway. "I'm sure I could chop vegetables for stew or a nice meat pie."

After a week of party planning and a morning of memories, Thea had been looking forward to a few hours of quiet. "Come back at dusk. Supper preparations begin then."

Once alone, Thea sat for a moment listening to the creaking planks and the breeze outside the window. While she'd lived at the vicarage most of her life, The Goat was her home in the truest sense. She had chosen every item, cleaned and scoured them to a shine over and over again. Her office and kitchen had recorded her successes and failures. For better or worse, she'd made all her own choices and slept under her own roof.

And her last decisions had been made here. Jenny and John would continue to run the inn. Polly would be the extra girl in the kitchen and learn a trade from Jenny. Rachel would be promoted to head housekeeper. If John could persuade Jenny to marry him, perhaps Rachel and Hannah could live upstairs in Thea's room.

In her *old* room.

Because she had agreed to move to another home where everything was familiar—but not. Where everything was hers—but not.

Until they left for Canada. Then nothing would be familiar.

The feeling had been lurking all week, as she had been introduced to parts of Felton House she'd never seen and been left feeling like a field mouse hiding from the snow. It had hit hardest today in Brandon, as she'd sat next to Jamey and spoken to Reverend Allen all while realizing her days with her son were numbered.

She was leaving him to raise a boy she'd come to love, but who wasn't hers. She'd spend her life with a man who was as overwhelming and wild as the forest he loved. In a marriage that was beginning in grief and disappointment.

All those years ago, while she'd waited for him to return, she'd harbored a fear of the outcome. The same fear had kept her from sending her letter, from using her paychecks to buy passage.

It had always lurked there—the fear that Oliver wouldn't have been happy.

And that, in the long run, was all she could offer. Because she had reached too high.

"Enough of this," she scolded herself as she stood and went in search of her broom. Chores wouldn't do themselves, and work was the best thing to keep dreary thoughts at bay.

Thea was in the middle of sweeping stubborn crumbs and dust from a tight corner when the front door opened behind her and heavy steps crossed the threshold.

"Can I help…?"

The words died on her tongue. She didn't recognize the man's face, but his size and shape were unmistakable. He was the larger, more dangerous, than the unknown arsonists she'd barely escaped in the woods. And he was no less terrifying in the daylight. "We aren't open until supper."

"Well, well." He sauntered forward, his leer widening. "This is goin' t'be more satisfyin' than I thought."

The giant stopped in front of her, and Thea cursed her slow reaction. With nowhere to go, she tightened her grip on her broom and swung it in a quick arc. "Leave."

She might as well have hit him with a dinner roll. He grunted a curse before grabbing the weapon with surprising speed and alarming strength. "By God if you don't already sound like a duchess, expectin' me to bow and scrape and by your leave." His eyes were as hard as the vise-like grip on her elbow. "I'll leave when I get what I came for."

Summoning all her nerve and strength, Thea wrenched free and kept from rubbing her arm. He smelled of beer, dirt, and his morning breakfast. "What do you want?"

"Your sister owes me money, and you're to pay it."

Of course this tied back to Millie. "If she incurred the debt, then it's hers alone."

"That's not how she sees it, nor me now that I've met you." The man widened his stance and braced his hands on his hips so that his elbows served as a barricade. "Seems you've interfered with her finances, and I'm thinkin' you interfered with mine." His eyes narrowed. "Maybe you found our money, after all."

As though she had time to snoop through the woods looking for things that weren't hers. Thea shoved his elbow aside and swept past, relieved to escape and careful not to show it. "If I had found money in the forest, I'd have returned it to its *rightful* owner."

For all she knew, Millie had taken it and double-crossed everyone. Thea refrained from throwing suspicion to her sister. The sibling loyalty was one-sided, true, but there was also their mother to consider. She'd need one daughter nearby to care for her.

"We earned that money," the giant growled, dogging her steps toward the kitchen.

"Take the matter to the constable, then." The back door was in sight, and she heard a harness jangling in the barnyard. John was home. Thea quickened her pace. "You'll get no satisfaction from me."

Her hand was on the latch when she was yanked backward and sent careening against the opposite wall. Before she could clear her head and race for the front door, the scoundrel had her pinned, pressing against her back. One hand grasped her skirts, baring her ankles and then her knees.

"There's more than one way to satisfy me, yer Ladyship."

His breath was as hot as it was rank, and grit coated Thea's skin. She'd swear she could taste it. Calling on years of fending off drunkards, she drove her heel into the top of his foot and reveled in his howl. "Get off me!"

"Uppity bitch." His fingers twisted in her hair, and the sting doubled when hairpins bit into her scalp. His other hand gripped her skirt and pulled. The resulting rip echoed in Thea's brain. "Pretend I'm a marquis if you'd like."

She'd felt like screeching for two days, and Thea finally gave in. Rage tinged with fear scalded her throat and emptied her lungs. She pressed her hands flat against the wall and pushed backward with all the strength and speed she had left, snapping her chin up at the last moment. Perhaps she'd break his hold. Maybe his nose.

Instead, she fell backward into air that was vacant but for a feral roar.

Free, flailing, Thea grasped the bench and tightened her hold until the edge bit into her fingers. As her breathing steadied and her pulse settled, a crashing chair fanned her indignation to life. As grateful as she was for a rescue, no one had the right to ruin her home.

"*Mierda.*"

The muffled curse made her spin to face the melee just in time to see Oliver fall to one knee. Blood oozed from his lip, and there was a bruise under one eye. The color was worsened by the angry flush under his dark skin.

She pushed herself straight, intent on confronting her attacker.

"Stay out of the bloody way," Oliver snarled as he barreled across the room much like a bull in a field. Catching the larger man around the middle, he propelled the villain through the open door and into the dusty barnyard.

Thea kicked free of her ruined skirt and followed them. The two men were rolling in a pile like wild dogs, arms and legs tangled until she wasn't sure which belonged to whom.

Simon was on the edge of the brawl, barely holding onto a yapping puppy almost his size. Beyond him, a squealing pig demanded to be fed or released. And all her animals were agreeing with him.

Thea ran to Simon, taking the boy in one arm and the dog in the other. "Let's go in the barn, dearest."

The child swung one arm as Oliver writhed free and sprung to his feet. "It's just a row. *Oncle* Richard says they're good for you." Simon continued to swing, coaching his father. "Hit 'im in the basket, Papa."

Oliver landed a solid punch to his opponent's stomach, doubling the man over. The crowd of John's boys, who had gathered at the stable entrance, cheered in response.

The dog, who was as excited as the boy, pulled the other direction and brought Thea to her knees. Sure either or both would rush into the fray, she was left with no option but to kneel beside them and watch.

Blows rained in a torrent of swings, some connecting, some missing as one opponent or the other ducked or danced away. Thea felt every blow as though it was aimed at her.

The Duke of Rushford was brawling in a barnyard like a common thug to save her honor.

Just like his mother had promised.

Riveted to the fight as she was, Thea didn't realize John and Jenny had returned until Jenny rushed to her side and John strode past them, intent on interceding.

Thea handed the dog to Jenny before running after him. "Don't. You'll get hurt. Let him finish it."

Because Oliver always finished what he started, and this was no different. He now had the upper hand. His opponent stumbled backward and collapsed to his knees, and Oliver's next two blows went unanswered.

The man's hands dropped, and Oliver continued to hit him. Even Simon fell silent, as though the boy understood that a dreadful line was about to be crossed.

"Oliver!" Thea commanded. "Stop!"

He shook his head like an angry animal, and for the first time in her life, she was worried for his safety. "Rushford!"

He paused, but kept his eyes on his prey. His shoulders heaved, and he swayed on his feet.

"I'm unhurt, Ol." Thea stepped into the dusty arena and rushed her words, hoping to finish her appeal before either man regrouped. "Truly, I am. And so is Simon, though it was all I could do to keep him from helping you."

As she had hoped, the mention of his son brought Oliver up

short. He gave a quick nod and stepped backward, wobbly though it was.

John joined them, carrying a length of heavy rope. He wasted no time binding the intruder's hands behind him. And he was none too gentle, given the man's grunts and swears.

Oliver ducked his chin. "Where the hell were you? Why was she alone?"

"Jenny and I—"

"Gather your things and get off the property, both of you. You're lucky—"

"Hold your tongue." Thea put herself between Oliver and John. "You may be lord of your manor, but you aren't the lord of mine."

"Yet," he grated.

"Never," Thea snapped. "This is *my* business, not yours. I built it without you, and I run it without your leave."

Oliver wiped his hand across his split lip, melding the blood from his face with the blood and dirt on his knuckles. His shirt was torn and filthy. He was ferocious in a way she'd never seen, and she was aware of him like she'd always been. The breeze lifted her hair and filtered through her skirt, reminding her she was in her petticoat.

Oliver raised his eyebrows, giving an extra sarcasm to his slight bow as he swung his hand toward the other two men.

Thea drew her spine taut. "John, put this ruffian in a stall and set a guard. Then please send someone for the sheriff and be sure to tell him his lordship is here so we have a magister on the premises."

"Oy," the tied man said. "He can't be fair."

"You should've considered that before you hit him," Thea said. She turned to Jenny. "Please bring Simon into the kitchen. We have biscuits from yesterday's tea."

Confident her requests would be fulfilled, Thea went into the house, stopping just long enough to retrieve her skirt before she climbed the stairs. She kept her head lifted and back straight, like she was leaving church in her shawl and hat rather than seeking refuge while exposing her underthings.

The façade crumbled the moment she closed her bedroom door and faced her mirror. Her braids drooped to her shoulders in places and frayed in others, and the lace hem of her petticoat was black with grime.

But worse were the handprints on her clothes. In intimate places. Too large to be hers.

Six years' worth of memories and words slid over her skin—her mother, the duchess, random presumptive men passing through Brandon, and those from today—mixing with the dirt and smell to worsen the mess until it crawled everywhere.

Choking back a sob, Thea scratched her way free of her clothes and dumped water into the basin, swearing as it splashed over the dressing table and onto the floor. She scrubbed with cold water, widening the puddles, and didn't stop until she was shivering and her skin was pink all over and splotchy red in places.

It wasn't just the unwanted touches of another man. It was the frustration that she hadn't been able to stop him on her own. And once word spread about Jamey, or worse, if she actually was increasing, it could be the first of many such scenes.

If not for Oliver.

No matter what she'd been able to accomplish, she was losing control of her life.

When her door opened without warning, Thea planted her feet in place and rolled her lips together. She would not scurry and cower like a mouse. Not in her home. Not anywhere.

Not any longer.

Oliver entered her bedroom, less dusty but no less beaten and torn, and her skin heated despite the icy bath.

"Do you always enter a lady's chamber without knocking?"

He blinked slowly. "No, but—"

"I am a lady, and I'll thank you for the courtesy." Thea pointed at the door. "I'll be—"

"Don't order me about like a field hand, *my lady*. I'll remind you that we're to be married and—"

"And we aren't married yet."

His smirk would have been charming if he hadn't rolled his eyes. "At least you're finally giving in on that point."

Thea bit her tongue. She wasn't nearly close to surrendering.

Oliver closed the door.

"What are you doing?" They shouldn't be alone, given everything that had happened downstairs, not to mention her state of undress. "Leave that open."

"No. I'd prefer no one hear you give me another dressing down when all I wanted to do was see after your condition." He thrust her robe at her. "Put this on if you're worried."

Thea pushed her arms through the robe and yanked it to her shoulders, but she fumbled the knot—twice. She looked down at her trembling fingers, half wondering if they belonged to someone else.

And then she was surrounded by warmth, strength, and the welcome smell of cinnamon and citrus.

"Ye gods, I'm an arse," Oliver murmured as he slipped his hands under her robe and pulled her closer. "You're freezing, *mi Pepinilla*."

"I couldn't wait for the water to heat," she said into his shoulder as she gave way to shivering. Maybe he would think it was due to her bath.

"I'm glad it's just that," he murmured. She could hear his smile. "I wouldn't want both of us terrified at once." Thea mimicked his position, sliding her hands to his back. His big muscles shook under her fingers, much like a horse after a race. "Shhh, *Mono*."

They stood like that until he swayed against her and she heard him gasp. "Do you think we could sit?" she asked. "There's a chair behind you and to the left."

He sank into it with a groan that the lumpy upholstery didn't deserve. When she would have left him, kept her perched on his thigh.

"I didn't come up here so you could nurse me." Thea lightly touched the bruised knot near his eye and winced when he did. "You can't fight the whole world, Ol." She moved her fingers to his lips to stop his argument. "But I am glad you were here. How did you happen by?"

He picked up her hairbrush. "We were taking Pinky home and—"

"Pinky?"

He might have blushed. "The pig. Turn 'round and let me help with your hair. It's a fright."

"Simon's named him?" She giggled as she obeyed. "You'll never have bacon."

"Not until we reach Quebec." He sighed as he undid her braids. "And Simon wanted to introduce you to his giant puppy, that he begged embarrassingly hard to get—that isn't true, the part about him. I realized it was Saturday and that I'd left you alone. I shouldn't have."

His touch was like alchemy. Bit by bit, he was erasing the filthy film that clung to her. Thea gave into it, tilting her head back so he could reach her crown. "You can't be with me all the time."

"Not now, though we'll speak about that." He teased a knot free with patience and care, nothing like the barnyard brawler from earlier. "This morning. To Brandon."

"Oh." Tears pricked her eyelids. She'd always imagined his return, introducing him to their son. It hadn't been anything like this. Nothing in her life was how she'd imagined it. "Would you like to go next time?"

"I would." He sectioned her unknotted hair. "Thank you."

This close, she could feel him inhale as well as hear it.

"Maybe we should marry earlier, before the party. Or you could move to the manor now. Since I don't live there—"

She wasn't living with the duchess. All the vagabonds in the world couldn't make her. "I'm fine here, Oliver."

He dropped the brush on the table and spun her to face him. "Do you have any idea what it did to me when I heard you scream? How did he get in here?"

"Through a door, I'd imagine."

"Don't be flip, Thee. If I'd been a minute later…"

She filled in all the lines he left blank. "He didn't want that, not really." She said it for herself as well as him. "He wanted money, and I'd refused to pay him. If you'd been later, I would have done it and he'd have gone." Or she'd have run a filet knife through his ribs.

"Money?" He narrowed his eyes. "He stopped by at random to rob you?"

The question showed her how much he didn't yet know, how much she'd forgotten to tell him. And, though she hated to be a source for yet more bad news, she needed to do so. "He burned your mill, Oliver. He's the one from the woods that night."

He took it much better than she'd expected. "And?"

"When he went back the next morning to find the money, it was gone. And Millie had something to do with it. He says she owes him. She told him to come to me for it."

"And you told him to stick it up his arse, I'm sure." His rueful chuckle shook the chair. "I have the money. I went through the woods on my way home that morning and found it. I had a feeling it belonged to me in the first place."

The sadness in his eyes broke Thea's heart. "He can tie them to it, Ol."

No more threats, no more blackmail or interference. They'd be free to do whatever they wanted. They could postpone the wedding and her courses would start. He could go back to Canada knowing she'd be safe.

And she'd be happier for doing the right thing. Really, she would.

"And I'd be the duke who sent both his mother and sister-in-law to prison days before his wedding." The sadness remained as he stroked his thumb over her cheek. "We can't fight everyone, Thee."

So her attacker would be free? Panic curled around her spine as she inched away. "He can't—"

"He won't go free." Oliver's eyes finally hardened. "He'll go to jail for what he did to you."

"But finished arson is so much worse than attempted r-rape."

He stood and brought her to her feet. "That is the most foolish thing you've said today, and there have been a few already. Pin your hair. I'm useless at that."

As Thea secured her braids, she became aware of the silent house. "Is everyone outside?"

"They're in the kitchen." He caught his bottom lip between his teeth, but it did little to hide his smile. "But I'm not sure who they're more frightened of, you or me."

Thea had to stop and recall what she'd said, and what she must have looked like while saying it. She covered her face with her hands. "Oh dear."

"We made a pair, I'm sure. Me covered and blood and dirt, and you so angry your freckles were sparking." He put his arms around her waist. "I haven't seen you that upset since the first time I plaited your hair."

"You braided me to a chair." She pushed his shoulder and, despite everything that had happened, enjoyed the solid feel of him.

"I had to do something to get a head start." He looked down his nose at her, his lips twisted in a wry smile and his eyes a mix of gold and green. "You always got the best of me."

It wasn't something Thea was proud of. For six years, she'd managed to keep a rein on her temper and her impulses. She liked to believe that everyone had forgotten, that she'd overcome them. It was just as false as everything else.

"Why do you insist on vexing me?"

"Because you're magnificent when vexed."

The words teased her lips before he kissed her. Firm mouth,

hot tongue—his heartbeat thudded against her palm, his knee brushed her skirt, and she was lost in a bubble where no one existed but them.

He caught her bottom lip between his teeth, pulling it slightly, reminding her how his mouth had felt on other parts of her body. The parts now hot and heavy, aching for him to do it again.

But Oliver was toying with her, teasing and tickling her, tempting her to play and building a more dangerous feeling than heat and want. Recalling what he'd always made her feel.

Thea nipped his bottom lip and reveled in his gasp. His skin, slightly chapped and gritty, tasted like fresh water, sweat, and earth, and a coppery hint of blood teased her tongue. Rather than repelling her, it added a wild flavor to an already reckless kiss.

Oliver gave a ragged groan and hauled her closer, his fingers flexing low on her hips as he rested his hard body against hers.

Heat flared from her center, outward, tightening her skin until her nerves sang and heightening her senses until she could feel his breath syncing with hers. Want became need. Need grew into craving. It was like smith's dust to a lodestone. She couldn't release him, wasn't able to move.

He cupped her breast through the thin fabric of her chemise and stroked his thumb over the sensitive peak. She melted into him with a sigh. She didn't want anything but this.

Him.

Oliver nibbled her ear, and his warm exhale tickled her skin as he pressed his thigh between her legs.

Thea's heart banged against her ribs, keeping time with her thoughts. *Yes. Yes. Yes.*

"Papa?" Simon called out as he rapped on the door. "Is Thea coming home with us?"

Home. What a spellbinding word.

The latch rattled, and the bubble broke as Oliver used one hand to push the door closed.

"What are you doing?" Simon asked.

"I'm kissing Thea." Oliver's lips were still wet, and his skin was flushed. "Give us a moment and I'll ask."

One look into his heavy-lidded gaze, and Thea wanted more than a moment. Wanted it so badly that her fingers shook as she tied her robe. "Is that wise to say?"

"He should get used to it." Oliver winked. "As should you. Go finish dressing."

Once behind the screen, Thea opened her wardrobe and paused in mid-reach for her second-best work dress. Instead, she chose a newer one she'd made for the village picnic last summer. Though it was plain and simple, the delicate print matched her improving mood. Besides, Oliver had never seen it.

"What are you supposed to ask me?" Making conversation kept her from thinking of him in her room sharing something this intimate.

"We're releasing Spot the Smaller into the wild today, and Simon—we—would like you to be there."

Thea sat on her dressing stool to do up her boots. She should stay well clear of him, of both of them, until she had her bearings. "Brownies won't do my chores, Ol."

The words belied the noise floating through the floorboards. Downstairs, Jenny was directing Polly on dinner preparations, and John had his boys bustling about to clear the damage from earlier. The claim also betrayed her reflection as she draped a delicate blue shawl over her shoulders. She'd never been less prepared for work.

"What are brownies?" Simon asked, far too clearly to be on the other side of the door.

Thea came around the screen to find the little boy on his father's knee and the father looking both sheepish and indulgent. "If I'd left him in the hallway, he would have told everyone what we were doing."

"And with both of you to charm me, I have little chance of refusing."

Thea couldn't help but think she'd need to get used to this as well. She also couldn't be bothered to care, especially not when

Oliver smiled at her and a fizzy feeling bubbled under her ribs.

Hope.

She smoothed her palm down the front of her skirt, and her traitorous heart gave a leap. What if…?

"Papa, what are brownies?"

"The house elves who fold your socks," Oliver teased.

"Are they brown?" Simon asked her. It was an irresistible invitation to play.

"Yes," Thea said as she knelt beside him. "And if you lick them, they taste like chocolate."

"You're silly." Despite his grin, his next question was very serious. "You are coming, aren't you? Papa wants to put Spot in the hedges, and they have thorns."

"I thought it a very safe place to live," Oliver said. "And he would be close to the door so you could see him on your way to and from school."

The worm would be barred from predators or an untimely end, but he'd be in a bitter and harsh environment.

Simon kept his eyes on her and chewed his bottom lip. Waiting for her answer.

So like his father.

So like her Jamey.

"Of course, Simon. Thank you for inviting me."

The child threw his arms around her in a hard hug that cracked more than her neck. Thea blinked back tears as she let him pull her forward toward the door.

The second it opened, the horse of a puppy bounded through, intent on joining the party.

Oliver wrestled to keep the dog at a safe distance. "Take this *demonio perro* outside before he knocks Thea down."

"C'mon, Brownie. Let's go home."

Boy and dog clattered down the stairs, and Thea grasped her skirts to keep from pulling the child back, telling him to be careful. The impulse worsened when a rough, tight cough drifted in his wake.

"You should stop at Murphy's and get—"

"Horehound. I know." Oliver tucked her hand into his elbow and covered her fingers with his. "It's just a cough, Thee."

Of course he knew. He was a good father who had carried his son into a forest full of wild animals and savages and brought him out the other side. They'd crossed an ocean together. She hadn't even gotten Jamey out of the village.

Thea pushed the thought aside, determined not to ruin a day he was already trying to salvage. She'd grieved once already. Maybe once was enough.

"At least let me get some arnica for your eye."

CHAPTER TWENTY-FIVE

THEA OPENED THE front door at Felton House and stepped inside. Her knuckles ached with the effort to keep from knocking, and her feet itched with the urge to run, to flee around the house to the safety of the kitchen entrance.

For the past week, everyone had scolded her for those impulses. Duchesses do not enter at the back of the house. Duchesses do not knock to enter their own homes.

She removed her hat and cloak and handed them to Lionel, who always insisted on greeting her himself. "Good morning, my lady."

Not Mrs. Smith, not even Miss Fowler. Thea resisted the urge to curtsey, reminding herself that he was no different than Martin at Tavie's house.

However, Lionel wasn't Martin and this wasn't Tavie's home. Lionel worked for the Rushford family, and Felton House had never been as warm and welcoming as Tavie's London townhome.

During childhood, Thea had hidden in this hallway, listening to arguments between Oliver and his mother, careful to stay in the background as they'd fought about her. They had all ended the same, and Oliver had often paid the price for his stubborn defense.

Over the past few weeks, with the encouragement of Lionel

and Hazel, and faced with Oliver's unyielding yet charming will, Thea was beginning to hope things would finally change.

That feeling doubled with the beginning of party preparations. Oaken chests full of silver sat next to folded linens on newly placed tables. In a few hours, the home would be full of guests for a party where they would announce her engagement.

Despite everything, happiness bubbled deep in Thea's heart.

As if conjured, the duchess appeared at the entrance to the drawing room, all in black like the Angel of Death itself.

"Mrs. Smith. Please come see me."

As Thea approached, the lady straightened her spine and looked down her nose. That look was the only thing Oliver had inherited from her.

"Your Grace." Thea limited her curtsey to a quick bob.

She followed her future mother-in-law into the room and took the chair indicated.

The years faded. She was back here facing the duchess in ill-fitting clothes and a guilty conscience, surrendering a letter for Oliver and asking for help. The words had been bitter on her tongue, but she'd had no other choice.

Of course I'll send it. But Thea, didn't Oliver tell you he was marrying? We found a lovely young girl, well-educated, of a good family. Their property in Quebec lies next to ours.

Thea was no longer that young girl. She smoothed her skirts before mimicking the woman's haughty posture. She could buy and sell this woman. She, in fact, had.

She was careful to keep eye contact, much like one did with a wild animal. "How can I—"

"You will end this farce of an engagement."

Well, that was to the point. Perhaps Oliver had inherited her forthrightness as well. "You underestimate your son's determination, Your Grace."

"I have never been deceived about my son's stubbornness, just as you have never been foolish about its consequences."

Thea pulled the reins on her tongue and wrapped her trembling fingers tighter. Admitting she agreed would be tantamount to betrayal in Oliver's eyes. However, antagonizing this woman benefitted no one. Aunt Tavie had taught her she learned more by listening.

"Dukes do not marry innkeepers," the duchess continued. "Just as second sons don't marry every village girl who lifts her skirts."

Thea sucked in a breath, chilled to the bone, much like jumping in the nearby woodland spring as a child. "He has other opinions."

"I will ruin him," the duchess said, her smile cold. "All I have to do is ruin *you*. How long do you think you'd have your position if your past was known? If the gossips discovered all the things you've done?"

Trembling in outrage, Thea anchored her spine to the back of the chair until it bit into her shoulder blades. The duchess would be seen as a mother protecting her son. Nothing would happen to Oliver, of course. Young men did foolish things. But her? The Goat would become little more than a brothel. The maids would be preyed upon. Their faces flitted through her brain, followed quickly by every wayward girl who'd passed through her kitchen on their way to better lives.

The duchess's eyes gleamed. "By the time I'm finished, you'll be his Doxy Duchess and he'll be the Disillusioned Duke. He'll lose any influence he has in this village or at lords to make the *change* he craves. He'll be forced into exile in Canada, a disgrace rather than the champion of his family he envisions. And now that travel is so much easier, as my husband constantly reminded me, that reputation will follow you both to Canada. He will lose everything. Tell me, *Mrs. Smith*, what would a parent suffer for the sake of their child?"

"That is quite enough." Thea bit out the words. "You have no right to speak of parents and children. Not to me." She drew in a deep breath. "Your son is worth twice, or more, of you. You discount his influence and his ethic at your peril, just as you discount mine. While I have no doubt of your capacity for vile rumor, I also doubt you would welcome the loss of influence and status that would come from your scheme."

Behind her desk, the duchess shrank back. Thea paused, recognizing for the first time how much this woman differed from the duchess-past, the one who had denied her everything. This small, frail woman had literally put herself in a corner and protected herself with her most treasured items. She'd picked a fight on her own territory.

This woman was frightened. Of all the moods in the world, Thea understood frightened best. She also knew cornered animals were the most dangerous. Showing fear, submitting to her plans, would mean certain death. Not just for Thea, but for Oliver and for Simon. She would have gained nothing in the past six years.

Thea stood. "Change is coming, *Your Grace.* Get accustomed to it."

She swept from the drawing room on shaking legs and closed the door behind her, careful not to slam it. Ladies never slammed doors.

To her left was the front entrance. Her hat and cloak sat waiting where Lionel had hung them.

She'd run from this house, given up, one too many times. She might have doubts about marrying Oliver, but she'd be damned if she'd let anyone tell her she *couldn't.*

Thea made a right toward the kitchen.

THE HOUSE WAS a hive of activity. Maids scurried across the foyer, carrying flowers hither and yon, positioning and then repositioning the bouquets under Lionel's watchful eye. Trays were heaped with sweets, and voids in the pattern indicated the pending arrival of baked goods. Empty glasses were stacked in intricate displays next to chilling bottles of champagne. Wine waited to be uncorked, and whiskey glistened gold in squat crystal decanters.

Everyday items sat beside family heirlooms and finery, working to fulfill ducal expectations while reveling in the ordinary things Oliver found comforting.

He stood on the threshold doing just that—enjoying a hall that didn't reek of dust and death. Every surface sparkled so that the chandelier cast a blizzard of rainbows on the walls.

For a moment, it reminded him of home. It was far grander than the house in Quebec, true, but he could see echoes in the architecture and decorations. The patterned rug he'd chosen for the stairs, the shape of the turned balusters, the curve of the ceiling—even the direction of the late afternoon sun.

Unlike Quebec, however, the manor was full of people. Some he recognized, some he loved—everyone he was responsible for. The weight settled on his shoulders, but it wasn't the burden it had been a month ago.

He'd sold his first pallet of native lumber today, and he'd walked home through a carefully thinned section of forest. The dappled sunshine hinted that the thinner, younger trees would mature properly and ensure years of profit. Simon—maybe even his children—would benefit from this summer.

"Thank God you're home, lad." Lionel strode the length of the hallway, deftly dodging decorations and servants. As he neared, his sweaty face broke into a broad smile. "I thought I might have to come down there and drag you back," he whispered.

"Not today." Oliver clapped him on the shoulder. "Did you hire more servants?"

"Just for the night. Lord Chitester's household could spare a few since the family will be here this evening. The duchess-to-be also had suggestions about others who would be useful."

Duchess-to-be. Not Miss Fowler and certainly not Mrs. Smith. Lionel had taken to calling Thea by her future title almost immediately, at least when no one else was near. As with every other time. Oliver caught a flicker of a smile.

"You like her then, *Tío*?"

"I've always liked her for you, Oliver." Lionel blotted his forehead with his handkerchief. "I believe we all have."

"Not everyone." Oliver raked his fingers through his hair, restoring some order to the mess caused by work and wind. "Is Mother upstairs?"

It was a rhetorical question. His mother was fighting her demotion to dowager by remaining in her room when Thea was in the house. As though that was a punishment.

"Yes. I believe she looked in on Simon before she began dressing for the party. The child's stewing about not being allowed down for the celebration."

He hadn't been keen on staying home from school either, but Thea had insisted because his cough was worse. Though Oliver thought she was being overly cautious, he'd agreed to keep her from worrying. Once she grew accustomed to the rough-and-tumble boy, she'd relax.

Once Simon got used to her being his…permanent, he'd sulk less about her care.

Once Mother…Oliver drew in a deep breath and strode toward the stairs, dodging tables and servants as he went. His mother would never get used to anything if he stayed down here and let her have her own way.

Outside her door, he paused long enough to straighten his clothes before knocking. Tightening his fist and strengthening his forearm, he made sure it sounded like a commanding rap rather than a childish scratch.

"You may enter."

She'd answered the same way for as long as he could remember, regardless of the time of day or the person knocking. Oliver briefly wondered if she'd greeted his father in the same fashion.

He entered the room and found her at her dressing table. Wearing black. Alice was nearby, as always. Once she saw him, she scurried for the door.

"Don't give me that look," his mother's reflection said to him.

"I am in mourning, and I'll remain there until I'm ready not to be."

It was all there in the determined line of her mouth and the precise way she placed her brush. A truce, even for tonight, was out of the question.

"Can you at least try to be happy for me, Mother?"

She faced him. "Happy that you've learned nothing of self-preservation in the past six years? That you're marrying beneath you because you let that woman trap you?" Her gaze simmered. "That you're covered in dirt and dust because you insist on turning your back on your family and your duty?"

"Tell me, Mother." Oliver moved forward, slightly vindicated when she shrank back in her chair. "Is it my *duty* to end up a wastrel like Garrett?"

"At least Garrett knew better than to sleep with servants."

"Because he'd rather sleep with other men's wives." He was a bastard for flinging that at her, but he was tired of keeping the peace.

"Who knew better than to get pregnant."

"Did they?" Oliver asked. "God, I wish just once one of them would've been stupid enough to give him a child. I'd be relieved of this mess, and of you. If it wasn't for my promise to Father—"

"What could he have possibly asked of you?"

"He practically begged me to come help right our finances and mend fences with my *family*. I must have been crazy to think either was possible."

"You have always been an ungrateful, spoiled child."

"Spoiled? I was second, as you constantly reminded me. Anything I had, would ever have, would have been at Garrett's whim. Even as a teenager, I realized there would be damned little left."

"So you ran and left that uppity wench and her whelp for me to deal with."

Oliver shoved his hand in his pocket and grasped Julia's rosary so tightly the faceted cross dug into his fingers. He would not lose control.

"I went to make a life where no one cared about lords, earls, or dukes. As for leaving Thea to your *care*, I never dreamt she'd come to you. She should have run in the other direction as fast as possible."

"Which is what you both intend to do now. You'll take my grandson and go back to Canada."

"I will take my family home."

"After you've played house in the dower cottage."

His lips twisted. "Oh no. I'm the duke and Thea is my duchess." He took immense pleasure at her pale complexion. "We'll be living here."

"I will not live under—"

"No, you won't. I'll not subject Thea to your poison any longer. You'll move to the cottage."

"No. The Bath house—"

"Sold two days ago."

"London, then."

"There are no servants in London, and you can't take any from here. Thea and I can't spare them."

Despite her hard expression, Oliver could see the tears building. He didn't know if they were sincere, perhaps borne of frustration or anger rather than sadness, or a ploy. For the first time in his life, he didn't care.

"The Bath house sold for enough to subsidize an extended trip abroad, if you'd like to go." He braced his hands on her chair and loomed over her. "As long as you behave yourself this evening."

After a moment, she jerked her chin in agreement. Resentment pooled in her eyes.

"If you say one unkind word, spread one whisper of gossip, I will not only banish you, I will tell everyone in attendance what you did to Jamey."

"I did nothing to that child. That girl was unfit to raise—"

"You knew where they were, what they were going through. You knew where he was *buried*." Oliver tightened his hold on the chair until the wood creaked in protest. "You let my son die just to spite his mother. After that *ondit* travels through the county, you'll be banished regardless."

He straightened and turned toward the door. "I don't care what you wear, Mother, and you can retire early if you'd like. But you'll be downstairs to welcome our guests, and you'll have a smile on your face for as long as you're there."

Oliver closed the door, careful not to slam it though his fingers flexed on the handle. He strode down the hallway, stopping briefly to look down at the party preparation. From this height, all the movement and color made him dizzy. He took in several deep, steadying breaths and backed away, continuing to Simon's room.

The boy was in bed, propped against a mountain of pillows. Brownie bounded to his feet with a yip, instantly alert. His wagging tail was less guard dog and more playmate. That was proven as he leapt onto the bed and snuffled along the covers to burrow under Simon's hand, licking and contorting himself until the boy giggled.

The laughter ended in a phlegmy cough.

Oliver made his way to them, careful to avoid the sticks, stones, and toys piled in the floor. The air smelled like the forest, which he attributed to the kettle placed over a low fire opposite the bed. Despite the heat, Simon was tucked under a coverlet, a blanket, and a knitted throw.

Oliver tousled his son's hair. It felt overly warm. "Have you been inside all day?"

Simon shook his head. "Thea and I went out this morning to get flowers for the party, and she helped me get things to build with." He sniffled and wiped his hand under his nose. "Did you see my stable?"

Sure enough, the pile of materials in the floor were the rock walls and stick roof of a small shelter, and the toy horse outside it, in a stick-built paddock, made clear its purpose. "What are the extra stones?"

"Brownie kept knocking it over, but Thea taught him a trick." Simon coughed again and then pointed his finger at the dog. "Brownie? Sit."

The puppy plopped to the coverlet, his tongue lolling out in a doggy grin.

"Good boy." Simon ruffled the dog's ears. "Thea said I have to make a fuss when he does something right."

"She's very wise about these things," Oliver said, happy to see the two of them bonding. He'd wanted to help train Brownie, but workdays had been long lately. "About the party—"

"Can I come?" Simon's question cracked at the end. "I don't feel that bad."

His glassy eyes reflected the windows, and his cheeks were pinker than normal. Oliver wasn't certain it was all due to the blankets. "I agree with Thea. You should stay up here with Brownie. Maybe Hazel could bring you to the landing to see everyone arrive."

"I don't want to miss the sweets," the boy's bottom lip trembled. "Thea said she'd invented one just for me. I wanted to tell everyone about how I 'spired her with my peppermint milk."

The tearful plea convinced Oliver the boy was indeed sick. He whined more when he was ill. "I'll bring you a plate piled high with sweets for you to enjoy all by yourself, and you can tell everyone your story at the next party."

Simon straightened his posture, no longer leaning against his pillows, as if to convince his father of his health. "But you promised—"

"I said you could go if you weren't ill. But you are, so my promise doesn't count."

A tear slid down the boy's nose, threatening Oliver's resolve. Simon would love the party, and he would make the whole evening that much more enjoyable. The three of them could be a proper family.

"What if I told you a secret so that you knew it before everyone else?"

Simon, still mulish, glanced sideways, and Oliver sensed a victory. Curiosity always bested a tantrum.

He leaned to the side so that his head was almost touching Simon's and dropped his voice to a conspiratorial whisper. "Thea is coming to live with us."

Sure enough, the tantrum ebbed. "Like *Oncle* Richard?"

Oliver coughed to cover his laugh. "Not exactly. She'll have the room next to mine."

The one that had been Julia's, and then Simon's nursery, and now sat empty save for dust.

"I have the room next to you. Where will I sleep?"

Oliver had to think about the layout of the Quebec house, his frown deepening as he had to think harder than when he'd first returned. "You have the room next to Uncle Richard, Simon." The boy had insisted on moving for his third birthday.

"At his house, but not at our house."

Our house. Oliver stared at the wall that separated his room from his son's.

His stomach tilted. "Simon, we aren't staying here. We are going *home*. To Canada. Thea is coming with us to live in Quebec."

"And Brownie, too?"

The dog wiggled on the bed, happy to be considered for the trip.

A dog wouldn't be bad to travel with, would it? "Of course Brownie, too."

"And Spot, and Pinkie, and Spot the Smaller?"

There was no way he could travel with a wife, a son, a dog, a pony, a pig, and a butterfly. "They have to stay here."

"But they'll be lonely," Simon whimpered.

"They won't. They'll have plenty of hay and sunshine while they wait for you to come visit."

"They'll think I don't love them. They'll forget me."

He hadn't even wanted the damned pony, the pig was supposed to be bacon already, and the butterfly would be dead by fall. "Fred and Emmett won't let them think that."

The boy's eyes widened. "Fred and Emmett aren't coming?"

"This is their home, Si." He wouldn't think about the chances of never seeing the older servants again or about how homesick he'd been for them during his first few months away.

"But who'll cook for them?"

"Hazel will." Something told Oliver he'd have to duel Fred to get Hazel away from the manor, as though the cook would leave in the first place.

"Hazel's not coming either?" Simon's whimper grew to a wail.

"We've never had a Hazel, nor a Thea for that matter, and we didn't starve."

Simon shook his head. "I don't want to go. Reverend Carson says we get to have a picnic after exams. We're going to play cricket."

Oliver swiped his hand down his face. He didn't want Simon playing cricket and thinking cooks were necessary for survival. "I can teach to you play cricket. In Quebec."

"Two people aren't a team. I want to stay with my friends."

"No, Simon."

"What about our house, and our garden?"

And Lita's memories, and his mill. Who would protect his investment—and Thea's—once he was across an ocean? Would his mother stay away long enough for the enterprise to have a fair chance? Would she come back simply to smash everything to bits? Ruin his promises again?

Oliver rose from the bed and tugged his shirt collar open, intent on drawing a deep breath.

"What about our brownies and our fairy? Thea said the house needs—"

He spun on the boy. "Brownies and fairies aren't real, Simon."

The child's face crumpled. "You said…"

Oliver's heart shrank by two sizes. He'd promised so many

things to Simon, even if he'd never said a word. Now he'd broken the most basic one. He'd ripped the boy's imagination away. "Si…"

"Go away." Simon had buried his face in Brownie's neck, and his sobs were part cry and part cough. "We don't like you."

Even the puppy seemed to judge him poorly.

Oliver left the room, trying to bolster his courage. Fathers had to do unpopular things all the time. This wasn't the first time he'd had to be firm with Simon, and it wouldn't the last. The storm would pass.

Still, when he heard the sounds of demolition from Simon's room—the skitter of rocks across the floor—he hung his head in shame.

He stopped at Thea's door and knocked, knowing she could help him sort things with Simon. He'd selected this room as hers for the evening. The windows overlooked the wildest parts of the forest and the worn hills beyond.

When she didn't answer, he opened the door. "Thee?"

The room was empty except for her dress spread flat on the bed. Dark green and gold, it looked less like a betrothal celebration and more like a fancy corpse.

CHAPTER TWENTY-SIX

OLIVER LEFT THE room and recalled years of practice as he descended the stairs double-time. "Lionel? Where's Thea?"

The butler's eyes widened at the use of the duchess-to-be's Christian name, but Oliver refused to cow to a formality that let everyone cling to a lie. They called him *lad* for God's sake. They could get over *Thea*.

"The last I knew, she was in the kitchen with Hazel making—"

Oliver rounded the corner and went through the dining room, barely noticing the tables set up for cards as he barreled into the kitchen.

Warmth and spices assailed his senses. Hazel was at the fire, stirring a large kettle of what he guessed was cider. A small cadre of extra staff was here as well, frosting and sugaring items, slicing fruit, or filling trays.

Thea was in front of the oven. In an apron.

"What in bloody hell are you doing?"

She spun, her hand at the base of her throat and her wispy curls dancing around her heat-pink face. It reminded him of all those years ago, in Lita's kitchen, when she'd been a vicar's daughter deemed unsuitable even for a second son.

"Go upstairs," he commanded. "You don't belong in here."

"Why?" Her gaze snapped.

Oliver ground his molars together. Was it something about

this house that made everyone in it contrary? "You can't entertain in an apron. Go upstairs and change."

"You first." Her flushed cheeks made her freckles brighter.

"What?"

"If I don't belong in here, neither do you." She put her fists on her hips. "And you can't meet guests in your work clothes."

"Don't be ridiculous. This is completely different."

She was smart enough to realize she'd be judged by everyone in attendance. Those with titles would determine whether she was worthy to join their ranks. Those who knew her would look to see if she was happy in her new role.

"How?" she demanded.

In turn, everything would be a reflection on him. On his choices. On whether he deserved her. Given that, he had little patience to argue with yet another fractious member of his household.

"Because I'm a—" *Duke.* "You're an—" *Outsider.* "This is—" *My house.*

With every turn in the argument, Oliver realized he'd talked himself into a corner. He was losing the fight without Thea saying a word.

Unlike their childhood, there was no gleam of triumph in her eyes, no witty smirk. All he saw was a quiet, sad, acknowledgement. An acceptance that left him cold.

"At last," she whispered.

"That's unfair, Thee."

One corner of her mouth hitched slightly. "We can agree on that, at least."

They could agree on much more than that if she'd let them. "It doesn't matter. Nothing matters except what's between us."

She tilted her head to the side. "And what if nothing's between us? What if I'm not increasing? How long will it take—"

"That isn't the point."

"If it isn't, then why are we going through this horrible charade? Why can't we—"

Stop this. He could fill in her conversation, too. The ending he anticipated stilled everything in him but his thudding heart.

"You love me." She had to. He couldn't be that wrong.

Thea's sad smile returned. "Not enough, Oliver."

He shook his head, trying to dislodge the words from his ears. This couldn't be happening. "What the devil does that mean?"

"I will never be able to make up for the people who will shun you for choosing me."

"They don't matter."

"Of course they matter, Oliver. They have *always* mattered. You've done everything in your life to prove to them that they were wrong, that you were different, that you were better than them because of the choices you made."

He reached for her hand, refusing to be daunted when she pulled it away. "When we get to Canada—"

"What happens when there isn't a child or, God forbid, there is never another one? How long will it take for you to question whether you were trapped into marriage with a servant?"

"You are not a servant! Not to me." He was damned tired of hearing this argument. Since when did Thea consider herself beneath anyone?

"If that were true, it wouldn't matter where I choose to spend my time."

"Dammit, Thea! I'm trying to make your situation better. You and Jamey should have been—"

Her chin tilted at a stubborn angle. "We didn't have a leisurely life, but it wasn't all drudgery. Just as yours wasn't all rose gardens. Your happiness didn't come at the cost of ours."

Thea looked past him. "Can you finish here, Hazel? I'm required upstairs."

Oliver reached for her arm. "Wait."

"If you keep at me, I'll say something I regret."

She avoided him with the grace of a fencer and left in a swirl of skirts and curls. He stood there, watching the door swing closed behind her, wondering at her lack of regret for everything she'd said so far.

The sickening, acrid smell of burnt sugar and lime filled the kitchen. A smell Oliver recognized from childhood. His stomach dipped lower as he retrieved a cloth and pulled the tray of burnt biscuits from the oven. Though the color was totally wrong, the shape was perfect. Lime biscuits.

For the first time, Oliver took stock of the preparations. The candies he'd expected. They'd discussed it. Mrs. Murphy had been working for a week to fill the orders of lemon drops, cinnamon chips, and peppermint sticks, not to mention biscuits of every flavor.

Lita's lime cookies were a surprise, not just in choice, but in number. There were piles of them, all perfectly done. Thea must have been working most of the day.

"*Mierda.*" Oliver tipped the ruined sweets into the bin. He could feel Hazel's stare. "She isn't right."

"She isn't wrong either, la—Your Grace."

He faced her. She was paler and smaller than usual, working the edge of her apron between her fingers. It was a nervous tell Oliver had learned years earlier. She did it when she had to deal with his mother.

"Don't call me that." He was Oliver. Just Oliver. Her lad. And he was more lost, more alone, than he'd been in years. He walked to her and took her hand, just like he'd done at Simon's age. "Please, *Tante.*"

Her sniffle was loud and watery. "You weren't raised to be this selfish, lad."

The hell he hadn't been. He was a Hawkins. "All I've ever wanted was to give Thea a better life, to make it so she didn't have to struggle."

"Does love figure into it at all?"

Surely she was joking. He met her gaze and saw the seriousness of her question. "How could you ask me that?"

"Because I've watched you since you learned to walk. The quickest way to get you to try something was to tell you it was against the rules or that you weren't capable of it. I'd wager your situation with Simon began the same way."

It hadn't. He'd wanted Simon near, to be the parent Julia would've been. It didn't matter that one nurse had said he'd fail on his own. She'd been too marriage-minded. And the vicar who'd christened Simon didn't count either. He'd laid eyes on Oliver exactly once, at Julia's funeral. And the banker had only been upset that Simon was colicky during a business meeting.

"You have always been determined to do things your way. I've never seen anyone more set on being poor and alone." The words were harsh, but Hazel's tone was gentle. "But you aren't, and you never have been."

She had no idea what life had been like in Quebec.

"You chose to make your own way, and that's not a bad thing. But the timber in Canada was your inheritance. You said as much before you left."

He had. Grandfather had won the vast, unseen acreage bordering Julia's family's property in a game of chance, and Father had never wanted it. Garrett was happy to be shed of it. Of him.

"And you could've come home at any time. Your family was waiting on you."

He shook his head. "I didn't want Simon near Mother."

Recent events had proven him justified.

"She's not the only family you have." Hazel touched his cheek. "You have no idea what it's like to be truly alone, my boy, and I'm glad of it. But don't judge Thea harshly simply because she has been."

The only person he judged harshly in this situation was himself. He'd been a selfish boy who hadn't considered the consequences and hadn't learned his lesson. Because if Julia hadn't gotten pregnant, she'd still be here.

Which just knotted the grief and guilt tighter in his brain. Without Julia, there was no Simon. With Julia, there was no Thea. Without Thea, there wasn't a Jamey. With Jamey, there was a guilt he couldn't heal, and with Thea there was…

Unbearable confusion and a pain that gutted him. Need that clawed him like a living thing. Light, play, peace, hope. Every time he closed his eyes, he saw her laughing in the garden or bedraggled and fighting for her own virtue. His memories were full of her playing with Simon and the look on her face when the boy touched her.

Which was all the time because she was the closest thing to a mother he'd experienced. So Oliver had failed in that, too. He turned for the door. He had to get out of here.

"Oliver!" Hazel shouted after him. "You can't possibly—"

"Just for a walk in the garden. I need to think before we're besieged."

Oliver left through the back door, relishing the feel of gravel underfoot. When he turned the corner of the house, the wind stole his breath. Truthfully, it was no colder than when he'd arrived home. Only now, he had a hollow spot in his chest that whistled with each gust.

If he had his way, he'd walk until he'd sorted everything—but that would take a trek to Scotland, maybe even to Wales. Instead, he was stuck dodging through the garden maze until he reached the large oak in the center.

Using the tree for balance, Oliver shucked off his boots and stockings. The round pebbles in the path pressed against his heels as the breeze chilled his toes and ankles. Both helped clear his thoughts, but the joy came as he grasped a branch. The bark bit into his palms, and then his soles, as his muscles pulled and stretched with effort. The higher he climbed, the easier he breathed.

He stopped when the branches were too thin to hold him. Sitting with his back to the trunk, his feet dangling, he stared up at the sky. He focused on the blue rather than the gathering clouds. He had more than enough storms in his thoughts.

Does love figure into it at all?

Hazel's question still stunned him. There had never been a time when he'd wondered what love was. Love was his *abuela* and Hazel. Love was Julia. Love was Thea.

Not enough.

How much did she need? She'd influenced every decision in his life since age eight. Even when he'd hated her for breaking his heart, she'd still been there.

The possibility of losing her left Oliver lonelier than he'd felt in years, even after Julia's death.

Which made him the worst husband in the world. Twice over.

It isn't a competition. This time, he heard Thea's words but Julia's sunny laugh.

Julia…who had deserved more than a husband with divided loyalties.

Enough, mon amour.

It was an old debate. The last time they'd had it was the night before they had announced their engagement. Julia had known she shared his heart. She said it only made it bigger. Right now, it hurt twice as much.

Oliver rubbed his knuckles across the stubble covering his chin and jaw. He'd been robbed of something precious. Twice.

Just as he'd been forbidden from sharing Simon with Julia, he'd missed sharing Jamey with Thea. He'd not been able to hold her the way he'd held Julia, or rub her feet, or tease her about the size of her dresses. He hadn't been here to comfort her.

He'd never seen her as a mother.

Except with Simon in the garden, and pony shopping, and with Spot the Smaller. Her worries over his minor coughs.

The laughter. The ache.

I wasn't prepared for it, Julia. How it would feel to watch someone else mother your child, how it would cut in places and fill other spots with…joy. How I'd be jealous watching Simon in her arms.

Lightning flashed, high in the clouds. Seconds later, thunder rolled toward Oliver—as though God was angry at him for omitting the rest of his confession.

We always talked about her as a part of my past, not my present.

Kissing her makes me hungry, love, but I wasn't prepared to have it drive you from my mind. I wasn't ready to wake with her name on my lips. Missing her in my bed instead of you.

Oliver closed his eyes and dropped his head back. The rough bark snagged his hair and scratched his scalp, but the tears leaking free had nothing to do with physical pain.

I'm sorry, mon lutin, but I feel more alive than I've felt in the last four years, as though someone's scraped sandpaper over all my skin. And it's not from work, or from coming home, or even being on this damned island. It's her.

She's alive, and she's warm. He lifted and dropped his head again, relishing the sting. He deserved at least this. If he'd never seen Julia, never touched her, chances were…

I have to move forward without you. Every bittersweet memory played out, reminding him what she'd saved him from, how she'd done it. It wasn't fair.

I miss you. Her smile was so like Simon's. *I will always miss you.*

But when he thought of his future, he saw Thea by his side. *I'm sorry.*

The wind brushed his skin, cool and soft, before ruffling his hair.

And then he was alone, with the lightning growing closer and the clouds darker, left to work out how to salvage the mess he'd made.

It had been easier a few weeks ago when he could blame Thea's plight on her imaginary sea captain. When he could point a finger and call the man a fool for not making adequate provisions for someone he claimed to love.

That's where Oliver's problems had begun—the past—and it was time to accept that he couldn't change it. For the most part, except for Jamey, he wouldn't change it if he could. Time to move forward.

It was past time to admit that his fate had been sealed before he'd ever arrived. He was a duke, even if he'd rather be anything else. He had a responsibility to an entire village that he couldn't fulfill from across on ocean. Even if he could find an iron-willed man of business, he'd never ask anyone else to deal with the chaos his mother would cause.

No tantrum he threw would convey him back to Canada. No amount of coercion would make Thea want to be a duchess.

The easiest way would be to cancel the party, but he—they—would be letting down the lending circle's charitable mission.

The second option was to not announce the engagement. However, that would mean making Thea his hostess, ensconcing her in his home, with no formal role. That was tantamount to making her his mistress, which is what everyone had thought for years.

While he couldn't change the past, he'd be damned if he'd repeat it.

Rain pattered the leaves above him in an irregular rhythm as he faced his third, and scariest, option. The only real choice. He'd talk to Thea and do what she wanted.

As he descended from his hiding spot, rain soaked his hair and slicked the tree bark. He didn't even bother with his boots. His stockings were wet already. Instead, he shoved everything under his arm and bolted down the path toward home.

Sharp, wet stones gave way to slippery kitchen floors and then to treacherous stairs. Oliver stood in the upstairs hallway for a moment, debating on talking with Thea now or later and deciding on later. He would appear much more rational when he was dry and dressed.

Oliver opened his bedroom door and Tipton, the valet he'd inherited from his father along with the title, paused mid-pace.

"Thank goodness, Your Grace. I was beginning to think the worst."

"Everything is fine. Thank you for waiting." Oliver dropped his boots and socks and shrugged free of his braces. "How quickly can we get this done?"

The valet frowned. "Party dress can't be rushed, m'lord."

"It can tonight." Oliver pulled his shirt over his head, grateful that a fire heated the room. "I have things to do before our guests arrive." He sunk his hands into a basin full of warm water. "Just make me presentable."

Presentable took almost an hour. Rather than letting the valet fuss over his jacket, Oliver waved him away. "Thank you, Tip. That will be all."

The other man hesitated. "Your cravat should really be…"

His cravat should be burned.

Oliver looked in the mirror. He'd surrendered to using his father's shirt studs and cufflinks but had kept his own watch and chain. They'd been a wedding gift from Julia, and he felt safer wearing them into social battle. The simple green-jeweled pin in his plainly-knotted cravat matched the heavy ring that spanned from the base of his finger to his knuckle. His grandfather's ring.

The trappings looked very ducal, and Oliver could help thinking his father was going to come in and catch him playing dress-up. Rain pelted the windows in sharp ticks and pings as he forced himself to relax. Terror, he had learned, only made him look taciturn and severe.

Neither of those would do now.

He squared his jacket, cuffs and then tails, before nodding at Tipton and forcing a smile. "Wish me luck, Tip."

The valet's reply was lost as Oliver left the room.

A few quick strides and he was standing at Thea's door. Truthfully, he could have saved the walk and used their adjoining door. However, that seemed too familiar and too risky.

Before he could knock, the door opened and Jenny Snow greeted him with wide eyes and a muffled curse before she bobbed a curtsey. "Apologies, Your Grace."

"Think nothing of it." He looked over her head and into the room. "Is Thea dressed?"

"Some time ago, sir. She mentioned going to look in on Simon."

If they were both together, it would save him some time

groveling.

"Thank you, ma'am." Oliver bowed slightly before he left her, lengthening his stride to beat the clock and right his wrongs before their guests arrived.

Simon's door was ajar, and a duet of giggles drifted out. Oliver paused to listen.

"They tickle," Simon said. "What do you call them?"

"I thought you should name them. Maybe Simon's, like your papa's candy?"

In the silence, Oliver could imagine his son weighing this important decision.

"Peppermint spots. 'Cause they have them."

"That's a very good name." Thea's steps tapped across the floor. "I'll put your sweets tray here for you to enjoy during the party."

"Can't I come down? Please?"

The request was ruined when he coughed between questions.

"I agree with your papa. You should stay in bed until you feel better." There was a pause, and then a soft squeak of mattress ropes and a rustle of bedding as Thea sat on the bed. "Don't frown so, Simon. Your face will freeze like that."

"Papa isn't right about anything. He said my fairy wasn't real."

"Oh…well. Perhaps he meant that your fairy wouldn't stay real if it crossed the ocean. Fairies don't like water. It ruins their magic."

Oliver fought to stay still. If he'd ever doubted, he knew better now. He did not deserve Thea Fowler.

"Then I want to stay here. With Hazel."

Oliver had made the same statement once, when he hadn't been much older than Simon. The more his mother had railed against it, the firmer his resolve had become.

"I think Hazel would love to have you stay," Thea said. "But your papa would miss you, as would I."

Again, there was a Simon-sized thoughtful silence.

"I've never been to Quebec before," Thea said. "And your papa will be busy working. I was hoping you could help me learn."

"I'll think about it."

Oliver grinned. Simon had picked up the phrase from the office. He used it often, and he thought about things far longer and much harder than any other four-year-old.

This time, the child's thoughts were interrupted by a loud yawn. A rustle of skirts indicated Thea had stood.

"You can talk to your papa tomorrow, after a good sleep. He'll be in a much better mood as well. I'm sure."

She said nothing of her mood, though.

Oliver was thinking of that when the door moved out of his reach. Thea stood there in a dark green velvet dress that made her skin glow, especially her bare shoulders. The neckline was draped in a froth of sheer green fabric joined above her breasts by a jeweled broach. The same fabric wound through her intricate curls and braids.

She was more beautiful, more precious, than any jewelry he wore, and he was terrified of losing her. Oliver took her fingers in his, and his heart ached at their coldness. That had always been her only indication of fear.

"Where is your favorite place?" he asked her in a whisper. "Where do you want to be?"

"Home."

Six years ago, her answer would have been wherever he was, he was certain, and Oliver was disappointed she didn't give it now. He had done that to her. There was also a stab of fear that she might never feel that way again, especially if they stayed here.

"Then pretend you're there. They're just guests in your dining room. Nothing more." He squeezed her icy fingers. "I—*we* will make this right. Together. After they're gone. I promise, Thee." He looked into her dark brown eyes and prayed she wouldn't cry. "Please trust me."

And then the bell rang.

CHAPTER TWENTY-SEVEN

"**M**Y DEAR? ARE you well?"

Thea sifted through the replies available. She was tired. Her face hurt from smiling, her feet hurt from standing too long in the kitchen this afternoon, and her heart hurt for far too many reasons to admit.

"I'm fine, Aunt Tavie."

It was a lie. Her nerves were so raw her skin tingled. She had expected Oliver to announce their engagement before the cards had begun, but he hadn't. It had left her teetering between hope that he'd finally seen reason and disappointment that he'd come to his senses.

"You should be quite proud of your efforts here. You and your duke have raised an impressive amount from so small a party."

They had, though the first rounds of *vingt-un* and *piquet* with such diverse groups had been tense. It had eased quickly, thanks to liberal draughts of whiskey and Thea's deliberate seating arrangements. Gentry had been kept together except for Augustus Chitester, who she'd paired with John so the two burly men could discuss business. She'd matched Lady Chitester with Hazel and Jenny, knowing the three could discuss cooking and recipes. And she'd matched Drake with Millie and Freddie, so he could counter their cheating.

"Everyone seemed to enjoy themselves," she murmured to her aunt.

Perhaps delaying the announcement had been a good idea.

But now it was late and everyone was milling about, clearly making plans for departure. If Oliver didn't speak soon, it would be all over the village by noon that she'd taken up residence at Felton House. *Hostess* would be interpreted as *mistress*. Old gossip would be resurrected and given the reverence of gospel. No one would care about the truth.

Oliver parted the crowd, striding toward her with a champagne flute in each hand and a grim expression on his handsome face.

"But he isn't my duke."

He wasn't. Not really. Oliver had been hers once. The handsome man dressed in finery that had cost more than her inn was slightly terrifying.

"Not for long, unless I miss my guess," Tavie said as she took champagne from a passing footman.

Oliver joined them and thrust a glass into one of Thea's hands. After turning on his heel to face the crowd, he grasped the other. No intertwined fingers, no reassuring squeeze. He held her like an ax he was afraid of dropping.

"Before you depart, if I could have your attention please."

All eyes focused on them, some of them narrowing. Ladies lifted their fans to hide whispers.

"I—we—would like to thank you for attending this evening, and for your generous support of St. Margaret's House. I have one last request, however." He cleared his throat. "Thea and I have agreed to marry. Please raise your glasses to my future wife."

He led the toast, lifting his champagne in a white-knuckled hand and holding it there for far too long.

Because few in the crowd were joining in.

Thea made herself meet their gazes, joining Oliver in the silent dare. However, picking out faces made her realize who was missing. The duchess had retired upstairs as card-play began, pleading a headache. Her mother had left soon after, without a goodbye at all. Millie and Freddie had vanished as well.

It was a ringing endorsement of this folly.

In the back, however, her friends had their glasses lifted high. Jenny and Tavie were dabbing their eyes. John and Drake were scanning the group, their expressions as dark as Oliver's.

"Hear, hear," chimed Augustus Chitester as he raised his glass and glanced around to his counterparts. "To an excellent match and a happy marriage."

Amelia crossed the battle lines first. She grasped Thea's shoulders in a brief warning before wrapping her in a hug. "Congratulations to you both," she whispered. "I should have known after that scene in your garden. I've never been so happy to be used as a tool to make someone jealous."

That was the farthest thing from the truth, but Thea didn't have time to argue because Lord Chitester was smiling as he congratulated them and Lady Chitester was right behind him. She took both Thea's hands in hers.

"I know it is a daunting thought, but you will make an excellent duchess."

It was as though Thea had needlepointed her dread for all to see. Which was laughable because no one would be able to read her stitching.

"Thank you, Lady—"

"Marian, please. You must call me Marian…Thea. Or will you prefer Theodora now?"

Oliver snickered into his glass, and Thea elbowed him. It only made him laugh louder.

"I'm taking that as a *no*." Lady—Marian—giggled. "We must do tea soon. I'll send a card."

Tavie was next. She hugged Oliver first. "Not her duke indeed. Lad, you'll take care of her or answer to me."

"Yes, ma'am." Oliver smiled. "As much as she'll allow."

"Good man. Good man."

She was still talking as she wrapped her arms around Thea. "Are you certain, child? This is what you want?"

How could Thea explain that she had imagined this moment for most of her adult life? Most of the time it involved Gretna Green and an announcement after the fact. She'd never fooled herself that their families would be overjoyed, but at least she and Oliver were happy.

Maybe fantasies and happiness belonged to vicars' daughters and second sons.

Innkeepers and dukes were relegated to large, drafty houses full of distant people. Trapped by duty, responsibility, and pride.

"I'm certain, Tavie."

The rest of the line was short. Their true friends had already celebrated with them, so their greetings were quick. Drake was last. To Oliver, he gave a firm handshake and steady stare. With Thea, he kissed her hand and held her gaze. He nodded once and waited for her to return it, which she did.

The remaining guests had used the celebration as an opportunity to retrieve their coats. The receiving line became a place for goodbyes. They migrated toward the door, and the cool, damp night air was welcoming. Fresh scents of damp earth and watered garden made Thea relax.

The Gerards, last in line, stopped to pay their respects.

"*Elle l'a piégé,*" Lady Gerard whispered loudly to her daughter, Margaret. "*Sinon, pourquoi emmènerait-il la pute de Fletcher chez lui? J'ai entendu dire qu'elle a été assez bien payée.*"

Fletcher's whore…it was an ugly insult, made in French because the Gerards thought she was uneducated and Oliver was stupid. Thea had had quite enough of both.

Oliver had told her to pretend they were guests at her inn, and she would never tolerate this sort of behavior in her place of business.

"*Au moins, le duc saura que je ne suis pas après son argent.*" Thea arched an eyebrow, adding a sting to her sneer. Marrying for money and a title was no less mercenary than trapping him with secrets and guilt.

The ladies paled, and it worsened when Oliver turned to them, his posture stiff as he ushered Lady Gerard to the door. Margaret followed behind.

"*Au revoir mesdames*," he spat from between his clenched jaws.

He pushed the door behind them, narrowly missing the hem of Margaret's silk dress. The heavy thud was still echoing as he tugged his cravat and cursed at the pin that held it in place.

"Before you ask, my French has not improved. But any man living in Quebec quickly learns the words you both exchanged." He kissed Thea's hair. "Well done, *mi Pepnilla*."

He lowered his voice to a whisper. "*Nosotros debemos hablar.*"

The transition to warm Spanish was welcome, but Thea still dreaded the words. They did need to talk, and she suspected the outcome. Too much had changed today. Things could not go forward as they had been.

She should be glad of her victory. It had been hard-won.

"We need to look in on Simon first."

Drake was at the entrance to the library, twirling the whiskey in his glass. "I thought I'd stay a moment or two longer."

He assumed he'd be needed as a co-conspirator, which meant she hadn't been the only one to notice the change in Oliver's temperament. However, his hand at her back, and the tingle it caused, made Thea wish she was only imagining things.

"We'll be a few moments," Oliver said. "Make yourself comfortable." He was quiet until they reached the top of the stairs. "The Gerards will spread the tale that you didn't deny their accusations."

"They would have spread it anyway." She put a hand on the doorknob, keeping her voice low to avoid waking Simon. "It was worth it for the looks on their faces."

It also was a ready-made reason for ending their engagement. Oliver wouldn't have to explain a thing. Her reputation would be damaged, but that wasn't as lethal as people thought.

Thea opened the door to Simon's room, careful to stay quiet.

The fire was still warm, and he had eaten about half of the sweets she'd left. He'd probably have a tummy ache tomorrow. His stick and pebble stable was still a mess. As she pushed the door wider, she frowned. His bed was empty.

Oliver pushed past her. "Simon?"

A quick search of the room yielded no boy.

They widened their search to Oliver's room. No boy.

"Fred. Emmett," Oliver called. "Take the grooms and search the grounds. Simon's gone missing again."

Thea quickened her pace, and the maids joined her search. She could hear Drake and Oliver downstairs.

"The last time he was angry, he ended up at the dower cottage," Oliver said. "He's probably sulking down there."

Thea stopped at the end of the hallway, at the duchess's door. Dread pooled in her stomach. As much as she loathed a confrontation with Oliver's mother, she needed to make certain Simon wasn't there. Maybe the boy went to his grandmother for comfort.

She knocked.

"You may enter."

Thea kept one foot in the hallway as she opened the door.

"What else could you possibly want of me?" the duchess asked from her chair. "Would you like to inspect your future rooms?"

Thea looked from her to the dour young nurse, Alice. "Simon isn't in his room. Did he come in here?"

The duchess's expressions flickered for a moment, and Thea recognized the concern there. Disdain returned in an instant.

"My son has made certain that my grandson fears me, and he's kept Alice from the child for months. I can assure you—"

"Your Grace, all that child, all *any* child, wants is to be accepted and loved. If he is afraid of you, you cannot blame his father."

"How dare you." The duchess rose.

Any other time, Thea would have welcomed the opportunity to fight over this subject. "I have no time to argue. Perhaps you could both join the search of the house?"

"I will not scurry about like a kitchen maid in my dressing gown," the duchess decreed.

Alice stood. "I will help. Have you been to the nursery yet?"

Thea shook her head and held the door wider for the girl. "Will you need assistance?"

"No." Alice, already several steps down the hall, plucked a candleholder from a nearby table. "I'll sing out if I find him."

Thea continued on her own, panic building in her lungs with every dark, empty room. Through the windows, lanterns bobbed across the grounds.

The front door crashed open and closed, and heavy boots thudded against the tile.

"Simon!"

Oliver's shout was frantic. Thea lifted her skirts and ran for the stairs. She reached him mid-way and put her hand on his chest. His heart thudded wildly under her palm.

"He's not up here, Ol."

"He's not downstairs either," Drake called up. "Where else could he hide?"

Emmett came in from the kitchen, carrying Simon's squirming puppy, a rope dangling from his neck. "He was in the stable with Spot the Larger, tied to the feed trough."

The boy would have never left his dog alone, much less tied him.

Close as she was, Thea was certain she was the only one who heard Oliver's shuddering inhale and the catch at the end that might have been a whimper. Everyone was staring at him, waiting on a command.

"Emmett," she said. "Please ask the groom to saddle the horses and fill lanterns for the ride. Tipton, his lordship will need a cloak to repel the rain."

"I'll saddle up as well," Drake said.

"Wait," Thea said. "When did Millie and Freddie leave the party?"

"About half an hour before your announcement. I won a large wager, and Millie lost a wager. Freddie took her out for air." Drake's eyes widened. "You don't think…"

It was exactly what Thea thought. She faced the man she loved. If her suspicions were correct, this would be the final cut to their relationship. He'd suffered cruelly, needlessly, at the hands of her sister. No one would want to be linked by marriage to a viper, even if there was a child involved.

Drake left the room without a word or a backward glance.

Once she was certain they were alone, Thea wrapped her arms around Oliver, and he crushed her to him. Her heart shattered anew as he trembled.

"I've lost my little boy," he whispered against her hair.

"He's not lost, *Mono*." She braced her body against his solid weight. "Millie's taken him."

"Mother—"

"No. She wouldn't put him in danger. She's genuinely concerned."

"Where would they go?"

With an hour's head start and a carriage, they could be halfway to London by now, but Thea knew her sister. Their unorthodox education had taught them both the same logic. All Thea had to do was twist it to think like a criminal.

Which she'd done for the last six years.

The farther Millie went, the longer it would take for a ransom demand to reach them, and for payment to reach her. She wouldn't go back through town, because someone would see her. That left the road to Brandon, which Millie would find funny.

However, she wouldn't stay in a public house or an inn. Being seen with Simon was too big a risk. The child was probably still in his nightclothes, and he most likely wasn't docile.

They'd stay hidden, but it would have to be reachable by gig. Millie never walked anywhere if she could help it.

"The Roman Road." She leaned back to look Oliver in the eye. "They'll be on the road, in the forest. They'll only keep him long enough to make us desperate to pay whatever they ask."

Hope glimmered deep in his eyes. "How can you be certain?"

"The same way you knew Garrett would cheat at curricle races." She kissed his bristly, stiff jaw. "Have courage."

He nodded and straightened his spine. "I don't want to wait for a search party."

"We shouldn't," she agreed. "The fewer people crashing through the trees, the better."

They all but ran to the barn, where Emmett was waiting with Jupiter. Drake was already astride his horse. Both animals were dancing across the hay, either startled by the weather or alarmed by the tension in the air.

Oliver swung into the saddle. He moved his feet from the stirrups and offered her his hand. Thea swung up behind him. He might need her, but no more than she needed to be with him.

"Give Thea the cloak, Tip. She can keep us both dry," Oliver commanded.

Thea tied the heavy garment and arranged it to cover them both as much as possible, then grasped the lantern Emmett offered. Once she was settled, she placed her hand against Oliver's stomach and tightened her hold.

"Let's go."

CHAPTER TWENTY-EIGHT

THE ENTRANCE TO the Roman Road was a yawning mouth in the trees with a faint dirt tongue that led them deeper into the bowels of the forest. Night shadows and stealth dictated a slower pace than any of them wanted, and Drake rode close enough that his heels scraped her dress. His gray horse was the only light spot in her vision.

Thea's backside ached from sitting bareback on Jupiter's thick, solid spine, and her position made it impossible to ignore all the places where Oliver's body touched hers.

His callused palm chafed her knuckles, sending sparks to her elbow. They went higher when his fingers curved to hold her hand. As he lifted it to his lips, the combination of the kiss and his breath on her skin made her sweat.

"You're freezing. You should have stayed at home."

She felt his whispered words more than heard them, both across her hand and through his back. "As if I'd let you have all the fun."

Rain splattered against the leaves and dripped onto her back, adding another layer of misery and worry to the night. Simon was out in this dreck, afraid, tired, and probably hungry because her selfish sister had put her greed above his health.

Anger shivered through Thea, and the breeze across her wet back doubled the tremble. She huddled closer to Oliver, stealing his warmth while hoping to keep him dry. She could at least do that.

Drake put up a hand and drew his mount to a stop. Oliver followed suit and held his breath. Thea did the same. Over the patter of rain, and the splash and tumble of rushing water, came the faint clatter of tin.

And a small, thin cough.

A glow on the horizon up the hill gave them a direction.

Thea slid from her perch, and Drake was there to cushion the last few inches of her fall. Oliver landed behind her with a hard thud, close enough she could hear his watch jingle in his pocket and his muttered curse.

"Thea," Drake whispered. "Stay here and—"

"I'm not staying with the horses," she hissed. This was her family's fault, and she wasn't going to let others resolve it.

"I want Papa," Simon whimpered through the cold shadows, stopping any argument. "I want to go home."

"But we're almost to Thea's." Millie's too-slick voice lilted the words. Trust her sister to treat Simon like an idiot.

"You're lying. We didn't go past the candy shop, and we do that on the way to her house."

"Good lad," Oliver whispered as he pulled Thea close.

His warmth only reached her ear as he bent to put them cheek to cheek. "You stay with me and do as you're told."

Thea nodded, not trusting her voice and not wanting to lie to him again. She'd caused him enough problems.

"Never should have agreed to this," Freddie grumbled. "Kidnapping—"

"We did not kidnap the child," Millie snapped. "You'd best get that straight. We went out for air between hands and found him in the stable, with no one around in naught but his nightshirt. We took him in to keep him safe."

"The boy's sick," Freddie argued. "At some point, we'll have to leave him behind to get out of here. He'll draw too much attention. Ought to just leave now. Can't even have a fire."

His voice was closer than Millie's. They were separated, and the glow was from a lantern. Millie would be blind for a few minutes without it. The trek here had given Thea the advantage—she was already wet and used to the dark.

The only problem was the plan hatching around her.

"I'll take Freddie. He has sneaky bastard all over him." Drake's grin sharpened in the lantern light. "Says another sneaky bastard."

"We'll take the other side of the bridge," Oliver whispered.

It was the easier climb, but it left them farther from Simon. Oliver was most likely sacrificing surprise for her benefit.

Thea considered switching sides and going with Drake, but there was no way she'd let Oliver do this alone. If that put an ice-cold river between her and Millie, so be it.

Drake whistled, sharp and shrill, mimicking an owl. A signal. Oliver repeated it in an agreement. Those would be her signals as well then.

"What was that?" Freddie asked.

"It's just an owl," Millie giggled. "Cor, but you're such a dandy."

"I didn't grow up a country lass like you, love. You've all sorts of talents, I think."

Oliver led Thea past a gig and a docile horse that didn't so much as flinch as he stroked its thick neck. They made their way up the embankment. Beside them, the river cascaded into a pool before rushing to town. Flat to the ground, waiting for Drake's signal, the cold from the rain and the mist from the river soaked through Thea's clothes and skin to reach her memories.

Oliver pressed a harsh kiss to her temple. "If something happens to me—"

"Hush." She wouldn't consider that.

"If something happens," he grated in her ear. "Take Simon home to Quebec. You'll have a place there and more than enough money to raise him. Richard will—"

Thea kissed him, both to keep him quiet and say goodbye.

"Give me a count of ten."

She scampered up the hill, yanking the hem of the cloak from Oliver's grasp and ignoring his hissed curses. Staying low to the ground, she kept to the shadows as she rushed across the road and into the trees.

One.

"Don't you know it," Millie crowed. "And I'll never have to set foot in this godforsaken place again once my bitch of a sister pays us what we're due."

Thea slipped in the grass and mud along the riverbank. The damp made twigs flex rather than snap, and the light from Millie's lantern was a beacon. *Here I am. Come get me.*

Two. Three.

"You're certain she'll pay?" Freddie asked.

"She'll bankrupt herself to give Lord Simon here back to his papa."

Four.

Thea stopped a few strides upstream from Millie's camp. From here it was easy to see Simon at the back of the grotto, curled with his knees to his chin. Millie sat on the other side, guarding from the road because no one would be foolish enough to come from the river.

"Anything for Oliver," Millie sneered. "She followed him around like a puppy until he took what she was too stupid to barter. For all her intelligence, she never understood the unique value of being a woman."

Thea untied her cloak; it would only tangle in the current, but she kept her shoes on. There wasn't enough time to unlace them, and they'd help keep her feet from being sliced to ribbons.

"Not like you, eh?" Freddie asked.

Five.

Water seeped through Thea's shoes stitching, then up her stockings and petticoats, through her chemise. Each inch stole another breath, but it wasn't bad. After all, she was already drenched.

Six.

The cold made her fingers immobile.

Seven.

The current swept her legs from beneath her and sloshed up her neck and into her ears, then across her scalp. Her velvet dress became an anchor as she fought her way to the other shore.

Eight. Nine.

Thea clung to the rushes to keep her out of the circle of light glinting across the rippling water.

"Not a thing like me. She wants to look down her nose at the way I live, while she raised a bastard and works like a dog for a man who will never—"

Ten.

One owl screeched, then another.

"Give me back my son," Oliver shouted from the bridge.

Thea climbed from her hiding place and crossed into the cold, dim light.

"Run, Simon."

He was already on his feet.

Millie charged forward.

The lantern burned Thea's fingers, but she kept hold and flung it into the river behind her, covering the area in darkness. Simon's nightshirt was a bright shadow, and she saw her sister lift him and heave him into the river.

Thea froze for a moment, watching the current, unsure how her sister had become such a monster. But as Millie's blonde hair glowed in the moonlight, it was clear she was sacrificing Simon to ensure her escape.

There was no time to fight or to plan. Thea snatched Millie by the waist and fell backward, taking them both into the river.

Since Thea was already soaked, the water wasn't as shocking as it was to Millie. Taking advantage of that, Thea tightened her hold on her sister and found Simon by his splashing alone. She wrapped her fingers around his thin wrist and yanked him to her just as Millie wrestled free.

"Interfering bitch," Millie screeched as she pulled free.

But it was only for a moment. Thea kicked Millie off her feet and dragged her sister back into custody by her hair.

"Greedy cow," Thea shouted as Simon wrapped his arms around her neck and his legs around her waist. "You'll not escape this, Millie."

The riverbed was uneven and slick, making the current more trustworthy. They re-entered it, and Thea kept her eye on the bridge and the shadowy brawl at its center.

"Papa!" Simon's squeal rang out.

"Freddie!" Millie shouted as she squirmed for freedom.

Thea's hem snagged, halting their progress, and Millie took advantage. Her boot landed in Thea's stomach, and she pushed Thea under as she broke free. Thea freed Simon to keep from drowning him.

Thea pursued her sister, screaming in frustration as she broke the surface and sucked in a deep breath. Millie's remaining pins stabbed her palms as she wrapped both hands through her sister's hair and dragged her back into the water.

"Let me go." Millie flailed backward, her nails ripping against Thea's skin rather than digging in.

"Thea! Help me!"

Simon's words were snatched by the river. He was too far out to reach, especially dragging Millie as dead weight. With a curse, Thea shoved her sister away and into the dark, and swam for Simon, stroking with the current to gain speed until she could reach Simon's ankle, then his knee.

"I've got you, Si."

Behind her, her sister's scream ended in a yelp that was swallowed by splashing and Drake's hearty swearing. Her cold, waterlogged sister would never be able to escape the drier, wilier pirate.

The bridge loomed ahead, and the current quickened. Thea forced her knuckles to curve and buried her fingers in Simon's trousers. "Oliver." The word was lost in the water slapping over her head. She bounced on the river bottom and pushed herself higher. "Oliver!"

Simon in one hand, she reached forward with the other. Oliver was her lifeline, reaching for her. She missed the first time and fought panic as the current tore Simon from her one finger at a time.

She latched onto Oliver's hand, but with every inch she gained, the river took another.

Then she was holding Oliver in one hand and nothing in the other. The water eddied around the bridge and swallowed Simon in a slithery, silent gulp.

No. I won't lose another boy.

Thea stopped fighting, releasing Oliver's hand, certain the weight of her clothes and the swift current would pull her free of him. The water washed over her, drowning his screams. Darkness pulled her forward, and she let it.

CHAPTER TWENTY-NINE

N O. Oliver stared at his empty hand.

No.

The river was empty, too.

"No!" He'd lost them both. Another little boy, another woman he loved.

And he could sit here and let it happen, or he could fight for them. He'd been doing it all day. His mother, his peers, kidnappers, a river—it didn't matter what it was. He'd brawl until he was bloody, broken, and cold.

A firm grip kept him from tumbling forward, and he reared backward prepared to kill anyone in his way.

Drake pushed him toward the opposite side of the bridge. "We'll catch them downstream."

Rocks bit into Oliver's palms and ripped through his trousers as he slid down the embankment. Shadows and limbs blended together, tripping him and snagging his shirt as he sprinted along the muddy bank.

"Thea!"

Nothing answered him but the rain.

"Thea." Her name ripped from his throat. "Simon." His shout echoed, mocking him.

"Here."

It was faint, but it gave him a direction.

"There." Drake pointed over his shoulder to a faint white glow, caught in a felled tree like so much flotsam.

Oliver splashed into the river, fighting the current to reach them. Drake was on his heels.

Thea's blue-white face matched Simon's shirt, and she had the boy on her stomach to keep him out of the water. She shoved him into Oliver's arms.

He handed his son to Drake, who was nearer to safety, and then hauled Thea close. She clung to him, her teeth chattering in his ear, and he forgot to scold her. Instead, he lifted her higher, keeping all but her hem out of the water.

At the shore, she sprang to life, clawing at rushes and limbs to get to dry land. Drake was waiting, holding Simon in his lap. Coughs racked the child's chest and shoulders.

Thea swept her hand under Simon's hair, then his shirt. "He's clammy."

What did she expect after a swim in the rain? "No doubt."

"Not wet. Feverish."

The words combined with the wild look in her eyes sent a chill across his already cold, wet skin. "What do we do?"

Thea had her hand over her mouth, and her eyes were wide. She was lost in a panic, and it was spreading.

Oliver closed his hand over hers, as much to hold on as to pull her back to the present. "Tell me what to do."

"We need to get him home," she said.

Oliver lifted Simon from Drake's arms and started for the horse and gig awaiting Freddie, who was in a heap on the middle of the bridge, and Millie, who was wherever Drake had left her. They'd be a handful once they were both awake and warm. "What about them?"

"Go," Drake commanded. "I have it."

Thea caught up and pushed Oliver aside on her way into the box. "I'm driving."

He was the better driver, the better racer. He always had

been. "Thee—"

"You're warmer." She blindly took the jacket Drake offered and shoved it over Simon. "Wrap him in that and hold him tightly." She snapped the whip over the horse's ear. "Come up." They lurched forward, and she snapped the leather again. "Like the wind, girlie. Let's go."

They climbed the embankment, tilting first one way, then back, before reaching the bridge. Thea then turned them toward the inn. Up one hill, down another, limbs snagging their clothing and hair, she guided the horse along the road which, in the moonlight and shadows, was nothing more than a footpath.

She took one turn too fast. With his arms full of Simon, Oliver had no choice but to slosh to and fro in the seat like a stranded fish.

"Who taught you to drive?"

"You." She stiffened her legs and pulled the reins to round another corner. The action slammed Oliver into her, threatening to push her from the cart and under its wheels.

He wrapped Simon tighter and shivered from both cold and macabre fantasies of what could have happened to his son if not for Thea. Everything she'd endured had shaped her into—

No. That wasn't right. Millie's harsh words careened through his brain. Thea had always been strong, smart, and determined, but he'd chalked it up to his influence rather than her skills.

Everything she'd been through had brought her to this point, yes. To where she'd remained calm and focused, held him together, and fought to save Simon.

"Never do that to me again." He braced his feet to stay close when gravity would have flung him away. "You just vanished."

"But I—"

Would she never understand her importance to him? Not for what she could give him, just because of herself?

"I'm sorry. I can't understand you for your teeth chattering." He put his arm across her back, warming her as much as possible. "Never again, Thea. Or I'll plait your hair to a tree."

By the time they reached the inn, it had stopped raining. Simon's rattling breaths were shaking Oliver to pieces.

"Get him to an upstairs room," Thea barked as they shuddered to a stop in her barnyard. "Strip him and rub him dry. Hard, Oliver. Get him under the blankets before you stoke the fire."

She vanished into her apothecary garden, and he did as he was told. Ignoring Jenny's anguished cry, Oliver banged up the stairs and into the first empty room he found. His heart pounding, Oliver worked until he was breathless and the boy was pink and warm. Thea swept in and put a kettle over a fire someone else must have kindled while he'd been working.

Pine-scented steam, smelling green and astringent, soon hung in the air like fog across the ocean, making him clean and dirty at the same time. He put his hand on his son's head just as another cough wracked through him. "Is he worse?"

Thea focused on Simon's bath, her fingers bright red against the cloth. "The steam helps soothe his lungs so he can breathe without rattling. Once the tea is ready, it will loosen the congestion, but he'll have to sit up to drink it."

He tugged the rag from her fingers. After their cold night, the water was scalding. "Go change."

"He needs—"

"A bath. I understand." He curved his free hand to the shape of her icy, delicate jaws. "Your clothes are still wet, and you're working yourself into a lather. You'll be sick next."

"But—"

"I can't do this without you." This close, she smelled of algae, wood, and fish, and the chill from her clothes soaked into his skin. It reminded him how close he'd come to losing them both. "Go get into dry clothes."

She left him without an argument, which was enough to

make him worry about the state of things. Rather than focus on the worst, Oliver finished bathing his son just as he'd learned to do when Simon was a baby. Starting at the neck, working his way down the front. Then the back, neck to heels, His face was next—the sharp nose and impish chin from his mother. His dark mass of curls was last.

"All dry," Thea said. "Your turn."

She was in her patchwork robe, and she'd scrubbed her face clean. Her hair hung in one thick braid. She appeared younger, more fragile, than just a few short hours ago.

"Drake's extra night shirt is on my bed for you. Go dry off and change," she ordered. "The tea should be ready by then."

Oliver clawed his soggy shirt over his head as he went down the hall, glad to finally pull the panic from his skin and let the air raise chill bumps.

His bath was quick, but it combined his scent with Thea's, making the room theirs. His boots were at the foot of the bed, and its spindly frame looked far too feminine. He hung his shirt on the rack near her dress, which was draped across a chair by the fire, its ruined green velvet limp as river moss against his fingers.

He pulled the nightshirt over his damp hair. The garment's long sleeves made him groan. It was already hotter than the fifth level of hell in that room. He'd be sweaty again in minutes.

"Oliver," Thea shouted.

Heart in his throat, Oliver threw open the door and charged down the hallway, expecting the worst.

What he found was Thea, standing between his mother and Doctor Anderson, brandishing a fire iron.

"Get the child away from that hysterical girl before she kills him." His mother shoved the doctor toward the bed. "I will not have her tend my grandson."

"You will not touch him." Thea swung the poker toward the doctor, who had the good sense to back away.

Oliver waded into the disagreement, gently tugging the weapon away before he faced his mother. "Neither of you are welcome here. Go now."

The doctor's eyes widened. "Your Grace. The child needs to be bled. It will ease his—"

"Bleeding will do *nothing* for him," Thea cried. "Nothing but weaken him until he cannot fight to cough and drowns in his own bed."

Her words sent splinters into Oliver's skin. They were too raw. She was too panicked.

This was how Jamey had died.

"Doctor Anderson. Thank you for coming, but you will leave Simon in the care of his mother."

"Your obsession with this woman is clouding your judgment," his mother snapped. "She let her son—"

"Our son," Oliver shouted. "Mine and hers, Mother. Your grandchild, whom you knew needed care but ignored. You are the only one not to be trusted in this room, and you will leave. Now. We have a sick child who needs our attention."

He grasped his mother's arm, and dragged her from the room, making sure Doctor Anderson was following close behind.

He didn't release his hold until they were outside. "Go home. I will send word when Simon is better. However, you should spend your time packing for travel. I would like you gone as soon as he is out of danger. I'll pay for a posting inn if necessary." He turned his back on her and nodded a goodbye to the doctor. "Take her away, sir."

Oliver stayed alert until the carriage disappeared and the clop of hooves faded, and then he stole a moment of solitude. Unaware of the drama brewing around them, bugs clicked and buzzed as they did every summer night. He wiggled his toes on the cool, wet grass and stared upward. The clouds had skated away, and stars pricked the velvet sky until it threatened to disintegrate and topple onto his head.

She's right, Julia. I know she is. But…if he heads your way, turn him back. Please, mon lutin. I need him. So does she.

He turned in time to see a shadow in the garden. Dear God,

what else?

"Only me," Fletcher drawled. "How is Simon?"

"Feverish, but he'll recover." He *would* recover. "Thea's tending him. I need to get back." Oliver stopped with his hand on the latch. "Millie and Freddie?"

"I left them at the constable. Millie is using every trick she can muster, but it's not working. And Freddie will be glad that Anderson is headed back to town, assuming that was his carriage leaving here."

"Why does Freddie need a doctor? I only broke his nose."

"I broke his arm." Fletcher's teeth glinted in the moonlight, making him look like a wolf in search of prey. "He resisted."

Laughter felt good. "Thank you, Drake."

"My pleasure." The smuggler leaned against the wall, flanking the door. "I'll stay out here for a bit, enjoy the air and the quiet, if you don't mind." He lifted a hand in salute. "Goodnight, Oliver."

Feeling much more secure with a pirate in the garden, Oliver latched the door and hurried back upstairs.

Thea was perched on the edge of the bed, humming the tune she'd always loved to play when they were children.

"You even miss notes when you sing." Oliver climbed across the mattress and lifted Simon into his lap. "Wake up, Si. You need to drink some tea."

The little boy's gaze was bleary, and his eyes drooped as he shook his head.

"Come now," Oliver chided. "Thea made it especially for you, and you don't want to hurt her feelings. Just a sip or two, I promise."

The bribe worked until Simon coughed on a sip, and it worsened into a barking gag. Thea moved closer, lifting him and thumping his back while she looked at Oliver. "This is good. He'll breathe better."

They worked in tandem, helping the child clear his lungs until he sagged, shivering against Oliver's chest.

"Whack for the too-ra loo-ra-laddy, whack for the too-ra loo-ra-lee," he sang quietly as he rocked Simon to sleep and willed the fever and the chill to soak into him instead. "Whack for the too-ra loo-ra-laddy, what for the too-ra loo-ra-lee."

"You're off key," Thea whispered as she brushed a hand through Simon's hair. "And that's a highly inappropriate lullaby."

"It's the only song Richard and I could remember in the middle of the night." Oliver started over and was rewarded when Simon snuggled tighter. By the end of the third round, he was quiet as Oliver put him on the pillows. "And I'm not off key. Love you, Si," he whispered against Simon's sweaty forehead. He pulled the covers to the boy's chin and then turned his attention to the quiet woman at his side.

Her hair was dry now, orange and gold to match the glow from the fire, and fine wisps curled around her face. She fingered the cuffs of her robe as she watched the boy's chest rise and fall with every wheezed breath.

"I'll send for the doctor," Thea whispered as she reached for her necklace. "If he worsens, I promise—"

Her flat voice and vague stare told Oliver she was years away, in some other cottage next to Jamey, watching him die all over again.

Oliver tugged her fingers until she followed him to the window seat. He sat, leaning against the wall, and made room for her between his legs. It would be a short, uncomfortable bed, but it was better than nothing. He didn't want to sleep anyway.

He found a distraction in the faded green ribbon Thea had used to tie her braid. Reaching dangerously close to her breast, Oliver twined his finger through the ribbon and tugged. "I remember the summer you bought these. You wore them every day."

"It was your second year at Eton," she murmured as if entranced. "I thought they were the same color as your eyes."

Oliver held his breath. Her exhaustion and worry were opening a door into their past, making way for a present. That's what he hoped, anyway.

"I lost one of them that fall, and it bothered me for months," she continued. "It was like you were wandering around school with a patch on your eye."

He brushed his lips across her cheek, and her curls stuck to his whiskers. "They're in Quebec. All of them. This one, the pink one that clashed with your hair, the blue one that matched my favorite dress."

Thea pulled away from him and turned, twisting her neck until she reminded him of an owl. Her wide eyes added to the impression.

"I stole them and carried them to Eton and then across the ocean." He tightened his arm around her waist to keep her from tumbling to the floor. "I wound them through my fingers when I was homesick."

She looked as though she wanted to punch him, but the efforts of her evening caught up with her and she sagged against his chest. Her sharp elbow struck him in the stomach.

"Ol."

It wasn't a rebuke. It was the same tired realization he'd come to in the tree. They'd lost so much time.

"Shh." Oliver closed his hand over hers and kissed her hair. "You should rest."

She shook her head, just like he'd expected.

"You've been an Amazon all night, Thee. I can take the first watch."

CHAPTER THIRTY

THEA TUCKED THE hot water bottle under the bed clothes, next to the poultice over Simon's chest. The little boy curled around it like it was a favorite toy, caught in another shivering fit that always followed his coughing spells.

The air in here was a mix of herbs, kindling, and now the pepper and mustard used in the poultice. The walls were so slick with steam the paint would soon begin to peel.

Dawn glowed gray through the windows, and Thea risked opening the one above the seat she and Oliver had occupied all night. He was still there, slouched against the wall in sleep. Even now, his brows were knotted with worry and his mouth drooped in a frown.

Bird songs drifted in on the breeze, and he inhaled deeply then exhaled on a sigh. "Thank God. I was dreaming about moldering." His gaze flew to the bed and the dark curls against the pillow. "How is he?"

"No worse, maybe slightly better." Thea stretched her back. "The tea is helping with his aches and encouraging him to sleep."

"Which you should do. It's your turn." He tugged her back to her spot. It was the last place either of them should wish to be, plastered against each other in a steamy room, but it was the only way either of them found comfort.

"I can now, since you aren't snoring." She tried to tease about it, but his first rattling inhale had sent her scrambling upright, checking his temperature while he'd been oblivious. "Jenny will have breakfast downstairs. You can go—"

Oliver draped his arms around her shoulders. "I will later. Is Drake still in the garden?"

"He came up a few hours ago." The sky overhead turned white-blue. "We had a talk about Millie's fate."

"Do you want me to intervene?"

She shook her head. "She should face the consequences of her schemes."

Just like Thea had reaped the consequences of her selfishness, of not thinking past claiming Oliver for her own, delighting that he'd wanted her, loved her. In return, she'd been punished repeatedly for keeping secrets and for being angry with him, his mother, her mother.

She should have climbed on a ship for Canada. She should have been brave and fought for what she'd wanted. She should have trusted Oliver.

She ran her thumb along the chain around her neck, curved her fingers under it, and lifted. One last consequence.

The catch on the locket gave easily, and the face sprang open, revealing the dark copper curl sealed within.

Oliver's deep inhale moved them both, and his exhale warmed her ear. She lifted his hand and put the treasure in his palm. It was all she had to give him of their little boy.

"Red-headed?" His smile soaked his words. "I should've guessed that much."

Thea stayed facing forward, not looking at him. She wouldn't be able to finish otherwise. "It was the color of maples in the fall, and it was thick like yours." She closed her eyes. "He looked like both of us. He had your eyes, but my penchant to freckle when he was outdoors too long. Which he always was."

Oliver's arm closed around her, his fingers shaping to her shoulder. Thea wrapped her hands around his thick forearm and clung to him as the words danced on the tide rising inside of her.

"He had your smile, and he was charming ladies from the cradle. Smart, stubborn, tall for his age. Good-tempered, most of the time anyway."

She swiped away the tears trickling down her cheeks. "His first word was *horse*. He loved the beasts from the moment he saw his first coach."

"Simon's was *dammit-to-hell*." Oliver's rough laughter rumbled through her. "How did you manage, dearest?"

"I got a kitchen job at The Crowned Lion in Brandon. The mistress there was pleasant, and she let me work as long as I could. I went into labor while I was peeling potatoes."

His hand slipped from her shoulders to her waist, and she guessed what he needed to know.

"I looked like the hippo we saw at the zoological exposition, and I waddled like a duck. I thought he'd break my bones to get free."

"Christ." He dropped his forehead to her shoulder and pulled her tighter. "And afterward?"

"I worked at The Lion until Lord and Lady Ebberley came through on a hunt. They were impressed and asked me to come to work for them at double my salary. But I couldn't take Jamey with me. There are rules about servants—"

"*Mierda*. You were no one's servant."

"There's nothing wrong with it, Oliver. I became their housekeeper and cook, and I made a good wage. They were kind. Jamey lived with an older couple nearby on a small farm, and we had almost every Saturday together." He was shaking against her now, and she closed her hand over his. "He was warm and safe, and he never went hungry. He didn't have to work except for regular chores. He was strong and healthy, and he'd never been sick a day in his life. Not until that winter. It was just so fast." She remembered running from Ebberley Hall to the farm, the snow soaking the hem of her dress, the cold air burning her lungs. Even now, she could feel it with every deep inhale. "I sent for the doctor, and I held out Jamey's little arm, and..."

She stopped clinging to Oliver and tried to push him away. She didn't deserve the comfort. She'd let them kill her son. Helped them do it.

Rather than letting her go, Oliver held on and, when she fought, buckled his arms around her. No matter how hard she twisted and kicked, he kept her close until she was sobbing, her head against his shoulder. "I tried. I did everything they told me, everything I was supposed to do. I worked so hard." She turned in his arms and curled against him. "I'm sorry, Oliver. I'm sorry."

"Hush." He stroked her hair and cradled her close, rocking her like she'd seen him do with Simon, like she'd done with her little boy. That thought made her weep harder, and it didn't help when he pressed his wet cheek to hers.

"You did nothing wrong, *mi amada*. Nothing. You were so brave, so strong. Thank you." His lips brushed her ear. "I am so sorry I left you alone."

"Thea."

Her name was nothing more than a whisper, but it had her scrambling across Simon's bed while she was still half asleep. He was cool and dry, and his breath didn't rattle against her ear.

Relief left her too weak to do anything but smile into Oliver's worried eyes. "His fever's broken. Let's get him out of this soupy mess."

While Oliver stripped Simon of his sweaty shirt and the poultice, she pulled the sickbed sheets from the mattress and tossed them into the hallway. By the time the little boy was clean and in a new nightshirt, she was putting cases on the pillows.

Oliver sat on the edge of the bed, his lips moving soundlessly as he doted over the sleeping child. Tears sprang to Thea's eyes at the sweetness of it.

Giving him privacy, she went down the hall and into her

room, full of their things now. It was a glimpse of what could have been, what might have happened, all those years ago. They'd lost so much time. The thoughts made her heavier than simple exhaustion could excuse. When her door closed, she could barely lift her head.

"You're asleep on your feet," Oliver crooned as he undid her robe and pushed it to the floor. Her nightdress followed. Thea couldn't resist, even when he put her to bed, stripped himself bare, and climbed in beside her.

"The sheets feel much better this way," he mumbled.

She had to agree. And she would. Later.

CHAPTER THIRTY-ONE

WHEN THEA WOKE, it was dark, and there was a moment's panic when she heard someone else breathing in her room. Then the mattress shifted, and a familiar hand slid over her stomach.

"Good morning," Oliver said against her shoulder. Even in the dark, she knew he was smiling.

"It's dark, Ol." Her sentence ended on a yawn.

He replied with one of his own. "Yes, but *goodnight* sounds wrong."

"What about *hello*"?

"Slightly formal considering we're naked in bed."

And just like that, she was aware of everywhere her body touched his, of the slide of the sheets against her skin, and the way her hair teased her shoulders.

It took her a moment more to recall everything before now. She threw off the covers. "Simon."

Oliver pulled her backward and covered her haphazardly. "He's fine. I've been to check on him. Jenny and Drake are taking turns entertaining him between naps. Emmett and Fred brought Brownie to stay. That mattress may never be the same."

So they were here, alone, naked in the dark. In an inn. Just like all those years ago. There was just enough light for her to make out his shadowy features. His hair was a mess.

He twined one of her curls around his finger. "I loved Julia. I swear I did. But there were mornings I woke and saw your hair on the pillow."

His broad chest was solid and warm against her palm, and his heart thudded in a steady beat.

"Did you read my letter?" he asked. "When you found it?"

She had tried, but she couldn't get past the first sentence. She had been afraid of what she'd learn.

When she shook her head, Oliver sighed and bent to kiss her. It was barely a touch of his lips against hers.

"Darling Thea, please tell me I haven't lost you forever."

His rich whisper filled the room as he pushed the quilt from her body and replaced its warmth with the heat of his hands.

"I miss you until I ache from it," he groaned as his lips found her ear, then her neck and her shoulder. "Only the hope of making a life for us, our own life, keeps me from your side."

Tears pricked Thea's eyes as she responded to him, widening her legs to welcome his body. Everything about him was gentle and compelling.

"I cannot do this without you," he continued. His kiss this time was deeper, longer, more heated. "Father has money for your passage. Please come to me. Yours always. Oliver." His fingers teased her open, slid inside and out until she was arching against him, begging him for more. "P.S. Pack warm clothes and heavy boots." His muscles were hard and long against her, and his hair was silk in her hands. He rested his forehead against hers, letting her take his full weight. "P.P.S. Bring biscuits."

Her laughter faded into a groan as he rocked his hips and entered her in one long thrust.

He set a slow pace, rocking against her, letting her feel every inch of him deep inside, building the heat under her skin.

In the past, their lovemaking had been desperate, storing up memories for separation or making up for lost time. This was different. It was an acknowledgement that they had all the time they wanted.

The beauty of it, of them, made her weep, and he kissed away her tears even as the pace of his thrusts quickened. "I love you, *mi alma.*"

Soul. The power of the word choked a sob from her.

Thea slid her hand across his back and lower, to his hips, urging him to finish with her. She wasn't broken, and she didn't need to be fixed, but she wasn't whole without him.

"I love you, *mi cielo.*" She rose to meet him, fought to keep him inside her as her heart pounded and her skin heated against his hands. "Please."

"God, yes. You have me. Always." He groaned as she climaxed around him, and then again as he followed close behind. "Always."

After a few long, languorous moments, Oliver slid to her side and Thea caught her breath. He kissed her collarbone, and she played with his hair. No titles, no work, no scandals. Just them at the beginning of something new.

Forsaking the warm comfort of his arm across her waist, she left the bed and crossed to her dressing screen to wash.

"Could we go to Brandon after breakfast?" he asked from bed.

"Of course." They shared Jamey now, like they shared Simon and everything else in their lives. And, after the last few days, it seemed natural to visit one boy and hug the other.

Thea ran a cloth over her most sensitive skin, smiling at the ache there. The smile faded when the cloth was splotched with pink.

Her courses were near.

Weeks of waiting and hoping. Of praying they would happen and save them both from a foolish mistake. And now…

She wasn't increasing.

Disappointment washed over her.

"Did you hear me?" Oliver asked as he peeked around the screen. "I asked… What is it?"

Thea shook her head, unable to speak the words because she would begin to cry in earnest. Not to mention, Oliver shouldn't be so…damned insistent.

"Oh." He gathered her into his arms.

"You shouldn't be back here." She pushed away from him and was mortified to see him *smiling* at her. "What do you find so funny about this, you…you…arse?"

Was he relieved? After everything?

He laughed harder and held her tighter. "Honestly, I'm pleased that you're upset about it."

That was the stupidest thing he'd ever said to her, and he'd said a lot of stupid things. "What?"

"We don't have to marry." He kissed her nose. "And you're upset."

She couldn't find the words.

"And you're speechless, which always happens when I'm right. Which means you want to marry me."

Despite herself, laughter bubbled on Thea's tongue "You are…insane. We're naked behind a dressing screen."

"Yes, and we'll have to stay in England and be an actual duke and duchess. It's the only way everything works. There's too much relying on us here."

It was true. She'd known it for a long time. Their businesses, friends, and families…nothing would succeed if they managed from a distance. The truth didn't make it less terrifying.

Oliver led her to the bed, where she perched on the edge of the mattress. He knelt in front of her on one knee, slightly more serious but still naked, and took her hands.

"You aren't carrying my child, and you'll have to stay in England and be a duchess, but I hope you love me enough to marry me anyway. Preferably today while we're in Brandon."

Love me enough. She heard the vague echo of what she'd told him only yesterday. "Ol, I didn't mean—"

"Why did you think I was rushing?" His Adam's apple bobbed and his smile faltered. His lashes hid his eyes. "You had to marry me. I didn't want to lose the upper hand. And now…" He kissed her fingers. "Please, Thee. Say yes."

There was no way to deny him. Her heart wouldn't let her. She didn't care if he was a duke, a farmer, or stuck in a tree. They could live here, in Canada, or on the moon. And it didn't matter whether he'd left her or she'd left him.

Her Oliver had finally come home.

Thea leaned forward and kissed him, shyly at first, then a bit bolder. He responded with a groan and a smile that made her restless in the best ways.

"Yes, Oliver. I would love to."

EPILOGUE

One year later

OLIVER STARED OUT the window, reliving memories from Simon's birth—the wails and screams and the unearthly silence that had followed. He crushed the drapes in his fist. The manor was far, far too quiet.

"Your Grace?"

The last word was still echoing as he sprinted down the hall and careened through the doorway. The doctor was saying something, he was sure of it. Doctors usually liked to tell you everything they'd done in excruciating detail.

All Oliver could see was Thea, her long hair floating around her as the breeze came through the open windows.

The maids moved across the hallway behind him and down the stairs, their arms full of sheets and towels, giving Oliver a clue as to why he'd had to wait to see his wife. Nothing kept him from her now, but his feet were rooted to the floor.

He cleared his throat and took one step. Then another. Her arms were empty and the room was silent except for the birds. Simon had screamed holy hell for hours after his birth. For months, Oliver's prayers had been for Thea's health, now guiltily, belatedly, he prayed for their child.

He finally reached the bed and perched on the edge. She was pale but warm, and her pulse throbbed steadily against his fingers.

"I'm fine, Ol." She burrowed her cheek into his hand and kissed his palm, and he could breathe again.

"You look tired."

"And you have sawdust in your hair," she teased. "We've both been busy."

Finally, from behind the dressing screen in the corner of the room, there was a hiccup that ended on a wail.

Jenny came into view, carrying a bundle that was all swaddling and waving fists. "Would you like to hold your daughter?"

Oliver's muscles locked. A girl.

The newborn's tiny head rested in the crook of his elbow, and her heels nudged his palm as though she was already trying to kick her way to freedom. It wasn't a surprise, though. She'd almost kicked him out of bed several times already.

Her face scrunched and reddened, making her light, thin hair stand out. The wail increased in volume. What was he supposed to—oh, right. Cradling her head and a bottom not much bigger than the lemons her mama loved, Oliver switched positions, bringing his daughter to rest on his shoulder.

"Whack for the too-ra loo-ra-lassie, whack for the too-ra loo-ra-lee." He winked at Thea as he sang. "Whack for the too-ra loo-ra-lassie, what for the too-ra loo-ra-lee."

The little girl finally quieted, and he got a better look at her. She was beautiful. "What are we going to name her?"

"Carys," Thea whispered as she leaned closer to stare at the tiny face. "Carys Carmelita Hawkins."

"It's Welsh." He buried his nose in Thea's glorious curls and kissed her ear. Lita would have been overjoyed with a great-granddaughter.

"Says the English duke with an Irish dog, a Shetland pony, a Spanish grandmother, and a Canadian son." She smiled as her eyes drifted closed. "Where is he?"

"With your mother, waiting for the all clear."

They'd moved Thea's mother into the dower cottage after

their honeymoon. The garden had mollified her, and Simon was working his charms. Last week, she'd even made him biscuits.

When the baby began to whine again, Thea took her to nurse. Oliver shifted, offering her support and watching, transfixed, as the infant latched on. Tears pricked his eyelids as he rested his chin on Thea's shoulder. "I love you, my duchess."

She elbowed him in the ribs. "You know I hate that."

This was his favorite game. "What would you prefer?" he asked as he kissed the soft skin at the base of her neck.

"Mrs. Hawkins."

And that was why he loved it. "Right, then."

"Don't gloat, Ol."

Ah, but he couldn't help it as he stroked his daughter's soft cheek and cradled her mother as gently as he could manage. "Lady Carys."

"If you call her Lady Carys, you'll have to call him Lord Simon."

"Lord Heathen is more like it. He's going to rebreak his arm if he's not careful. I caught him trying to balance on Spot's back, like the rider we saw last month at the circus. Took five years off my life."

"You did the same thing, except yours was a handstand."

"Don't tell him that." Oliver yawned and burrowed into the pillows.

"We need to write your mother and tell her. Is she still in Morocco?"

"I believe so." Distance had helped them call a truce, so long as they only talked of painting and the weather. "Will you be well enough to travel to London? I'd hate to brave lords without you."

Thea's answer was a snuffling snore.

Oliver lifted his fussy daughter to his shoulder and covered his wife. His muscles ached from work and his brain buzzed with ideas for his speech on child labor. Both his girls snuggled closer, and his son's giggles floated up on the breeze.

The Duke of Rushford was home.

ACKNOWLEDGMENTS

I hope you've enjoyed Oliver and Thea's story.

I was encouraged to write historical romance by friends who knew it was my genre of choice when I read, and by the kind, talented, and generous authors I consider friends: Taryn Leigh Taylor, Carrie Nichols, Brynn Kelly, Nancy Sartor, C.S. Smith, and Victoria Elliott.

I was *inspired* to write it by my fan girl "keeper shelf" of authors who have entranced me for years. One book by Grace Burrowes almost made me miss a plane.

Thank you to Patti, Sherry, and Melinda for *so* many lunches and coffees where you had to listen to adventures about imaginary people. I could not do this without you.

No romance writer is without a hero of her own, and I have mine. He never complains that I'm reading too much, spending hours at the keyboard, or that there are books in every room of the house. He talks to our cats like they're people, makes sure I get off the couch for a regular walk, and has been known to suggest a plot idea. Our HEA doesn't involve a castle, but I love it just the same.

ABOUT THE AUTHOR

Peri Maxwell has lost herself in reading romances all her life. She began writing as a challenge to herself and wrote her first historical romance on a dare, and now she's hooked. She prefers to write heroines who can stand toe-to-toe with a hero, challenge society's rules for good reasons, and find love with heroes who admire an equal (even if it's a little reluctantly).

She enjoys history, humor, and a good mystery. An armchair historian, she also has a background in women's studies.

Peri lives in Arkansas with her husband and the two cats who rescued them. When she's not writing or reading, she's working her day job or spending time with her family and friends (the same ones who dared her to write a historical romance).